Rebel

The Shattered World Saga
Book 2

by

Dennis K. Hausker

Published by
Melange Books, LLC
White Bear Lake, MN 55110
www.melange-books.com

ISBN: 978-1-61235-649-5 print

Cover Artist: Caroline Andrus

Rebel
Dennis K. Hausker

Aron's peaceful life on his father's farm ended abruptly and he struggled with galling captivity in the palace while he formed a fearsome corps of expert fighters. They managed to escape fleeing into the wilds but their new life is tenuous with daily challenges merely to survive. His problems seem to mount on a daily basis with his personal struggles with the significant women in his life, the barbaric savages living in the wilds, and then the shocking discovery that threatens the world with a nightmare resurrected. Their limited understanding of their whole world has left them vulnerable. Can Aron and the allies rise to meet the challenge? They don't know the answer to that question, and they fear the worst under the circumstances.

Rebel
Dennis K. Hausker

Aron's peaceful life on his father's farm ended abruptly and he struggled with galling captivity in the palace while he formed a fearsome corps of expert fighters. They managed to escape fleeing into the wilds but their new life is tenuous with daily challenges merely to survive. His problems seem to mount on a daily basis with his personal struggles with the significant women in his life, the barbaric savages living in the wilds, and then the shocking discovery that threatens the world with a nightmare resurrected. Their limited understanding of their whole world has left them vulnerable. Can Aron and the allies rise to meet the challenge? They don't know the answer to that question, and they fear the worst under the circumstances.

Chapter One
~ Hidden Motives ~

Aron moved briskly along the trail from his fortress construction site back toward the Erati camp. Frigid winds blowing down from the north filled the air with flecks of snow as a major winter storm approached. Aron squinted at the strong wind blowing in his face. He'd broken his own protocol by traveling alone because the messenger had said Tasha needed to meet him urgently.

He was worried. A gang convert courier had come to Aron; a man often in the company of Radigan, and someone he wasn't sure he could trust, but when it came to Tasha he wasn't always rational. Distress over Radigan's ongoing pursuit of Tasha never receded, but at the same time, he had duties and needed to function in his many roles as leader of his people. As he hurried along the path he realized he should have told someone where he was going, and why. He'd made himself vulnerable and suddenly felt uneasy. This whole situation had a strange feel. Tasha almost never called for him and always left it to him to come to her.

With dusk approaching, he increased his pace to a jog as the light receded. Footing was treacherous on the slippery snow covered ground. He hurried around a sharp curve in the path by a heavy stand of trees when suddenly a crunch rattled the bushes beside him. A huge ice cat leaped out of the undergrowth and knocked him down before he could react. He tried to pull his sword, but was knocked onto his side lying on the weapon with the heavy cat pinning him down. The cat snarled and tried to bite Aron's neck. Aron grabbed the creature's head to keep those fangs away. The cat clawed at him, but fortunately Aron's heavy leather coat kept the talons from breaking through to his skin. He wrestled with the powerful cat to get it off him so he could move. He was partially successful, but the cat nicked him with its claws in numerous swipes and managed a thrust with its face which wounded Aron's cheek and forehead.

The sight of Aron bleeding spurred the cat's ravenous appetite. Aron tried to knock the cat away with swings of his elbows, but it was too big, too strong, and he was pinned down. The animal smacked him in the head with a power swipe of its paw, stunning him and then tried again to bite his throat and end his life. Long claws opened serious wounds on his scalp and neck. Aron's consciousness faded so he wasn't aware when the cat stiffened and shuddered as an arrow struck it with a killing shot.

Radigan jogged up to the scene along with his thugs.

"Why didn't you let the cat kill him?" asked one of his men. "We were about to ambush him anyway."

"This is an unexpected opportunity," Radigan replied. "If we'd killed him, the blame would have fallen on me as the prime suspect. Here, I've saved his life and this will oblige him to me. Now I've saved the lives of both Tasha and Aron. He'll be less able to object to my actions in camp and with her. If I can win Tasha with deeds and still retain my façade in the camp, it gives me many more options."

"He's bleeding badly," said the man. "He may not survive these wounds."

"If he dies from the attack, it would be fortuitous. Gather him up and we'll carry him back to the main camp. It will be a great boon with Tasha. She'll be very grateful I've saved him. I had a feeling this would be a good day."

Tasha hurried along with Aron and Brock's mothers to meet Radigan's patrol carrying Aron's limp body. Distressed, she was unsure if he was even alive; Liani and Belisa weren't far behind them in arriving at the dire scene and were accompanied by Enna and Biala.

"I'm not sure why he was out there alone on the trail," Radigan explained. "He was attacked by a big ice cat. It was fortunate we were nearby and heard the shouts or he would have been killed and dragged away into the brush to be torn apart."

Radigan looked at the women, all of whom had looks of shock and pain.

Brock and Trent hurried up and looked at Radigan skeptically.

"That isn't right," said Brock. "Aron wouldn't have gone off alone.

There's something we don't know."

"I have no explanation," Radigan replied with a look of innocence. "I agree it doesn't make sense, yet here we are. Aron's injuries are obviously from a cat. You're too quick to seek blame for those who are innocent, Brock."

Brock glowered, but said nothing.

Galean arrived and examined Aron with concern.

"Take him to the medical tent. These wounds are very serious. Everybody, please go back to your business and let us take care of him. When we know something, I'll send word."

Radigan eased his way over to Tasha. She looked at him directly.

"It's a sad day, Tasha."

"Thank you for saving his life."

"I'm here for you in any way I can help, Tasha. You know my feelings, but I'm not going to force you. Remember what I said when I saved you. I'm the person best equipped to safeguard you and yours. I'll never allow you to be in danger, ever again. When I say I truly love you, perhaps you'll start to believe me. I know you still have strong feelings for me. If you'll stop resisting them and let nature run its course, the problem of choosing between me and Aron may resolve itself. I've told you I'll be patient to allow you to consider what you want for your life, but I won't stand idly by without letting you know I care a great deal. Aron hasn't shown you a fraction of what I have. I'm sure there's a certain amount of rustic charm with his humble roots and his efforts to overcome hardship. That doesn't make him a person of my caliber. You know this already. You've lived a higher life beyond that of a mere villager. Life as my wife would be such a delight for us, Tasha. I would devote myself to your happiness. You've tasted that fruit. I don't think it's so easily dismissed. Would you prefer the clumsy bumbling advances of Aron? In that way, he's still a youth. I'm the romantic man for you."

She looked away contemplatively.

Tasha's father walked up eyeing Radigan dourly.

"Come along, daughter, there's nothing here for you to concern yourself with."

He scowled at Radigan who put his arm around his daughter. Radigan smiled slyly.

For days Aron lay unconscious from the trauma of the head blows and blood loss. Galean was constantly stopped and asked about Aron's condition.

"He's stable, but at this point I don't see any improvement. He had serious injuries and a long distance to carry him back here. The bleeding complicates everything. I'm sorry, but all we can do is to wait until his condition changes. As I said before, when there's a break in his condition, I'll let everyone know."

Radigan basked in the gratefulness for his "rescue." Nearly everybody expressed indebted feelings, except Belisa who was very suspicious.

"What have I done that's earned this caution, Belisa? Have your tender feelings for me evaporated? I don't understand?"

"Radigan, those feelings have nothing to do with my concerns. I see you very clearly for who you are. Even then, I knew you were using me for your purposes, but it didn't matter. I had no prospects to escape life under the control of the prince. Like Tasha, you were a pleasant diversion, and in a way a means to secretly taunt the prince cheating right under his nose. He foolishly trusted you. That's a mistake I would never make. I can't foresee any circumstance where I would trust you, and yes I still have warm feelings for you."

"You wrong me unfairly, Belisa. I hold nothing but the deepest love and respect for you."

"Hah, respect? That's a laugh. You would never respect any woman. We're objects for your use and nothing more. Do you think we're mindless fools? Because I allowed myself to be used in the past, don't make the mistake to think it gives you free license now, or that I'm in your thrall. I know you want to take Tasha away, but I don't think you'll succeed. She's no fool either."

"I've never denied I desire to marry her. I can't marry you, Belisa, because you're the Arreck princess, but my love for you is undiminished. I do have genuine feelings for Tasha and for you. Do you see me pursuing any others?"

He watched her closely and noted an emotional reaction to his statement. She couldn't hide her own feelings and he was a master at playing a woman. He smiled in appreciation of his prowess. Elcou and Trache moved close; each took a place on either side of Belisa and seethed as they glared at Radigan. He made elaborate bows to them.

"Perhaps we'll talk further about this later, Belisa."

She eyed him dourly as he walked away.

"Your highness, you should allow us to eliminate this man," said Elcou.

"It would be our pleasure," Trache added.

Belisa chuckled.

"Problems are not so easily dispatched. You shouldn't underestimate him. He's dangerous and no fool. He'll have protections and safeguards in place. It wouldn't be so easy a task as you think."

"We would prevail," Elcou uttered grimly.

"You should use great caution in your dealings with him, princess," Trache added. "He has no true feelings. Women are objects for his use to advance his goals, nothing more. Don't be deluded by his glib words. They're as false as he is. The incident with Aron is very suspicious. That they were miraculously at hand to save his life is hard to believe. If he can get you and Tasha into positions to his advantage, he'll exercise no scruples at all. He's a vile man."

Belisa shrugged. "I understand all of it. I think you had a need to speak it for your own feelings. I know what I'm doing."

Trache looked at Elcou in unspoken agreement the princess didn't know what she was doing.

Radigan's discussion with Belisa opened new possibilities and motivated him to grow bolder in his actions. He went that evening to invite himself to dinner with Tasha and her parents. Her father stared at him in undisguised anger. Tasha's mother attempted to be conciliatory.

"I want to express again our thanks for your brave action in saving Aron. He's vital to this rebellion, but more than that he's dear to us. With also saving Tasha, I want to extend the hospitality of our home. I'm sorry for my husband's mood. What happened to our daughter in the palace isn't something we can easily resolve. I beg your pardon, Radigan."

"I understand completely and believe me when I say it isn't a problem for me. In your position I would have similar feelings. I'm not going to try to excuse my past behavior. I can only say, the life there is different than probably anywhere else on the planet. The way the prince lives his life, it bleeds into his staff and into society. I admit it was too easy to sink down to base emotions and ill conceived choices. As bad as it may seem, without our liaisons I wouldn't know Tasha, the woman I hope to make a life with."

He smiled benignly and was interested to see Tasha's father fight with his emotions. It was clear he'd argued with his wife before the visit and undoubtedly she'd given him a pronouncement to be civil. Tasha's mother put on an expression of welcome, though it was easy to see it was a façade as she fought her own battle against lashing out at Radigan - despoiler of their daughter.

Tasha was surprisingly serene in the midst of the boiling emotions around her. Though she wasn't solicitous toward Radigan, tonight she wasn't resistant. She'd even chosen to wear an attractive form fitting dress instead of the plain, drab garb she usually wore around him.

"This is very nice sharing your evening. I lost my family when I was a child, so this is something I've missed out on most of my life."

"You never mentioned that," Tasha replied curiously. "What happened to them?"

"They were palace courtesan's who were caught in a bad situation. A visiting noble was caught in a compromising situation with the wife of an important royal figure. Since the noble was a key ally, the king decided to spare him, but they looked for scapegoats. My parents were charged with unseemly acts and executed to keep their mouths shut. I was taken into the royal household to be raised. It elevated my position in the royal order, but it cost me my parents. Had they lived, I wonder how different a person I'd have been. I wonder if I'd have been respectable and decent. I know how you feel about me. I wish it was otherwise. I can only say I've tried to become a better man, someone worthy of Tasha. With time perhaps I can sway you to reconsider your poor impressions of me."

He glanced at Tasha. She'd looked at her parents to gauge their reactions. Radigan looked too. They both looked doubtful, unconvinced by Radigan's subtle manipulation. Those challenges didn't daunt him. He was supremely confident he'd eventually achieve his goals and that Tasha would pick him, and he'd defeat Aron both in love and as the leader of the rebellion. He'd even begun to imagine a post-Aron plan to assume leadership and impose his own vision for the resistance to the prince.

Tasha continued an even temperament, neither embracing nor rejecting Radigan. The same was true for this particular evening. The other key women, Belisa, Liani, Enna, Biala, and even Cherine, spent considerable time at Aron's bedside even though he was still unconscious. Tasha went to be with him much less than the others.

"I just can't see him that way," Tasha explained in her own defense, but nearly everyone took it as a sign her affections were elsewhere. That she could possibly prefer Radigan over Aron seemed inconceivable to the others. Away from her, the women whispered worriedly.

"Belisa, what's your opinion? You've been in the same circumstances and as a woman you've known Radigan. Is it possible Tasha could love this man in spite of his obvious flaws and ulterior motives? I have experience with him also, as you know, but I'm not under his thrall. Tasha is incredibly beautiful and she's smart. How can she not see what's glaring to the rest of us?" asked Cherine.

"The only idea I have is sometimes our feelings can't be controlled. Though we might have a desire to go in one direction, it doesn't always work out that way. Radigan has a definite level of appeal. He carved out a place in my affections. That doesn't stop me from seeing the truth of him and taking protective measures. What I know of Tasha is she'd do the same thing. I hope we're not reading too much into this."

"We can only judge by what we see, Belisa," Liani added. "I don't hide the fact I'd gladly take her place in Aron's heart, but it isn't something a person can cause in another person. Aron would need to make that choice. If Tasha chose Radigan I can't say it would make me sad. It makes me a small person to say this, but I won't lie about it."

"I do understand Liani and believe me none of us hold your feelings for Aron against you. As a matter of fact, I've been impressed at how tastefully you handled the issue. I think if I wanted a man, I'd be less worried about the feelings of my competition. I've considered talking to Tasha about it, but it doesn't feel right to me for some reason. I think she doesn't want the interference of others. She's the one who'll ultimately pay the price for her choices."

"Do you propose we let nature run its course?" asked Enna. "I feel protective of Aron and I don't want to see him hurt."

"I think we have no choice about it," Belisa replied. "We can't go to Tasha as a committee to settle this. If she wants to be with Radigan in her heart, that's what will eventually happen. Our interference won't change it."

"I don't like this," Biala added. "With Aron in distress, Radigan has a free hand with Tasha and she doesn't seem disposed to stop him. It isn't right. I don't understand what's in her mind."

"Remember Biala, the life she's lived and the experiences she's had are far different from yours. You and Enna are virgins. You don't understand the emotions that go along with intimacy. Someday with your own experiences you may have a different view of this."

Biala looked at Enna and shrugged. "Perhaps, but I'd like to understand."

"I can't speak for Tasha, but in my case let me say I'm no longer the person I was before my captivity in the palace. The pride I felt in being Arreck royalty is gone. I was humbled in so many ways. My great transformation is much the same as Tasha told me about hers, in our spirits. It wasn't that unseemly, unstoppable things were done to us which troubled us so much, it's that over time, our resistance eroded away. It was too easy to acquiesce, to give in, because we believed we'd never escape. Our own weaknesses haunt us still and neither of us feels worthy any longer. Other people can excuse us, forgive us, rationalize away our lives there, but we know the truth. What Radigan has is knowledge of that dark truth. We know he took advantage of us, but we too easily allowed ourselves to attach to him emotionally and then to develop a love bond. Worthiness is something which when it's lost, I don't think it can ever be recovered. Tasha doesn't feel worthy of Aron who's shown himself to be a great moral man. Tasha doesn't feel moral any more than I do. Does that help you understand?"

"So, Tasha would choose to make a life with a person responsible for that condition and ignore the person she wanted to be with?" asked Liani, incredulous. "That's tragic and seems so needless. Who's chastised her about those days? Nobody I know of. She's done this to herself and with how she acts around Radigan one would think it's her preferred choice to be that way. "

"No one needed to say anything," Belisa replied. "It's about us, not the perceptions and opinions of others. In our emotional state, until we resolve our inner doubts and issues, we can't really be fit mates for a life partner. It's unfortunate, but that's how things stand."

"I find it hard to be sympathetic to her," Liani added.

"I'd like to slug her," said Enna.

The women all laughed.

"It might make you feel better, but I doubt it would solve any of the issues, Enna."

"Perhaps we could all get together and slug Radigan instead."

They laughed again.

Tasha came walking over to them at that point.

"What mischief are you ladies doing? You look awfully guilty."

They looked among each other ruefully.

"Ah, I see, I'm the topic of conversation, again. I can't say I'm surprised with circumstances being as they are."

"I'm sorry Tasha," Liani advised. "We're not against you. We're just confused by your indecision. Belisa explained how you were damaged in the palace emotionally. I, for one, am sorry for what happened, but isn't it time to put it behind you? You're no longer in their control. You have the opportunity to take control of your life. Your paths are clear. We don't understand why you hesitate."

"I don't feel disposed to try to explain my feelings to you. It's my life and it's my options. From your viewpoint, I understand your opinions. You can't see things from my viewpoint because you haven't walked in my shoes. Once I feel I'm ready, once I know what I want, I'll make that choice everyone is pressing on me."

"We don't intend to pressure you," said Enna, "but you should know we're on Aron's side."

Tasha smiled contemplatively. "Aron is a good person. You can't go wrong supporting him. I don't see that as a problem for me. I'm a supporter of Aron's also, in case you don't understand it. I hope you ladies don't see me as an opponent or a danger to him."

"Of course not," said Belisa. "We want you to know we're here for you, all you need to do is ask."

"I appreciate that, Belisa. I love you like a sister. I can say I love all of you, but about this part of my life, I must travel this path alone. I know you want to help, but I ask that you respect my wishes and back off."

Expressions of agreement or satisfaction did not appear after Tasha's declaration. No one said anything outright, but it was no secret they were in stark disagreement with her.

Tasha looked at each of their faces. "I believe I'll go over to see Aron. Has there been any change?"

"None," said Biala.

"Have a pleasant day, ladies," said Tasha in parting.

"I'll walk with you," Belisa advised.

They left the other women behind. Tasha could feel their eyes on her back.

"For some reason, this reminds me of when the men of the camp turned on us and nearly attacked, Belisa."

"No Tasha, they were distressed and we had a hand in it. They didn't understand what we were going through and we didn't understand how we came across to them. Here, we're all worried about Radigan. I was in the royal suite along with you so I understand where these feelings began. I admit I still feel an inner fire now, but I've evolved enough to recognize things in him I didn't pay attention to back then. I think what he tells you are lies to gain his goals. I know you have doubts."

"I do and I'm no fool, Belisa. He's very persistent and that's gratifying. I don't have many questions about Radigan. He acts as I expect him to. What I don't understand is Aron. I'm not a woman who pursues a man. What is it he expects me to do? He wallows in self pity, he misreads signals, and he makes no attempt to woo me. Is it so wrong of me to expect him to make an effort to win me? I've never rejected him. At least I've said nothing to drive him away. When we left Nephora we were all in shock. None of us were at our best. I will tell you this, darling. It isn't impossible in my mind to imagine being wife to Radigan. You know what I'm saying. He can fill that role very well. I'm not choosing him at this point, but if Aron continues on his aimless path, where does that leave me?"

"I believe Aron is haunted by many demons, some of his own making. He has an imagination of you as his mate, but he's never taken the next step. His experiences have all been in combat. Radigan has considerable experience elsewhere. If Aron tried, perhaps he is charming, but he fears to look the fool when compared to Radigan who's dashing and supremely confident. Don't forget also, he's burdened with heavy responsibility as our leader. He doesn't have free time like Radigan does. When you say you're on Aron's side, maybe you can see there's another way to support him too."

Tasha shrugged. "I'm a flesh and blood woman. I don't crave to be worshipped from afar. I want to feel the embrace of a man who loves me."

"My darlings," they heard from behind them.

Radigan came up and put arms around their waists. "You've

brightened my day with your radiance. What man could want more than what I hold in my arms right here. I feel blessed."

He kissed each of them on the cheek.

Though both women resisted, they're cheeks flushed - a natural reaction they couldn't stop.

He whispered an idea, a lure from the old days. It took an effort of will on their parts to properly respond to him.

"No, Radigan, we cannot," Tasha whispered.

"Perhaps another time," he replied, undeterred by their rejections. He sensed how difficult it was for them to say no, which was his intention.

He let them go as they turned into the medical area and went to Aron's tent.

Aron was still unconscious and very pale. Galean had a worried look and approached as they walked close to the bed.

"Tasha, Belisa, I wish I had good news for you, but he's unchanged. Perhaps it's a good thing he isn't declining, but we haven't seen a sign of progress. I'm at a loss at what to do. I'm sure blood loss was a major factor in his weakness."

Tasha sat on the edge of the bed. Aron, a man now, was no longer the youth she'd fancied. Even in sleep, worry creased his face. On impulse, she took his hand into hers. Aron responded with REM sleep, rapid eye movements and moaned softly. She felt a twitch in his hand.

"Aron?"

He moaned again and moved slightly.

"Galean, come over here," said Tasha.

Galean hurried close along with Belisa.

"Aron!" he said sharply.

Tasha felt his hand squeeze hers. He moaned louder and started to thrash, like he was stuck in his coma.

"Strike him sharply!" Galean ordered.

Tasha hesitated a moment before she slapped his face jarring his head.

Aron's eyes flew open in panic and he flailed about wildly. Galean, Belisa, Tasha and some of the nurses grabbed him until he gasped and focused his eyes on Tasha.

"Tasha?" he whispered. "Am I dead?"

Tasha chuckled. "No Aron, this is my hand you're crushing."

He released her hand and blinked.

"I was in danger… attacked…"

"You were saved by Radigan," Tasha explained. "He happened along and shot the ice cat. You were gravely injured, but they carried you back here. You've been unconscious for over a week."

"A week," he muttered faintly. He looked again at her and whispered affectionately, "Tasha."

"I'm right here, Aron," she answered to sooth him. "You're safe amongst friends. I think the worst is behind you now."

Chapter Two
~ Leadership Games ~

Aron's awakening was joyous news, but in his weakened state he was in no condition to resume leadership duties. This left a void as to who would fill that role in the interim.

"No Aron, I don't wish to assume that responsibility," said Galean. "I know we must have a leader, and I would seem to be least offensive to any competing candidates, but I'd also be the weakest choice. I fear my orders could be more easily ignored by those with other plans and motives. You need a stronger voice. Whether you consider Trent, Brock, your father, or another warrior, you must pick a person as a defender, a person who can meet challenges from outside and inside of the camp. I know you wouldn't ever choose Radigan, but he's a strong person and an example of what we need."

"He's universally despised," Aron replied, "not the least of which is by me. How could we trust him? Most of us believe he's still a follower of the prince."

"I understand, Aron. I'm not saying you should choose him. I'm saying his good qualities are those we need to search for. I acknowledge his bad side, but who doesn't have a bad side?"

"I'll think about it, Galean. If I appointed him regent in my stead, perhaps it would make Tasha happy."

"Aron," Galean chided, "you should see her when you're asleep. She watches over you lovingly. That's where you need to look. Radigan is competing for her hand, but don't assume she leans toward him. I don't see it that way at all from my observations."

"When do you think I'll be recovered enough to get up and around?"

"I think physically we can start exercising now. The blow to your head still worries me, Aron."

"Perhaps it's a good thing if I've forgotten my past. There's an awful lot I'd like to forget."

"Do you have a thought about your replacement, a person you favor?'

"As I think about it, what do you say to my appointing Cherine?"

Galean eyed him skeptically.

"There's no doubt she'd be a good leader, Aron. What I worry is women are seen in a subservient role in society, regardless of our wishes for it to be otherwise. It's a choice you can make, but I'd say think about it a great deal. Remember what the prince did that pushed her into our camp. No one intervened to spare her and she was surrounded by her own masters. There's a social flaw we mustn't ignore. Someday it may be remedied."

Aron said nothing. He had a regretful look on his face.

"I hate the prince," he muttered. "He's been the cause of so much suffering in my life and to those around me I care about. Call Cherine here to see me. I'll ask her if she's willing to do it."

"As you wish, Aron..."

Cherine was in the field that day so she didn't come to Aron's tent until evening after the supper meal.

"What is it, Aron? Galean sent word to me about an urgent matter you wish to discuss?"

"I want to ask you something, Cherine. Maybe I'm asking you for a favor. I've talked a great deal with Galean about someone to take my place while I'm recovering."

"Of course, Aron, I've thought about this too. There are a number of qualified men to fill the role."

"Cherine, I want to ask you if you'd be willing to take the job."

"What? Aron, you're asking me to assume leadership of the camp and of the movement? I'm a woman."

"I am asking it of you. I've been struggling with the decision and I feel you're the person I trust to handle the responsibility."

"Do you anticipate the men will follow my orders? I'm leader of the masters, but they respect me from my years training and fighting with them. These former scoundrels we've turned to our side have always seen women with different eyes, and much different feelings. I don't reject your request, but I want you to know you may be creating a new set of issues if you put a woman in charge."

"I'm saying I'm willing to take that risk, Cherine. I respect you as a combatant, but I also respect your mind to recognize and react to problems which might arise. Do you agree to become my regent?"

He saw a slight smile. She chuckled. "How strange with what I've experienced in my life at the hands of men I could be put in charge of them as their leader, even if only temporarily so."

"Is that a yes, Cherine?"

She laughed. "I'll do it, Aron, though I wonder where this will lead us."

"Let Galean know and we'll announce it right away. I know you'll do a great job."

"I owe you a great debt, Aron. Don't say I owe you nothing. I intend to repay you in a significant way. No man has been willing to extend such a gift to women."

"You do owe me nothing. I don't know what you think you could do for me. It's honor enough for me to have your respect and friendship. You're the one who's a great person and an inspiration to me. At heart, I'm still just a village farmer. I've been made to seem like much more than I really am. Do you think we should create some symbol of leadership? Maybe we could create a bonnet for you to wear."

Cherine laughed heartily. Galean smiled when he came in the tent.

"What's this?" he asked, smiling and chuckling.

"Aron's blow to the head has addled his mind. He proposes we create a bonnet for me to wear as a sign of leadership."

They all laughed.

"It could be a fierce bonnet, Galean," said Aron with a smile.

"Let's forgo the bonnet idea, Aron," said Galean skeptically.

"It was just a thought, Galean. If you've got a better idea for a symbol of leadership, let me know."

Galean got a curious look on his face. "Aron, we've all wanted to ask you something. Why were you out on that trail alone?"

"I've thought about it, Galean. I don't remember. Whatever was the reason, the blow to my head knocked it out. It does seem very foolish on my part. Apparently I was going to the Erati camp, but there would have been nothing there for me. Everybody was here at the time."

"Trent and Brock have suspicions regarding Radigan. They're quietly investigating the whole incident."

"Good, we should never trust Radigan about anything. That goes beyond my personal issues about Tasha. Just on the basis he could be working for the prince in our camp, he's someone who should be under constant scrutiny."

"It just doesn't make sense," Galean reflected. "If he was planning your demise, why did he save you? You nearly died as it was. He could have simply left you to the cat."

"I agree, Galean. We know why he would save Tasha, but saving me is a mystery. I'm the last person to believe he could change his nature. Cherine, I don't need to tell you to watch him. You do that anyway. We'll get you that new bonnet, but assume you're in charge as of this moment."

"Aron, you're a nut," she replied with a smile. "I'll do my best, but get back on your feet as soon as you can, and forget about the war bonnet."

* * * *

They trooped out an hour later to a gathering of the camp.

"I'd like to say a few things," Aron began. "First, I want to extend my thanks to Radigan who saved my life. We haven't always agreed on everything, but an act like this can't go unmentioned. So thank you, Radigan."

Radigan took a step forward, smiled and bowed to the assembled.

"The second thing I want to explain is I'm not fully recovered and we need someone in charge. I've discussed this with Galean and we've decided to appoint Cherine to take my place.'

Surprise and relative silence spread through the crowd. A female leader wasn't a concept they had experience with. Suddenly Radigan walked up to them and turned.

"I pledge my full support to Cherine. I've known her for a very long time, I've seen her in fights, and I've seen her wisely handle some very adverse situations. I plan to offer her my time and my personal counsel."

Polite applause followed initially, and then others led by the masters shouted their acceptance of her leadership too.

Cherine looked at Radigan.

"You don't need to thank me," he said innocently.

"We'll talk later," she replied ruefully.

Cherine stepped over to Aron's side. He wasn't paying attention to

Radigan. He was watching the reaction of the women who were in a small group and in particular the expression on Tasha's face. She smiled at Radigan before she glanced at Aron. He turned and wobbled back to the tent. Vertigo made him very unsteady on his feet and sick in his stomach. Cherine followed him and so did Radigan. Aron sat down on his bed.

"Did you have any orders for me?" she asked.

"No, just look about and do what needs to be done."

"My offer of assistance extends to you also, Aron," said Radigan.

Aron glanced at Galean who had a doubtful expression.

"Radigan, I thank you for your offer, but I won't be doing much, and I'm sure your own business will keep you fully occupied."

"That is certainly true," Radigan replied. "Do you have a problem with my working with Cherine?"

"I don't, you'll have to ask her what her feelings are on the matter."

"I have no doubt we can come to an agreement," Radigan replied, looking expectantly at Cherine. "We've worked together closely in the past many times."

Cherine appeared uncomfortable. "I'll take that tour of the camp now, Aron. Thank you for the faith you've shown in me."

Radigan walked out at her side.

"I just hate that man," Aron muttered.

Galean chuckled. "I'll keep my eyes on him. Cherine won't be easy prey, Aron. She's dealt with him before. I won't be the only one watching him either."

"Tasha and Belisa dealt with him before too and their ultimate choices are still in question which way they'll go, Galean. Now that he saved my life, I've got to be nice to him."

"Life can be strange, that's for certain, Aron."

* * * *

Aron took his time with his recuperation; not so much that he needed it as he was in no hurry to resume the responsibilities. Leaving the decisions to Cherine gave him an excuse to shirk leadership, a goal he secretly coveted.

He strolled out one evening with the idea to spend some time with Tasha. When he arrived at her parent's tent they frowned.

"I'm sorry, Aron. She went to walk with Radigan. He's at her constantly," said her father unhappily.

"I see," he replied. "It was nothing important, sir. Tell her I'll speak with her another time."

"It's important to me, Aron," said her father pointedly. "She walks with him because he asks and there's no one else wooing her. Aron, don't be timid about this. I shudder to think of her life with such a man. She's too young to have been forced to face ugliness in her life, but it happened. She doesn't think we understand, but we know how a person can sink to their weaknesses instead of rising to their strengths. Even with the life of a villager, there are tests we face."

"I'll remember that, sir."

"She knows how we feel about this man, but we can't make her choices."

"I understand, sir."

Now motivated, Aron walked about the entire camp without finding them. It didn't give him a good feeling that she would go away with Radigan out of sight. The reasons for her doing so weren't reassuring, none of them were good. He decided to return to his area after a time. Finding them, at this point, had grim possibilities he could do without.

As he walked along he noticed Galean in the center of a gathering of his staffers speaking intently. He made a detour and sat down beside Liani. She smiled at him but her attention was focused on Galean. Aron listened to their ongoing dialogue.

"It's my conclusion this is a significant find. I've decided to allocate our full attention to this."

He noticed Aron for the first time.

"Aron hello, you probably wonder what I'm talking about. In our excavations at the new fortress site we dug up a strange object. As we continued to dig, we found much more of interest to us, which was equally inexplicable. Below this hill there were structures, like a settlement from the distant past. We just ran onto this today so I haven't had a chance to advise everybody. I wanted to get an idea about the find before I came before the leadership council."

"I understand, Galean, it isn't a problem. What's this all about? What did you discover?"

Galean nodded to an assistant who hurried away into the gloom returning after a short time carrying an object covered in a blanket.

Aron stood up in curiosity. He looked at Liani who'd remained seated.

"Come with me," he said, reaching out his hand to her.

She smiled again and stood up with his help.

They walked over to Galean who took the blanket off the discovery. Aron was puzzled, whatever it was and whatever it did, he had no idea. It was round, heavy, appeared to be metal and had colors and letters. The word formed by the letters was unknown to the onlookers.

Aron looked at Galean who was fascinated by the ball. Galean looked back.

"I have no answers, Aron. I don't know what it is or its purpose. I have a suspicion there could be much more buried in this hill. This is why I wish to reallocate our workers. I realize we need to complete the fortress, but this is a huge finding. I know you understand the importance of this."

Aron picked up the object and was surprised at its heavy weight.

"I don't disagree, Galean, but we've been building this fortress for nearly a year and we're still working on the lower regions. There is still no foundation lain for the outer walls."

"I realize it, Aron, but I would say in our defense we've made great progress with what we are working on. Building the escape tunnels, the storage rooms, water system, and the other specific rooms we've discussed is not a task we can accomplish quickly."

Aron glanced at Liani who was staring at the object.

"Do you have any ideas, Liani?"

"No Aron, I'm as mystified as everybody else and this discovery makes me curious about what other things we'll unearth. Perhaps they'll give us some clue to the purpose of this item."

"Have you shown this to the Arrecks, or Abdurka? Possibly the Uripeans may have some opinion."

"We've just discovered it, Aron. Of course we'll include the others. I haven't had a chance to speak to them yet."

"I was just thinking out loud, Galean. Sorry, I didn't mean to sound pushy. You know what you're doing. Perhaps I'll try to make myself useful by joining the diggers. It will help with rebuilding my strength and stamina. I'm curious too."

"Aron was there something you needed?" asked Galean. "I didn't ask why you joined our meeting."

"No, Galean. I was out to see someone who wasn't in, so I wandered over here."

Galean glanced at Liani. She turned towards Aron, glanced behind him and her expression changed. He turned his head to see Radigan walking beside Tasha coming out of the woods. Tasha seemed to sense their stare and looked toward them. She got a scowl on her face. Radigan smiled smugly at Aron like he scored another victory.

Aron felt dark, strong emotions.

"Aron," said Liani sharply to get his attention.

He blinked and turned his face back to her.

"We're going to do some further research, perhaps you'd like to join us?" asked Liani. "I have a text which may be helpful with these hidden objects."

"Good… yes," he muttered absently, trying to control his roiling feelings.

"Come with me!" She took his hand and pulled him into motion. He followed her away, still thinking about Tasha. He knew it wasn't a good choice to try to go to her now. The possibility of anything good happening was remote at best after seeing her come out from her secret time with Radigan. He could only think the worst.

Liani kept talking as they walked. Aron made a point to try to shift gears to focus on her instead of Tasha, but it wasn't easy for him. Galean walked at Liani's side and they talked about their theories.

Aron glanced back once, but they were gone out of his sight. He attended the session of the scholars - a good choice - calming him and diverting his attention back to important matters.

Liani was particularly attentive the entire night which he appreciated in his current depressed mood.

"Do you think this is an isolated object, perhaps dropped by a traveling band in the distant past?" Aron asked.

"Although that's a possibility, my feeling is no," Galean replied. "This discovery has a feel of great portent for me, though at this point I have nothing to support it. If we find nothing further, then perhaps you're right, Aron."

"What other thoughts do you have, Galean?"

"Another idea we're looking at is this may have been the site of a prior habitation, whether an individual structure, or a greater settlement. I've thought to expand the area of our digging and to dig deeper. That's the surest way to answer our questions in my opinion."

Liani was staring raptly at Galean like he was delivering the secrets of life which made Aron smile.

"I can't really take exception to your proposal, Galean. As long as we devote adequate manpower to our primary task of completing the fortress as soon as possible, I would say it's fine to pursue this other search too. I'm as curious as everyone else about this mystery."

"Excellent, Aron, I knew you were a man of vision."

Aron laughed along with the others in attendance. Liani smiled warmly.

"This is much better, Aron," she whispered. "Deal with what you can affect. Perhaps other matters need to work themselves out on their own."

He shrugged his shoulders noncommittally and walked over to examine and ponder the strange object again.

The next morning Aron attended Cherine's staff meeting for the officers. Radigan sauntered in at her side talking intently to her as they arrived. Whatever he was saying, she was listening closely. When Radigan completed his conversation, he looked directly at Aron with another self satisfied smile. Cherine looked to be somewhat discomfited.

"Good morning," Cherine started. "I've been told the prince has begun consolidating his control over the borderlands. Our hope that he would return to Nephora doesn't appear to be his plan. They're making preparations for a long term campaign and we're the obvious target. Our attempts to keep in touch with the Uripeans in Graysauld have been interdicted. Apparently they understand we have an alliance. I don't know of any strikes into the swamp, but at the same time, their ability to come to our aid is all but eliminated. Radigan has expressed the opinion we should discount them from any further part in our plans."

Aron's eyes narrowed as he looked around. Radigan had managed to change his perception in the camp where now his thoughts and suggestions were taken under consideration rather than simply dismissed because they were his. In spite of his past actions, and the possibility he still was an agent of the prince, he was ascending in the camp leadership hierarchy which displeased Aron. Brock came over and sat beside Aron.

"Brother, it's good to see you back amongst the living. Why aren't you up there helping Cherine instead of that viper?"

"I get a good view of things from here," Aron replied. "You've got to give it to him. He's good. He's done more than I could have if I tried to infiltrate the prince's camp. I don't trust him, but he's winning a lot of trust from the others here. It surprises me."

"I think he's a good planner," Brock answered. "That doesn't make him special in my eyes. He came among us with definite goals and he's determined in pursuing them. I don't think we'll be so easily conquered. I've had my fill of life under the royal boot. We're getting stronger by the day. There are many of these gangs coming to us voluntarily now. We've grown into a sizeable military force, and the masters are incredible at the training and the instillation of discipline. I think a great number of former criminals have grown to feel genuine loyalty to us. Life under our leadership is so much better than what they had. I think Radigan has a large following among those groups he's lured to his ways, but we greatly outnumber his people."

"I hope you're right, Brock. If we got into a major battle and he executed a mutiny, it could lead to our downfall."

"I can eliminate that problem any time you want, brother."

Aron chuckled. It drew the notice of the gathering.

"Did you have something to share, Aron?" asked Cherine with a scowl.

"I'm sorry," he replied. "My brother has a way with words. Please continue, Cherine."

Radigan eyed them closely. Brock and Aron stared back coolly.

"There's been another report I need to mention," Cherine continued. "One of the groups that have recently joined us comes from far to the west in the wilds, an area well away from any of our patrols. They state there's activity to the west of them. We'd never considered the wilds having a far border, but apparently that's the case. Whatever is beyond that border has taken notice and there have been probes. I think this is an important matter. The border gangs living there have been retreating rather than resisting that force. It strikes me as ominous if they're so fearsome as to drive away those criminals without even a fight to protect their territories."

Cherine looked at Aron.

"Possibly Abdurka can shed some light about them. Nobody else has any experience out there," Aron commented.

"Abdurka is occupied with Galean and his people digging in the ground," said Radigan, who didn't appear to be concerned about the unknown threat from the west. "I'll dispatch someone to seek him out."

"Thank you, Radigan," said Cherine, nodding to him. "I guess I should tell everyone I've decided to accept Radigan as an officer on my staff and an advisor to me. I know some of you won't understand, or agree with my choice, but there it is."

She looked straight at Aron for his reaction. He simply shrugged his shoulders. "It's your choice, Cherine. I trust you."

She smiled gratefully.

Trent and Brock turned and looked at Aron. Their opinions about the development were clear. Aron smiled wryly at their disapproval, like vicariously he was at fault for Cherine's risky decision.

After the meeting, Aron was unpleasantly surprised that Tasha showed up to meet Radigan, apparently to share the midday meal in his company. She looked at Aron like she was waiting for a response, but he was interrupted by Liani dragging him away on a pretext.

"What is it, Liani?"

"Lord Galean thought it wise that you dine with us to discuss the western problem."

"Did he? Though it's strange I don't see him present to have heard of the news. How did he receive word?"

"I don't know, Aron."

He stopped and turned her to face him.

"I'm sorry, Aron. It's too painful to watch Tasha's actions punishing you."

"Thank you for caring, Liani, but it's something I must deal with."

"Aron, simply watching from a distance is not a good plan. You must intercede with your feelings for her, or Radigan will simply take her away. You can't allow it, or else you need to decide to move on. You know there are others who would gladly seek your attentions."

He smiled at her. "I know that, Liani. Don't think I'm not considering those other options. I can't explain it. Something about Tasha, it's like we're fated together."

"Perhaps that fate intends for her to be your friend, Aron."

The theory struck him. He'd never thought of it that way. He didn't want to imagine a life where Tasha wasn't his wife.

He glanced back to see Radigan embrace Tasha. He then took Tasha and Cherine away with him.

"Maybe that's a good idea of yours to eat with Galean, Liani."

He followed her toward the fortress site. Galean was filthy from the digging far down from the surface. Abdurka was there working diligently.

They climbed down the ladders to the latest excavations and walked over to Galean.

"Aron, what is it? Has something happened?" asked Galean.

"There's word about incursions to the west."

Abdurka abruptly stopped his work and hurried over.

"This is dire news, Aron. Beyond the borders of the wilds to the west there are no friends, but there are forces capable to causing great havoc, forces about which we must be wary. Have there been any fights?"

"Not that I'm aware of," Aron replied.

"Good," Abdurka continued, "we must fade away before them and give them no reason to come farther. If they think it's a worthless wasteland here, we may have a chance. If we give them reason to think there's anything worth pursuing, they'll come back in force. I've told you the world outside of you is a dangerous and brutal place. The strong devour the weak."

"Why would they come now, Abdurka? What drew their notice?"

"It's impossible to say. Perhaps someone or something was spotted, or perhaps it was nothing more than restless soldiers exploring unknown regions. Regardless, our situation must be one of total avoidance at all costs. With the threat of the prince before us, drawing yet another enemy to our backs places us in a vulnerable position, a position where we could be wiped out."

Liani looked at Aron, like he had the answers.

"I guess we should start heading west to consolidate the tribes that live there and let them know what you said, Abdurka. I'll tell Cherine later so she can organize our forces accordingly."

"Later?" asked Galean.

"Cherine appointed Radigan to her staff as her advisor. She was going off with him and Tasha the last I saw."

Galean looked at Liani and then Abdurka. "Perhaps I've done enough down here for today. I'll clean myself and then join you, Aron."

Aron shrugged. They walked to the ladder and climbed up to ground level.

Galean went off to bathe.

* * * *

"Do you have any idea about Tasha, Liani?" asked Aron. "I don't understand."

She paused before she answered. "I can't speak for her and you already know I think you've been too passive, but if you're asking what draws her to Radigan, I think you should know with women, sometimes the rogue in a man is a lure. It isn't we don't see his flaws, because no woman could ever miss the glaring flaws in every man. We have a feeling we can fix them, make them better. Do you see what I'm saying?"

"So if a man acts outlandish such as Radigan does, this is stimulating to women?" he asked, incredulous.

Liani laughed. "No Aron, it isn't we want men to act badly, it's that we expect such behavior, but feel we can do something about it."

"I don't see it. It makes no sense to me. Someone like Radigan acts how he does because he wishes to act that way. He's not interested in being fixed, he's interested in, well, you know, getting what he wants from a woman, or I should say from women because he's not a man to be content with just one. If he ever manages to capture Tasha, that won't be the end of his dalliances. He's not much different than the prince in that regard."

"I agree with you, but in the case of Tasha, she has a history with him. It isn't something to discount. Aron, she's never known you closely. You never put her in a position to see you with your guard down. You never show her how you feel. You speak nobly enough for the public to hear, proclaiming your intentions, but then you never do anything further. Can you not see how frustrating that is for a woman? Perhaps she hasn't acted the best to your contacts, but Radigan ignores her moods and states his case. Aron, what are you waiting for? If you want Tasha, go and get her. If you want me, here I am."

Aron wasn't expecting that from Liani, a bold statement expressing her own desires.

"I, eh…" he stammered.

"You see what I'm saying. You're very frustrating for a woman, Aron."

Aron turned his head.

"You're right, Liani. I have been too passive. I'm going to change my ways."

He looked up as Abdurka walked up from behind them.

"You smell like dirt, Abdurka."

"That's not so bad a smell, I think, but I'll take a little time to cleanse myself since you folks are so sensitive about such unimportant things."

Aron chuckled and looked at Liani who had a look of disdain at his reference.

"Men," she muttered, shaking her head dismissively.

Chapter Three
~ Deepening Mysteries ~

Aron's decision to change his ways towards Tasha had to wait when everyone became focused on a second object unearthed by their diggers. It was equally inexplicable for them, but substantially more intriguing. The discovered item was large and cylindrical, and also made from metal. Makeshift winches and a crew of men were required to hoist the hefty item out of the ground.

Galean eyed the thing with a perplexed look.

"Do you have any ideas?" asked Aron.

"No more so than the first object. What I will say is this adds to my belief we're standing over the ruins of an important find. I think below us was a city of an ancient people. If these two objects are samples of their civilization, I suspect they may have had great knowledge about things we've lost over time. I'm inspired to devote even more effort to delving into the mystery. I know we must build our fortress, but for a scholar this is irresistible, Aron. I can't help myself."

Aron chuckled. "I understand, Galean. Do what you must, we'll adjust accordingly."

They walked around the cylinder studying it closely.

"Can you translate these words on the thing, Galean? What is the symbol? Have you seen such in your old books?"

"I haven't, Aron. As ancient as are our histories, it's possible we're looking at life prior to that time. I have no way to know how long these artifacts have been buried here."

"Are they dangerous in any way?"

"I don't know that either, but it's a good idea for us to be very cautious about them. I hate to say this but I think we should have limited access to any of our discoveries. I'm not saying we withhold the facts we glean, but the uninformed laying hands on these pieces would not be good. Some may think there is potential profit to be made here."

"I agree, Galean. I think we should assign a place to collect and store them. Maybe we need to add a new room to your construction plans."

"That's easily enough accomplished, Aron. I like that idea."

He glanced up at the rim of the surface ground above them and noticed Cherine and Radigan talking intensely. Aron scowled.

Galean was intent on the object and didn't notice. "Aron, the outer foundations are going to be prepared this next week. After that, obviously, we can begin to erect outer walls and create defenses. It won't interfere with what we're doing below grounds."

"Good, Galean. I'll see you later."

Aron climbed out of the excavation, but by then Cherine and Radigan were gone.

Aron wandered over to join Trache and Elcou who were sitting near Belisa who was talking to Liani.

"Hey guys, are you staying busy?"

"As busy as you," Elcou retorted.

Aron smiled. "I'm sorry if you don't think I'm pulling my weight, but stepping back has been just what I needed."

"We don't reflect on you," Trache pointed out. "We're concerned Radigan has been given authority in the camp and access now to many important people. If he chooses to work some scheme of the prince, we could suffer serious harm."

"I know that. I wouldn't have chosen him, but it was Cherine's decision and I trust her judgment. She may have him on a shorter leash than you realize. She's no dummy. There was a reason I picked her."

"Let's hope we don't rue her choice," Elcou reflected. "Controlling a rabid dog may not be so easy, even if it's your dog and you think it follows your instructions."

"Radigan, the rabid dog," said Aron, chuckling. "I like it."

Belisa and Liani turned to them.

"Hello, Aron."

"Ladies..."

"What brings you to us?"

"I just left Galean. They're looking at the newest discovery. There isn't anything I can do to help. I'm curious, but it's better if I get out of their way and let them work. What are you guys talking about?"

The women looked at each other.

"Women things," said Belisa evasively. "It's nothing to concern you, Aron."

"Right," he said, unsatisfied with the non-explanation.

"I have something I must take care of," said Belisa. "Please excuse me." She turned and walked away briskly.

Aron turned to Liani whose expression seemed like she felt guilty about something she didn't want to share with him. It didn't give him a good feeling.

"Is something wrong, Liani?"

"No, nothing is wrong."

"Why do I have trouble believing that?"

"It's just your imagination, Aron. Sometimes you see things that aren't really there about women. Your inner turmoil is clear to us, but that doesn't make your thoughts, suspicions and fears correct. Not everything involves you. Sometimes things happen to others that have nothing to do with you."

Aron shrugged. "I guess you've got a point, Liani."

"It's difficult for us to deal with you," she continued. "None of us want to add to your misery, so we try to be careful around you. It's a burden."

"I never realized that. Why didn't you say so before now?"

"You've had more than enough on your mind and with the attack of that beast you were in even worse condition."

"I'd love to resign as leader here. I'm happy to have Cherine continue to lead."

Liani smiled. "That isn't going to happen. You're going to be resuming authority, probably sooner than later."

"That's great news," he replied sourly.

"Do you have any tasks for us today?"

"Not really, I was going to work on the construction of the wall."

"Aron, that's not work for you," Liani chided.

"I need mindless labor sometimes. It helps me relax."

Liani scowled at him.

"If that's what you're doing, I have things I can do with the women.

If you need me, you can find me there. I think Tasha was organizing a group of women to care for the injured and the ill."

"That's fine. I'll see you later, Liani."

He watched her walk away. Liani was a beautiful young woman and his affection for her was continuing to grow.

Aron glanced around the camp as he walked back toward the construction site. He noticed Radigan talking to a group of men. Radigan looked up and saw Aron. He nodded amicably. The men with him had dark expressions. Aron nodded back and continued his walk.

He picked a place surrounded by laboring Brutans. They were diligently fervent about the construction. He nodded to them and pitched in, burying his worries and thoughts with hard work. The day passed by quickly. Since he'd conquered the Brutans, they had gradually tolerated Aron and even began to accept him to an extent. For a closed group it was fortuitous for Aron to gain their trust and loyalty. He had no illusions they'd magically transformed into model citizens, but for the time being having them be non-threatening to the rest of the camp was a big improvement.

Aron left work as the night grew dark. Covered in grime, he walked slowly to the nearby stream to bathe. Washing quickly, he was about to leave when sounds of movement carried across from the other side of the stream. The night was too gloomy to see anything so he squatted down motionless. He waited patiently until he again heard movement and then a growl. Freezing with fear, he drew out his sword. At that moment a large group of Brutans came up behind him to bathe. The predator suddenly turned and raced away. The Brutans stopped and watched the brush move as the creature ran along.

"Thank you," said Aron. "I seem to be good at drawing animal attacks."

They nodded and eased up to the stream cautiously. Aron hurried into the camp. His parents were sitting with Tasha and her parents. Aron walked over. Tasha got up and served him a plate of food and coffee.

"Thank you," he mumbled.

"You're welcome," she replied softly.

He noticed her father's avid stare,

"Did he make you do that, Tasha?"

"No," she replied, but he felt she was lying.

"Listen, you don't have to do anything for me you don't want to do."

"I didn't mind, Aron."

"Good, then I'm doubly thankful."

Tasha chuckled.

"Can I sit beside you, Tasha?"

She looked at him doubtfully. "Aron, I'm the same person you ignored when we were kids."

"I'm not ignoring you now."

She blinked her eyes and turned to go sit down.

He followed her and sat between her and his own mother.

"I heard about your organizing efforts, Tasha. That's a good thing you're doing."

Tasha smiled warmly. "Thank you. It's not much, but at least it's something."

"Are you feeling stronger, Aron?" asked her father. "That was some blow to the head you took."

"I'm much better now, sir. Thank you."

Being with Tasha was enjoyable, but in this situation where it seemed her father was coercing her toward him, he couldn't be sure if Tasha would have made any overtures on her own.

They talked for a time reminiscing about their village days.

"Do you still hate Coraline, Tasha?"

"I never hated her. I was jealous as a girl. Our experiences at the palace changed us all. Now I feel sorry for her. I can't believe she stayed back to honor her wedding vows to him. I think she made a poor choice. She'll never have a good life as his wife. He'll never change and he doesn't even want to change. Him I will hate to my dying day."

"I don't want to pry, but I think you know Radigan is a thorn in my side. I don't understand you two. I know you have a past, but I don't get the present. It's easy for me to think you prefer spending your time with him."

"That's a conclusion you concocted, Aron. When I'm with him it's because he makes the effort. He's actively pursuing me. You say you want me to be your wife, but all I see is your back as you're walking away. You view me with suspicion, you don't trust me, and you nearly drew your sword on me and threw me out of the camp. I think you can do better than that if you mean to romance me. Am I wrong? Why don't I draw a sword on you and see how you like it?"

Aron chuckled. “When you put it that way, I am pretty lame.”

Tasha chuckled also. “You’re beyond lame, you’re hopeless.”

“About him…”

“Aron, why do you want to talk about Radigan? Can’t you think of a better topic?”

“I’m sorry, he bothers me a lot, Tasha.”

A calculating look came over her face as she studied his. “It’s strange how I chased you around all those years and now the role is reversed. It’s weird to me that you don’t act normal toward me. I’m just a village girl.”

“No Tasha, you’re much more than just a village girl. Look at the effect you have on men. Radigan risks his life daily for you. The Uripean chieftain saw you amongst all of the other women. Don’t you remember, you, the dark haired woman? He saw you as another wife. The prince is ignoring his kingdom, and Coraline, incurring vast expense with the army in the field chasing after you, and I can’t look at you without my heart skipping a beat.”

Tasha chuckled. “You actually said something almost romantic, Aron.”

He scowled playfully. “You better stop messing with me. I know where you live.”

They both laughed.

He hadn’t felt this good in years and felt hope for the first time. His long lost rapport seemed to be sneaking back, in spite of his awkward romancing mistakes - a moment in time he desired to preserve.

He looked into her eyes hopefully.

“What are you thinking, Tasha?”

“I’m thinking maybe I could beat you if I draw my sword. I’m getting pretty good in my training.”

Aron smiled. “I would love to train you if Cherine will turn you loose.”

“Maybe,” she replied with a smirk. “Cherine is really good.”

“And I’m not?”

“Naw…” she answered chuckling.

He grabbed her impulsively and she laughed. His arms around her was immensely compelling. He hugged her tightly.

“I hope you understand my feelings,” he whispered into her ear.

“I’m starting to,” she replied. “This is better, Aron. Don’t forget that

I have feelings too. How you act affects me. I never do anything to hurt you, but I can't make you come to me. You've got to do it yourself. I'm sorry you're threatened about Radigan. What do you plan to do about it? That's what's important."

"You're right, Tasha. When you and Belisa acted cold that first night after we escaped, I didn't handle it well. I know that with my head, but in my gut I just couldn't cope. I felt like you blamed me and wanted me out of your life."

"Actually I understand that, Aron. I can see how you would feel that way. The problem is you couldn't understand how I felt. What you went through gave you no insight into what we went through. There's nothing in your life to give you that insight. Other women can understand us. That's why we talk together so much. It isn't to exclude you, it's to support us. When a woman goes through what we did it affects you to your core, and changes you in spite of what you want to happen. The long term erosion of spirit and resolve with that kind of life is terrible. Do you hear what I'm telling you? It makes it impossible to love someone else when you can't forgive and love yourself. That's why we needed separation, to try to crawl back from the dark abyss of shame. You can say you understand, but you really can't. I'm not ashamed for what was forced on me. I couldn't prevent it. I'm ashamed because I eventually gave up and gave in."

"I'm truly sorry, Tasha. I'm sorry I couldn't prevent it and protect you. It doesn't change my wish to marry you."

Tasha turned her face and they kissed tenderly.

"Do you understand me now?" she asked softly. Aron crushed her in an embrace.

Both sets of parents tried to pretend they weren't paying close attention. They smiled happily to each other.

"Let's take a walk," said Aron standing up and extending his hand to Tasha. She took it and let him pull her up. "We'll be back a little later."

Radigan watched the encounter from not far away. He simmered with anger as his plans were in real jeopardy. For him, Tasha was the most critical issue and the only one he really cared about. He wanted Tasha exclusively.

Radigan went off to gather his confederates. He had some radical ideas in his mind.

Meanwhile, Aron felt giddy with Tasha walking at his side holding his hand. He was particularly happy because she seemed to be happy too, a development he worried could never come true.

"When you walked with him it was all I could do to keep from chasing you down I was so jealous, Tasha."

She shrugged. "I'm sorry you suffered, but do you realize you had yourself to blame? It could have been you walking me instead of him all along. You forgot I was smitten with you, Aron. Staking your claim wasn't a difficult task. If you had to work a bit, hey, I think I'm worth it. The chief of the Uripeans sure thought so."

They chuckled.

"He definitely had a goal in mind for you."

"What's your goal for me, Aron?" She stopped and turned to him.

He felt sweat beads on his forehead and his face flushed. This was new ground for him.

She watched him and waited patiently.

"You'd race into the deadliest battles outnumbered and in peril, yet I'm so frightening, Aron?"

He shrugged his shoulders. "About you, I guess I'm vulnerable. I don't want to make a mistake and lose you. With my sword I'm confident because I know what I can do. With you, I'm not experienced in love so I'm afraid I'll look foolish compared to Radigan."

"Aron," she said in frustration, "this isn't searching out the secrets of life, and it isn't difficult at all. Why don't you just relax? We can sit over there under the tree and just be together. I'd like that."

He smiled sheepishly and let her pull him into the obscured place where they could be alone - a good choice on his part. Now they were able to change the nature of their relationship and strengthen their feelings for each other. Aron felt Tasha's love for the first time in terms he could understand.

They returned much later in the darkness to their families, both sets of whom had retired to sleep. Liani was already resting comfortably when they got into their bedrolls beside her. Belisa was staying with the Arreck soldiers that evening.

Aron smiled before he dozed off. At last his situation was improving.

Later a band of men slipped out of the camp and headed toward the border with the kingdom.

"Go directly to the prince," said Radigan as they left. "Don't get caught. If you are, I'll disclaim any knowledge of you, do you understand?"

They nodded silently and departed.

Radigan hurried back to the camp. He smiled deviously as he crept over to where Tasha was sleeping beside Aron. He placed his bedding boldly right beside her, close enough so he could 'body up' against her. She moaned slightly as he pushed against her back, but she didn't awaken.

In the morning the rising sun on the distant horizon was dim in the camp as a large rainstorm approached. Aron opened his eyes first and glanced over at Tasha. He was stunned to see Radigan sleeping with her in his embrace. She was also still asleep. Aron's old anxiety flared up in spite of his prior night with her. He carefully got up and went to take care of his morning business; warm feelings had quickly drained away leaving him in a sour mood.

Aron nodded to the closest sentry as he headed for a nearby tree. Lightning flashed and thunder rumbled as the fast moving storm closed in on them. Aron hurried to get back just as the first raindrops fell.

Tasha was talking to Radigan when he came back. She looked up at Aron with a smile, but saw the look on his face. It wasn't difficult to surmise he'd drawn some conclusions. She shook her head in frustration.

Aron stood a moment pondering what he should do.

"Good morning, Aron," said Radigan magnanimously. "You improve noticeably each day. This is very good."

"Radigan," he replied neutrally.

"Tasha, I think our friend could use a strong cup of coffee."

Tasha bristled at his attempt to exercise ownership of her. Aron eyed him coolly. She stood up and walked stiffly over to the cook fires. She came back with the coffee and handed it to Aron, but she also put her hand to his back and rubbed him possessively. Aron blinked his eyes at her gesture.

"Thank you, Tasha," he said, smiling at her.

"Yes, thank you, Tasha," said Radigan, as if her action at his behest was a validation of his claims on her.

Tasha looked at Radigan pointedly.

Both sets of parents came over at that moment to join them for breakfast. Radigan did not leave. Instead he sat amongst them and ignored the dour looks maintaining his aloof and untroubled mood.

Tasha sat down beside Aron. Radigan was unfazed. He smiled warmly and chatted amicably to no one in particular. It irked Aron that Tasha kept her eyes on her food, but eventually she smiled and made eye contact with Radigan. His ongoing conversation didn't require an audience, but when he got her he pounced.

"Today has a momentous feel to it, does it not, Tasha. I have duties to attend serving Cherine, but later I'll be free if you can find time in your schedule. I know you have a great deal to do with your project, but we must eat, so perhaps we can break bread together."

Tasha stared at him contemplatively. She glanced at Aron.

"I'm sorry, Radigan," he ventured. "Tasha has plans with me today."

"Certainly," Radigan replied without showing any concern, "perhaps another day, Tasha."

Aron was about to add she'd be tied up for the rest of her life, but a messenger hurried over to them and went straight to Aron.

"My lord, the prince has begun to punish any villagers he catches who are trying to escape into the wilds to join us. Trent wishes to know what we should do for them."

"What did Cherine say?" Aron asked.

"I'm sorry, I was told to come straight to you. I haven't advised her of this yet."

Aron scowled.

"Please speak to her. I'll give her my opinion, if she asks."

"Yes, my lord."

He hurried away.

"You're going to need to resume your old job, Aron," said Tasha. "You know you should have done so already. It isn't that they don't respect Cherine, but you're our leader whether you like it or not."

Aron glanced at Radigan. He had a pleased smile. "I'm afraid she's right. The mantle of leadership will follow you around, Aron. It's clear you need to consider our future path. If we try to dispatch fighters to protect the villagers in the open, we'll be easy meat for the royal host. The prince wants to provoke you into precipitous action. You know he will go to any lengths to achieve his goals. If you don't answer this challenge, he'll continue to increase his offenses until you can no longer ignore them."

Aron got up. "I guess I better go see Cherine. I'll see you later, Tasha."

He was surprised Radigan got up also to walk beside him.

"I'm sorry to disturb your convalescence."

Aron did not sense genuine regret. Radigan was pleased, again and that made Aron suspicious.

They walked to the far edge of the camp where Cherine was talking with a number of the masters.

"I heard," she said as they sat down beside her. "I fear there is little we can do. The prince is offering bait to lure us into his traps. He still has unlimited manpower to face us. We're a larger force now, but not on a scale to face the prince in open battle."

"I know, Cherine," Aron replied.

Cherine looked at Radigan.

"Do you have any ideas?"

"If we're to do anything, it must be a surprise to the prince, something he wouldn't have anticipated."

"What could we do?" asked Aron curiously. "What could possibly surprise the prince?"

"If we send a large force it will draw their notice. My idea is to send small teams to slip through their lines in the darkness to get behind them. Those teams must be familiar with the surrounding area, to know where the occupied villages are. They must infiltrate and give those villagers instructions on escaping and then lead them to safety. Obviously the Black Fist would need to be prominent in that plan. No one else knows the layout of the villages."

Instantly, Aron's suspicions were aroused - that plan could lead to wiping out the Black Fist. Dispersing them greatly increased their vulnerability. Aron glanced at Cherine who appeared to have the same reservations.

"We'll consider your idea, Radigan. Thank you for sharing your thoughts. Aron, do you have any alternatives?"

"Not really, Cherine, I'm sorry. I'm not much of a tactician."

"Perhaps we could even out the personnel on those teams, some of them Black Fist to direct their routes, some masters to support them with their battle skills, and then add some of our trainees," Radigan added.

"I'll need to think about it," Cherine replied. "I'll make my decision and let you know, Radigan."

A brief look of calculation came over his eyes before he smiled and bowed his head to her. “Of course, Cherine, I’m at your service.”

“Why don’t we ride to the border and talk to Trent directly. He may have some ideas of his own,” Aron ventured.

Cherine nodded her head. “We’ll take a sizeable force with us. Something bothers me today. I want to be ready for anything.”

“Good thought,” said Aron.

“Gather some troops, Radigan,” she ordered.

After he left, she looked straight at Aron.

“There were many suspicious about the circumstances of your accident and here I feel those same worries. Radigan distresses me a great deal. He could be such an asset, but I get the feeling there is always something dire in his mind.”

“I’m glad you said that, Cherine. We all feel that way. I was worried he…well.”

“That I could fall under his thrall…? I keep a close rein on my emotions with any man, not just Radigan. With him I’m especially cautious. He thinks he’s too shrewd for me, or any other woman, that he can win us over with his charm in the end. That will not happen.”

Aron chuckled.

“What’s funny?”

“I’d never count on charming a woman into anything. I’ve got to give it to Radigan in that aspect. He’s a step beyond me.”

“You’re too critical of yourself, Aron. Other people, women in particular, don’t see you in weak or negative lights. You just don’t understand us.”

“No argument here.”

Radigan returned with a force of Black Fist, masters and men loyal only to Radigan. Without delay, they left for the borderlands.

They rode steadily on a road Aron had ordered to be created for rapid travel with horses. Clearing away the barbs and brambles had been difficult and painful labor – a considerable amount of time for sure, but the end result was worth it in speeding up travel to and from that critical place.

Only a week passed to get to Trent’s camp. Trent was surprised to see them ride in.

“Greetings, my friends, what brings you to see me?”

“We got your message about the prince,” Aron replied.

"It's good to see you back in action, Aron."

"Cherine is still in charge, but I'm making myself available. This is a tough problem. I'm sure the prince thinks he has us over a barrel. What's he doing to them?"

Trent looked grim.

"After they're tortured, he stakes them out exposed to the sun and elements. Bound as they are, they have no way to ward off predators. The prince's forces are always close enough to watch for our intervention. So far I've only gone once into a fight with them. I took more fighters than they anticipated, but they had reinforcements to call up so we exited quickly. Some of those poor souls didn't make it. They'd been staked out for many days without food or water. The young ones were in tough shape. The old ones didn't have the stamina. I'm sorry I couldn't do more for them, Aron."

"There's no fault on you, Trent. You did what you could. It's the prince who'll answer for all of this."

Aron noticed Radigan staring out at the horizon.

"Do you see something there Radigan?"

"I see a haze. I don't know if it's from their fires, or if it's a cloud kicked up by moving soldiers."

They all looked; something was moving out there.

"What do you think, Trent?"

"I've not seen such before. I don't know."

"Let's send some fast riders," said Cherine.

Everybody agreed and soon after five horsemen sped away heading toward the foggy mystery.

"I've got small camps positioned in both directions along the border," Trent explained. "Their instructions are to send word to me, not to confront the enemy. We're spread very thin, so I don't want small units overwhelmed and outnumbered in fights with the royals."

"Excellent, Trent, I've said all along, you're the man for leadership," Aron advised with a smirk.

"That's not going to work, Aron. I have my role and so do you. My role is not yours. You can't change that reality as much as you seem to want it."

"I just think we'd all be better off if I wasn't the one in charge and making decisions for the group, Trent."

Chapter Four

~ Escalations ~

Instead of following the script conceived by Radigan, Aron decided to lead a significant force himself to spring the prince's trap. He took a great risk by including Trent, Cherine and Radigan in that force. If they were killed or captured, it could be a death blow to the resistance movement.

Aron watched Radigan to gauge his reaction. As always, he was a mask of neutrality. Whatever his inner thoughts and feelings, he didn't betray them for Aron to see.

Over five hundred troops gathered in their assault unit and left at dusk departing the concealment of the wilds. Riding rapidly, Trent had locations already mapped out for the royal camps and where the captives were being held.

Over an hour passed to reach the closest of the imperial forces. The royal forces were watching for him, but Aron attacked with such speed and with superior skilled forces they cut through the imperial outer defenses like paper. Aron's force raced into the main camp and attacked the startled enemy. A sizeable force was on hand, but Aron had surprise and the advantage of mounted forces shredding infantry troops. The battle was never in question. The royal commander surrendered fairly quickly. All of them eyed Cherine, knelt to her, and humbly apologized for the fight.

"I know you feel loyalty to the crown fighting for your country, but you know this isn't about any danger to the kingdom. Any danger from us is reserved for the monarchy alone. I don't question you serving in the army, but how can you countenance these atrocities you do to innocent and helpless villagers simply because he orders you to do so merely to draw us out. What did these people ever do to warrant such treatment? If it were your families, your wives and children exposed to this outrage, would you sit idly by?"

The commander was daunted and ashamed.

"Who was I, or any of us, to contradict the prince? What power do you imagine I could have to do anything about it?"

"Was I not in that same position, commander? You know the price I paid at the hands of the prince. I took action and you can too."

The commander looked up at her and then at Aron.

"What are you saying?"

Cherine looked at Aron. "You've got to decide about this?"

Aron glanced around at the others of his forces. They eyed him quietly.

"Commander, I haven't done this before so you'll be the first. When we conquer barbarians, we give them the chance to change their ways, to live better lives and to join us. I'll allow you the same opportunity join us too, but my thought is to keep you here on station to pretend you'rc still following Agar's orders. Meanwhile I want to possibly extend a network of royal soldiers secretly loyal to my cause. You can use Cherine as a rallying point. She definitely warrants your high regard and she has the notoriety throughout the kingdom. If you must interdict villagers to maintain the façade, that's fine, but treat them humanely and only pretend the torture if the prince comes around to check on you. We'll establish a communication network to bring you into our planning. What's your reply?"

"I will gladly accept your offer, Aron. For your information you are well regarded in the ranks too. It is a very tenuous hold the prince has on the army. Each man must make his own choice because some fear retribution against their families back home, some see themselves as patriots regardless of what the prince does, and others are like me, wishing for a better world and worthy leadership. The choices of the prince are galling to so many but we've felt powerless to do anything about it. We see what he does and say those poor victims could be our wives or daughters in the future with this misguided man. I personally have no problem at all with pledging allegiance to you, Aron, if you truly are the principled person they say. If your aim is to save the kingdom, I think you'll find a great many are with you."

"You know the commanders along the front. Our plan was to strike quickly before the alarm is raised to rescue suffering villagers, but if we can avoid those fights and loss of life, I would be grateful. Please stand up commander, as well as, your men. I never want people kneeling to me. I'm not the prince."

The commander stood up. "Thank you, my lord. I could travel about and speak on your behalf to the other camps. I know which ones to avoid. As I said, there are some who are blindly loyal to the prince, no matter what."

"If we can spare the innocent, that's my overriding wish," Aron explained. "We already have a network and allies we were building before we came here. I'd like to begin to connect both forces and eliminate needless casualties, do you agree?"

"Of course, my lord... You've been more than generous in sparing our lives. As I stand here with you hearing your plan, I feel hope. It's something I didn't think possible in this realm."

"I'm extending my trust," Aron concluded. "It may be a good idea to secretly explain to the villagers the wisdom of staying home. We're not in a position to accommodate great numbers of refugees right now. We have a great deal left to do to get up to minimal standards and be a deterrent to the prince."

"I understand, my lord."

"In the near future, we'll bring you and the other leaders who pledge to us to our main base in the wilds to explain some things."

"As you wish, my lord, consider us your loyal servants now..."

"Good, I'd like to talk to your prisoners now."

The commander led Aron, Cherine, Trent, and Radigan to a single large tent. Inside were huddled twenty gaunt and terrified people: fathers, mothers, and children. They were gaunt and terrified.

Aron sat down beside a little girl with large round brown eyes.

"Hi," he said gently.

"Hi," she whispered.

"I want to tell you everything is going to be okay now. My name is Aron. You folks were coming to join us. We came here to save you, but the royal forces in this camp have decided to switch sides. From now on they're going to protect you. I'm asking you to bear with me and help perpetrate a ruse to fool the prince. You'll be here pretending to be suffering captives, but you'll be fed and safeguarded. If the prince shows up you act as if you're in torment until he leaves. Can you do that? I don't intend this to be your permanent home, but we're not ready yet to contest with the prince on a large scale. We're going to try to convert the entire frontier, or at least as many as we can sway. If you'd made it to my camp I want you to know life there is very primitive. I'm building a place of safety, but it's a long way from being finished. I'm going to have a communication link established here so if you need to get word to me, you can do so. I'm sorry for what you've been through, but better days are on the horizon for us all."

"Thank you, my lord," said the little girl's mother. "We thought this was our end here. I couldn't accept such a fate for her. She hasn't had a chance to live yet. We'll do as you ask of us."

Aron kissed the little girl on the forehead. She smiled shyly and looked at her mother.

"It's all right, darling," she whispered. "He's a good man. He's protecting us."

When they walked out of the tent, Aron stopped and turned to Radigan.

"I want to say something to you. It's no secret I don't trust anything you say or do. That's not the point, regardless of what you've been through in your life and the things you've done because you could. It's my honest belief that down deep, everyone has a conscience. You saw those poor helpless people in there. They didn't deserve this. They've done nothing wrong. It's the prince's doing. Either you're a part of it as his agent, or you're with us in resisting it. Think about it, and don't bother telling me some expedient answer. I wouldn't believe you anyway. What I judge you on are your actions. I don't hold your pursuit of Tasha against you. We both know she's a rare treasure that every man would want, but I will not tolerate what happened to these villagers and if you have a hand in it, I will seek retribution on the behalf of those who have no power. Don't be standing on the wrong side on that day, Radigan."

Radigan was daunted.

"You don't have to give an answer, but realize I always watch what you do, Radigan. You may think you can beat me in a fight, but if I were you I wouldn't bet my life on it. You can be as arrogant as you want, but at the same time you'd better use your head. You take some needless chances in your life. If I truly saw you as an ally and a person to trust I'd see that as a big detriment."

Radigan glanced at Cherine who eyed him critically. Trent had never been friendly to him.

"I understand, Aron," he said finally.

Aron's force stayed that night in the camp, but got up early in the morning to return to the wilds.

"Do you have any doubts about the imperial soldiers, Cherine?" asked Aron as they rode side by side.

"I don't, Aron. I felt he was being honest. He's right, there are many who wish to resist the prince, but have no ability to do so. This is a good idea to secretly wrest away control of his forces. The prince isn't a person who could see it coming. Even with his paranoia, he truly feels his power insulates him and the other royals from their consequences because it's been true for all of their lives. No one has ever successfully mounted a challenge to that way of life."

"I feel overwhelmed by this whole movement. I worry because we can't afford to fail, but I'm in charge and I know how incompetent I am."

Cherine chuckled. "I've always lived around arrogant self absorbed men. To hear you castigate yourself so foolishly, it amuses me. It adds to your charm, Aron."

"Buffoons are charming?" he asked astonished.

She laughed heartily.

"You just don't see how others see you. People see you as a great man."

"You're right, Cherine, I don't see that. They're misguided."

She laughed again. "Aron, it's one of the great pleasures of my life to be your friend. I hope you can take that in the spirit it's given."

"Cherine, it's my honor. For me, you're a great inspiration. I've faced challenges, but what you've had to overcome in your life impresses me to no end. I'm still just a farmer so to be in the company of people like you is amazing."

She eyed him contemplatively and finally shrugged.

"I think we can dispense with this charade of my leadership, Aron. You've been capable of resuming control for a while now."

"Actually, I don't want to resume yet. Being in this position gives me a unique chance to view some things out of notice. I know you want to be rid of the burden, but I ask you to bear with me a little longer. I think having the men adjust to seeing qualified women in leadership is a very good thing."

"Don't wait too long, Aron. I'm not an ambitious person. Leading the masters is all the authority I want right now."

"If I get killed off, you'll have experience to step in and take my place."

"Don't even say that. Aron, you're more than our leader, you're our hope and our inspiration. Without you, there would never have been any rebellion and without you this all collapses like a tent in a storm. There are precious few who can defy the prince and you're one of them. Without you, I'd still be the prince's play thing. Think about the world we can build rather than about your demise. You make me feel all crazy."

"Is that good or bad?"

"Both, silly man... Maybe you should stop talking."

Aron laughed.

They rode into the wilds and continued toward his base. He was glad Radigan was riding with him unable to take advantage of Tasha.

* * * *

Meanwhile, the reports coming to the prince were uniformly similar. The village captives were docile and Aron had shown no response to the prince's latest ploy, the idea he'd gotten from Radigan's messengers.

"Granor, this strikes me as strange. Radigan implied this would provoke Aron into action. There's no sign he even notices what we're doing, and these villagers reactions aren't normal. We've dealt with villagers before and they're not a tame lot. I wonder what's afoot in our midst."

"I agree, sire. They made that initial raid, but they've done nothing of consequence since that time. Perhaps they suspect Radigan and followed his messengers. I expected more from them too. I can go to our outposts to see if those commanders have any feel for the enemy plans. It may be there are low level actions occurring they didn't feel warranted reporting to us."

"Make it clear I want word on even the smallest of actions from the rebels. I'll decide what's important, not them."

"As you command, my prince..."

Granor rode out an hour later with a very large troop and did a sweep along the entire frontier. At each stop, the commanders followed

Aron's instructions and mimicked loyalty to the crown. The "prisoners" put on a nice show of their "suffering" until Granor left, after which they had a good laugh. Granor was aware of the unusual similarities in every camp, but kept it to himself. With nothing on the surface to point to, he was convinced this situation needed further investigation.

When he returned to the prince they met in secret without his generals present.

"Sire, I have nothing I can give as proof, but there was a strange feel to the camps, like I was being misled. I'm not sure what it would mean. They would seem to have nothing to gain. Maybe the long term effect being away from home and family is manifesting in this way. They aren't disobeying your orders, but what they are doing I can't grasp yet."

"Thank you, Granor, I trust your instincts. I think we need to create a secret plan for this. I want you to decide who is truly trustworthy and loyal to me. We'll make them a force at my disposal in case of unexpected events. Honestly I question if we can trust all of the people wearing my uniforms. Go about this discreetly, but as rapidly as you can. I no longer depend on an oath to the crown to guarantee trust."

"As you command, sire..."

He thought about his wife, Coraline, after Granor's comment about the troop's homesickness. He actually felt a desire to go home to her. His pursuit of Tasha after so long a time was losing its urgency. Belisa was dismissed from his mind now that she was back in the presence of her Arreck soldiers. All that remained was his stubbornness about being defied.

His father, the king, had recently sent word of his concerns that Agar's campaign was taking too long and costing the realm too dearly in treasure. Agar was both angry and worried. Failure wasn't acceptable, but Aron was proving to be an incredibly difficult opponent. There was no simple solution and putting a time limit on his campaign was the last thing he expected. The king had also advised him about troubling developments elsewhere in the kingdom. There were increasing reports of unrest scattered across a wide area - not outright rebellion, but to have any resistance at all was a new development.

For once, the prince thought about situations other than his personal agenda. It wasn't so much that he'd grown as a man, but now realized he was vulnerable. Events he caused and failures he authored could come back and endanger his future ascension to the throne - a sobering detail.

He sought out Granor. He suspected Granor was there to judge Agar's actions and report back to the king.

"I find it prudent that we return home to counsel the king. He has concerns I need to address and I must admit I would like to see my wife again. We'll maintain our positions along the border. I don't think the rebels will pose a threat in the interim. They're building their nest and consolidating the criminals of the wilds under their control. I'll return when it's practical for me to do so. Do you have any questions?"

"No sire, I'll protect your position here until you return. That's clear enough. I agree it's wise to return to the capital and to the king."

The prince nodded and went to pack his things for the trip. He took a very sizeable contingent as his escort. He wanted no surprises along the way he couldn't handle.

* * * *

When Aron rode into camp, he and Brock both noticed Barmon and Sirina sitting together talking. Brock's half brothers Damor and Bren were sitting beside them listening to the conversation.

Brock dismounted and walked over to them.

"Father, mother... It's nice to see you together."

His father had a distant look. His mother slowly turned her face to look at Brock.

"Did I interrupt something?" Brock asked frostily with a grim look.

"We've been talking about, well, the situation," Sirina started. "I don't want to distress either of you. I know you don't understand my feelings. I don't know that I could explain them to you. Brock, I haven't rejected your father. It's just that I can't ignore what happened afterwards. I was the mate of Straga and here are his sons. It isn't possible to simply go back to the life we had and pretend I don't have two families. Can I be a wife to Barmon again and deny Straga?"

"Sure," said Brock. "Do you think his stealing another man's wife is something to honor and to uphold? I don't. What's your issue, mother? Is it that you prefer the barbarian? Those vows you made as a maiden freely and without coercion to my father, do they mean nothing to you now? Because we were torn away from you by force, does it make us inconsequential? I don't advocate ignoring your other sons, I advocate you acknowledging all of your son's needs. Is it so difficult to love and respect the goodness in my father in favor of the arrogance and brutality of your captor? I don't see any dilemma for you to continue to ponder. I think you don't want to tell us your choice you already made."

Barmon looked at Sirina who was emotionally distressed.

"I hear my sons words very clearly, Sirina. I loved you then and I love you still, but if there's truth in what he just said, speak it now and be done with us. I've waited patiently for you to come back to me. I'll wait no longer. If you've come to love this other man and your feelings for me died somewhere along the way, it's better for you to tell me the truth. I've dreamed of the time we could have a life again, but I think maybe that was my dream alone."

"Barmon, I didn't stop loving you," she whispered.

It surprised both of them. Brock looked at Barmon.

"What are you saying, Sirina?"

She looked at her other two sons.

"I've struggled to find a way to accommodate both of you, but it's clear there is none. If I must make a choice this minute, I choose you Barmon."

They both anticipated the opposite choice so it took a few minutes to realize what she'd actually said and to react. Sirina looked forlorn and fragile staring back at them.

Barmon moved close and took her in his arms.

"Thank God," he muttered over and over again. Sirina hugged him tightly.

"I don't know what to say to Straga. He'll be very angry."

"Don't worry about Straga. We'll deal with him if he tries to cause trouble. This is the price of his thievery. You never were his except in his mind, Sirina. Everything will be better now, I promise."

Brock went over to the boys.

"I know this is confusing for you. If you're agreeable, as of this moment, you're fully my brothers and I will treat you such from now on. You must treat my father as your father too. He's a good man. It's not that Straga is no longer your father. Now you have two fathers. There could be bad blood from him, but he stole my mother. That can't be allowed. Do you have anything you want to say?"

The boys looked at each other and shook their heads.

"We're going to move in with my husband, Barmon," said Sirina. "We'll live with him now. You'll still see Straga, but I won't be living with him ever again. Do you understand?"

"Yes mother," they whispered.

"You can learn a great deal from Barmon and from Brock, things Straga would not teach you, important things about character, integrity, and compassion for others."

They looked at Brock.

"I will teach you," he affirmed.

"Yes, brother," they retorted softly.

"Sirina, I didn't think I could ever feel happiness," said Barman.

"I'm sorry for the pain I've caused you, husband. You deserve a better wife."

"I want no other than you, darling. Let's go home. Come boys."

Aron smiled as he watched the reunited family leave. He glanced around and noticed Tasha staring intently at him. She walked up to him.

"What did you learn from that, Aron?"

"I guess there can be happy endings after all."

"Does that include us?"

Aron smiled and embraced her warmly. "Yes it can."

"Can you put aside your doubts and your suspicions, Aron? Can you believe what I tell you instead of following your fears about me?"

"I can't stop being a dunce, Tasha, but I can give you the promise of my love and devotion."

She chuckled. "I know you're a dunce. I'll just have to live with it."

"Hey," he objected. "You're not supposed to agree with me. I was trying to be humble."

"You succeeded, Aron."

They also walked away, arm in arm.

They spent the evening with their families. Radigan still came to join them acting as if he was still a key player for Tasha's affections. Tasha smiled politely to him, but her attention focused on Aron. At that moment, Aron felt like perhaps he'd won at last.

* * * *

Galean hurried to the digging site. Another object was unearthed which they'd said was urgent for him to see. He was curious and excited.

A large mass of diggers were gathered around, so he didn't initially see what they were looking at. He hurried down the ladder from the rim.

"Excuse me," he said numerous times trying to push through the crowd to get to the object. Four men were bent over trying to extract another metal thing. This one was square on the corners, but mostly still buried. They couldn't budge it in the slightest. They looked up at Galean.

He squatted down and slid his hand over the surface which was smooth on the top, and strangely warm to the touch. He held his hand on it and felt a tiny vibration.

"Dig down on all the sides to expose it," he said. Men crowded forward with shovels digging frantically.

The uncovered top was a six foot square. Galean backed away so his men could work. Brutans were at the head of the workers digging frantically. As they gradually worked their way down exposing the sides of the thing they made a further shocking discovery. One side of the thing was an opaque panel with lights flickering inside. As they dug down to the base, ten feet lower, a low sound emitted - a steady hum.

The object was totally mystifying. Galean had no idea what the thing was and wasn't sure if it was dangerous.

Down at the base, they discovered the object was rooted into solid but smooth flooring extending in all directions. The flooring material was also unfamiliar to them.

The men looked at Galean for guidance, but he just shrugged his shoulders.

"Keep clearing away the soil to see where this goes. Don't touch this pillar until we determine if it's dangerous."

Galean sent word to Aron who was relaxing in his newly blossoming relationship with Tasha. They were sharing a picnic lunch in the warm sunshine when the messenger raced over to them.

"Come my lord, Master Galean has made an important discovery. He bids you come quickly."

"Go Aron, I'll clean up here and come shortly," Tasha insisted and began picking up the picnic leftovers.

After the messenger departed, Aron jogged back to the construction site. He hurried down the ladder. At his arrival, the square metal pillar was clear and the workers had dug out a six foot circle around it. The strange flooring continued in all directions.

Galean half smiled when Aron came up to him.

Others of Aron's inner circle were arriving quickly and came down to join them.

"Don't bother asking me," said Galean. "I have only questions, no answers about this thing."

He led them over close to it to see the clear panel with its flickering lights and the hum, which had grown slightly louder. They stood for a long time fascinated at the marvel.

"I feel excitement," Galean explained, "but for some reason I also feel worried about this thing. I wonder about its purpose. Something meant to help or to harm…?"

Aron felt a chill run down his spine. They had no way to cope with this object if it unleashed dangerous power through their awkward probing.

"I'll continue to watch it for changes, Aron," Galean added. "I don't want to sound dire, but I think we should use great caution."

"I agree, Galean."

"Keep digging, men!"

Aron went back up the ladder just as Tasha arrived with the other women.

"What did he find, Aron?"

"We don't know. I suspect we'll find more items we don't know. There's a flat bottom which was manmade, though we have no idea what it's made of or how it was done. It's becoming clear this was a location of an older race which dwelt here. It appears they had knowledge which died with them. We'll keep excavating to see what else we find."

"I haven't seen Liani lately, Aron. Is she working with Galean on this project?"

"You're right, Tasha, now that you mention it. I haven't seen her for almost a week."

"She's your assistant so I'd assume she'd tell you if she was going to be away, Aron. She was working with us on my medical organizational efforts. One day she didn't show up and I haven't seen her since."

Aron furrowed his brow. "I just assumed she was working with you. Now you've got me worried. I'll talk to Cherine right away."

"I'll come with you, Aron."

They walked away together. Tasha took his hand in hers. Aron happened to notice Radigan eyeing them from afar. Something in Radigan's look struck Aron as strange; he didn't have his usual look of confidence.

"He's not happy I'm being with you, Aron," said Tasha.

"I wonder if there's something else going on. I've never seen him act flustered before."

Radigan turned and left quickly, which definitely drew Aron's notice.

They saw Cherine talking to some of her people and hurried over to her.

"What's wrong, Aron?" she asked.

"We haven't seen Liani in almost a week. Do you know where she is?"

"I don't. I've been busy with this new threat from the west. I'm sorry. Do you believe there's a problem?"

"I don't know. It isn't like her to go off without telling anyone. She never said anything to me. I just saw Radigan and he looked odd. I don't know if that's connected. I can't think of a reason he would carry away Liani, plus the fact he's still here."

"Radigan has been handling a matter at the border. I can send for him."

"That may be a good idea. If something is wrong and she's been kidnapped I want to know right now."

Radigan had suddenly left the camp and was heading to the border.

"He took a troop with him and just left," said the messenger.

"I'll go after him, Aron," said Cherine. "We're speculating he had something to do with Liani, but he may simply be going back to his assignment. I'll take sufficient numbers of the masters with me, just in case. Somehow, I don't think this is him at work. I don't think he'd do something to reflect back on him. He's too shrewd."

"I hope your right, Cherine. I'll start my own search here. If any harm has come to her…"

Tasha took his hand with a look of concern on her face. "Let's get to work and find Liani, Aron."

"Do you think Radigan did this, Tasha?" he asked as they walked away.

"I don't, Aron. I can't speak for him, and I'm not defending him, but as Cherine said, he's no fool. What would be the benefit for him of taking Liani? It doesn't strike me as something he would do. If there is a reason, I can't imagine what it is. Do you understand? Aron, I'm on your side, I always have been. Right now, Radigan is a friend and he's my past."

"I wasn't trying to go down that road again, Tasha. I was trying to piece this together in my mind. I do trust you and I do believe I finally know your real feelings. At the same time, I'm a cautious person. I've made enough errors in judgment. I try to be thorough in my considerations. I can't afford to make any more mistakes. People pay serious prices for my mistakes."

"Let's hope she just decided to take some time away to relax and gather her wits. Hopefully it's something totally innocent."

Chapter Five

~ Deepening Mysteries ~

Galean was very concerned to hear Liani was missing, but he forged ahead with explorations at the dig site. Within a week a second metal pillar identical to the first one was discovered. It also had active blinking lights and the same low pitched hum. When the second pillar was completely cleared of encumbering soil, the underlying sound in both pillars increased slightly, followed by a series of bright blinks to the lights inside the panels.

Their digging also revealed increasing numbers of other objects, all of them equally inexplicable. Several more of the heavy cylinders were found. Galean had them carried to a guarded collection room. Their inventory of the unknown was growing rapidly. Nothing in the archives back at the royal library would give him insight into what he was finding. Convinced the discoveries predated the ancient histories, he was no longer speculating.

This caused him to redouble efforts in clearing out this site and drew workers away from construction of the walls. Aron wasn't there to object; he'd gone around to various camps to be certain none of the gangs had captured Liani and started with a trip to see Straga.

"You can suspect me, Aron, but I've had no hand in this. I don't know what happened to her. She isn't the woman I would have taken, you know that. You've forced me to accept my wife and sons going to that other man. You should feel fortunate I didn't react violently to that affront. That matter isn't closed, but I've taken no action about this woman of yours. If you search here, you're wasting valuable time."

Aron grudgingly accepted Straga's explanation.

"Thank you, Straga," said Cherine. "If you hear of anything about

Liani, please inform us immediately. We're very concerned about what happened to her and what it could mean for the rest of us."

A circuit of all of the tribes in the area revealed nothing useful. There hadn't been any other kidnappings so it didn't appear to be a trend.

"Perhaps it was an individual and a crime of opportunity," said Cherine.

"I don't know," Aron replied. "We've found no clues of any kind. That strikes me as odd."

"If it wasn't a kidnapping, perhaps she had a natural mishap, or a predator may have taken her. You were caught, Aron, by that ice cat."

"I hope that didn't happen to her. I can't imagine she would've been out walking alone somewhere to be vulnerable to animal attack. She's a smart woman and she knows what happened to me. I could believe a crazy person on the loose working mischief. I've seen the work of such people before. I shudder to think of her at the mercy of such evil."

Cherine looked very upset at the thought. "I, too, have seen such horrors. That people can do monstrous things to other living beings is sickening and disturbing."

"I'm at a loss at what to do, Cherine? We can continue this sweep of these camps, but I don't feel the answer is there."

"I agree, Aron, but I too have no answers."

Aron stood wrestling with the stalemate staring off at the forest. In frustration he turned back to Cherine.

"Let's go back to camp. This is accomplishing nothing out here. We need a lead of some sort."

"I'm sorry, Aron," she said sympathetically. "Something will turn up. I feel confident it will."

Aron was angry because once again he was in a position of helplessness about a friend. He had no idea if Liani was in imminent danger at that very moment, or if she was even still alive. Old feelings rumbled to awakening, feelings of despair and incompetence. No one else would blame him, but he blamed himself.

Galean came to have dinner with Aron, Tasha, and their families. Cherine was on her way after Radigan.

The occasion had the feel of a funeral with concern over Liani.

As they finished their meal Enna and Biala rode into camp from a mission to their home in Graysauld swamp. They walked determinedly toward Aron.

"Ladies," Aron said. "I'm glad to see you safely back with us."

"A perilous journey, for sure Aron," Enna explained. "Getting through the prince's lines was hazardous and the travel through territory they hold was perilous too. The villagers who remain behind are cowed and huddling in terror believing they'll be next to be used as pawns to try to lure you out, Aron. There's no travel between villages and therefore no commerce. Many are desperate to feed their families."

"How are things with the Uripeans?"

"We're unaffected by the royal occupation. What weak attempts they made to enter our swamp, led to disaster for them. They quickly gave up any plans to invade us. Our king bids us pass on his regards to Tasha. She's always welcome in his hut."

Tasha laughed heartily. Aron smiled ruefully.

"He's a man who doesn't easily abandon his goals," she chuckled. "Good for him. That's why he's a great leader for your people."

"That's very entertaining, Tasha," said Aron sourly.

"Aron, stop acting so put upon. My hope is someday you'll stop feeling so fragile about our relationship. I think I've made my feelings sufficiently known. I'm standing right here at your side when I could be elsewhere."

Aron looked at Enna and Biala. They had amused smiles listening to Tasha chide him.

"You're right, Tasha."

"Of course I am, and don't forget it."

All of the women laughed, including Aron's mother.

Aron shook his head resignedly.

"Is there trouble in the camp? Everyone seems astir," asked Biala with a look of concern.

"Liani has been missing for at least a week. We have no idea what's happened to her," Tasha answered.

"What can we do to help?" asked Enna.

"We have people looking everywhere but we've turned up nothing," Tasha explained.

"We'll join in the search," Biala replied.

"Get some food first," said Aron. "You had a long ride back from your swamp."

* * * *

Liani opened her eyes and glanced around fearfully. Her mouth was gagged, hands tied behind her back and surrounded by fierce looking men in strange uniforms who spoke in an unfamiliar language.

Her head hurt from the blow taken during her capture. They hadn't bothered to treat her wound which had finally clotted and stopped bleeding on its own.

As she watched them a major debate was going on and she assumed she was the topic. What to do with her was their question. It wasn't hard for her to see which of them wanted to leave her behind as a body for the animals to feed on. What the other side proposed she wasn't sure, but she doubted it was a much better fate. What she didn't see in any of their eyes was sympathy.

She had no idea where she was other than she was still in the wilds somewhere. If she'd been taken far away from Aron's camp she had no way to know. The thought of escape crossed her mind, but how seemed impossible. These weren't soldiers to make mistakes of inattention and she certainly couldn't overpower them. They looked like the type itching for an excuse to slaughter her.

She thought back to her fateful decision to stretch her legs and take a walk alone into the woods. The ambush had happened after only a short trek, so she knew they'd seen Aron's camp. Warning him was a supreme need for her, more so than escaping. She started to think about options. If she was meant to die, she wanted to have a purpose in her demise.

Her captors stopped talking and they all looked at her. Two guards yanked her to her feet. The man who was the leader came over and took her face in his hand. He moved close to her face and spoke to her sharply, though she didn't know what he said. He gave her face a contemptuous shove before they packed up the camp and quickly started to move toward the west.

Liani felt instant panic as she realized she was being taken farther away from Aron and the camp.

They trotted on foot and expected Liani to match their grueling pace. She was in distress almost immediately both from the physical strain and the gag in her mouth didn't allow her to breathe.

She made a muffled cry which caused them all to stop. The leader came over to her with murder in his eyes.

Liani quickly talked even though her words were muffled. The leader got a calculating look and took out the gag.

"If you mean for me to run with you, I must be able to breathe," she huffed, panting heavily.

The leader smiled.

"You speak in the old tongue. Does it surprise you I can understand your words?"

"I hadn't thought about it, or you," she replied defiantly.

Her captors laughed.

"You have spirit, but I ask you, is it wise to antagonize those who hold your life in their hands?"

"I don't have a life any longer. You didn't treat my wound so it's pretty clear you don't intend to keep me alive. What does it matter if you kill me now or later?"

He glanced at his men and smiled.

"I like her. I would not have thought that."

He nodded to one of his men who came over to clean out her head wound and then applied a salve.

"Do you see, we've allowed you to continue breathing? You should be grateful to us for that. What's your name?"

"What's your name?" she retorted boldly. "Your letting me live, am I supposed to think that's a good thing?"

He laughed. "My name is Drang-ku. I repeat, what is your name?"

"Liani," she said softly.

"Brothers, here we have, Liani!" he bellowed expansively holding out his arms.

They all did a martial shout.

"If you've rested sufficiently, we must keep moving, Liani."

"Where are you taking me?"

Drang-ku smiled. "You're not being taken; you're accompanying us back to a greater gathering of my brothers."

"I don't remember asking to accompany you," she snapped.

"Minor technicalities," he replied. "Be content with the honor of joining us as a fellow traveler. You wouldn't like the alternative."

She followed him as they resumed the trek.

"You're from outside, aren't you?" Liani asked.

He fell back to walk beside her.

"What do you know about outside of this wasteland?"

"I know you're a bunch of cruel, heartless, barbaric nations competing to demonstrate which among you the worst possible society is. You have no compassion, no concept of higher planes of reason, or of human dignity. What do you devote your life to, Drang-ku? How much blood spilled does it take to sate your killing lust? The sooner you all devour each other, the better for this planet."

"How do you know anything to even have such an opinion?"

"I work with great scholars who have extensive historical records, and also we've…"

"You've what?" he asked. "What were you going to say that you thought better of?"

"Why would I share pearls of wisdom with such as you?"

"You live here in this backwards sty and think yourself better than me?" he asked in astonishment. "If all of your people are like you filled with such self importance, I wonder if you can do anything other than admire your own reflections. Whatever flaws we have as a people, I think our accomplishments far outweigh them."

"What accomplishments would that be?" she asked scornfully. "You constructed taller poles upon which to put the heads of those you've killed?"

Drang-ku chuckled.

"I like you, so I'll give you this advice. You should not be so vocal with your derision. Where we're going it will not impress our leaders and it will only bring you severe punishment. It's best to try to learn and to assimilate into a new life. Though I question my sanity for saying this, I'll do what I can for you, but it must be a shared effort. If your only thought is to die in the most painful ways, there is nothing I can do for you, and I place myself in jeopardy in the process. Are you listening to what I'm saying? You must stop looking back at your past. They can't help you now. Your future is here, with me, and with my people, the Chenese."

Liani felt a cold chill run down her spine. The idea she would have an ongoing life as a captive hadn't occurred to her. She'd assumed a quick death was in her near future.

"You need to make a decision, and quickly," he added.

"I don't really have any choice," she replied. "I don't think any person hungers for death. Staying alive in the short term is better than ending it. With life there is always hope."

He glanced at her thoughtfully.

"Do you have a mate and children, Liani?"

"Not yet."

"This is good. I'm not heartless, for your information. I would feel badly if you left a family behind. Understand me when I say there will never be any going back. If through some quirk your people discovered us, they would all die. It's best to put them out of your mind. As far as your impression we're ignorant, you're wrong. There is a great deal you don't know."

"It seems I have all the time in the world, Drang-ku. Feel free to enlighten me."

"Do you never silence yourself? Do you demand the last word in every discussion?"

"That's probably true. Deal with it."

"You're such trouble for me, Liani. I already know this in my head yet foolishly I'm drawn to you. I think this will not have a good outcome for either of us. All I ask is when we get to camp keep your mouth shut. There is real peril there."

Liani glanced at him. He no longer appeared to be a ruthless blood thirsty killer. Now he was merely a man following his orders.

She shrugged her shoulders. His men grumbled as they listened to the exchange.

"What are they saying, Drang-ku?"

"They have the same worry I told you, that your mouth will lead to the end of all of us."

Liani smiled.

"You're truly a demented woman if you take pleasure in that," he objected sourly.

She chuckled. "You can always let me go back."

He shook his head.

"By the way, why did you hit me? Does your society abuse women?"

"When you surprised us, we didn't know you were a woman. You were just suddenly a stranger emerging from the trees, too close for us to hide. No, we don't abuse women."

"That's at least one good answer from you."

"Tell me about your people, Liani."

"Let me explain to you that I won't do or say anything to betray them. If you mean to war against us, I'll always be your enemy and it would probably be better to kill me here and now."

"I'm just asking about your life, your friends, and your loves. You know you'll be asked those other questions at the camp. I can't protect you about that. If you choose to try to defy them, there are those who are cruel and ruthless. That's true of any society. You also have bad apples in your world."

"That's true. What would you suggest I do, Drang-ku? I'm no less a patriot than you. If I must die to protect my people, I will."

He looked genuinely distressed. "Perhaps you should think of plausible answers to tell them rather than endure the pain. If there are things you can say that have the ring of truth, yet don't jeopardize your people, that may allow you to survive for a time. As you said, life is sweet so preserving your life is a goal you must have as your highest priority. I take no joy in the suffering of others, even those who are deadly enemies. You didn't answer my questions about you and your life."

"There isn't much to tell. I wasn't high born, so back in the imperial city I lived a life of mundane tasks and avoidance of notice by the royals. Beauty is a curse for a woman in the palace. One day like so many others of us, my luck ran out and I found myself being brought before the princes. They argued as to who would get me as a servant and fortunately for me, Lord Galean was in attendance that day. He needed nimble minds for his research in the library. I answered his questions and he took me away before, well, you know. The fate of most women is usually not so fortunate there. We've learned to live with it over the centuries. Their power is unquestioned and unchallenged, at least until Aron came along."

"Aron?" asked Drang-ku.

Liani got a look of distress. "I've said too much. You're right; my mouth will be the end of us."

"Is Aron the man of your heart?"

She got a distant stare. "If only that were the case, Drang-ku, his heart belongs to another woman. I can't blame him, she's remarkable. Everybody wants her, including the crown prince. I was merely his assistant. I cherished the time I could spend in his company. I question if Tasha is worthy of him, as entrancing as she is. He's the one that has no peer."

"Aron and Tasha," he uttered.

"I'm going to stop talking. I'm saying things I don't wish to share with you and your leaders."

"Listen closely to what I said, Liani. You need to have answers to give to the questioners. They won't be gentle with you. There are those in the world who shouldn't be free to roam about and cause such pain."

Liani felt concern at the prospect of torture. She wasn't sure what he was trying to tell her with his last comment, but it felt like a dire warning. He certainly had a serious look of worry on his face.

"How long do we have before we arrive there?" she asked soberly.

"Less than a week, I'm sorry, Liani."

"If it's that bad, Drang-ku, I'd prefer if you or one of your men take my life now. From how you're acting, I think it would be more humane. I'm not a coward, but what rational person would choose to endure torture?"

He looked stricken. She looked back at the others. Uniformly, they all looked regretful.

"You've heard my request. If you put me into the hands of such men, it rests on your souls. This isn't waging war to do such things. There's no justification for monstrous acts in any society."

"I wish conditions were different, Liani. I sent word to them about your capture that first day. I must bring you in. I don't have other options."

"Drang-ku, I'm just a single solitary woman. What terrible threat do they think I could possibly pose to the Chenese?"

"I'm sorry I don't have any good answers for you. We can hope for the best. I will do what I can for you."

"Is this what you'd offer for your mother or your sister? Somehow I don't feel reassured."

He looked at her remorsefully.

* * * *

As the dig continued, Galean wasn't surprised to discover additional metal columns uniformly spaced on each side of the previous two unearthed - a recognizable pattern. Each additional device discovered caused a reaction where the lights grew stronger and the underlying sound became louder in all of the mechanisms. With four of them cleared of dirt Galean saw they were roughly in an arc shape which led him to believe they were built to surround something. Digging forward, they reached the edge of a building also long buried under earth and debris. The structures wall was impervious, completely smooth with no sign of a door or windows. Continuing their digging at an accelerated pace more of the metal columns was found spaced equidistance from each other, encircling the strange building. Further excavation of the building revealed a structure circular and convex in shape, and huge.

Aron came to see the structural marvel, but couldn't fully focus without knowing Liani's fate. When Cherine returned with Radigan, Aron talked with him enough to realize he had no hand in the mystery. Radigan was genuinely distressed.

"Although our first thought would be the prince, most of the frontier commanders support us now. If she'd passed through their camps we would have been told. The prince is not even there. He's returned to the palace to speak with the king. Speculation is the king will put an end to this campaign. There's no real passion amongst the royals for the prince's little excursion. Now that they're incurring substantial cost, and with unrest developing all across the realm, there's strong pressure to bring the army back. Putting them in peril is the best defense we have, Aron. What we couldn't have accomplished with force of arms can happen vicariously with the actions of others. I think there is some new factor in play regarding Liani. There is a possibility she was caught by a predator and devoured. If that happened, we may never know. Other than that, if one of the gangs took her, we would know. We have people everywhere and those gangs have come to be very loyal to us. You said there is trouble to the west. Perhaps we need to look that way for answers."

"Radigan, your thoughts make a lot of sense," Aron agreed. "What do you think, Cherine?"

"I tend to agree with his evaluation. I can begin our search of the far western areas immediately."

"I may come with you. As fascinating as Galean's work is, I'm driven to find her. Who knows what's she's facing."

"As our leader, it's too risky for you to go and put yourselves in harm's way when we don't know what we're facing. Remember, the gangs in that area fled without a fight against this new invader. We need to approach this matter very carefully."

"All the more reason for me to be there to assess that threat, I'm going, Cherine. I'll leave Brock in charge back here."

"No, you won't," Brock said as he walked up to them. "I'm a

fighter, not a leader. I'm going too. Pick someone else. Why not your father…?"

"He's told me numerous times, he doesn't want positions of responsibility."

Cherine looked at Radigan, who smiled and said, "I'm at your service in any capacity."

Cherine looked at Aron. He eyed at Radigan ruefully.

"Don't do anything exotic, Radigan. The camp runs itself. You don't need to institute any new plans. Just be here to keep an eye on things."

"Of course, Aron, I understand my role perfectly."

"We'll leave at first light tomorrow. I think we need to take a large enough force to meet any threat."

"I'll gather a force tonight, Aron," said Cherine. "We'll be ready tomorrow."

Brock scowled at Radigan who simply smiled back.

"Cherine, I've got an idea," Aron added. "Include Straga and some of his people in our forces. I think we should take some Brutans too. They're fierce fighters and they've proven to be really loyal to me."

"As you wish, Aron, I'll send for them right away."

Aron left with Brock to talk to Galean.

"I can't just sit here and leave Liani to her fate. We're going on a mission to the west, which seems the best possibility to solve the mystery. You don't need me here for what you're doing, Galean. If you need to make any decisions, you're better qualified than me. Like Brock said, he's a fighter and I feel the same way."

"It's unwise, Aron, but I know you won't heed my advice."

"I do consider what you said, but there's a certain amount of peril you must deal with. Being too safe can be just as hazardous as not being safe enough."

"I don't agree, Aron, but you'll do what you want to do. I'll keep at the work here. By the way, we've decided to add a space and construct an inner wall and then fill that space with soil. This will make our outer walls far sturdier and less likely to be breeched. It will take much longer, but the added security may pay off in the end."

"Good, Galean."

* * * *

Predictably, Radigan came to dinner to join Tasha that evening with the families. Because it appeared Tasha had made her commitment to Aron, Radigan was tolerated somewhat, but Aron's anxiety towards Radigan and Tasha never went away.

On this evening, Tasha chatted pleasantly with Radigan, which didn't help Aron's mood. She seemed oblivious to Aron's feelings of turmoil. He fought the impression that she was unconcerned.

Radigan was charming to all of the women present, which was his forte.

Aron said little which caused Tasha to pay more attention to Radigan's banter. After the meal, Aron arose. "I hope you'll excuse me as I have an early departure tomorrow, so I'll bid you all good night."

"Good night, Aron," said Tasha with a perfunctory glance. She turned back to her conversation with Radigan.

"Safe hunting out there, Aron," Radigan added.

Aron nodded stiffly and walked away feeling like he'd lost a battle. He went to sleep amongst the masters and Cherine that night, bringing all of his gear with him.

Cherine eyed him as if she could read his mind.

"You are your own worst enemy, Aron."

"No argument here, Cherine."

Trying to sleep, Aron tossed and turned fitfully as he tormented himself about Tasha's past with Radigan and the prince - a senseless and a useless mental experience, which fed into insecurities regarding her, his greatest vulnerability.

Dawn broke to a cloudy dismal day which matched Aron's mood. He sat up groggy and ill tempered. A cup of strong coffee helped and he quickly gathered himself. This mission was too important to be out of sorts.

They hadn't ridden long before a steady soaking drizzle started. Aron rode beside Cherine and let Brock take the lead. Days passed before reaching regions they hadn't been in before.

Cherine recognized Aron's mood and left him be.

A thousand men accompanied them; not a minor probe, this was reconnaissance in force. They weren't expecting to sneak up on anybody.

The camps they passed eyed them with concern.

"Have you sworn allegiance to me?" asked Aron time after time.

"Yes," they all exclaimed, whether it was true or not. Because he didn't attack any of them went a long way toward gaining allegiance.

"What have you heard to the west?" asked Cherine.

The answer was always the same.

"There's great trouble coming. It's time to flee rather than face sure annihilation."

"Are you going to flee?" she asked.

"If we can expect mercy from your people, yes we will."

"All that I ask of you is to abandon your thieving, and the other terrible things you've done and live better lives. We'll welcome you into our midst, but only on our terms. If you cause us trouble, we'll be swift with our punishment. Do you agree?"

"Of course," they all said, but Aron didn't felt a great deal of sincerity. He couldn't afford to be distracted from his mission though, so he let it slide.

Aron noted that every single camp they entered, the whole populace knew and feared the Brutans. This pleased Aron that they were daunted, the fact he could corral such lethal killers into complete devotion to him and his cause.

The Brutans always looked on the verge of mayhem and tended not to mingle with the others in the force, staying separate to eat and to sleep. They would allow Aron in their midst, but the only other person where they showed any deference was Cherine. To Brock they gave grudging respect to his prowess and his single minded determination in any task.

Brock tended to ignore them - a good symbiosis.

They traveled until dark each day trying to cover ground rapidly. The terrain remained the same with tall thick foliage, barbs and brambles all about, limited visibility and the threat of predators.

At the last camp, a man named Arka, volunteered to lead them back to where his original camp had been.

"I'm not happy my people fled and gave up our homes to these invaders without a fight. If you intend to give a strong answer to this challenge, then I am with you."

Aron looked at Cherine. "It wouldn't hurt to have a guide familiar with our destination."

"As you wish, Aron..."

"Thank you for trusting me," said Arka.

Chapter Six
~ Dire Circumstances ~

With each day that passed Liani's fear increased. As much as she tried to ignore her anxiety, she couldn't stop thinking about her fate. That Drang-ku was visibly distressed heightened her own terror.

The day they finally walked into the Chenese camp she felt ill. A great host of Chenese soldiers were all around and the way they gazed at her, she hoped for a quick end.

Drang-ku led her to the great central tent and took her inside where a number of older men, obviously the leaders sat. They looked at her like she was not worth their time and notice.

The elders conversed in their native language. Drang-ku did a great deal of explaining, but Liani didn't feel optimistic. One of the leaders spoke sharply to Drang-ku after he made an impassioned plea. He bowed his head meekly and turned to leave.

"I'm sorry," he whispered.

"Drang-ku tells us you speak the old language," said the leader. "Do you understand me now?"

"Yes sir," she replied.

"Good, then there will be no misunderstandings. You will tell us everything about your people, where they're camped, their weaponry, their numbers, and anything else we ask of you. Do you agree?"

She thought for a moment.

"May I ask why you want to know this?"

"No, you may not ask any questions. Our reasons are of no concern to you. If you don't fulfill our requests promptly and fully, we have ways to persuade you. You don't want to provoke me, woman. To us, you're an enemy and as such you're not entitled to the same considerations as our citizens."

He nodded to the doorway. An incredibly huge man came in, clearly the person Drang-ku feared. He looked at her with contempt, seemingly avid to be freed to do his work on her.

Liani couldn't suppress a shudder. The man walked up to her and put hand to her chin and the other behind her head. He twisted her head to the side as far as it would go.

"It would be the easiest thing to snap your neck, but there is no such quick escape from life for you. I can prolong your life in abject agony for as long as I wish. Do you understand?"

"Yes," she whimpered. He released her head.

"I think she would like to answer your questions, my lord."

"Thank you, Wu Hang. Please help yourself to refreshment here at my table. I'd like you to observe the interrogation."

He nodded and wandered over to pour a drink from a pitcher on the table.

Liani felt miserable, vulnerable, and alone. She tried to imagine Aron storming into the tent with all of the masters and the Black Fist to rescue her.

"You know what we wish to hear from you. Start talking now," said the leader.

"Ahead of you lies the imperial kingdom. They rule this land other than for outlaws and rebels who've taken up refuge here in the wilds to live free of imperial rule. As far as their numbers, the royal host is vast. I have no way of knowing their total number. The wilds are populated by numerous camps of criminals. Once again, I have no way to know how many there are, where they're located, or any other of these things you ask. I'm just a woman and I'm not a person of importance. Women don't hold power in the kingdom. Their weapons are the same as yours. I'm telling you the truth because I fear your butcher. What do women know in your realm? They probably know nothing also."

The leader smiled.

"You're well spoken. I think perhaps you're more than a mere woman amongst your people. Who is this Aron?"

She looked at him defiantly.

"I think you had a foolish thought. They tell me your name is Liani. Wu Hang is no illusion. He is very skilled at his work. I've warned you not to test me. This will be your final warning. Believe me, you will tell Wu Hang everything he asks of you. Don't expect pity from him."

She felt another bout of cold chills as Wu Hang smiled at her wickedly.

"Aron is the leader of the rebels resisting the prince."

"You were a part of his camp. Drang-ku caught you there."

"Yes."

"We know roughly where they are, and I have an idea of their numbers. What I'd like to know is will he come searching for you?"

"No, I'm just a camp woman who cooks his food."

"You're lying. That was a mistake, Liani."

Wu Hang arose slowly and came over to her.

She shut her eyes in terror and tried to steel her courage. He lifted her to her feet like she was weightless.

"Come, my precious," said Wu Hang. He led her out of the tent to another tent not far away. Liani nearly fainted when they walked in to see what was arrayed there, implements of torment and devices designed to wrack the body.

She was whimpering and couldn't stop tears from rolling down her cheeks.

Wu Hang acted gentle with her although she was so frightened it didn't dawn on her.

"Please take them off," he said nodding to her clothes. She paused only a moment before following his orders.

He fastened manacles to her wrists and her ankles leaving her helpless to protect herself.

"Do you think me a monster for my work?" he asked.

"You already know the answer."

"I'm not. Though what I must do is gruesome, I do regret that anyone must suffer. I have my duty, as do you. You won't be permitted to keep your secrets. Two guards came into the tent.

Liani felt a cold sweat of utter fear.

"You're a very beautiful woman," he continued. Yes, I recognize beauty. Often beautiful women are also vain about their looks, like they're above others not so blessed in appearance. Men look at you with great desire because you evoke it in them with those looks and with your alluring manner. What do you think potential husbands would think if your beauty is marred?"

He picked up a poker from the fire. The tip was red hot.

Liani closed her eyes and gulped in fright. Wu Hang and the guards walked behind her. She waited for what seemed an eternity, but was actually a short time.

Something pressed against her back, then the sizzle of frying meat, accompanied by the smell of charring. She moaned in agony, but the pain wasn't the overwhelming shock she anticipated. She felt fluid rolling down her back.

Wu Hang walked around in front of her holding a cube of ice. The two guards behind her had pressed the hot poker against a steak to simulate the sound and the smell.

"Do you think I'll continue to toy with you?" he asked. "Would you like to answer our questions? You can live without all of your fingers, or with just one eye. We can shed some of your blood if you like."

Badly shaken, she nodded affirmatively to him.

"What is your relationship to Aron and will he come looking for you?"

"I was his assistant. He would want to look for me, but I don't believe he knows where to look. Was there a trail to follow? I don't know that."

"I think that was a truthful answer. See, we're making good progress. A monster would have tortured you simply because he could, and for no other reason than the love of suffering in others."

"Do you have any other questions, Wu Hang? I'm on the verge of getting sick and I'm afraid I'm about to faint." She couldn't stop the involuntary shaking in her body.

"Let me fetch our leader to see if he wants to resume his questions."

The guards stood by watching her. A short passed time before Wu Hang returned along with the old man.

"I'm happy you decided to be reasonable, Liani. I didn't wish for your pain, but we do what we must. My opinion is if Aron is deserving of his leadership, he'll find a way to follow you here. How can we best lure him into a trap?"

"Use me as bait. I'm what he would be looking for. If he sees me, that's where his attention will be focused, not on what's around me."

"That's true, Liani. You realize we don't plan for him to survive the encounter. If your idea is sound, it could mean the end of your friend and your rebellion."

"What else can I do hanging here in shackles like this? I don't pretend to be brave. I just want to survive the moment."

"You have hopes he will come and rescue you. Understandable feelings, my dear, but impossible, the Chenese don't lose battles."

"Then you have nothing to fear from me. I've answered your questions. May I be freed to get dressed?"

He muttered something to the guards. They came over and released her from the restraints. She quickly donned her clothing and looked at Wu Hang to see what was next. He merely made a small bow to her.

"May you have good fortune, maiden."

The guards led her out of the torture tent, and then she was taken to the tent of the leader. They fastened her to a pole and left her there. The leader didn't return for many hours. Darkness had fallen when he finally arrived.

"Am I to exist here without food and drink? How do I see to my needs?" she said darkly. "Why am I here in your tent?"

The leader looked at her sternly, but he sent away a servant. They returned with a plate of stew and coffee. After she dined, guards took her to a place to handle her needs and bathe. When they brought her back she was chained again to the pole for another uncomfortable night of cramping and troubled sleep.

"Did you expect to stroll freely about our camp?" asked the leader.

She glared at him, but wisely said nothing.

* * * *

Galean watched as two more columns were unearthed. The sound was now a constant deep hum heard everywhere in the camp. Much more of the circular building was uncovered. After darkness fell, Galean stood on the rim looking down and noticed the lights now pulsed in rhythm and was bright enough to illuminate more than just the building.

The building continued to be uniform in profile. Nothing but smooth solid walls arched into the area still buried in the ground in perfect proportion.

Galean felt they were potentially getting into something over their heads, but his curiosity was too strong. He wanted to see this through, regardless of consequences. The same was true of the workers, especially the Brutans. This discovery was like uncovering their true life's mission and they were driven to complete the task.

Trent rode into camp just back from the border. He walked over to Galean.

"Any word from Aron…?"

"No, they were moving fast and I think they wouldn't waste a messenger until they have something of significance to tell us," Galean replied.

Trent glanced over at Biala and Enna. "He wouldn't let you go with them?"

"Obviously," said Enna frostily. "He puts too much value on our lives. We didn't come here to sit uselessly on the sidelines while others bear the risk."

"Ladies, you could have much worse problems than being left behind in safety."

"Is Liani safe?" Biala huffed. "She needs our help."

"We hope we can help her," said Galean sadly. "You must accept the possibility she's not a captive. She may have been predator prey."

"Until we know that, I choose to think she's still alive," said Enna.

* * * *

Though disturbed about Liani's disappearance, it didn't deter him from his chance at time with Tasha while Aron was away.

Tasha's father was always suspicious of Radigan and unfriendly when he came around. This didn't bother Radigan in the least; his only concern was the responses he could evoke in Tasha. Lately Tasha was a much bigger challenge because she had made a significant decision toward Aron and was not easily swayed -an area of concern. She acted 'taken' so Radigan had to be particularly careful in his approach and actions.

Tasha's mother no longer acted rude to Radigan - a great feat on his part. Winning her acquiescence was gratifying and gave him hope he could still prevail in competing with Aron for Tasha.

"This is so nice spending time with you," he extolled. "As I've said, my parents are gone, so I have no family of my own. In spite of past misunderstandings, I think we've come to an accommodation. I've never been a threat, though I'm often wrongly portrayed as such."

"We've had time to get to know you," said Tasha's mother. "We judge you on your deeds, Radigan. It's the only way for you to deal with the rumors and dire speculations. If you don't have deceit in your heart, the truth will show through for all to see."

"That's exactly right," he agreed. "As I said, I can't change what happened in the past. I wish I could. I hope my current actions merit some level of forgiveness. I'm not a bad fellow once you get to know me, right Tasha?"

She smiled mischievously. "You leave yourself open for whatever I might say. Do you really want to trust your reputation to that?"

"I fear no barbs from you, my dear. You of all people know me like no other. I'm willing to entrust my reputation and my life in your hands."

The emotional conflict he caused in her pleased him. She glanced in the direction Aron's mission had gone.

"We all wish him success and safety, Tasha," he added. "I never would've thought I would look upon him as a friend, but I do."

She looked back skeptically.

"It's true. I haven't lost my passion for you and I haven't given up my hope to make you my bride, but I don't see Aron as an enemy. If that seems ambiguous, I'm as surprised as you I feel that way. My thought is recovering our dear Liani and bringing her home to safety and out of harm's way."

Tasha's eyes revealed a question.

"You don't believe me?"

"As my mother said, we judge you on your actions, not glib words. You say I know you as no other. I do know you and I haven't forgotten anything of our past. Perhaps you are a much changed person, but there are sides of you that troubled me then and trouble me now. I'm not saying I was a blameless victim. I admit I had a part in my past mistakes, but you had a part too and that wasn't a good thing. It's taken me a long time to recover a sense of dignity and worth. I value that and I won't see it taken away from me ever again. Whatever you have in your mind, I warn you to tread lightly because I'll have no patience for what was our history. You can come here as often as you wish, but I've chosen my course and it won't be making me your wife."

To control his emotions and keep from lashing out at Tasha, Radigan paused. She surprised and angered him when he was feeling in control of her.

"Nonetheless," he said finally, "you can't take away my hope, Tasha. I love you still and I always will. I desire no other, so there it is."

She shrugged casually and looked at her mother who was staring at him keenly. Her father came out of the tent at that moment.

"What's going on here?" he growled.

"Nothing father," said Tasha. "We were talking about our concerns for Liani."

He scowled at Radigan who smiled back pleasantly.

"That's a matter Aron will see about," he muttered gruffly, like a challenge to Radigan.

"We all pray for his brave venture," Radigan replied evenly. "On that we can all agree."

Tasha looked at him closely. He could still evoke feelings in her, feelings she wanted to deny. She recognized the façade he put on for everyone else and could comprehend how he manipulated people. Astounding to her was the fact Radigan could work a woman to where she didn't mind being manipulated knowing full well what he was doing. Even now with her growing love for Aron, she still couldn't totally erase her feelings for Radigan. His obvious pride at being appointed the leader in the camp, even though just temporarily, amused her like he was a peacock preening before her. Secretly too, she was gratified by his unending romantic pursuit. He wouldn't give up on her and that can affect a woman.

After stating her intentions for Aron, which she thought would deter him, he just brushed them off. Tasha further annoyed her father by agreeing to go walking with Radigan.

"It's such a pleasant evening, wouldn't you say?" he asked her father. Tasha's father just turned and stormed into his tent.

"Why do you want to torment my father?" asked Tasha, as they walked away.

"I don't know what you're talking about," he replied smugly.

"If I had chosen you, how would you act then?"

"I care about you, Tasha, and only you. What anyone else chooses to think or chooses to do does not concern me."

"Someday I think your arrogance is going to catch up to you, Radigan."

"Until that day, I'll do what has always worked for me."

"What's that?"

"Love you, Tasha."

She shook her head, but Radigan's words evoked feelings again.

"Of all of the village girls in the world, you pick me to chase around and annoy. It doesn't make sense, Radigan."

"It doesn't make sense to you, but to anyone else, it's very clear. Someday, I think your life will catch up to you and you'll no longer be able to pretend you aren't a significant person. Measure yourself by the stature to the people pursuing you, and then try to tell me it doesn't make sense."

She had no answer.

* * * *

At the same Tasha walked into more secluded areas with a man she knew could put her emotional situation at risk, Galean hurried back to the dig site following the messenger.

"We've discovered twenty of these things and it appears we're about halfway around the building," said his chief assistant. "As soon as these last two were clear, it started."

Galean could clearly hear thc difference. The sound was no longer a single tone, but different sounds emerged matched by corresponding fluctuations in the lights in the panels. More startling was the faint glow to the wall of the building.

"When we went close to the wall we could feel warmth radiating and could no longer touch it, like an invisible barrier was protecting it. I've never seen or heard anything like this. When I moved close, I experienced great fear until I backed away. How is this possible? What is this place? What is its purpose?"

Galean climbed down the ladder and approached the wall of the building. Within ten feet he felt the fright his assistant had described. He tried to go all the way up to the wall, but it was impossible. With each step closer, the feelings of fear intensified; increasing markedly to the point of being physically painful. He retreated.

"What should we do? Are we in danger if we completely unearth this thing?"

"I wish I knew," Galean answered.

"Should we keep working?"

"For the time being," Galean directed, "but inform me immediately of any further changes."

"As you wish, my lord..."

Aron pressed ahead doggedly. He could only think of Liani. In light of his experiences in the palace, he didn't think she should be exposed to peril any longer than necessary.

Arka was a great help. He was knowledgeable of the area and enamored with being allowed to be a part of Aron's crack units.

"Aron, do you allow good men to join your elite ranks?"

"We deny no one, Arka. It isn't me you must impress, it's Cherine."

"Can she be impressed by anybody?"

Cherine answered. "So far, by just one man and you're riding beside him."

"That's encouraging," Arka answered with a shrug. "I would like to be considered to join you."

"We'll see, let's see if we survive this mission first. Do you have a guess of what's up ahead and how close we might be? If there is an enemy force, they're certain to have sentries and patrols. I don't want to stumble into a trap. I'd like to maintain the element of surprise as long as we can."

"My guess is we're within a day of the best place to form a large camp. The wilds are tough terrain, but their pretty uniform. Not many places stand out over another. If it weren't for the vegetation, a person could see great distances as there isn't much elevation. That's my opinion anyway."

"Is that where you're leading us, Arka?"

"Yes, I could think of no better destination if you wish to find your companion."

Cherine looked at Aron.

"I don't think it's wise to send men ahead in country we don't know. I prefer to meet our opponent with all of our forces present."

"You don't need to ask me, Cherine. You and Trent got training I never did. I have no problem deferring to your knowledge of tactics."

"Thank you, Aron. I hope I warrant your trust."

The scout in the lead suddenly put up a fist and the command halted and slipped off the trail into the brambles and brush. A fast moving band of twenty riders raced from the same direction Aron's troops were heading. When the riders got into the middle of Aron's troop they suddenly burst out to trap them.

The riders were competent looking brigands, but they put up no resistance surrounded by a thousand elite troops.

Arka rode up to the rider's leader.

"Arka?" the leader asked, "Why do you ride with these strangers?"

"They captured us, but gave us the option to join them - a wise choice not because they spared us, but because they offer a much better life."

"We don't have time to haggle. We have pursuers who are uncanny trackers. We've barely eluded them a number of times, and lost some good men. I sent our women ahead of us, but I don't know if they've been taken. We've not found them and been too hard pressed to look."

"If you want our protection, it comes at a price," said Aron. "Anybody is welcome to our cause, but they must guarantee to live better lives and give up the criminal ways. We'll even try to find your women."

"Then you have our loyalty. My name is Reston. I warn you, don't underestimate these enemies. I've never seen any better. You may outnumber them, but I don't think they'll care."

"Is there a better place to meet them, Arka?"

"What do you say, Reston. This is your territory."

"Perhaps just up the trail, there's a place better to have a fight than here."

They rode quickly to the place and Cherine deployed the men.

"Stay clear of the battle unless there is no other way, Reston. Let us handle this. We need prisoners."

"Be my guest," he replied with a chuckle.

"Stay with him Arka."

"Yes, my lord."

They set the snare and waited. It didn't take long, but they weren't met by a force marching openly down the trail. Some of the scouts had actually slipped well into the midst of Aron's hidden forces before they noticed them. The enemy's main force hurried along, but well under control, vigilant at all times. A soldier who appeared to be their leader suddenly looked around and the enemy froze in place, like they could sense the trap.

Aron gave the silent signal and waves of the masters, the Black Fist, Brutan warriors and assorted others of the converts charged out of concealment. They cut off the retreat and left no place for the strangers to escape. Their leader gave a shout and they attacked savagely.

It took all of the skill and the prowess of Aron's elite force to keep their lines intact from the withering enemy assault. Each side fought for survival as the sudden attack turned into individual contests. Aron could not sit back and watch. He charged into the middle of the battle to get to Cherine's side. The enemy seemed focused on her and they were a potent force. Aron struck at the back of the surrounding enemy noose meant to take down Cherine. The Black Fist suddenly appeared all around him and they battered ahead forcing the deathly vice grip open. Cherine and five masters stood back to back in a circle offering no openings to the enemy trying to keep from being killed at the center.

Aron gave a loud shout and got a martial reply from the Black Fist with a roar and a blistering attack. The enemy continued to fight doggedly and seemed unconcerned about dying in the fight. Aron personally broke through the final enemy soldiers and led Cherine out of the trap.

Now the enemy was encircled. Their leader shouted encouragement as they fought mightily to preserve their lives. Aron was impressed. He signaled silently and suddenly all of his forces stopped fighting. The enemy was confused but wary.

Aron rode forward with Cherine and Brock.

"Surrender, we have no desire to shed blood needlessly."

"We don't surrender," said the man.

"You think dying is the honorable thing to do?" asked Aron.

"We don't surrender to any foe, we don't live as prisoners, and we do think it honorable to die here, if need be."

"My name is Aron." He was surprised at the reaction from the man.

"You're Aron?" he asked.

"You know me? How is that possible?"

"I was told about you," he replied.

"By who…?"

"Liani..."

"Where is she," Aron barked, "what's happened to her? Who are you and why are you here?"

"My name is Drang-ku, I captured her."

"Drang-ku, I don't know you, but if she's been harmed in any way, your life will be forfeited, do you hear me?" Aron was steaming with rage.

“Aron, she’s at the main camp. I did what I could for her, but I’m not a soldier of great importance. Our leaders have her. She was given over to Wu Hang when I was sent from the camp. I don’t know her fate.”

“Is it the way of your people to savage women? If that’s why you’ve come, we will show you no mercy. You have great battle prowess, but you’re in our lands. We’re fighting to protect our families and the innocent. You won‘t prevail in such a war.”

“When Liani told me about you, she spoke with great respect. I’m not surprised at the skill of your fighters, but you shouldn’t overestimate what you can do in a war with us. We have fought wars for nearly our entire existence. We don’t fear to die. We’re a mighty nation and our army numbers more than the stars in the sky.”

“Why did you take Liani?”

“An unfortunate circumstance... She stumbled into our midst. We couldn’t allow her to betray our presence to you. I regret I had to take her to them. Wu Hang is a terrifying person.”

“I’m happy to give you a chance to rectify the wrong you’ve done. Liani didn’t deserve to have this happen to her. I’ll offer you and your men the same chance we give to any others. If you decide to join with us, you must agree to live your lives differently to live a higher and a better life.”

Drang-ku looked to be genuinely distressed.

“You don’t understand, Aron. We don’t have an option to leave our people. We’re patriots too. Betraying the cause isn’t something we’d consider.”

“I’m not asking you to betray anything. I’m not asking you to fight against your own people. What I’m offering you is a chance at a different life. We’re all from a wide variety of backgrounds and beliefs. I get the feeling you’ve had a lot of questions about the society you live in. If they tolerate a person like this Wu Hang, who I gather is a demented person, that’s a problem for anybody. You don’t have to accede to it any longer. I’m giving you an option. You can believe whatever you want, I don’t care, as long as you don’t infringe on others and force your will on them.”

Drang-ku stared at Aron.

“I understand now what Liani said, and why she was so faithful. Aron, I don’t know if they hurt her. I can’t guarantee she’s still alive.”

"If I have to fight my way into your camp to rescue her, I'll do it gladly. We don't fear death either. I don't have time to wait here so you need to make a smart decision. If there's a way to rescue her without having to fight your people, tell me what it is? I don't seek out battles, but I'm not going to shy away from them either. If you've met Liani, you know what a special woman she is. Saving her life doesn't violate any true rules if they're just. Your army's success won't revolve around one lone woman. I'm sure I'm the person you're interested in. I get the opinion your people are vain about your fighting skills. Anyone can be beaten, including your army. Wouldn't it be better to talk and maybe become allies?"

"You don't know what you're dealing with, Aron. The generals wouldn't listen to you. They have no interest in the people here. They're the ones who retain the Wu Hang's of the world. As far as us here, we're low level soldiers. What you're asking is for us to abandon our people and our families, and the cause."

"If you die needlessly here and now, you'll not see your families, Drang-ku. Are you willing to keep living with the possibility of a good life or would you prefer to sacrifice your men too?"

Chapter Seven
~ Our Precious Liani ~

Radigan wasn't the only man who used that term to describe her. She became beloved by another unexpected person.

Drang-ku was no idiot about his predicament. He looked at his men who awaited a signal about what to do.

"Aron, Liani told me she just wanted to survive the moment, I think it was her way of saying she wanted to live and keep a hold of hope. Whatever gauntlet she faced, her goal was merely to get through it because she thinks you'll come to save her. I'll follow her advice. We'll go with you, and if there's a way to save Liani without fighting our own, we'll not stand in your way. If it comes to a fight at the camp, I can make no guarantees. We aren't traitors to our people."

"That's good enough, Drang-ku. Will you lead us to save time? If Liani is in the control of this bad man, this Wu Hang, I want to do something about it immediately."

He looked at his men.

"We'll let you keep your weapons as a show of good faith," Aron added.

"This way," said Drang-ku.

"Is this wise, brother?" asked Brock as they rode along behind Drang-ku.

"We've got no choice. Lord knows what condition Liani is in. Brock, if they've tortured her, I'll level that camp, no matter how many of them there are."

"Careful Aron, we feel the same way, but remember that was the attitude that got you thrown into prison walking into the prince's suite before we were ready."

"You're right, brother. Keep reminding me when I do things like that. They may have an army like the royal host waiting at that camp."

Brock smiled. "Finally, you admit I'm the better man."

"Brock, I'm going to brain you."

They both laughed.

* * * *

Liani expected more days of misery lashed to the pole, but guards came in and released her. They took her to bathe and take care of personal things. When she finished cleansing, they replaced her dress with a different one, a stylish and expensive one. She had no choice but to put it on. The dress was too tight for her taste and portrayed her in a sensual way.

They took her for a meal dining with the leaders and sat her down beside the leader and the person who'd kept her chained in his tent.

"We've decided to show you we aren't barbarians like your people. You'll be allowed to share companion time in our esteemed company." The other men just snickered.

"What do you say to the honor I've given you?"

She fought back a sharp retort. "Thank you," she said meekly.

"If you are the assistant of your leader, do you spend time in his company?"

"Of course..."

"Does he show you respect and regard? As a barbarian, does he merely take what he covets?"

"I'm not his woman, if that's what you're asking." Pleased looks on the faces of the others bloomed. They were toying with her, but she didn't want to risk retribution. Wu Hang was a terrifying deterrent.

As if on cue, Wu Hang entered the tent and took a seat beside Liani. She felt a cold chill run down her spine. He acted genteel, but he was a man who did horrific things, who looked upon things no human should.

"Our precious Liani... It's good to see you again in more pleasant circumstances."

"You've been addressed, Liani," said the leader. "Does your culture not respond to civil contact? This won't do in the camp of the Chenese."

"Hello, Wu Hang. Thank you for your greeting and I agree these are more pleasant circumstances."

She couldn't bring herself to look at the massive man. Just to be close to him was frightening.

"As a companion, I suspect you'll require some instruction on proper behavior around us. I'll see about finding someone to tutor you in our ways. First, it's proper to bow to your superiors. Do you understand?"

"Yes, I understand."

"Women are the lesser of men. You'll bow to any man who addresses you."

She kept her head down staring at the table top.

"We take women into our care and control to safeguard them. Chenese women don't walk about without fathers, brothers, or husbands. Since you're currently unmarried, I'll extend my protection over you, as will Wu Hang. You couldn't be safer. It isn't outside the realm of possibility you could become a wife and aspire to a family and a life in our homeland. You're young and strong, and pleasing to the eye. There's no reason we can't teach you to be an obedient wife. I'm sure that gladdens your heart. I expect we'll quickly conclude this campaign so we can return home in triumph. What do you say about this?"

She pondered a scorching retort, but only in her heart. Wu Hang seemed to know everything she felt and thought so she wanted to give him no opportunity of any kind to punish her.

"You're very generous with a slave," she replied.

"Don't think of this as slavery," he replied magnanimously. "You have a chance to achieve an equal footing with a Chenese woman. That's a great honor."

"Thank you, sire."

The men chuckled.

"That's your term for your nobles, very amusing, my dear, very amusing. We're not barbarian lords. Tonight you won't be attached to the pole. We'll provide you a better arrangement. There are already those who've expressed an interest in you, and I mean a keen interest."

She glanced up at him and saw Wu Hang was eyeing her intently. She nearly got sick on the spot at the thought of being given to him.

"Ah, here's the food," said the leader as servant women carried in trays, platters, and pitchers of beverages. She didn't get a choice of her food or drink. Wu Hang filled her plate and poured a tankard of strong ale for her to drink.

She tried to eat without drinking.

"You must try this brew, it's a special recipe I favor," said Wu Hang.

The swill was potent and burned all the way down her throat. Before the drink was half done, she felt light headed.

Wu Hang laughed. "You're too little a person. This is a man's drink."

"You're welcome to mine."

He smiled again and downed the balance of her tankard.

When the "festivities" concluded, she tried to stand, but wobbled and nearly fell down. Wu Hang grabbed her to keep her on her feet. He propped her up and led her out of the tent and directly to his sleeping area.

"Oh no," she moaned as he escorted her inside. He looked at her. "Please don't," she moaned.

"This is merely where you'll sleep. You misjudge me, maiden."

She couldn't keep the tears from flowing.

He led her over to a bed. "This is yours alone."

"Thank you," she said honestly and gratefully.

"You're here to be under my protection, Liani. Is this not better than being chained to that pole?"

"Yes," she whispered. Her anxiety never receded. Totally at the mercy of these strange men was unnerving.

"Stay here, Liani. I have my work to do. I'll be back later."

She waited until he was gone before she crept to the door of the tent. There were two guards standing on duty. Returning to the bed, she crawled in and dozed off so she didn't hear the screams of Wu Hang at work serving his master's orders.

When he returned to his tent, darkness had settled in and Liani was fast asleep. He looked at her sleeping peacefully. She was a breathtaking sight and touched him deeply, a tiny moment of beauty and tranquility in his otherwise horrific life. He cleansed his arms and face in a bucket of water and then crawled into his own bed. He was clean on the outside, at any rate. It was always difficult for him to sleep. He couldn't simply dismiss what he'd done from his thoughts and memories. The agony of his victims tormented him even in his dreams.

* * * *

Aron was surprised that once Drang-ku agreed to accompany them, he actually cooperated. Some among his men were openly hostile, but did nothing to incur a response from their captors. They approached the large Chenese camp at dusk. Estimating their total numbers was impossible, but clearly they had more troops than Aron's thousand.

"What do you propose to do?" asked Drang-ku.

Aron shrugged and looked at Brock and Cherine. They shrugged also.

"If you want to avoid bloodshed, Drang-ku, this is a good time to make a suggestion. All that we want is Liani. Slipping in and out unseen would be great."

Drang-ku pondered the problem.

"I know of no way for you to go into our camp undetected. The only idea I have you will not like."

"What's your idea?"

"You can allow me and my men to go on your behalf."

"Do you think we're idiots," Brock snarled.

"It involves trusting people you see as enemies, I understand. Would it be better to try to storm the camp? You don't even know if she's still alive, or where she might be. If we alerted our brothers, you'd be no worse off than with your attack."

"Why would you think it's safe for us to trust you, Drang-ku? If you killed me, you kill the leader of your enemies."

"That's true. All that I can offer you is we've never been shown mercy in a fight. It made us think about the life you offer us. I personally have never met a woman like Liani. I won't stand by to let her be tortured and abused, assuming she's still with us. I want to protect her too."

Aron looked at Brock.

"You can't possibly be considering this, Aron."

"He's right that we have no idea where she is, or if she is alive. If we charge, it will be no worse than them attacking us."

Brock looked at Cherine for support.

"Not you too," he complained. "Am I the only one that's not insane here?"

"If you go into the camp, do you want to remain there?" asked Aron.

"I have a desire to try this new life," he replied. "I can't speak for all of my men."

Aron accompanied Drang-ku to talk to the captives.

"You know what has been offered to us," Drang-ku explained. "It's a generous offer we could expect no where else but here. They honored our request to avoid fighting our brothers. They only want Liani to be rescued. I say it's fair on their part. The only other option is that we go into our camp to find her if she's still alive and to bring her out here. Aron has asked me if I wish to stay in the camp. I've told him I want to go to this new life he offers. That is a choice for me. I'll leave it to each of you if you want to stay or go."

Dead silence and stone faces ensued. Finally one of the men spoke.

"I'll go with you, Drang-ku. I'll try this life of freedom too."

After that, most of the men opted to go with Aron. Those who wished to stay in the camp were taken aside.

"We'll release you when we leave," Aron explained. "If you try to interfere with the rescue to warn the camp, you'll be killed. Do you understand?"

They nodded.

Drang-ku collected his volunteers.

Cherine was standing beside Brock as Aron walked up.

"Aron, this is a terrible idea," said Brock.

"Do you have a better plan, Brock?"

Brock scowled.

"I didn't think so, brother. Let's get ready if things go south."

They crept toward the camp and positioned the masters and the Black Fist for quick action.

Drang-ku took a deep breath and nodded to Aron.

"Thank you for trusting us. I can't know what will happen in there, but we'll do our best."

Brock started to say something, but Aron stopped him.

"Good luck, Drang-ku."

He watched them make their way through the darkness into the camp. The sentries challenged them briefly. Aron was surprised to see how skillfully the sentries were hidden. The sentries who came out of hiding weren't anywhere near the total number safeguarding the camp. The others were well camouflaged and obscured from sight. Aron and his men followed Drang-ku's movements as long as they could, but the camp was big and he was soon out of sight.

"We're going to regret this, Aron," Brock whispered, to his side.

Aron glanced at Cherine. She was intent on the movements in the camp, coiled like a predator cat ready to spring into action.

* * * *

Drang-ku tried to move purposefully. His troops followed trying to act casual, but everyone was nervous and worried. Drang-ku sauntered over to a couple sentries.

"So, what happened to the captive woman? Did they give her to Wu Hang?"

"In a way," the sentry replied. "She must have sung like a song bird because the interrogator didn't mar her. She was chained in the leader's tent for a while. Now Wu Hang has her in his tent. We've heard no screams so I think he didn't harm her there either."

"She's fortunate," said Drang-ku, immensely relieved.

He led his men in a circuitous path, ending up at Wu Hang's dire tent near the leaders, so they had to be particularly careful. There were numerous guards in the area where the leaders were concentrated. Two guards were stationed at the entrance.

"I heard Wu Hang took the woman into his tent?" he whispered to the guard.

"It's been completely silent in there. I don't know what he plans for her. I wouldn't want to be in her shoes. I don't even like being this close to him."

"I understand," Drang-ku agreed. "He's a dangerous man."

Drang-ku continued to talk softly with the guards. Meanwhile he had men slip around back and cut through the tent wall. Creeping over, a soldier put a hand over Liani's mouth.

"Silence, don't wake the interrogator. We're here to take you to Aron," he whispered.

Liani stopped struggling and allowed them to take her cautiously out of the tent. Quickly putting a uniform over her dress, they edged away.

"Good fortune to you," said Drang-ku and edged around to the back of the tent. He led his men out to the sentry line.

"We're supposed to do a night sweep," he lied. "Don't shoot us when we return later."

They eased out of the camp fearing exposure at any moment. Once they cleared the sentries, they angled back toward Aron.

Trying not to make sounds to alert the edgy sentries was harrowing and dangerous. When they finally got to the allied forces Liani saw Aron and leapt into his arms.

"I dreamed you would come for me," she whispered. "I thought they would kill me."

"You're safe now. Let's get out of here."

She suddenly turned to Drang-ku and hugged him.

"Why did you save me?"

He smiled sheepishly. "I, eh…" he stammered.

"Thank you for my life."

"Did the interrogator harm you Liani?"

"He scared me to death, but no, he didn't touch me. I don't understand. I feel fortunate to be alive."

"I've never seen him show compassion for any other person. You're a unique woman, Liani."

* * * *

Sleep wasn't a priority when lives hung in the balance so they just traveled back the way they'd come. Arka and Reston moved close to Aron.

"We wish to pledge to you, Aron. I wouldn't have believed that possible if I hadn't seen it with my own eyes. Getting enemy soldiers to act for you against their own kind, it's remarkable," said Arka.

"Everybody dreams of freedom, Arka. There's nothing special about me."

Arka chuckled. "I wish I could be as un-special as you."

"You'll swell his head," said Brock. "It's already too big."

"I'd be happy to swell your head with my fists, Brock," Aron retorted playfully.

* * * *

Aron's rear guard held the prisoners silent to give him time to establish some distance from the camp. When they released them, they sprinted away, heedless about the sentries. The released prisoners hurried to alert the leaders. Wu Hang found out Liani was gone and was enraged. He was terrifying when he was docile. In this mood, even the leaders feared to come near him.

He growled in frustration and went to the leader. "I'll go to bring her back."

The leader started to contradict him, but saw murder in his eyes.

"I'll send our best trackers with you. She won't get away, Wu Hang. Don't harm her though. Bring her back here and I'll decide what's to be done with her. She's a fool for trying to escape."

Wu Hang gave him the merest of nods and quickly armed himself for the pursuit. He didn't wait for the other men. They had to try to catch up to him. He was single minded of purpose and driven to recover her. Liani was an important person in his life, unlike any other person. For his first time, he cared about someone. He wasn't going to give her up to anybody. He attached something to her that had always been foreign to him, hope.

* * * *

Aron's rear guard flew along the trail to escape, but unfortunately, they were like a beacon for Wu Hang to follow. Neither force wanted to stop so their relative positions didn't change, but both groups were gaining on the main body that had finally stopped to rest and have a meal.

Liani stayed at Aron's side. She couldn't tolerate him being out of her sight for even an instant. He was equally protective of her.

"Liani, I'm so sorry this happened to you."

"I was lucky. They're very dangerous, Aron. We'll see them again."

"We'll be ready, Liani. I'll never allow you to be in danger again. No more walks by yourself."

She smiled sheepishly. "I was a fool. I'm lucky I didn't pay with my life for my stupidity."

Aron took her into his arms. He couldn't resist the urge. It had been too harrowing an experience with her in jeopardy.

"Welcome back," he whispered into her ear. "Besides, I'm not one to judge. I almost got eaten by an ice cat. We're both fools."

She chuckled. "We are fools."

"Let's close our eyes and rest a minute. We can't stay long. They'll be after us with a vengeance."

She curled up contentedly in his embrace and was asleep in minutes. He held her warm petite body against his feeling like he'd set the world right again.

* * * *

Two groups of riders thundered their way relentlessly.

They slept an hour, though it seemed like only minutes. The allies mounted up and resumed their trek back to Aron's camp.

* * * *

More of the strange alien columns were cleared and with each one uncovered the corresponding reactions were noticeably stronger. The increased sound was so distracting people were moving farther away from camp to avoid the hum.

Galean stood with Radigan and Tasha looking at the building which was also markedly more reactive.

"I'm afraid of this thing, Galean," said Tasha.

"I have my doubts too. I'm afraid it's too late for us not to finish the work. It triggered some fanatical impulse in the Brutans and drives them to work nearly round the clock to complete the digging. I don't understand it."

"Other than the annoying sound, I've seen no sign of anything dangerous," said Radigan.

"Nor have I," Galean agreed. "What I fear is if we trigger some event, we'll be in no position to control it or to escape any bad effects."

"That's troubling, Galean. Perhaps we should suspend the digging until Aron returns."

"I doubt I could stop the Brutans now, Radigan. It may also be that what we've started cannot be stopped now. See how the Brutans congregate around. It draws them like moths to a flame."

"What do they say about it?" asked Tasha.

"They know nothing. They can't explain their feelings either."

Radigan shrugged his shoulders. "If anything happens of note, advise me immediately. Come Tasha."

Galean nodded. He didn't fail to notice Radigan's renewed rapport with Tasha. Her reactions to him, that of acceptance and acquiescence hinted at something more - the very thing Aron had struggled mightily with. Those subtle touches not discouraged and the ease they shared together evoked concern in Galean.

"Tasha," he muttered shaking his head in dismay. "This isn't good."

Radigan's "rule" over the camp had been surprisingly successful. For as much as he was distrusted throughout the camp and his continuing pursuit of Tasha, he managed to avoid confrontations of any kind and even improved the security in the camp, decreasing the ongoing offenses of the people of low character.

* * * *

Tasha's father maintained his eternal repugnance of Radigan, but nothing came of it. Radigan was always affable and pleasant around her family. Tasha's mother continued to warm to Radigan.

Aron's parents kept away from Tasha and Radigan, unwilling to judge her to risk a possible argument. Nonetheless, they recognized the evolution in the relationship. Tasha was again drifting away from Aron.

Brock's mother saw the whole scene unfolding and knew keenly what Tasha was trying to cope with. She still had strong feelings from severing ties with Straga.

Sirina decided to go against better judgment and have a talk with Tasha.

"If you don't wish to speak with me, I'll understand, Tasha. I offer my thoughts if you're of a mind to listen. You know we share a similar problem. Though I've chosen to return to my first husband, I haven't forgotten my life with my second husband. I would never tell Barmon because he's still too fragile about me. Do you understand?"

"I do, Sirina."

"For me, it wasn't a matter of picking the better man. Both of them were good to me and each had their own strengths and qualities which attracted me. Barmon still tries to subtly question me if he measures up to Straga. I say things to soothe his ego, but it's an annoyance to have to do so. Straga never questioned his own worth and prowess. I liked that. He was strong and confident. I didn't like some of his barbaric dealings with others, but with me he was always good. If it were possible, I would split time between them. Doing that would kill Barmon's heart, so I keep it to myself. I can't say this is a good plan or that it will continue to work for me."

She looked at Tasha.

"Is it so obvious to everybody that Radigan is, well…"

"Tasha, you're Aron's woman. You'll always be the object of attention in the camp. You're a woman who is unique, who draws men merely by being. People will put their own thoughts and feelings on you. It isn't fair, but it's a reality you must accept. I can't tell you what to do; only you can decide that. I know you're struggling with coping. I know how you can have strong feelings for two men. Even outwardly making Aron your choice, within the secrecy of your heart, I can see you still have stubborn feelings for Radigan too. That doesn't make you a bad person."

"The same issues keep coming up, Sirina. I think I've closed the book on them, but Radigan just has a way about him that cuts through any defense I put up. I can't pretend we haven't been together. Those are good memories, I'm ashamed to say. They're good memories because Radigan made them good. He's a very skilled man in that way."

"You're worried about making more of those memories, aren't you? I understand that. I haven't forgotten being with Straga in that way either. It isn't something I could explain to Barmon, so I know you don't want to speak of it with Aron. In a way, our men are similar in being worried about their competitors. Neither Straga nor Radigan would ever have those worries. That self confidence is compelling, I know that, Tasha."

"I feel like a failure so often, Sirina. Within my head, I say don't go walking with Radigan, and the next thing I know I'm doing that very thing. I don't know how to rectify this problem. When Aron gets back I'm sure there will be plenty of mouths bending his ear about my actions. If he asks me, do I lie?"

"You must search your heart, Tasha. Who is it you think about, that you can't imagine living without? Who makes your heart skip a beat? If it's Aron, I say it's better to be honest with him. Your true love can forgive you your mistakes, as long as you see them as mistakes. If the real truth is Radigan owns your heart, these dalliances will continue to happen. I'm not saying that to judge. I could easily be in your predicament. Straga had a way as a husband. Barmon is a wonderful man, but much different than Straga. Do you know what I'm saying? Straga knew how to treat me about some things, ways which I liked and miss. I don't want Barmon to be so cautious around me. I'm his wife, so treat me as such."

"I do see, Sirina. You're right in that you can conceive of my situation. I don't want it to be this way, but it is. I feel like I'm weak."

"It serves no good purpose to punish yourself Tasha. I would counsel that you not let it go on this way. If Aron is your choice, end it with Radigan, or else tell Aron he isn't the one."

"I thought I had ended it with Radigan, a number of times, but then my feelings end up in turmoil and I'm back in situations where I shouldn't be. I can say it's his fault for keeping it going, but I think if I truly wanted to end it, I should be able to do so. I saw the look in Aron's eyes when he left on this mission to rescue Liani. He wanted to feel secure about us, but he didn't. Now he has reason to have had no faith in me. It would have been better if I had been taken away rather than Liani. She is a woman worthy of Aron."

"I regret the pain you feel, Tasha. I understand how difficult it is to resolve this trouble. I'm here for you to talk to anytime. I'll support you no matter what you choose."

"Thank you, Sirina. That means a great deal to me. There are no others I can talk to about this. They would all have strong opinions about what to do. They would have me kick Radigan away. I've tried to do it, but it hasn't worked. He won't give me up."

"It's gratifying to a woman when you see a man so taken with you. We all want to feel we're the universe to somebody. In our case, that's true with multiple men. In your case, its many men when you add in the prince and even this Uripean chieftain you spoke of."

Tasha chuckled. "That chieftain makes me laugh. He was intriguing in his way. How can I be swayed by these different men? I tell you I'm a weak woman."

"How could you not be swayed, Tasha. They're all important men of great influence in the world. Being appealing to such men speaks admirably of the incredible woman you are."

"If I was incredible, I'd be like Liani. She has none of these silly dilemmas. She knows her mind, sets her goals, and then strives doggedly to achieve them. She is something of a hero to me. I've never told her that."

"Tasha, you don't seem to realize how others see you. I'm sure I wouldn't have to go far to find women who see you as their inspiration. You've overcome so much. You inspire me."

"I've done nothing of note, Sirina. If people could have seen me in my past, they wouldn't have been inspired by my actions, believe me. My history is the story of failures, not successes."

"You're too hard on yourself. I've been there, remember. I've chosen to put my past away. It's over and can't be changed. What's important is what I do from this point forward. The same is true for you, Tasha. You're a gorgeous young woman with great possibilities ahead for you. Embrace your future and don't dwell in your past. Isn't that reasonable?"

"Yes, Sirina, I agree and that's what I'll do, but my truth is I continue to stumble along."

Sirina embraced Tasha.

"I think everything will work out as it should. Why don't we put our worries aside for now and see about what wonders await us with each new day."

Tasha kissed her on the cheek.

Chapter Eight
~ Complicated Matters ~

When the rear guard caught up to Aron's main body they arrived at the gallop. Their leader hurried up to speak with Aron and Cherine.

"We got away cleanly, but there's a force close behind in hot pursuit. We didn't stop to face them so I have no idea how many are in their party."

"That was wise," said Aron. "If there is to be a fight, let's have it with all of our strength and give them no advantages at all."

He sent for Drang-ku.

"We're being pursued by a fast moving unit. Who would they send? I don't want needless bloodshed, but we may not be given a choice."

"Aron, I can't say who it might be. To be this close it must be a highly motivated person leading them."

"Who do you think it is, Drang-ku?"

"It had to be a hastily assembled small force. We're very good, but to instantly spring to the pursuit, it would take a little time to form the force and assemble the cache of supplies. I could only guess about who it would be leading them."

"I know you don't want to fight against your countrymen, but if you're casting your lots with us, you may be forced to choose a side. If you think any of your men will turn on us in a fight, say so now."

"They would have been those who chose to stay behind. I trust all of my men here."

Aron glanced at Cherine who seemed to be pondering the matter. Brock didn't trust the Chenese, any of them, but then again Brock didn't trust anybody.

"Aron, we can't place our trust in them at this point. It's too risky."

"What would you have me do, brother? We have no choice but to extend our trust."

"I warned you," Brock huffed.

"Duly noted, Brock..."

They continued to ride along, but Aron dispatched significant scouts to spy on the pursuers and report back. Dusk came before they returned. Aron had called a halt for the evening and set up a temporary camp.

"We didn't let them see us, Aron. There were twenty of them led by a huge man."

"Wu Hang?" asked Liani, looking at Drang-ku in distress. "Would he be the one they'd send to chase after me?" She looked a wreck at the prospect of meeting the interrogator again.

"It could only be him," Drang-ku replied, "but I have no idea why he would be leading the pursuit. He's not one of the field soldiers. He's normally kept close to the leader as his enforcer and protector."

"Maybe he couldn't accept that Liani could escape right out of his tent," said Brock.

"Aron, he's a really dangerous man," said Liani with a shudder.

"I don't know of any person ever escaping Wu Hang before," Drang-ku advised. "Perhaps you're right. Perhaps he's driven by the affront and stain on his honor. Honor is very important amongst the Chenese."

"Do you think he'd come charging into our camp, Drang-ku?" asked Aron. "Surely he doesn't think he could prevail against all of us. Is he contemptuous of us as an adversary? That would be foolish and I don't assume he's a foolish man."

"Wu Hang is a unique person. What he can accomplish, I can't say. I would take every possible precaution. Liani is right that he's a very dangerous man. He evokes fear in us and we're his countrymen, or at least we were."

"Do you have any suggestions?"

"I think we should conceal Liani from his sight. He won't know where we have her. He'll assume wherever we have troops massed, she'll be the reason."

"I don't want to increase her risk by having no guards on her."

"We'll guard her, but carefully." He turned to look at Liani. "Do you trust me?"

"I do, Drang-ku."

"Would you trust me and my men to take you away from this fight? Since we have no wish to fight our brothers and you shouldn't be in camp for Wu Hang to find, it's the best solution to the problem."

She looked at Aron. "I have no wish to be parted from you ever again, Aron, and I trust you and the prowess of our forces, but I've been in the control of the interrogator. It's beyond any fear I've ever felt. I don't want him to see me because I fear he'd be unstoppable at that point in reclaiming me, no matter the odds. I trust Drang-ku to safeguard me until this matter is resolved."

"I'm surrounded by insanity," Brock spouted in disbelief. "Liani, what's to stop them from changing their minds about betraying their people and simply taking you back?"

"Nothing... I'm telling you I'm willing to take that risk, Brock."

"Am I the only person in this entire camp who sees reality?" Brock grumbled.

"Perhaps you are," Aron replied. "Keep telling us your thoughts and feelings. I need to have all viewpoints of a crisis."

"Even if you totally ignore what I say?"

"You may not think so, but I do pay attention to your concerns, Brock. In this case, it's another calculated risk. Liani has been with Drang-ku enough to feel trust. I'm using her instincts to guide my judgment about a person I don't know well enough yet."

Brock wasn't satisfied at all. "If you're going to do this, we should include some of our people in the force guarding Liani."

"That won't be a problem for us," Drang-ku advised.

"Do you want to go with them, Brock?" asked Aron.

"You know better than that, Aron. If this Wu Hang is so fearsome, he's somebody I want to tangle with. We're pretty fearsome too."

Drang-ku shrugged, skeptically.

"You put a lot of stock in this man," said Brock. "He's just a man."

"You can judge for yourself soon enough. I tell you again to be very careful."

"You doubt us?" Brock objected. "We managed to conquer you and your invincible Chenese soldiers."

"I don't have worries about you. It's the interrogator I have thoughts of. I share Liani's fears about being in the sights of the most frightening man you'll ever meet. I fear his retribution too. You'll know what we fear after this fight. I hope we're all still here to talk about it."

Even Brock paused at Drang-ku's chilling assessment.

"Drang-ku, gather your people." Aron advised after a short pause. "We'll send some of the master's and Black Fist with you. If through some incredible quirk, the interrogator found you, the more competent fighters you have, the better your chances to escape and continue to our main camp."

"We'll be prepared shortly, Aron. He might charge straight into camp here, but I doubt it."

Aron turned to Liani. The tears forming at the edge of her eyes affected him.

"Everything will work out fine, Liani. He'll keep you safe."

"I don't want to leave, Aron. When I was a captive, you were my solace. I can't lose you. Don't fight him directly."

Aron smiled. "Go with Drang-ku. We'll see you later after this battle is over."

Liani stepped close and hugged Aron tightly before she turned and followed Drang-ku away.

Cherine called the masters to gather around her. The Black Fist gravitated to Aron without his call. He looked at them grimly.

"We've had plenty of warning about our adversary. My rules of engagement are always the same. Don't take life needlessly. Kill only when we must. These men are as ardent for their cause and their country as we are. If it's possible to capture them, that would be the best outcome. At the same time, take nothing for granted. We outnumber them a thousand of our finest to twenty and still Drang-ku and Liani are worried, so therefore let's exercise ultimate caution. I never want to lose any of us so don't take unnecessary risks and don't try to fight this Wu Hang by yourself. Hopefully, Brock, Cherine or myself will get a crack at him. Leave him to us, if possible. If we can't beat him, I don't know who else can. If the worst happens, get out of here and get Liani back to camp."

"We will not abandon you, Aron," said one of the Black Fist.

Aron shrugged and chuckled. "I was hoping you'd say that."

The men all laughed, reducing the tense feelings in the camp and restoring feelings of confidence.

"Bring on this lout," said another of the men. "Let him be schooled by the Black Fist."

The entire camp shouted.

Aron glanced at Brock who was bursting with pride and fighting frenzy. The masters were equally provoked. Cherine, too, looked to be pleased.

"Deploy the men, Cherine," said Aron, according to the array we discussed."

They waited patiently into dusk as it started to darken. They maintained a perfunctory appearance of camp routines, though a considerable number of men were hidden from view. The direct attack on the camp didn't happen. As dusk transformed into total darkness, they continued to wait. The bait Aron set: a collection of men in the center of the camp pretending to safeguard Liani didn't fool the interrogator.

When Wu Hang arrived at Aron's camp, he took only a short time to assess the threat, and their state of readiness.

"This is a trap," he whispered to his men. "They've taken her elsewhere. Spread out and search the areas all around the camp. There will be another gathering place where they hope to keep her safe. I don't see any of the traitors. They're probably holed up there also. If anyone betrays our presence here through mistake or even by chance, you'll answer to me. I will tolerate no failure."

His men nodded and filtered away.

Wu Hang remained with a few of the men to study his enemy.

"You're careful, Aron," he muttered. "It will do no good."

Wu Hang headed in a wide arc around the camp. He could sense each of the hidden men watching him. They navigated the trap and began to make their way eerily closer to where Drang-ku waited in fear with Liani huddling in terror beside him.

Aron felt concern when so much time passed and nothing happened. He crept out of his hiding place and motioned to the nearest of his men.

"Somehow, he's discerned us here and slipped through. Let's go to Liani before it's too late."

As he hurried past, other Black Fist members, and masters, jumped out and joined him racing to where Liani was hidden.

When Aron arrived, panting from the long sprint, he heard the sound of fighting.

"Hurry," he yelled and they raced to close the remaining distance. A pitched battle was in progress. The Black Fist and masters in Drang-ku's party were leading the fight. Drang-ku had Liani behind him as he faced the largest man Aron had ever seen. Even from a distance in the dark,

Aron could see Drang-ku quaking. Aron raced over to stand between Drang-ku and the interrogator.

They eyed each other momentarily.

"Wu Hang," he said with a nod of his head.

"Aron," Wu Hang replied with a smile. "Hand over Liani to me and we can dispense with needless pain and bloodshed."

"If role was reversed and I asked you to release her to me, what would be your answer?"

Wu Hang chuckled. "That is an interesting point, but I think you don't understand the nature of the Chenese when it comes to duty and honor. I can't abide what was done. Liani was placed in my care to safeguard with my life. The leader will not accept this failure on my part. I was foolish to take for granted her safety so close to me in my very own tent. I didn't foresee the intervention of these traitors. That's a mistake I'll never make again."

"We're not traitors," Drang-ku replied sharply. "Aron is unlike any leader we've ever encountered. He's offered us something no Chenese has, freedom to live our lives as we choose. Have you ever had such an offer, master interrogator?"

"You put a great deal of trust in a stranger, Drang-ku. What guarantees do you have when you get to his camp? You choose for more than yourself. Your men will pay the same price you've incurred on your own head. You know the army will come to Aron's camp. We will wipe them out. There's no question about that battle."

"You seem to have an opinion about our battle skills," said Aron. "You're welcome to your opinions, but what are you basing it on, Wu Hang. I would never underestimate any protagonist. When it comes to strangers, I use maximum caution. Do you think slipping around my camp proves your superiority? Here I am standing between you and your prey. Liani is what to you, a stain on your honor, and a breach of your orders from your superiors? For us, Liani is precious. Perhaps you're incapable of understanding that. Your job is to torture, after all."

Wu Hang was silent. He stared at Liani who was peering at him ashen faced and terrified.

"Perhaps it's you who can't understand, Aron. Even a man such as me who must do the grisly work, I too can cherish. Liani for me is…"

Aron looked at him and then Liani.

"Did he hurt you, Liani?"

"No Aron," she replied soberly. "I feared they would, but I was touched by none of them. I don't know what their ultimate plans were."

"Are you trying to say, this isn't about recapturing her for your leader? That this is about feelings you have for Liani?"

He looked daunted for the first time. Aron stared in amazement. He looked at Liani. She was incredulous.

"What did you think, master interrogator?" she asked. "What woman do you believe could reconcile what you do? Any of us would live in fear you would turn on us one day out of insanity for that's the only possible end for a person who rends flesh daily."

"You've summarized the horror of my life. I'm cursed to live alone with no hope of a life and no one to share it with. I'm not saying I was a worthy man to woo you, Liani. You gave me the dream of a different life. Even I can dream of being loved and of being a father to my children."

"I, eh," she stammered. "I don't know what to say. I can't pretend you haven't shown me such terror in our brief time together as I couldn't have imagined before. The thought of anything else, it seems impossible. I'm sorry, Wu Hang. I don't want to antagonize you. The truth is the truth. You frighten me down to my core."

"I don't want a fight, Wu Hang," Aron interjected. "Whatever the outcome here, I think its best we talk about it. Will you agree to that?"

"I will not leave without her," Wu hang replied.

"I think the issue is if you want to return back there at all. I don't know you, but I can see the profound impression you make on other people. My offer to any who wish to join us is that you be willing to discard your past, your old ways, and live a better life. I don't expect perfection because we all make mistakes. I know all about mistakes because I've made more than my share and other people have paid a price. We don't have work in our camp for a torturer. But if you're willing to try something else, I think it's a better option than a meaningless death here and now. Each of your men will have the same choice to join us or return to your people."

Wu Hang looked longingly at Liani. She shuddered, but stood her ground bravely.

"If you want to talk privately with your men or in conjunction with Drang-ku, I'm willing to let you camp with us tonight," Aron advised. "You say you're men of honor so I'll ask all of you on your honor to postpone any ongoing feud with us until tomorrow. We'll settle this one way or another then."

"We accept," said Wu Hang.

He walked over to Liani, who seemed on the verge of fainting, while everyone else tensed. He gently touched her shoulder before gathering his men. They all went to Aron's camp - an unlikely end to what started as a deadly confrontation.

Brock and Cherine stood looking on in amazement.

"You've captured him without any losses?" asked Cherine. "How did you do that?"

"We spoke as two reasonable opponents. We've agreed to make a decision tomorrow."

Brock stepped close to Wu Hang. "We would have beaten you tonight and we'll beat you tomorrow if you choose to fight. I'm not afraid of you."

Wu Hang merely smiled, but the smile was terrifying.

"Sleep well, brother of Aron."

Brock was shaken. His bravado seemed a needless taunt at a supremely confident and potentially deadly man. Wu Hang didn't act worried about a possible future fight with them and he truly was the most frightening man they'd ever seen.

"Good night, Liani," said Wu Hang. "It's good to see you again.

"Night," she whispered. She couldn't mask her fright. Her face was pale.

Liani almost crawled into Aron's bedroll that night. She pressed against him for her feeling of security even though they were in separate bedding.

Aron put his arm over her and whispered. "It's going to be all right, Liani."

"Thank you, Aron," she whispered back and kissed his hand.

The master interrogator had chosen to sleep close to Liani. She was unnerved, but he made no threatening moves and soon fell asleep. After that she was able to doze off and Aron was already asleep.

Distracted by his thoughts and ready to dismount his horse after the long journey back from the borderlands, the prince rode to the palace entrance. He'd thought about Tasha the entire trip and indirectly about the annoyance of Aron's successes. As he walked through the palace doors, he shifted mental gears. He was anxious to see his wife again, and he had his father to deal with.

He'd gotten most of the way to his suites when Granor approached. Arriving a week before Agar, he'd ridden ahead to speak to the king.

"Welcome home, my prince," he said with a bow.

Agar eyed him suspiciously; suspecting Granor's whispered accusations in his father's ear was part of the problem.

"You've moved up in the world, Granor, good for you."

"Thank you, sire," he replied with a self-satisfied grin. "His majesty wishes you to attend him at your earliest convenience."

"Am I not allowed to see my wife after such a long separation?" His steely glare left no doubts with Granor he understood the subtle contest for power.

"Of course you must see to your wife, his majesty is not insensitive. But we see this as a vital issue, one not to be delayed."

"We?" asked Agar. "Are you a prince now, Granor?"

"I was saying the royal we, sire. I wasn't including myself. As you note, I'm not of the royal family. I merely serve at the king's pleasure."

"I'll hold you no further from your duties, Granor."

The prince turned sharply and walked away without looking back."

Granor eyed him grimly and thought, "*We'll see who's still standing in the end, Agar*."

The crown prince burst into his suite and saw Coraline waiting. She was breathtaking.

"Welcome home, husband. It's been a long time awaiting your return."

"You gladden my heart, wife. If there is a more beautiful woman in the realm, I've never seen her."

"Thank you, my prince. I hoped to brighten your day."

"I must meet with my father, but I'll come back as soon as I can so we can spend time together."

"I'm yours to command, Agar."

"I'd take you along, but I fear Granor has poisoned my father against me. This could be a difficult and contentious meeting."

"If you want me to come and speak on your behalf, just tell me, Agar."

He smiled. "I'll handle it, my love. You shouldn't be exposed to these exercises of intrigue and ambitions from lesser people. In the end, the king is my father and he'll understand what I say. Granor's plotting and schemes will come to nothing."

Agar paused a moment and looked at his wife.

"Has Granor caused any problems for you, my dear?"

"I'm often in the company of the queen. We do see him. He's a main counselor for your father, but no, he hasn't caused me any problems. He goes his way, and I go mine."

Agar pondered her answer.

"Be on your guard about him, Coraline. I don't yet know the nature of his plans, but you need to safeguard and protect our family in my absence. I'm sorry to put such an odious task on your shoulders, but there is no other to do it. Do you see?"

"Of course, my prince," she replied with a bow.

Suspicious of everyone by nature, an aberrant life style gave him good reason to distrust those around him. Though he'd given his trust to Coraline, a part of him could never fully trust any other person. With Coraline, he was vulnerable for the first time in his life and it rattled him. He felt anyone could turn on him sooner or later.

Leaving Coraline alone to cope for long periods of time was another concern. Though Tasha still occupied a major part of his interest, increasingly he looked backwards at the woman he'd chosen to leave behind. Since he couldn't imagine going without intimacy, it was hard to imagine that Coraline could either. Yet, this was the situation he'd left her in. Whether she'd been celibate during that absence, he struggled with. He could only see life through the filter of himself and his urges. That another person might be able to control their impulses was inconceivable.

He was stirred up when he left for the audience with his father, imagining all sorts of unfortunate possibilities.

Coraline watched him leave. She had a sense of his feelings and suspicions. From Agar's mother, the queen, Coraline trained to be very good at looking and acting placid. Like the queen, she'd learned how to cope successfully with the challenges of life and marriage. The queen was possibly the dearest of her friends and a good mentor about life as an elite person in the kingdom. The queen, she trusted completely.

"*Coraline, dwell on the things that are good in our lives. Those things we abhor are out of our control anyway. Don't waste time thinking about them. We have each other and the others of our women friends. In that group we carve out our lives. It's the only way to survive the traps in our path. There is no ideal life possible to royal women. Acknowledging and accepting that fact will allow you to achieve some measure of peace in your life, dear. There aren't any other alternatives, do you see?"*

She was the only person Coraline had chosen to place any trust and take the risk of sharing her truth.

"*Agar is your son, so it's probably unwise to tell you this, but I need to trust someone and admit my mistakes. I've done some things for which I feel shame. Agar is gone so often, I...*"

"*I know what you're going to say, Coraline. I was a young woman too, and I also was a lonely woman then. Agar is like his father; they have no qualms about sewing their wild oats, and felt no shame about soiling their marriage vows. It angers a woman and it makes it easy to lash back at them in a number of ways. You don't need to tell me about being with Radigan. We all know about it and we aren't surprised. If you could see a list of all of the women he's been with, I think you'd worry less. I've been where you are, darling. We aspire to live within the promises of our marriage vows, but none of us have denied ourselves in the end. You've done much better than most. Don't think any more about it because it matters not to any of the rest of us. Frankly, many are envious of you and would gladly have taken your place for a night with a masterful lover. He has a reputation he's earned with his prowess and his successes. What our husbands do in shaming us, those things have a price for them, though it's in secret so they never know what we do for revenge. It gives us power to smile blithely at them and know we've scored an affront they'd find intolerable without their discovering it.*"

"*This isn't what I expected for my life, your majesty,*" Coraline replied. "*That isn't acceptable behavior in the village.*"

"*It isn't acceptable behavior anywhere, yet I'll guarantee it happened in your village too. Human weakness isn't something exclusive to the monarchy. Probably not to the extent it happens here, but there are disillusioned and disgruntled wives everywhere. They look for secret thrills to counter the drudgery and the disappointment in their lives.*"

"*I didn't think of it that way. I don't know that it makes me feel better about my mistakes, but I appreciate your efforts to comfort me.*"

"*Coraline, you already know this, but I'll tell you again anyway. You must not allow Agar to discern your distress. You must wear your façade and show him the fantasy he wants you to be. You've seen how your life will be with him gone frequently, so it's a matter of perpetrating this ruse for periods of time until they inevitably leave again. After enough time, it becomes an automatic response you do without thinking.*"

"*Is there never a time when you are truly honest with your husband, that you can share your inner feelings and goals?*"

"*There never was for me. I'm sorry, dear. With the king, we're closer at this stage of life, but it isn't the same as close. I've envied peasants so often for their marriage bond of true love and devotion. It's something I'll never have. All of the comfort and the riches don't fully offset my losses in my relationship.*"

"*Your majesty, that's really troubling to hear.*"

"*You made a difficult choice to be bride to the crown prince, Coraline. It's a tradeoff and I can't say we're the better for it.*"

Coraline got a contemplative look.

"*I've felt that same thing, Coraline. There was a young man in my youth too. I still wonder what my life would have been with him. I wouldn't have been rich, famous, and pampered, but often I'd wished to trade places for the love and devotion a good man can give. Your Aron is a remarkable man. Your life with him, I think it would have been fulfilling.*"

"*It's too late for that. He wants Tasha now, I can't disagree. She's a much better woman than I. All I have is great beauty. She has beauty and all of the inner qualities I envy. See how my husband pursues her.*"

"*Don't say that, Coraline. You know the mistakes she made when she was here. She made poor choices too. She isn't innately better than you.*"

Coraline smiled and hugged the queen.

"*Thanks for trying to make me feel better, your majesty.*"

* * * *

Agar entered the throne room firmly and confidently. Granor was standing beside his father who was seated on the throne. Agar went straight to his father and completely ignored Granor. He had a plan in mind to vary from what his father expected.

He walked up to the king, went to a knee, and then stood up and grasped his father in a welcoming embrace.

"It's so good to see you again, father."

The king was stunned and moved. His son wasn't one to show affection.

"I'm glad you're home too, son."

"It's been a perilous time in the field, and I hear it's been difficult in the kingdom. I've had ample time to think about my campaign. Retroactively, a rational mind would have to question the wisdom of it. I think many elements looked to take advantage of the situation with me away and our resources stretched."

"I'm so happy to hear you say this, Agar. You know I've tried to allow you a certain level of authority and decision making, but I fear you've put us all at risk."

"I'm sorry, father. The affront to the realm from Aron and his rebels was too strong a provocation. I didn't properly assess the cost of my response. For that I'm sorry. I want you to know I stand ready to follow your counsel on the matter."

"Son, I share your outrage at what Aron has done. Granted I see it from a different perspective, but I'm equally motivated. The problem is the kingdom. You'll one day be king, Agar. You've got to learn you can no longer act the petulant child. The entire monarchy is at risk from this pursuit of a village woman. You may have strong feelings for her, but if it means losing the kingdom, it has to dawn on you your making a serious mistake. The unrest we're currently experiencing across the whole realm is unprecedented. I've been told Aron began to establish pockets of resistance as he traveled about on royal tasks with the Black Fist unit. Since he traveled extensively, the scope of his mischief is widespread. I'm sorry to tell you, we can no longer afford to have the army sitting idly at the border to the wilds while the rest of the kingdom erodes into disarray. I fear we're close to outright rebellion. That's a matter that can't be ignored."

"I understand, father. We can begin to redeploy our forces as you see fit."

"I've talked with Granor at length on the subject and he's offered some solid options."

Agar bristled, but outwardly nodded in acquiescence.

"Of course, father. Tell me what you'd like to do."

The king looked closely at his son. "I must say, I'm pleasantly surprised that you're so agreeable to these necessary changes. I've feared the worst that you might turn to obstinacy and argument. You give me hope about our future. I've always thought you could be a competent and a smart ruler. Even with a king, Agar, there can be humbling occasions. A person must persevere and overcome those disappointments. If Aron foolishly concludes our withdrawal of forces is a sign of his victory, he'll be ripe for a response that will end his little rebellion in flames and ruin. Let him try to be bold and seize the initiative. Let him try to face us in the open field. The royal host has never lost a war and we won't lose this time either."

Even in his cynical heart, Agar was inspired by his father's words. He'd never really felt or even sought a close father son relationship. Now he regretted it.

He glanced at Granor who had a calculating look.

"Let's talk about your plans," said Agar.

Chapter Nine

~ Impending Decisions ~

Aron opened his eyes, to the morning sun. Liani had somehow managed to wiggle into his bedding during the night and was still asleep resting peacefully. Aron smiled and glanced up to see Wu Hang staring at him. Aron nodded. The interrogator nodded back.

Liani opened her eyes and smiled at Aron.

"Morning," she whispered. "I'm sorry if I didn't give you room to sleep."

"It's fine, Liani."

She looked over at Wu Hang who stared at her in silence.

"Good morning," she said. That made him smile.

"Maiden…"

The camp stirred and moved about, preparing breakfast and assembling for the trek back to camp.

"Did you make a decision?" asked Liani. "I don't want any bloodshed over me. I abhor violence."

Wu Hang looked at her and then Aron who had seated himself beside Liani, along with Cherine and Brock.

"I've decided to go with you. I'll let my men choose as they wish."

Drang-ku walked up and smiled broadly. "Master interrogator, I'm glad I don't have to face you as a combatant. I don't feel certain about the outcome of that fight."

"I don't seek needless conflict either. Perhaps I can be seen in a new light as I discard my old life." He looked directly at Liani. She had a 'deer in headlights' look as she sipped her coffee. Conceiving Wu Hang as anything other than terrifying was difficult. His potential romantic aspirations were an untenable step at that moment.

After eating Wu Hang called together his twenty men. None of them chose to return to the Chenese camp. Drang-ku's men gladly accepted more Chenese converts and combined forces.

"Do you wish to be our leader, Wu Hang?" asked Drang-ku.

"No," he replied without elaboration.

"So be it," said Drang-ku with a shrug.

Aron's remarkable luck overcoming adversaries without the need to kill them off continued. The diverse range of people pledging loyalty to him was remarkable, especially in light of their former animosities.

Aron led the march to his camp. Wu Hang positioned himself near to Liani, prompting her to hustle up to Aron. She didn't say anything, but didn't need to. Aron glanced back at Wu Hang and nodded. Wu Hang returned the gesture.

They traveled rapidly assuming the balance of the Chenese forces would give pursuit. Aron wanted to have that fight on his home grounds.

* * * *

Radigan got the word of Aron's approach when they were a day out and went to talk to Tasha immediately.

"I'm told Aron was successful in finding and rescuing Liani. It's nothing short of a miracle. There is a large force pursuing them. We know nothing of them other than they're from beyond the wilds."

"We need to tell Galean and Abdurka, Radigan."

"I've already sent word to them. I want to talk to you before he arrives."

She glanced around nervously. "I believe I know the topic. This isn't the time or place to have your talk. In spite of, well, our recent times together, I'm Aron's betrothed still. Though I'm a poor choice on his part, he seems to want me, no matter what. I can't ignore that..."

"I understand all of that, Tasha. What I wanted to say won't wait. Let's take a short walk so I can speak my mind."

"Taking walks with you is what leads me into trouble, Radigan."

"This time I truly want only to talk. Please come with me, Tasha. We'll be back very soon."

She eyed him suspiciously.

"None of your tricks," she hissed.

They walked away into the nearby trees for privacy.

"Tasha, I'm not going to lie to you. This is too important to me. It's not a ploy or subterfuge. I'm baring my soul to you. Aron would be a wonderful husband, but he isn't me. You know what I'm saying. In your heart you love me. You loved me back then and you did something no other woman has ever done. You caused me to love you back. You know I've pulled up a great many dresses and skirts in my time. Right now, the only dress I ever want to raise again is yours. We have a connection, a rapport, and an unmatchable union you get nowhere else. Aron was your childhood love, albeit adolescent. You've known mature love with me. I think you pick him because you think it's what you should do, the right thing for the resistance and the wishes of your family. Can you honestly say you crave Aron like you crave me? I have no thoughts in my head but you, darling. I know you, I know what you like, what you need, and what you want. Aron meanders through your life clueless. Of course he has feelings for you, but remember darling, his first love was Coraline. You were his second choice."

Tasha's expression darkened.

"I will do anything for you, my love. You will never have to worry about me with another woman. You're the only woman I want. My old life is over."

She was troubled. He tried to embrace her, but she put up her hands.

"Radigan, I won't lie to you either. Yes, I do love you, but you too easily discount that I love Aron. I could be a wife to you and I have no doubt you'd make me happy. I have that same belief about Aron. I think you've made an assumption about my feelings because I'm a weak person who is too prone to mistakes with you - a mistake on my part, not a revelation of my deepest love. I don't think I could ever get you out of my system, but that doesn't mean I don't want to explore a life with Aron. You compliment me with your persistence, but I can't accept your offer. I want to be with Aron."

She looked at his face - a frozen mask of conflict. She wasn't sure if he would turn on her and felt concern. He blinked his eyes and grimaced eventually, took a deep breath and forced a smile.

"I'm a reasonable man, Tasha. We're not really in a different place than we've been all along. My feelings for you aren't going to change. I wasn't planning on standing in your way, but understand, my darling, I'll never give up loving you."

Tasha relaxed. "I feared that very thing, Radigan. If you were a vengeful man, you could go to Aron with stories of my missteps to poison him against me. I'm sure you know that wouldn't be a wise path. It certainly wouldn't endear me to you, quite the opposite. I would hate you forever for such a betrayal. I've told you consistently I want to be with him, not you."

"You have, Tasha. I acknowledge that, and no, I would never do something underhanded to harm you. I still hope to win you back to me with my deeds and accomplishments. Who else could walk alone into the camp of a dire enemy without consequence and eventually rise to a position of trust and leadership? This temporary role I've been given isn't the last time you'll see me in charge."

She looked at him, and then shook her head. "It will not sway me, Radigan. We must return to the camp now. I've been gone too long already. People may notice us come out of seclusion together and make assumptions. I don't want that. I'll walk out now, alone, and you can circle the camp and come in from a different direction."

Radigan nodded his head.

"Thank you. I'll probably always love you too, but my mind is made up about this, Radigan. From this point forward, we're friends only. No more walks in the woods. I think it would be wise if you start to look at the other women in the camp. There are many great women who'd be excellent partners for you, worthy women, far better than me."

"There are none better than you, Tasha, but I won't debate you now. As you said, we should get back to the camp."

He turned and walked away rapidly through the trees. Tasha watched him for a moment before she went out of the brush and into the camp. People were stirred up, moving busily and preparing for the imminent triumphant return of their esteemed leader. Tasha hurried away to join her and Aron's mothers. She wanted to look her best for Aron.

* * * *

Galean was helping to dig and covered in soil when they came for him.

"Master Galean, Radigan has called for you and Abdurka to come immediately. There's word from the west for you to consider."

"I'll be there shortly."

He stretched and put a hand to his aching back before climbing up the ladder and out of the excavation site. He looked back at the emerging spectacle of the large concave alien building. More columns were found, all in a continuous circle and equidistance from each other. With no escape from the sound and thrumming sensation, the pervasive hum was now so strong it seemed to bore through a person's skull.

He left to bathe and when he emerged Abdurka approached.

"Good day," he called affably.

"What's this important news we're supposed to hear about, Galean?" Abdurka replied gruffly. "I was busy."

Galean chuckled and patted Abdurka on the shoulder. "It's a heavy burden being a person of import."

Abdurka grumbled.

"Come along, my friend. Let's see to this and then you can return to your work, Abdurka."

They walked to the headquarters where Radigan was talking with a scout who had just arrived from Aron's troop. Radigan and the scout turned and nodded as Galean and Abdurka walked up.

"Good, thank you for coming promptly," Radigan advised. "I'll let this messenger explain why I've called for you."

"My lords, Aron sends word they've encountered a new force who called themselves the Chenese. They've come in force and they're moving our way. The Chenese are very good fighters so we need to begin to make preparations to defend the camp. This could be a serious fight."

They all looked at Abdurka. His gruff expression was gone, replaced by a look of concern.

"What is it?" asked Galean. "Apparently you know of these people."

"I do indeed," Abdurka replied. "Among the competing nations of the world, the Chenese are among the fiercest. They're numerous beyond counting and sacrifice their own extravagantly to achieve their aims. This isn't a good turn of events. If we can prevail in a battle against them, it won't be an easy victory and will cost us dearly in casualties and supplies. The battle won't be over until the last of the Chenese are dead or the last of us because I can't guarantee our victory against this force. If they return to their homeland to report us, it could unleash a chain of events leading to our end and the end of this entire realm. This is a very serious matter, Galean."

Galean looked at Radigan who eyed them closely.

"I think what I read in the royal archives pointed toward this outcome, my friends. I didn't see any stories of the outcomes of individual battles. I only saw the final battle against the beast. My opinion is we'll survive this test, but I have nothing to support that opinion."

"What thoughts do you have about the defense of the camp, Abdurka?" asked Radigan.

"The Chenese try to overwhelm their enemies and don't employ subtle tactics - most likely a full frontal attack in waves. We must construct obstacles to slow their charge. Our men shouldn't be exposed to man on man fights any more than is necessary. If we move about and don't give them stationery targets to focus on, I think it will go better."

"The Brutans in particular won't want to shy away from battle. They have reckless courage, Abdurka," Radigan pointed out.

"There will be fewer Brutans then," Abdurka answered. "The Chenese train for battle from the time they can first stand up and toddle about as children. Their society is based on honor so they would never run from a fight. For them it's better to die in the attempt than to go back home in defeat. If a soldier was ever disgraced, his family would pay the price in suffering, blood and eventually in death."

"Perhaps you should have a talk with our Brutan friends, Abdurka," said Galean.

"I can do that, if it will do any good, Galean. Of all of the possible enemies in the world for us to face, the Chenese would be my last choice."

* * * *

Aron smiled as they rounded the last turn and saw his camp in the distance.

"See Liani," he said. "I told you we'd get you home to safety."

She smiled.

He glanced back at Wu Hang and Drang-ku. They were surveying the layout of the camp in military terms- the defensibility of the camp placement, and array of available fighters.

"When you first came here to spy on us Drang-ku, what were your conclusions?" asked Aron.

"Aron, you must understand no Chenese soldier looks on an opponent as invincible or too daunting. We simply assess our adversary and then prepare a plan for their destruction. When our main forces arrive, it will be no different. No matter what preparations you've made the Chenese will attack without pity. We either kill all before us, or enslave any for valuable services they can provide. The Chenese seek only one outcome, total victory. I'm sorry, Aron."

"Will you join your countrymen in that fight?"

"No," Wu Hang answered. "When we joined you, we became traitors. Our army will slaughter us, if they can."

"I'm glad you're on our side, Wu Hang. I wouldn't want to fight against you."

"I'm but one man, Aron. I will be a fierce challenge for any opponent, but I can be slain like any other."

"In my camp, we fight as parts of a single unit. Each of us protects those around us. You'll be afforded the same bond of brotherhood as any other. I guess I shouldn't just say brotherhood, because we have females as key parts of our fighting forces. Cherine is more than a match for any man."

"We thank you, Aron," said Wu Hang. "We'll not disappoint you in the battle."

They rode until entering the camps to the cheers of the masses who called out Liani's and Aron's name. The pair smiled and waved to the crowd, wishing they weren't the center of attention.

When they stopped at the command tent, Radigan was standing with Galean and Abdurka. Abdurka looked at Wu Hang in shock.

Tasha emerged along with Enna, Biala, Belisa, the mothers' and others of their female circle and quickly embraced Liani, exclaiming over her happily.

"If you ever do this again, Liani," said Enna, "we will personally hunt you down and skin you alive."

Liani laughed and hugged them.

Finally Tasha turned to Aron.

"Welcome back. You did an incredible job. We're all very proud of you."

He took her in his arms and hugged her firmly.

Abdurka went straight up to Wu Hang. Wu Hang nodded to him with a sly smile.

"My life has become a series of wonders. I'd never thought to see a Chenese again, and certainly not without crossing swords."

"My own life has gone in directions I could never have foreseen," Wu Hang replied. "How is it you're here in this backwards land?"

"Probably the same reason you're here. We were exploring uncharted realms. My companions fell to various calamities. I'm the only survivor, but the new life I have with my friends, I wouldn't trade for anything."

"I understand that. Aron offered us companionship and brotherhood. It's something no Chenese has ever received before."

"Usually any new person you meet is slain on the spot, Wu Hang."

"True," he replied with a smile. "I'll try a different approach in the future."

"You're the biggest man I've ever seen. It's unsettling. I'm not a person who's frightened of others, but I'm frightened of you."

"I've lived with that mantle all my life, Abdurka. I can't change my appearance, so I'm going to show people a difference in my ways. Perhaps it will be sufficient."

He glanced at Liani. She stared at him wide eyed before she turned back to her women friends and left the area.

As they walked, Tasha couldn't let it pass.

"Liani, what is this with that huge barbarian? I was told he tortures people. His frightful appearance defies description. He looked at you with tenderness, like he's besotted."

"It's through nothing on my part, Tasha. I can't even look at him without quaking in fear. If he has a desire to woo me, that would be the most difficult task any man has ever attempted. I don't favor him in any way. I'm happy when I manage to be apart from him. He follows me everywhere and chills my blood. I can't ignore what grisly things he's done to people."

"I think he hopes otherwise, darling."

"Who are you to talk, Tasha? I suspect Radigan will never abandon his romantic aims about you. Of all people, you should understand how trying this is for me."

"Liani, I didn't mean this derisively. It's just you're such a petite little woman and he is so massive a man, the disparity is comical, in a way."

Liani looked at the other women and they shrugged and smirked.

"I'm sorry to lash out at you, Tasha. I'm not quite myself. This trauma has been a terrible test for me. I thought I was going to meet my end in the interrogators tent. His attempts to be romantic are, well, I can't think of an appropriate word. I may never be the same again if he is always near me."

"I don't think he means you any harm," said Belisa. "Arrecks see people a little differently. I believe what he said was totally honest. I would have sensed any attempt to mislead us."

"Why don't you marry him, Belisa? I would feel a lot better then," Liani huffed.

All of the women laughed.

"It's an interesting concept, Liani, but I'm not disposed to go in that direction. Having the interrogator as consort to the future queen of the Arreck, that doesn't strike me as a sound idea. Beside the fact he terrifies me also."

"There you have it," Liani retorted. "See, it's not so difficult to understand my feelings and my reactions, ladies."

"We understand you very clearly, Liani," Tasha interjected. "Please don't take offense because none was intended."

Obviously still perturbed, Liani scowled and then shrugged, which made the other women chuckle.

* * * *

Radigan, a patient and a confident man was also perturbed. This was his first experience with failure. He'd always gotten everything he wanted in his life. The prospect that Tasha might slip through his fingers when she was so tantalizingly close, irked him to no end. He had to exert a great deal of effort to keep from taking ill-conceived actions. Mistakes were another area of unfamiliarity and he had no intention to start now.

Although preoccupied and sullen, Radigan accompanied the other leaders to discuss the defensive plan for the impending Chenese attack. Cherine detected Radigan's foul mood immediately.

"Radigan, whatever is your problem, this isn't the time or the place for it. Get control of yourself," she whispered tersely, pulling him aside for a moment.

"Of course, Cherine, you're right, I need to focus."

Tasha's suggestion that he should look at the other women of the camp crossed his mind. There couldn't be a more impressive woman than Cherine. He pondered such a move for only a moment before shifting gears to consider the issue at hand: a fight against an overpowering foe.

Aron stepped to the forefront. "There are many more qualified to stand here and make our strategy. I wish you would, but regardless, I've thought about the advice of our new Chenese friends. I say we should incorporate those ideas into our plans. Perhaps we can station numerous mobile teams to sweep into and out of the battle. If we continue to lead our enemy this way and that, they won't be able to concentrate on any one spot. We can lace the opponent with archer fire from all around and cull their numbers. I'm confident we're the measure of any others fighters in the world, but I'm not going to discount the prowess of our enemies. We couldn't afford a mistake of arrogance that could cost us the lives of our families and loved ones. We cannot accept defeat. If our foes are dedicated to annihilating us, we must be willing to do the same. You all know I would avoid violence if possible, but it appears we have no choice."

He gazed around at silent faces.

"Would anybody like to add anything?"

Again silence...

"You all know how to fight. I don't need to talk about that. Our fighting purpose always stays the same. You're fighting for those who can't. You're fighting for your comrades, and you're fighting for the ideal of freedom. It's something many of us have rarely had, some never had and is worth putting our lives on the line for. I wish I was a great speaker with words to inspire you, but I'm just a farmer who wouldn't take no for an answer."

Everybody chuckled.

"Let's get the obstacles put together and put into place. After that, it's just a matter of waiting for them to make their move."

* * * *

Digging continued around the strange building. Much of the structure was uncovered and the circle of columns was mostly exposed. Aron had considered showing the Chenese the site, but a little warning signal inside his head restrained him.

The appearance of their enemy didn't occur as rapidly as Aron anticipated. A week passed before scouts reported signs of their stealthy approach.

"The leaders are cautious in unfamiliar territory," Drang-ku explained. "The additional peril of our aligning with you and divulging their plans slows them too. It won't stop them though."

Aron deployed the camp. The civilians had been moved away for safety

Aron guessed Chenese numbers at five thousand based on what he'd seen and what Drang-ku said. Currently, Aron's troop strength was far beyond that with the continuous influx of new recruits. He could field five times the number of Chenese, but in these close quarters, he'd have his men stumbling over each other.

Instead, Aron set waves of reinforcements close at hand to react in any direction. The initial points of conflict would have roughly equal numbers on both sides, so he put his best fighters there in hopes to carry the day.

Aron watched the approaches to the camp from an elevated platform built in the trees. Cherine was there too, along with other staff members. Radigan stood beside Cherine.

Aron thought if he went down in this battle, it wasn't impossible Radigan could vie for the role of leader. He'd been very successful in running the camp and much of the antagonism against him had drained away. Radigan was seen much more favorably these days than Aron would have thought possible not so long ago.

Galean had asked to participate in the fight, but was quickly overruled. He and his staff were sent away with the families and the other civilians.

Aron had placed the Brutan fighters into the reserve on the advice of every one of his staff members because they were too much of an uncontrollable force to depend on. Their actions in a battle could cause as much harm as help.

The Brutans argued strenuously, but he wouldn't be swayed.

"Don't think there won't be fighting for you, but we need to control the initial phase of the battle before we see where best to put you. All that I ask of you is a little patience. We can't be frantic out there and lose control of things."

The Brutans were surly at the perceived snub and affront to their dignity, grudgingly following Aron's orders and retiring to a secondary position only because Aron asked them.

"What do you think, Wu Hang?" Aron asked. "Is there anything else we should be doing?"

"Like you, I'm no strategist, Aron. Battle ultimately comes down to each man finding a way to defeat his opponent. I'm sorry I can offer you nothing better."

"I'll keep you and your people away from the fighting as best I can, but if they break through, can we depend on you to do what you must?"

"Aron, I've told you our comrades will seek us out in the battle. We're traitors and that makes us the first victims to slay. I wish to live as much as any other man. That's the best guarantee I can think of that we'll do our best. Also, I carry a small cloth of Liani's as a reminder of what I'm fighting for. I won't allow them to lay hands on her. They don't see her as the miracle she is. She's just a pawn to be used as they see fit."

"That's good enough for me, Wu Hang. Thank you. Stay safe."

"Aron, I can say the same for you. It was easy enough for us to see what a key role you play here and in this rebellion you speak of. You're the main cog they'll be looking to eliminate. Be on your guard constantly and never be alone. Keep considerable forces close by you. I'd offer my own services, but I know you have other plans for us."

"Don't think I didn't consider it, Wu Hang. You'd be a great deterrent to anybody coming after me, but I want you guys to help protect our vulnerable, the civilians and our women. If we lost them, it would gut us all. I don't know if there would be a resistance after such a disaster."

"As you wish, Aron, we'll stand by if you need us elsewhere too. Fight to your utmost. I know you prefer to avoid death and hope to transform all of your opponents into allies. Believe me you can't do that here. You and your forces must be as ruthless as they. You'll get no mercy from them. If you show them mercy they'll merely see it as weakness. If you allow any to escape, they could return home and raise an army to wipe out the entire kingdom."

"I understand, Wu Hang."

"May good fortune smile upon you, Aron."

The wait for the Chenese invasion came to an end. They heard the sound of drums and trumpets blaring loudly accompanied by shouts of the army building to battle frenzy.

Aron glanced at his people. They were all experienced fighters, but none of them had fought in a battle against an army before. Aron felt rattled with the cacophony of shouts and discordant noise. He glanced back to see Wu Hang hurrying with the other Chenese converts to their assigned station.

Brock punched him in the arm suddenly.

"Buck up, brother. This is just another fight. We've had plenty of fights and this one will be no different."

Aron smiled at his brothers attempt to settle him down. He patted him on the shoulder.

His camp remained passive, there were no frightened fighters thinking better of the battle and fleeing to save themselves.

The loud noise continued unabated until suddenly they began their charge. The allies could hear their noise as they stormed through the underbrush, though they were still out of sight.

Aron looked all around to be sure he wasn't missing anything in case there was a ploy to distract them. Movement stirred behind them and then the clash of weapons. A large force of the enemy had unerringly located Wu Hang's troop and were assaulting them ferociously. Aron saw Wu Hang scything his way through the attackers, ejecting their bodies like mown grass. Aron was about to dispatch a reinforcing unit, but the main attack broke through the brush charging into the camp.

Aron signaled and the archers began their deadly barrage. Chenese soldiers dropped to the ground slain, but they ignored their losses and kept charging forward.

Aron heard sounds of fighting in other places as secret attackers came upon his reserve teams.

He stood watching the progress of the assault, unsure if he should take action.

When he started to move, Cherine grabbed him.

"Not yet, Aron..."

As difficult as it was, they continued to watch as the Chenese forces surged ahead searching for entrenched opponents to fight. They already covered much of the settlement area.

"Now, Aron," said Cherine.

Aron signaled and his teams of fighters attacked from all sides, but didn't close and grapple with the bulk of the Chenese. Executing hit and run strikes, they continuously moved not allowing the enemy to bottle them up.

Between attacks and continuous pelting from the archers, the Chenese were losing sizeable numbers of men.

Aron stood frozen in place, worried for his people as casualties mounted on his side too. He felt helpless to save them, like he was a failure, once again. His inner doubts never left him and now was a part of his fabric as a man to look at everything pessimistically. The only thing bolstering his spirits was the competence in his fighters. They matched the Chenese frenzy with spirit of their own. They weren't intimidated or cowed by their fearsome opponents. This would be a battle that could go either way.

Chapter Ten
~ The Battle of the Camp ~

Aron watched closely, gauging individual fights. His Black Fist and the masters all did well as expected, but the battle got dicey with the rest of his forces. The villagers were brave and fought smartly, protecting each other. Giving ground rather than absorb casualties, they depended on reinforcements to recoup lost ground. The convert gangs were competent fighters, but looked first to self-preservation and worried little about the flow of the battle. This also Aron expected. Jumping into and out of fights worked well to keep them around in the fight rather than fleeing at the first sign of adversity.

The sound of the peripheral battles increased. The Chenese commander didn't commit all of his troops to open battle with the predictable barrage from the archers. He'd sent significant numbers to flank Aron on both sides.

Aron had no way to know how the fights were going out of his sight and it worried him. Wu Hang's force was under severe pressure trying to hold off Chenese reinforcements. He was a focus of their wrath.

"I think we need to do something about that situation, Cherine. If they break through there, they've got a clear path to the women and children.

"One of us needs to stay here, Aron. Let me go down there."

"Cherine, I can't stand this. I've got to go down and do what I do best. I'm sorry, but I need to get into this fight. You're better at directing things up here than I am."

"Oh Aron," she replied in dismay, shaking her head.

Aron hurried down from the loft where a hand-picked force was waiting at the base of the structure.

"We're going to go break that noose squeezing on Wu Hang, men. Our families are at risk so we can't lose this fight."

They sprinted after Aron as he raced toward the desperate battle. Wu Hang towered over everyone else and numerous bodies were strewn all about. Wu Hang's force had suffered losses of Chenese men, and also some of the other troops Aron had included in that troop. Wu Hang was flanked by two of the Black Fist and two masters. What remained of his force was behind him in a defensive fight and was being hard pressed by the attackers.

Wu Hang's force was outnumbered at least two to one.

Aron silently rushed into the rear of the enemy and tore into them. As both sides tried to avert death and take down their opponents, the fight became increasingly savage. Aron fought skillfully, dwelling only on the moment to moment shifts in the battle and letting his fighting instincts take over. They fought their way through to split the opposition and open the way to Wu Hang.

"I told you we'd protect you," said Aron as he made it to Wu Hang's side. Wu Hang lunged to deflect a blow aimed at Aron's back.

"I'll protect you too," he panted.

Aron's arrival turned the fight back into a stalemate as more Chenese continued to arrive to replace the ones Aron's people were killing.

The sounds of fighting all around continued at a high level. Aron was absorbed in his own plight, so he couldn't pay attention elsewhere. The strategy of the battle was in Cherine's hands which made him very happy.

Cherine brought up more reinforcements to offset the Chenese ferocity. The Chenese surge had been stymied into a meat grinder of individual fights. Both sides were taking terrible losses, but it no longer seemed inevitable the Chenese would win this battle.

The leader of the Chenese sent a new arm of attack to bore through the congested mass of Aron's forces protecting the center of the camp - a calculated risk on his part, but with the battle hanging in the balance, he tried to tip the scales in his favor. They were his fiercest most skilled fighters and they drove back the defenders steadily.

Cherine watched the move and realized this was the key point in the battle. She left Radigan on the platform to oversee the fighting, but descended to personally lead reinforcements to stem the enemy surge with Masters surrounding her.

"Now we must prove if we're worthy to survive, my friends."

The men gave a martial shout and charged toward the critical point. The fight went on for hours as each side strove mightily to prevail. The Chenese that Cherine fought were as skillful and determined as any men she'd ever faced. She was in fear of her life often as she narrowly averted disaster. Cherine got nicked multiple times, but each of her opponents went down in the end.

The desperate Chenese strategy gradually ground to a halt and Cherine dug in with her men to throw up an impenetrable wall of swords. The fight reached a tipping point when Cherine's continuously arriving reinforcements versus the number of Chenese still standing moved in her favor and they began to drive them back. The battle became a killing field as none of the Chenese would surrender.

After fighting most of the day, the entire camp was littered with the dead and dying. Neither side could retrieve their wounded.

Aron saw the surge of his reinforcing forces attacking in response to Cherine's orders. The Chenese attacking him were beset from both sides, but wouldn't retreat. Aron battered his way forward with Wu Hang, the Black Fist and the masters. The enemy resistance stiffened trying to preserve their lives as they saw their end was at hand. Too many of them had fallen to have a hope to win and they fought to the last man before the mêlée was over. The same scenario played out everywhere else in the camp.

Aron stood with quivering muscles from the strain of the protracted lengthy fight. They all took deep breaths, thankful they'd survived the terrible battle.

Aron hurried to try to get to Cherine to ascertain the state of the conflict. The din of fighting around them was greatly reduced. Aron hurried up to the platform. Cherine was talking with Radigan and turned to look at Aron. She was bloodied and bruised.

"You look exhausted, Aron."

"I am, but so do you, Cherine. What of the battle?"

"We've basically won, but there is a great deal of mopping up to do. None of the Chenese will surrender. The Brutans found the Chenese leaders and fought a savage fight. The Chenese fought to the death with a tragic loss of life all around. We had to restrain the Brutans afterwards from dismembering the corpses for trophies."

"The Chenese were brave," said Aron. "I hope we've seen the last of them."

Brock walked up with Abdurka. Both showed injuries from the battle.

"Bad?" asked Aron.

"We lost a great many souls," Abdurka answered. "War is a tragedy. Even most of the Chenese wouldn't have chosen to die today. They had families too. I'm getting more sentimental as I age and doesn't take much to evoke strong emotional responses. Pity was a feeling foreign in my youth. Now it's an integral part of my psyche."

"We've suffered a big setback, Aron," Brock added. "The newest trainees took the greatest losses and unfortunately that included villagers. The Black Fist and the masters came through the battle with injuries, but no fatalities. Wu Hang lost a number of his people too. We'll have a big job burying this many bodies."

Aron looked troubled.

"Aron, you'll need to toughen up about our losses which were going to happen sooner or later. You can't save everybody."

"Those villagers came here for a better life. If they'd stayed back home, they'd still be alive. Now there are too many widows and children in mourning. I can't casually ignore that, Brock."

"Feel compassion, brother, but with the understanding there's no other way. There's a price to pay for our rebellion."

"Feel thankful we're still standing," Cherine added. "That was a great victory, Aron and could have easily gone the other way. We could all be face down in the dirt."

Wu Hang came up to the group and bowed to Aron. Drang-ku was right behind him with the rest of the surviving Chenese who also bowed.

"Have we proven ourselves to you?" asked Wu Hang who then looked at Brock.

"We're glad to have you with us," Brock replied. "You've proven your loyalty to my satisfaction."

"I didn't think we could prevail in this battle," said Drang-ku. "I'm amazed to still be alive. I thank you, Aron, for everything you've done for us."

Aron nodded soberly and didn't feel like celebrating, nor did anyone else.

"We need to bring the civilians back. We can't withhold the bad news about our deaths any longer from their families. I hate this job."

"Drang-ku, do you think we got them all?" asked Cherine. "Would they have sent men back to report our position?"

"It's possible they sent couriers, I don't have an answer for you."

Cherine looked at Aron. "I think we must establish a new line of defense along the western border to the outside world to watch for further of these incursions."

"I agree, Cherine. I'm afraid we may need to create fortified posts to keep a permanent watch out there."

"We'll need many more troops," said Abdurka. "We can't be weak there. The threat from the west is far greater than any threat from the prince in the east."

Aron shrugged. "We may need to create a new position, someone to be in charge in the west. It's too great an expanse for us to direct things from here in this camp. As far as more people in our army, we're growing at a steady pace. I hesitate to send out a call for more villages to resume migrating here. With the royal army aiding us, they're no longer in peril and we need for them to plant and grow new crops. We can't sustain this camp without steady supplies from them. It's not like we can grow crops here."

"Did you have someone in mind for that position, Aron?" asked Brock pointedly.

"I'm open to suggestions, brother. Trent is basically in charge of the eastern border. He's done a great job there. I need someone I can depend on in the west to get that job done too."

Brock glanced at Radigan and Aron smiled back at his brother's question. He wondered if he could solve a problem by putting distance between Radigan and Tasha, or if it would simply create a new problem.

"Who would you think would be the best choice, Cherine?"

"Brock could do it," she replied. "I have confidence in him. There are a few others too. Right now our big problem is diverting workers building our forts, and then supplying them on top of it. Our work here is going slowly enough with the dual projects of the fortress walls and Galean's strange discovery."

"Galean's excavations seem to be nearing their conclusion," Aron replied. "That will free up a large group of workers. The civilians should all be back later today, so we can speak with him about it then."

"As you wish, Aron," she replied.

They dispersed to survey the condition of the camp, tend the wounded and collect the bodies of the fallen.

Wu Hang, Drang-ku and their Chenese comrades were somber and respectful of their dead countrymen. After the bodies were collected, they performed a religious ritual to bless the departed before the internment in a mass grave.

When the civilians and families arrived a great deal of wailing and agony arose as wives found husbands gone forever from the world. The carnage was excruciating for Aron, who blamed himself for the battle and loss of men. Women of significance in his life approached him and he couldn't look in their eyes.

Tasha sympathetically put her arms around him, knowing enough to not say soothing things. She understood his grief and feelings of guilt.

Liani was close by them. Aron saw her shudder as the interrogator came near.

"I've lived through this terrible fight, maiden," he said. "It gladdens my heart to see you."

Liani's eyes were wide with concern.

"I'm glad you prevailed, master interrogator," she replied, averting her eyes.

"Would you permit me to dine with you this evening?"

She looked like she was going to choke.

"Perhaps we could all gather together to share a meal of thanksgiving for our survival," said Aron. "In the meantime we have somber tasks seeing to the dead and their grieving survivors. We live, but this is a grim day for too many of us."

Liani glanced at a smiling Wu Hang and then looked at Aron. She was flustered and whether that meant she was upset with him for his offer, he couldn't tell. It was too late to rescind the invitation.

As the camp went about the necessary final preparations for so many, the afternoon turned grim. A great number of widows were present, most who had children - a distressing development for which Aron had no answer. Women could always remarry, but here, the pool of potential husbands was dominated by former thugs. Whether any of them could change enough to be good husbands was debatable.

Aron highly doubted the more bizarre and radical of the tribes could provide any viable candidates. The Brutans and the Erati were seemingly too lost in their heinous ways to assume normal lives, especially raising another man's children. In spite of Sirina's success being married to Straga, Aron felt that was the exception rather than the rule.

The single joint service for the bereaved was difficult as the shared emotions were very powerful. Aron said a few things about the courage and the devotion to family of the fallen men, but he left the bulk of the ceremony to Galean, an excellent speaker for such occasions.

Cherine spoke briefly. Her homily was short, but inspirational and filled with hope. Aron didn't want to rush the proceedings, but was glad when they were over. Death was a part of living but a difficult part for him to cope with.

The men were buried right afterwards in hasty makeshift graves.

The evening was solemn when they tried to have Aron's 'thanksgiving' meal, but the usual issues were still there. Tasha sat with Aron. Radigan followed Tasha and sat on her other side. Liani sat on Aron's other side, but the interrogator claimed the place beside her. His attempt at civil pleasantries left her with a reduced appetite. She picked at her food and chatted with Tasha often. She wasn't rude to Wu Hang, but at the same time she wasn't solicitous. His presence was an ongoing test for Liani.

Aron noted it all: Tasha's artificially overboard manner with him, Radigan's enchanting the women with his affable personality while Tasha pretended not to notice and Liani's stilted mood responding to Wu Hang as little as possible - a surreal undercurrent for him on such a dire occasion. Though he had a vested interest in the people around him, on this night he couldn't invest his emotions there. Truly moved by the pain in the camp and the staggering losses suffered, he was tempted to stand up in the middle of the feast to creep away and avoid the inane. So many widows and children needed comfort and support at that moment and he felt guilty he was one of the fortunate to still be alive.

He looked up to see Brock studying him, like he could read his mind.

"Do you want to take a walk, brother?"

"Sure, Brock, I would."

Tasha eyed Aron questioningly as he stood up to walk away. Radigan talked to her to get her attention. Liani looked alarmed to be left alone beside Wu Hang.

"I'll be back. We just want to check on the survivors, Liani."

She looked like she would get ill on the spot and slid over to where Aron had been sitting beside Tasha. Wu Hang moved toward her slightly, but left her a little room.

Their tour ended up being not so brief. Stopping to converse with families, they got side tracked and talked a great deal to try to ease their pain. In a way, this was more healing for Aron as he witnessed the courage of the widows and the resolve to stay strong for their children.

"Thank you, my lord," said one of the younger women who had two small babies. "We knew the risk of coming here. You shouldn't feel responsible for my husband's death. It was our choice. He was proud to do his part."

Aron was moved to absolute compassion and couldn't help but hug the young woman.

"If there is anything you need, I want you to come to me personally. Will you do that?"

"My lord, you're too busy and I'm of no more importance than any other widow."

"I'm telling you, I'm going to watch over you. It isn't negotiable. What's your name?"

"My name is Jenn and my daughters are Emma and Winifred, we call her Winny."

Hugging their mother's leg, the fragile, tiny girls stared at Aron with shy wide eyes, which further melted Aron's heart.

"If you don't keep in touch with me, I'll come looking for you," Aron said with a gentle voice and a warm smile, touching her on the shoulder.

"Yes, my lord," she replied and gave him a bow. "Thank you."

"Do you have enough food?"

"I do, my lord."

"I wish you would call me Aron, I'm not a lord."

"Yes, my lord."

Brock chuckled. "Good evening, ma'am," he nodded and pulled Aron away.

"Aron, why did you take an interest in this widow out of all of them?"

"I don't know, brother. She's so young and her road ahead alone seems so daunting. Seeing her with her little daughters, how much love survived and how good they were, I know they had a wonderful father. It just struck me as particularly tragic to lose such a good man. Those little girls will never have a chance to know him. I hate war, Brock."

Brock didn't immediately reply, but thought about what Aron said and how it affected him too. He wasn't one to show his emotions, but that didn't mean he didn't have them. He shook his head after a moment to collect himself.

"We can't give our personal attention to all of them, Aron. There are too many, and the ones we didn't see might feel ignored and rejected. It would be worse for them at a time they've got their hands full with grief."

"I know, Brock, she just touched me in my heart. I couldn't ignore her."

"Well, it's done now, so we'll just have to deal with it."

"Have you thought about having children, Brock?"

"I think there's a step in between, unless I'm wrong, getting a woman to marry me. I'm not the greatest prize in the world, Aron."

Aron chuckled.

"I'm just talking about being a Dad. Have you thought about it?"

"I think every man thinks about it. With the unstable environment we have, I wouldn't want to go in that direction. I need to be mobile. Don't get me wrong, I fully intend to woo a woman at some point, but I don't know how soon that can be. If I had a wife and children and I fell in battle, you saw the result, Aron. Having a family would make me vulnerable in battle trying to be too cautious. If I thought about my wife at a time I was fighting for my life, it could tip the scales against me. I'm better to be as I am for the moment."

"Maybe I should adopt that approach. Ditching these worries I carry around, would be a good thing. I never thought about Tasha making me vulnerable, but I think because of her I took off on that day when the ice cat got me. I'll have to think about it."

"I think the same is true for women fighters, Aron. Cherine has her pick of any man she wants, but keeps her eye on the mission and ignores romantic entanglements. It's a good move on her part. I'm not telling you to abandon Tasha, but you can understand what I'm saying?"

"I do, brother, and I appreciate your trying to look out for me."

"If you've decided to start taking advice from the rest of us that would be a major step forward for you, Aron. I always feared your hard head was too thick for intelligent ideas to get through."

"Shut up, Brock," he replied, chuckling and punched Brock on the arm. "If you want to talk about thick heads, you should start with your own. By the way, you need to head over to get those cuts taken care of. You don't want infections to set in."

"If you insist, brother... What are you going to do now?"

"Visiting more widows for a bit, then I'll go see Galean. Seeing their troubles helps me forget my problems."

Aron meandered away in no particular direction. Just as he was about to join a group of people, a loud sound rang out like a bell had been struck and the deep echoes were going across the globe. Everyone looked around in alarm.

Aron hurried to find Galean, running all the way to the excavation site. Galean stood on the rim of the dig along with Abdurka, Wu Hang, Drang-ku, Belisa, Enna and Biala. Elcou and Trache were standing just behind Belisa. Others of the camps leadership raced up to join them.

"I don't know what the sound was, Aron," Galean explained as Aron stopped beside him. "We've unearthed portions of all of the remaining columns. Somehow I think they've linked together, though I have no explanation how it could happen, or what it means."

Cherine, Radigan, and Tasha hurried to Aron's side. Aron shrugged. "Don't ask, we don't know. These structures have some sort of connection. All I can think of is a tuning fork."

"That's very good, Aron," said Galean excitedly.

Liani arrived and stepped over to Galean.

"Hello, my dear," he said. "Aron has given me an idea. Can you spare some time to work with me?"

She glanced at Wu Hang. "Of course, Galean, you know I'll come whenever you need me."

The pair climbed down the ladder and walked over to the guards warding the ring of columns. Aron climbed down after them which started a stampede of the curious.

"Galean, the space between the columns is hazy," Liani noted and picked up a small rock and tossed it into the haze. A zap and a spark shot out as the rock hit the nearly invisible barrier and caused the entire series of columns to react, like they were being switched on. The few columns still partially buried hummed loudly and suddenly the remaining earth around them was blown away. When they were totally clear of dirt, the columns turned a deep red which was matched by the now visible current barrier running between them. The building flickered and turned a menacing red also. Another deep sound rang out. Being so close, the noise was deafening and everybody scrambled out of the crater. When the last was away from the barrier, the red hue faded to a softer light with only a slight hint of red.

Stupefied, gaping at the wonder, no one moved for a long time. Finally Galean turned to Aron.

"I need to borrow Liani, and I need all of my staff. I think we need answers quickly. Something significant is happening, but I have no advice about what we should do."

"Certainly, Galean, take anybody else you want too. I think Abdurka, and maybe Drang-ku might have some thoughts that could be helpful."

"Come, my friends," said Galean. "We have urgent work to do."

Liani glanced piercingly at Aron before she followed Galean away. Aron felt a little emotional tingle and sighed quietly, watching her petite form and dainty gait. Liani was another incredible woman in his circle of acquaintances - a true treasure.

In contrast, Aron glanced to see Tasha talking intently with Radigan. She was supposedly Aron's betrothed? In spite of what she said, Aron always had that question when he saw them together. Though whatever they were saying could have been totally innocent, just like the alien building, Aron got a bad feeling watching them.

Aron turned to Cherine.

"I think we better keep the guards up here from now on. I feel that thing can harm anybody who gets close to it."

She nodded.

Wu Hang stood staring at the structure and showed no signs he was going to leave any time soon.

Aron walked over to him. "What is it?"

"A story in Chenese history goes all the way back to the beginning of time about the creation of the nations of the world. A great power wielded then which caused the world to change. We know nothing of what was before, but a dire event ended that world and brought about ours. This is like nothing I've ever seen or heard of. There's a bad feel to it. I think perhaps it would have been better left buried under the ground."

"I feel it too, Wu Hang, but it's too late now. Even if we decided to cover it back up, I don't think it would allow us. Suddenly a frightening entity has come to life."

"This is troublesome, Aron. I'm moved to flee away and have no sense of anything good coming from it."

Aron stared at the menacing phenomenon. The most terrifying man in the world, the interrogator, was frightened - a sobering matter indeed.

Aron could see the haze of the aura extended to completely overlay the building. The barrier protected all approaches, both from the side and top.

* * * *

The prince was pleased his audience with his father had gone well, much better than he anticipated. He accomplished all of his goals: he'd avoided Granor's snare, improved his standing with his father and decreased Granor's standing in the process, and he'd been given support to proceed as he saw fit.

He returned to the suite and smiled at Coraline.

"I take it everything went well with his majesty?"

"I told you I would handle everything, my dearest. I feel festive. Let's have a feast tonight, perhaps invite guests, Coraline."

"As you wish, husband... I'll see to the arrangements right away."

"Make the arrangements promptly, my darling. I want to spend time with my wife. I've sorely missed you during my long absence. I won't be gone that long ever again. Although there had to be an answer to Aron's treachery, I could've handled it more wisely. His majesty had valid concerns for the kingdom we shall inherit. I must train myself to think in bigger terms from now on. I'm sorry, Coraline. I know I haven't been the best husband, but I desire to change. I've made serious mistakes in the past, I finally see that. My father overcame his failings and became a better man. I intend to do the same thing. Do you see? I do love you."

Coraline had a look on her face Agar couldn't fully translate. He wasn't sure whether to feel reassured or concerned. After a moment she smiled at him.

"This is welcome news, Agar." Her tone was serious with none of the deference she normally portrayed. He got a glimpse of the real woman he was married to. "I'll see to the arrangements and I'll be back shortly."

She walked away and left the suite. Agar sat down to ponder his situation. His marriage was suddenly a new area requiring scrutiny. With his proclivities and paranoia, it was easy for him to imagine activities he would not have been happy about by his lonely wife. His nature was to blame her, but for some reason, he was cogent at that moment and grasped a major hand in his own travails - an unsettling development.

"*I must deal with this smartly. Coraline is too important a piece in this play to ignore any longer. I need her.*" His ruminations continued until she returned.

"I think you'll be very happy tonight, husband. I've included your parents in the invitation. I thought it wise too to send an invitation to Granor. I think it best since he's been humbled and he's your father's main counselor, if we win him to our side. If we treat him well it can't hurt, right?"

"He's not a man I would seek as a friend, but I like your ideas. As you said, we need to protect our position and our standing. I think I made a breakthrough with my father, perhaps I can also reassure my mother that I do have potential for the future."

"We have the afternoon for whatever plans you have, Agar."

He smiled and pulled her into his embrace.

* * * *

Meanwhile, Granor received Coraline's invitation with mixed feelings.

"What are you up to, Agar," he muttered. "Is there some hidden meaning here, a danger I haven't grasped? I'm no fool. You think you've won, but I say this matter has just begun. I have surprises of my own. We'll see who's still standing in the end."

"What reply do you have, my lord?" asked the messenger.

"Give them my thanks. I would love to attend their little gathering."

"As you command," said the messenger with a bow.

He hurried away leaving Granor sitting with his close circle.

"Nothing is changed." Granor explained. "If we've suffered a setback, it's only a temporary thing which we'll overcome. Maintain our usual façade. I'll go to this soiree and prosper. I've been doing this royal dance all of my life. I know how to survive and to persevere. They're not smarter than us. They're fools who just happen to have power."

His people chuckled.

"If Aron can accomplish what he has, you know we can do better. He was just a farm boy, yet he's managed to thumb his nose at the might of the kingdom with impunity. We'll show them all. Trust me."

His people gave a shout and Granor smiled.

He gazed at the prettiest of his female associates.

"Put on your best dress and accompany me tonight as my companion, Lilith. We won't let these royals show us up. We can be as ostentatious as any of them."

"As you wish, my lord," she replied, eyeing him provocatively.

"Yes, Lilith, that's exactly what I want from you tonight, to be the most alluring woman in the room. You've never failed me in the past and I expect your best efforts tonight."

"As you command, my lord..."

Chapter Eleven
~ Ominous Changes ~

The sound emitted from the revitalized barrier permeated the camp and the surrounding area like a threat of death. Animals in camp pens bellowed and shied away from the sound, testing the fences holding them in. Wild animals could be seen hurrying away from the sound and leaving the immediate area. The color of the barrier began to change, gradually shifting throughout the colors of the rainbow. The sound was a steady deep note and the populace had trouble blotting out the noise no matter how they tried, even blocking their ears didn't help.

"Aron, we need to reduce the length of the guard shifts at the site," Cherine advised. "It's too terrifying to stay there for long spans. The guards are very disturbed when they come off duty."

"Of course, Cherine, do whatever you need to."

Abdurka came walking over along with Galean and Liani.

"That barrier could keep anybody from getting into that building," Aron commented.

"I'm not sure about that," Abdurka replied. "Are you sure it wasn't meant to keep something inside from getting out?"

"That's a very scary thought," Aron answered. "I hope you're wrong because if it got out, I wonder if there are any alive today who can stop it."

Liani looked ill and gazed at Aron.

"I'm sorry if I seem weak," she said. "I'll admit I'm not the strongest woman in the world."

"We're all worried, Liani," Aron said. "If you're not afraid of this, you're a fool."

"Galean has discovered something of our situation that may be enlightening, Aron," Liani explained. "Talking with Abdurka and the Chenese, there seems to be a similar thread in their archival histories. They see our world being formed out of chaos and ruin. We're survivor descendents of ancient peoples. The records of those people are lost through the eons, or destroyed, so we can only speculate. What we've uncovered in artifacts and this intact structure, lends credibility to that theory. Galean discounted some things he read in our histories, but in light of what we've discovered, he agrees with that assessment of history."

"I'm not surprised," Aron replied. "It is the nature of people to war. The strong always look to subjugate the weak. I guess it doesn't matter who won or lost with a war. The result would be the same, the victors trample the losers. Both of them probably were ruthless. It's discouraging to imagine. Do we have it in us to be better? Am I asking something of these people we convert that's beyond them? Is living in goodness just an impossible dream of mine?"

"I hope not, Aron. You inspire us to try. That's got to count for something."

Aron shrugged. "I think you picked too faulty a person to place your hopes in, Liani."

"No, Aron, I didn't." She looked at him very intently. Again he felt a tingle. He smiled at her and she smiled back. It wasn't hard to have feelings for her. How she felt was very clear to him, and she showed no inclination to back away from her feelings, in spite of Tasha.

Liani glanced to the side; Aron turned to see the interrogator coming toward them.

"Relax, Liani," Aron whispered. "He's really is trying to turn over a new leaf."

She still watched him with concern.

Wu Hang nodded. "Greetings, Liani. It's nice to see you today."

"Thank you, master interrogator," she replied stiffly.

"That was another life. Do you not think it would help us to get past that if you start calling me by my name?"

"As you wish," she answered meekly.

"I know it was a terrible fright for you then, Liani. I can continue to apologize for the rest of my life, but intimidation was my role in the army. I had no choice. I had to make you answer the commander, but I never wanted to hurt you. I thought my solution was very ingenious. Do you agree?"

He smiled warmly. She looked at him and returned a small smile.

"I'm afraid I require more time than the average woman to recover my wits. I apologize, Wu Hang, and I do acknowledge what you did was a merciful act. I think if you had actually hurt me, I would have died on the spot from terror. I don't handle pain very well."

"I can't imagine any person wanting to hurt you, Liani. You are a rare treasure."

Liani glanced at Aron who smiled. "You *are* a rare treasure, Liani," he added. This was a comment that could be construed a number of ways. For Aron, it was like drawing close to a flame and running the risk of a serious burn. With his professed love for Tasha, and their supposed betrothal, Liani continued to grow in his esteem and affection. Tasha never felt like a sure thing to him, regardless of what she said. That had nothing to do with his love for her, which was as strong as ever. The ever present threat of Radigan was the unsolvable issue for him. Tasha could smile at Aron, but her feelings for Radigan were something she couldn't gloss over. He still mattered to her, and therefore it mattered to Aron.

He tried to shake himself out of his stupor. Liani had a sly smile, like she could read his thoughts. Wu Hang studied both of them closely.

"I guess I should talk to Galean," said Aron. "Did you want to join me, Liani?"

"Of course," she replied with a pleased smile.

"You're welcome to come, Wu Hang," Aron offered.

"I have other duties, but thank you." He bowed his head and walked away.

"See, that wasn't so bad, Liani. Give things a chance and you can get to a good relationship."

"He wishes to be more than a friend," she replied looking into Aron's eyes.

"I know, but Liani, you're really beautiful. Of course you're going to draw male attention."

"His is not the male attention I wish to draw," she answered, bringing the issue into the light.

Aron was at a crossroads - not an easy choice.

"Are you going to make me say it, Aron?"

He never had to answer the question as they arrived at Galean's side. Liani leaned over to him.

"This isn't over."

With the feelings she was able to stir in him, he agreed.

The ominous escalations in the strange alien structure did not end, but instead increased. The next development startling and frightening the camp was a sudden deep blast of a warning tone followed by the lights intensifying until they were too bright to look at. A huge beam of light shot up into the air and began to search across the heavens until it stopped, like it had located something in the sky. Another loud tone higher than the first blasted out followed by a sequence of various tones before a sudden flash of light shot into the sky. The beam shut off and the alien complex returned to the previous state with alternating colors of lights in the protective barrier, but the building started to shimmer.

Suddenly a different bright beam of light scanned across the frightened crowd setting off cries and shouts of fear. The beam didn't harm anybody, and took a moment to realize Liani was missing - disappeared.

"Liani…!" Aron shouted in alarm. "Galean, what happened to her?"

"I don't know, Aron," he replied in confusion.

"Was it that light? Could it make her disappear? Was she slain?" he asked frantically.

"I'm sorry, Aron, I have no answers for you."

"What can I do?" he asked in frustration and helplessness. "We've got to find her."

Wu Hang, distressed and angered, appeared at Aron's side.

Again a sound arose from the complex. The underlying hum from the barrier grew sharp and suddenly stopped. The vast concave metal of the building began to move like an iris. The entire covering rotated and retracted rolling into itself and exposing the interior. The barrier receded completely in only a few minutes. Inside sat a building of metal and thick glass. A large doorway slid open and Liani walked out. They were so awed it took a moment before anybody reacted. Aron and Wu Hang hurried down the ladder and rushed up to Liani. She was standing, but appeared to be in a trance.

"Liani?" asked Aron.

She turned and walked back into the building. Aron and Wu Hang followed her. She led them through the building to a room where a machine with blinking lights was positioned. A clear covering was draped over a man was lying asleep on a table surrounded by a foggy cloud.

Liani walked to a console and began to touch various buttons and panels. The machine responded with different tones and flashes of light. The gas cloud quickly drained away and the cover over the man receded just like the cover over the main building. Liani walked over to the table and began disconnecting wires attached to the man. When the last connection was removed, the man's eyes blinked and opened. He looked at their faces blinking to clear away the cobwebs. His eyes sharpened like his faculties had returned and sat up.

The man spoke in a deep resonant voice, but in a language not understood. Liani replied in the same tongue. The man smiled at her and then looked at Aron and Wu Hang. He put a device over Liani's head. She stood a moment while her brain was scanned before the man took it off.

"Who are you?" asked the man.

"I'm Aron, this is Liani and Wu Hang."

"My name is Damien. What of the war?"

"I'm not sure what war you're talking about," Aron answered, glancing at Liani. She still looked to be glassy eyed. "What's wrong with Liani?"

"I'm sorry, the device that safe guarded me touched her to fulfill some required actions which had to be done on my behalf," Damien replied with a magnanimous smile.

Aron got a feeling of worry. This man was like Radigan on steroids.

"What does that mean? Why is she not herself?"

"This is a temporary condition and will pass. Her mind had to be acclimated to the technology in order to perform her tasks. Don't concern yourself."

"I'm sorry, Damien, but I am concerned. Liani is a person dear to us."

Damien looked at Wu Hang who looked on the verge of tearing the Damien apart.

"You're a fierce man, I know your people." Damien said amicably. "Good for you. I gather considerable time has passed since I was cryo-preserved."

"I don't know what you're talking about. Our only concern is having Liani freed of this malady and returned to us unharmed."

"Malady?" asked Damien chuckling. "This isn't a malady. She's unharmed. She'll be back as you know her soon enough. Now will you tell me about your world?"

"I think there are others of us better suited to speak with you," Aron replied evenly.

"You're the leader here," it was not a question.

"How do you know that Damien…?"

"I can tell from your demeanor, your command presence, and the deference I sense in this other one."

Aron took Liani by the hand. "Liani, can you hear me?"

Damien laughed. "Of course she can hear you. Come Liani."

Liani faced Damien and nodded. She took her hand out of Aron's and walked beside Damien which bothered Aron a great deal, but bothered Wu Hang even more who then boldly stepped in front of Damien.

"You should tread very carefully, stranger. If you continue to hold Liani in your sway, I will not accept it, and I will take action to free her."

Aron worried the two men would fight. A frightening look of insane rage crossed Damien's face for a moment before he once again got a placid look.

"An admirable trait, my large friend, I can appreciate your protective instincts for this lovely little female, but I'll give you this warning one time. I'm not a person to trifle with. I give you leeway because none of you know me. I will change that soon enough. Liani is safer with me than she has been in her life. You're a frightening man who has his uses. Against me, you're not dealing with these primitive people you intimidate. I'm well able to defend myself and those close to me. Now step aside. It's time that I see the world I've awakened into."

Wu Hang stood for a moment before he moved.

"A wise choice," said Damien.

Aron quickly walked over and put a hand on Wu Hang's shoulder.

"We need to learn about this man," he whispered. "Until we know his risk, we can't make proper safeguards."

Wu Hang nodded stiffly, still enraged.

Damien was already walking out of the building and looked up at the sea of faces staring down at him from the rim of the hole. He smiled.

Damien had returned to the world. No one grasped the gravity of the event at that time.

Liani remained at his side, still seemingly oblivious to anyone but Damien.

They all climbed up the ladder. Damien smiled magnanimously and nodded all about.

"Greetings, my friends, it's good to be here amongst you."

"My name is Galean, sir. Can we offer you food and drink? Perhaps we could have a talk to answer some questions."

"Of course, I thank you for your hospitality. My name is Damien."

Galean looked at Liani.

"Liani, are you unwell, dear?"

"She's experiencing a temporary disconnect," Damien explained. "It will resolve shortly. Our Liani will soon be herself again. She's in no discomfort or peril. Please lead me, Galean. We both have many questions."

Galean looked at Aron who'd just walked up to his side.

"Lead away, Galean," said Aron. Wu Hang walked at his side, his eyes constantly on the unresponsive Liani.

Aron was so intent on their worries about her, he walked right past Tasha and Radigan without noticing them. Tasha noticed though and scowled at the perceived snub.

Radigan put a hand to Tasha's back guiding her forward and she didn't resist. They joined in the procession following the stranger.

Everybody came to the food tent in curiosity. Belisa came forward with Enna and Biala to Aron's side. Damien had sat down with Liani and attacked the food on the table ravenously.

"I'm afraid it's been a long time between meals for me. This food tastes very good. Thank you again, my friends."

Liani took small portions of food and drink and ate daintily. It evoked Aron and a great number of other people. Aron felt like she'd been stolen, just like by the Chenese, but this time he was far more worried.

Meanwhile Damien chatted expansively. A man with charisma, Damien had the same attributes Aron hated in Radigan, but so much more of the new stranger gave Aron cold chills of concern.

Galean sat down on the other side of Damien. He sipped on a beverage and studied the stranger.

“Thank you for the meal, Galean. Now let’s have our talk.”

“Obviously, Damien, we’re curious about you,” Galean began. “All of this, what was your word, technology, it’s beyond us. We’re a simple society. Perhaps we appear simplistic to you.”

“You shouldn’t feel the lesser, Galean. You live in your own time and your level of development is not what was mine. I’m here as your friend, and I hope to be your mentor. We have before us the possibilities of a new golden age. The wonders of my society were dazzling. We can exceed those heights and achieve a state of bliss beyond your wildest dreams.”

“That’s a very intriguing notion, Damien. We are beset with more than our share of challenges.”

“I’ll look to see about that, Galean, but I can offer more than just triumph over your enemies and mastery of your realm, I can offer you enlightenment, a view into the higher planes of existence, into the destiny and the purpose we’re here. I’m uniquely able to shoulder that heavy mantle of leadership and direction for the world.”

“I see,” Galean replied evenly. “Are you of a mind to tell us about your world? I gather you came from our past. Our records probably post date your time, so we have no knowledge of you or your civilization.”

“You’re very astute, Galean. I like that. I think as we progress, I can see a position for you in my council of advisors. Though many of the issues I’ll be dealing with surpass your knowledge and experience, your shrewd and discerning mind can be a valuable asset for me.”

“Thank you,” Galean answered. He glanced over at Aron, with a skeptical look barely concealed.

“Tell me of your world, Galean.” Aron noted he never answered Galean’s questions about the past.

Galean paused a moment before answering.

“We live within a kingdom which is flanked by mountains on three sides and the wilds on the fourth side. Unfortunately the king and the noble class are not particularly mindful of their subjects, seeing them more as objects to fleece, use and discard rather than as partners to help the realm flourish. Their power resides in the royal host enforcing decrees and demands, and odious taxes. Since none have the power to conquer such a mighty force, we’re left with the scraps off the royal table and demeaning lives of subservience and abuse. It’s a life without hope for our children and futures and that’s the most damning aspect of all. As individuals, we cope with our fates as best we can, but no parent wants their children to have lives worse than the parents. It's brought us to this situation."

"What situation are you speaking of, Galean?"

"Resistance against the crown, Damien, Aron is the leader of the rebellion."

"Is he now," Damien replied, eyeing Aron thoughtfully.

Aron felt mildly disturbed by the perusal, like Damien saw him with contempt and dismissal and with Aron's usual self doubts it was an uncomfortable moment. He glanced at Liani who stared straight, still impervious to any but Damien. Then he glanced over at Tasha and Radigan who'd chosen to stand apart. Tasha was eyeing him darkly. Radigan looked to be very intrigued by Damien.

"What resides beyond the mountains, Galean?"

Galean looked over at Abdurka. "Would you like to explain, my friend. It's your world he's asking about."

"You come from outside?" asked Damien avidly. "Are conditions there the same as I see here? Is there any residual from my world?"

"I've not traveled the entire globe," Abdurka replied. "From what I have seen, conditions are all about the same. Whatever was your world, is gone now."

"Interesting to hear this, my friends, I think that's a very good thing for us all."

"Are you speaking of your enemies?" asked Galean innocently.

Damien chuckled. "You are a smart man, Galean. I think we all have enemies. If mine have perished for all time, the world is the better for it. They were ruthless and heartless brutes having dull brains and no redeeming values. Their fate was set by their own failings and shortcomings. They had no capacity to see the bigger picture being driven by their own small cravings, greed, and ignorance. I tried to open the pathway to enlightenment, but they rejected logic and good sense in favor of barbaric ways and petty intrigues. They were useless then and deserve none of our time now."

Galean's expression was neutral, but Aron knew him well enough to recognize when he was disturbed. What Damien was saying wasn't putting Galean's mind at ease.

"You said you know of Wu Hang, and the Chenese?"

"Chenese?" asked Damien. "Time does cause change, some things subtle and others not so subtle. That's an interesting decay in the name."

"What do you mean, Damien?"

"It's not important. You call them Chenese now. That's good enough for me. Chenese they are."

Wu Hang walked over to Liani.

"Would you like more food or drink, Liani?"

She sat for a moment, blinked and looked around for the first time.

"No, thank you, I've had enough." The spell seemed to have been broken. She looked around like she was confused.

"You've had a bad time," Wu Hang said to her. "Are you feeling better?"

"I feel well." She looked at Damien who smiled pleasantly.

"Hello, Liani," he said.

"Hello."

"You've been invaluable helping me to return from my slumbers. I want to thank you for that. If you're agreeable, I'd like you to assist me further during my transition into this world. Will you do that, Liani?"

A glazed look came over Liani.

"I, eh…"

"Thank you, my dear. I assure you, we'll have you back with your friends at the earliest possible moment. My requirements are simple enough. You're the only one at this point who's been prepped by the system."

"What does that mean?" asked Galean.

"It's technology. I couldn't really explain it to you without considerable time and a great deal of teaching. She'll be back at your side before you know it. Don't worry about her."

Aron walked over to Damien.

"Just before the covering over your building opened, a great light shot up in the air followed by a sharp flash of light. What was that?"

Damien smiled and sat up.

"This is more good news. Perhaps something of my world yet remains. I need to return to the complex to check this. I'm sorry I must cut this visit short, but if it's true, it could greatly speed up our efforts at progress."

Damien suddenly got up. Liani followed and they both went back to his building. Wu Hang followed Liani.

Damien glanced at Wu Hang with annoyance, but didn't stop him from going into the building. Aron decided to follow them too. As he stepped forward, Tasha stepped out.

"It's admirable, the loyalty and the feelings you have for Liani, Aron."

A hard glint set in her eyes.

"Thank you, Tasha, she seems like she's under a spell. I don't think she can protect herself. That's why Wu Hang, I and the others are trying to intercede."

"Of course, Aron, I understand." The challenge in her eyes said she didn't believe his explanation, or motives. "I won't hold you any longer from your task," she said tersely.

Tasha turned abruptly and walked away. Radigan smiled, nodded to Aron and followed her. Aron's stomach roiled again and he pondered whether he should go after Tasha, but ultimately chose to go to Liani where he felt the danger and the need for intervention.

"Aron, I'll join you," said Galean. Abdurka came along as well as Belisa, Enna and Biala.

They all went to a different room than the one where Damien was discovered. Damien was sitting at a large console with many buttons staring at a flat screen. As he punched various keys, the screen responded. A sound emitted outside the building and the screen responded with a view of a planet from space.

"Excellent," said Damien. "This is much more than I could have hoped for."

"What's that we see?" asked Galean.

"A view of this planet from space... As you can see, the world is round like a ball."

"Astounding," said Galean in awe. "I've thought this, but was never in a position to explore the possibility. If the royals didn't like your theories, they were very peevish and wasn't unusual for them to apply painful measures to silence a person."

"They're meaningless fools. Think no more about them. A new day has dawned for the world."

Damien's eyes gleamed with ambition.

"This is frightening to behold, Damien, these powers you wield."

"I'm the perfect man for this time and this place. Don't fear our technology. I have complete control."

“Who controls you?” Brock whispered to Aron. He’d arrived just in time to see the screen and hear Damien’s pronouncements.

“Good point, brother,” Aron replied.

“Why is Liani with him?”

“He said she was touched by his technology and is recovering.”

“I think we might need to touch this Damien fellow with our technology, Aron.”

Brock brandished his fist. Aron chuckled.

“You are such a bone head, Brock.”

“I don’t like him. He reminds me of someone else.”

“Don’t rub it in, Brock. I got the comparison all on my own. He’s a worse version of Radigan.”

“Speaking of Radigan, I just saw him going…”

“I know, Brock. Tasha got mad at me and left with him.”

“Okay Aron, it’s your choice about what you do, but he keeps flaunting…”

“Brock, I can’t think about that now. We’ve got more urgent trouble right here.”

Brock shrugged. “Maybe I should apply our technology to you, Aron.”

Aron laughed softly.

“It probably can’t hurt with the way things are going.”

Damien shifted the view from space and then sent a tracer and discovered a few more satellites remained in orbit and functional. He pulled up views from them too. None of the others had any inkling of what this meant for them. It was a dazzling and concerning display.

“Do you see, my dear Liani, we have resources beyond our wildest hopes. There can yet be a good outcome from that terrible war of old.”

Liani stared at the screen, but said nothing. Wu Hang stood at her side glowering at Damien.

“I wouldn’t want Wu Hang as my enemy,” said Brock. “This Damien thinks a great deal of himself. That arrogance can be a valuable tool for us, if we need it.”

Belisa came over to Aron.

“I know you realize there is peril here. This strange person requires close scrutiny and constant monitoring. Arreck histories coincide with the others, but we have similar prophesies as Galean found in the royal archives. I think this person is a sign of the terrible end times. I fear this will be a test of ultimate survival for all who live on this planet."

"Belisa I agree, but there is so much we don't know. I think we need to learn what we can from him as fast as we can. With what you're seeing here, how could anyone fight him?"

"I was just saying, the Arreck will have eyes on him constantly."

"Good, Belisa. I don't trust him either."

Damien continued punching the keys and shifting the views from space. Studying the shots of the ground, he tried to ascertain what remained from his world, if there were still cities and the like. Only a few remnants of that world remained. Most of the structure of his past was wiped away as if it had never existed.

Aron and the others were shocked to discover their planet had vast oceans. No one said anything; they just gaped at the marvels - an unexpected revelation.

Damien turned to look at the onlookers. "There is a great deal you don't know about our world. I will be the one to provide you that which you lack."

"At what price…?" Belisa asked quietly.

"I wonder that also," Aron added.

Damien looked slowly across the entire crowd. He stopped when Liani was in his sight.

"This is the beginning of great things, my dear Liani. You have the chance to stand with me leading the people to glory."

She turned her head to Damien with a strange expression. Aron was confused and concerned.

"I'm going to go and slug that guy," Brock muttered.

"I think she's not fully free from her spell," Aron said.

"I'll try to talk to her and perhaps take her away," Belisa replied. "Getting her parted from Damien may help her to recover."

Wu Hang put his hand firmly on Liani's shoulder which caused her eyes to blink. She looked up at him, seemingly back to normal. Wu Hang stared at Damien grimly, daring him to intercede.

Again, Aron noticed a quick flash of rage before he calmed and returned to a placid smile.

Belisa took that moment to walk over to them.

"Liani, you've experienced difficult times. I think soaking in a bath tub, and some sleep is what you need. I'm sure you understand, Damien. We'll bid you farewell for the moment."

Liani stood up and allowed Belisa to lead her away from Damien.

Damien turned back to the machine. The spectators started to drift away. Aron walked over to Wu Hang.

"Come, my friend. We have work to do."

Damien ignored them.

Staring at Damien Wu Hang paused, considering whether he wanted to take action. Aron realized this and tugged at Wu Hang, avoiding a confrontation.

"Have a pleasant day, gentlemen," said Damien distractedly, like they were inconsequential.

Aron pushed Wu Hang into motion and led him out of the building.

Chapter Twelve
~ Troubling Choices ~

Aron went to check on Liani. He'd paused only momentarily thinking which woman he should seek out first. He remembered Tasha's ire about his concerns for Liani.

Liani was with Belisa, Enna, and Biala. She acted totally normal as if nothing had happened to her, talking pleasantly and smiling warmly when she saw Aron.

"Are you feeling yourself again, Liani?"

"I'm well, Aron, thank you. I believe my distress has passed. I appreciate your concern."

"I don't mean to intrude here, but we're all worried. We know nothing of Damien's ways and feared he'd harmed you."

"I feel fine. If there's some residual consequence of what happened to me, I don't feel it."

Aron glanced at the other women who were staring at him intently. He felt suddenly uncomfortable. Liani had a satisfied smile, again like she'd scored a victory.

"Was there something you wanted to discuss, Aron?" she had a mischievous look.

"I, eh…" he stammered. "I'm going to let you have your time with your friends. I've got some other things to do. I'm glad you're better."

"Remember what I said, Aron," she whispered before he left.

As Aron left to find Tasha, he saw Wu Hang approach Liani. Liani was slightly less uncomfortable, but she wasn't at ease around him.

Aron went to Tasha's parent's place where she was sitting talking with her mother. Radigan was seated beside her and her father was working gathering firewood.

"Hello, Aron," she said as he walked up. "Have you seen to Liani?"

"Thankfully, she seems to be doing better. Getting her apart from Damien helped. She's with Belisa and the other women."

"What did you need from me, Aron?" she asked curtly.

"I need nothing. I was just coming to spend time with you, unless I'm interrupting your plans."

A hostile look came over her. "What plans would that be?"

"Tasha, stop it," said her mother. "I'm sorry, Aron. She's in a sour mood."

"Am I, mother?" she huffed. "If I'm in a mood, is it possible I might have a good reason? In case you hadn't noticed, I'm not a little girl any longer."

"There's no reason not to be civil, Tasha. We don't need to burden others with our problems."

Tasha eyed Aron grimly. He had no trouble comprehending who she was angry with.

Radigan had an amused and smug smile on his face. Aron looked back at Tasha who'd noted his glance which further angered her at the implication.

"Well, perhaps it's best if I stretch my legs," she said frostily. "I'll be back later."

She got up and walked away. Radigan quickly joined her. Aron stared at the ground and when he looked up, both her parents were looking at him like he'd failed them again.

"I guess I'll be going," he said.

Tasha's father looked like he would slug Aron.

When Aron left them, he heard a whooshing sound and looked to see another vast beam of light go up from Damien's equipment into the sky generating another flash of light. This time an echo of sound boomed out from whatever was up there. It rolled across the heavens like a clap of thunder. A second multicolored burst of light occurred quickly causing an even louder burst of sound.

The rumble echoed across the countryside rattling windows.

Aron was curious, but not enough to walk back to the site. He was still embroiled with feelings about the failed visit to Tasha and his unending stress about their rocky relationship. He knew Galean would be there watching Damien and he was imminently more qualified than Aron to deal with the new threat.

Agar stared at Granor across the table at the banquet because he was making no attempt to hide his perusal of Princess Coraline. Coraline didn't pay attention, acknowledge, or even seem to notice Granor's unseemly look. Agar considered if this was a ploy, or if Granor was bold enough to imply a threat toward Coraline. Agar would be leaving again at some point in time which would leave his wife unprotected. This was a new contingency Agar hadn't encountered before. Just like the threat of Aron's spreading rebellion, hazards were popping up that hadn't existed before for the class of royals.

After his failure to reclaim and recapture Tasha, Agar wasn't in the mood for new problems. Tasha still evoked him, but the idea of further lengthy fruitless chases struck him as too costly and pointless. Belisa, was written off in his mind some time ago.

Coraline was chatting pleasantly with the queen, oblivious to the currents swirling all around her. Granor's attractive female companion for the evening was eyeing Coraline darkly. She whispered with Granor frequently, like they were assessing enemies for their threat level.

Agar glanced at his father who sat on his throne confident in his rule, and secure in his marriage to the queen. When the time came to replace his father, Agar too wanted this security.

In the banquet hall, the walls were lined with royal soldiers silent and unmoving in their dress uniforms. As Agar pondered Granor, he wondered what plots and schemes he'd devised and if any were in play at that moment. What did Granor say in the dark and in secret? Were those guards threatening to him? Could they be trusted in their loyalty to the crown?

These troubling problems weighed heavily on Agar's thoughts.

The doors opened and a troupe of musicians and dancers entered the room. The scantily clad shapely young women would normally have been the prime focus for Agar and probably would have evoked a detour on his way back to his suite, but tonight he ignored them. Instead, he took Coraline's hand. She turned her head in surprise and smiled. A public display of affection wasn't what she expected.

"Agar?" she asked softly.

He smiled warmly.

The gesture nearly floored her, was unanticipated, out of character and put a question in her mind. She glanced around at the other attendees. Granor's companion was staring at her like a predator. Coraline nodded her head pleasantly. The expression of the woman softened and she nodded back. She whispered to Granor who then nodded also.

"Is there something I should know about, husband?" Coraline whispered.

"I have everything under control, my dear. Return to your conversation with my mother."

She took one more look at Granor and his companion before turning back to the queen who also was looking at Granor.

Granor stood up. "I'd like to propose a toast to our crown prince, safely returned from the front. It's good to have him back home."

"Here, here!" the crowd replied.

Agar smiled ruefully, lifted his glass and nodded to Granor.

"Thank you, Granor," said the king. "You're an attentive associate and invaluable to my personal agenda. With you at my side, I have no worries about problems getting the best of me. I've never been as organized as I am now. Thank you."

"Here, here!" said the crowd.

Musicians began to play and the diners drifted away from the banquet table and many started to dance. Granor made a beeline to Agar and Coraline.

"My prince, may I request the honor of a dance with your wife?" Granor's companion edged close to Agar.

"Would it be presumptuous of me to hope you'd dance with me, my Prince?"

Agar was no fool. This was a beautiful woman displaying herself openly. They were trying to take advantage of his well known proclivities of "bedding the wench." She was clearly meant to be tempting bait.

Agar nodded graciously, but to her surprise, he kept proper decorum and didn't embrace her salaciously. He acted a perfect gentleman and kept his distance as they danced. He chatted amicably, but kept an eye on Granor who was talking intently and continuously to Coraline. Coraline was saying very little to him in response. Agar was consumed with curiosity and with concern, but this was a time he had to have faith in his wife.

When the dance ended, Granor continued talking. Coraline looked and listened to him before she broke off and returned to her husband.

"May I have this dance, princess?" asked Agar.

"Of course, husband."

The music began again.

He left it to her to explain her encounter with Granor.

"I know you wish to hear what he said. I'll tell you later in private, husband."

"Should I be concerned Coraline…?"

"I'll let you decide after we've talked. It's a complicated matter, not one to air here for curious ears."

"We'll make it a short evening, my dear. I've been to enough banquets in my day."

"As you wish, husband..."

Coraline next danced with the king while Agar danced with his mother.

"What was that about, son?"

"I don't know. Coraline said she would tell me later in private. I wonder that Granor could feel emboldened enough to challenge me outright. It's a big risk on his part and he has a lot to lose, in spite of having my father's ear."

"Intrigues are an unavoidable part of our lives, son. There will never be an end to the legions of those who envy our positions, wealth and power. I can't imagine he'd do something flagrant. He's not immune from consequences for his actions."

"That's my thought. Is there something about Coraline I should know, mother?"

She paused a moment before her answer.

"Let me say this, Agar. I couldn't have picked a better wife for you. No person is perfect, but she's the best wife any man could hope for. I hope you'll keep your wits with whatever she chooses to share with you. Without her, Agar, who could you find to replace her? There is none of her caliber. I'm not perfect either. We women have difficult lives and cope as best we can in our situations in the kingdom. That doesn't mean every choice we make is a good one. Can you apply the same critical standard to your own behaviors that you'd hold against your wife?"

"I think you can see I'm a changed person, also not perfect, but I assure you a much more reasonable one then I was not so long ago. Being humbled has a sobering effect on a person's viewpoint, mother. I see things much more realistically now."

"I cherish Coraline above any of my own daughters, Agar. That should tell you how I feel. If she's made mistakes…well, so have I."

"I'll take it into consideration, mother. This matter is going in a different direction than I anticipated."

"I always had hopes for you, son. I hated your lifestyle, but down deep I felt the seed of a better person. What I'm seeing and hearing from you is very encouraging."

"I'll admit I have much to learn, but I think at last I have my focus on higher goals."

"Cherish your wife, Agar. She is truly a gift."

"Thank you, mother, I do cherish her."

Agar took his wife away from the party soon after the dance and returned to his royal suite.

Coraline took her time in their dwelling. She changed clothes puttered around at a few tasks before she finally sat down with Agar. He waited patiently, not a trait he'd been noted for.

"Coraline, don't feel threatened by me. I want you to know you can be totally honest. We need to work together and trust each other. I'll say, if you're worried about telling me private things, you know about my legion of mistakes, so I'm not here to be judgmental."

"Truly, Agar…? A woman in the kingdom lives her life in fear most of the time. We see pettiness, vengefulness, arbitrary decisions, and a host of other troubles. We're vulnerable every minute and men are often the danger. Do you hear what I'm saying? You're my husband and I've tried to do my best in the role of your wife, but I could never be sure that one day you might cause me harm on a whim. If I no longer pleased you, I could be discarded like old clothes. It makes it so difficult to feel secure and to have contentment and peace. In your case, your choices with other women are a daily test for me. Chasing after Tasha is galling and diminishes me. I had no opportunity to remedy that stain."

"Coraline, I understand and I'm sorry."

"Agar let me finish, please. In spite of anything you do, it didn't give me the right to take petty revenge. I didn't have the option to soil my own marriage vows. Agar, I haven't been blameless during our marriage. I did let my hurt at your affairs rule my choices and I have been unfaithful on some occasions. I'm not proud of what I did. I don't expect you to forgive me but what's important now is Granor knows about my dalliances. That's what he brought against me as we danced. He hopes to use it as a lever in his contesting with you. He wants to blackmail me into being his spy, and more."

"More, Coraline…? What more?"

"You know, Agar. What do men want from women? What did you get in your liaisons? Granor's a man like any other hoping to rise above his station in life. The wife of his chief rival, the crown prince is a prize he's chosen to pursue. He anticipates you'll go after Tasha again and he proposes I accede to him when you're gone."

"That snake," Agar hissed. "Who else have you brought into my bed, wife?"

"I don't want to give you names, Agar, anymore than I want to know who you've been with. I will say there has been no steady stream of miscreants to soil our marriage bed. There have been only a few, and it hasn't been frequent. I've not done that for a quite a time. Your mother has been very helpful for me in that area. I was honest with her, though she already knew of my mistakes. She helped me with how she coped. She's been down my road and understands everything. I truly cherish her as a mother, Agar. Can you forgive me?"

"Coraline, I know you expect me to be the person I was, arrogant, uncompromising, arbitrary, and unfair. I, of all people, understand about needs and intimate issues. I was a fool to go off and leave you alone for all that time. I wasn't always faithful, so how can I blame you seeing to your needs. I do forgive you. It's I who needs your forgiveness, wife. The list of my mistakes has no end."

Tears welled at the edges of her eyes. She looked vulnerable, dainty, and it evoked strong feelings of love and protectiveness in him. He hugged her before they continued their conversation.

"I can't guarantee you I'll never make further mistakes, Coraline. I can only tell you, I'll try my best. So, I don't expect you to be perfect, though I trust you'll do much better than I."

"About Granor, what should I do? He's a man of some import in the kingdom. If I spurn his advances, what will happen to me? He has the king's ear, Agar."

"It's a problem I'm going to solve, Coraline. I'll go directly to my father. You should tell my mother so she's an additional buffer to protect you. I going off soon for another lengthy campaign which is Granor's dream, that's not going to happen. If I'm forced to leave, it will be a well planned matter and I'll not leave you unprotected. If Granor has turned the palace guards, I will have my own personal guard to ward you. I'm not sure about his end game, but whatever it is, I will have an answer."

"Thank you, Agar. I was afraid of this day, admitting my sins. I feared it would lead to the end of me."

"No, Coraline. I was a fool, but I've finally started to see the light. I know you're unmatchable. I want to give you the best life possible. I don't want you to worry, to live in fear, or to be vulnerable at the whims and cravings of the men around you. Granor will not achieve his goals and he certainly will never crawl into my bed with you."

Coraline smiled warmly. "I was afraid of that very thing. Thank you for caring and for safe guarding me."

"From this day forward, neither of us will look backwards at what's been done. We'll only look forward to what we're going to do. I promise to be there for you, Coraline. You will have guards accompany you at all times. This is not to spy on you, but to keep others away to keep you safe. Do you understand?"

"Yes, husband. I agree to this whole heartedly."

"You're a good person, Coraline. You've lived a life of goodness I could only dream about. Your example gives me hope of something higher to aspire to, darling."

"I don't feel like an example for anybody, Agar. I suppose I'm like anybody else. I don't think about things I've done that are considered good. I dwell on my mistakes, failures, and weaknesses."

"I wouldn't trade you for another woman in the world, including Tasha. I've been too long getting around to telling you this."

"You've said it now. That's good enough for me, Agar. You've made me feel warm. Any woman wants to be the center of the universe for her husband. I haven't felt that before now with you."

"These aren't just idle words to mislead you, Coraline. I actually feel better about myself than I have ever in my life. I can't undo what I've done, but I can control what I do from now on. Let Granor try his schemes. He doesn't understand his influence with my father doesn't raise him above me. I'm going now to speak to my guards. My best soldier is Marin. His new duty will be you exclusively. I'll bring him to meet you shortly. If Granor tests Marin, he will rue the day. Marin reminds me of Aron. He's a deadly fighter and he's perhaps the only person left I have complete faith in."

"I'll be here waiting, Agar."

"One other thing and this may be difficult for you to hear and understand, but as I said, I'm not perfect and I don't expect you to be. If there is an occasion where I'm forced into another lengthy separation, and if you have, well…I only want you to turn to Marin. I'll tell him he is to see to you with everything you need."

Her face flushed. "Agar, I thank you for the offer, but it isn't something I plan to do. I feel shame enough over my past mistakes. Those liaisons weren't what I needed. I can't be with a person where I have no love for them. Besides, your mother has taught me about her accommodations and I'm doing fine. It's just the kind of person I am, husband."

He smiled. "I was hoping you'd say that, but hear me. The offer still stands. Sometimes things don't work out the way we'd desire and you find yourself in circumstances you wouldn't choose."

She shrugged.

Agar left the suite quickly. He noticed more palace guards arrayed near his suite than usual - double the number.

He hustled to the barracks.

"Marin, we need to talk..."

Agar returned to his suite an hour later. Marin walked at his side with an entire detachment of his personal guard. They deployed at the doorway and eyed the nearby palace troops closely. Neither side made any hostile moves.

Coraline took a deep breath as Agar brought Marin into her room.

"My dear, this is Marin, the most trusted of my guards. This is my wife, Princess Coraline."

"My lady," Marin bowed.

"Hello, Marin. I'm happy to meet you."

"Coraline, Marin is going to move into the suite and take a room so he is never far away from you."

"I hope this doesn't vex you, ma'am," said Marin. He kept his eyes on the floor.

Coraline smiled. "You can look at me, Marin. I'm just a woman. I want to thank you for your protection. It puts my mind at peace to know you'll be close by."

"I aim to serve," he replied. "You're not *just a woman*, highness."

She couldn't help but notice Marin's good looks and broad

shoulders. He was a man women looked twice at; and being comfortable with martial skills showed in his self confident manner. He glanced up at her with his deep blue eyes and dark blond hair and she felt a tingle. His eyes were pools of passion she could fall into and be lost forever. Thoughts of her times with Radigan flitted through her mind before she forced down the seductive memories. It took an effort on her part to corral her tantalizing thoughts.

"I've stationed troops outside our door, Coraline," Agar explained, ignoring the spark between Marin and his wife. "If you go anywhere, they go with you. Enemies watch for our vulnerabilities and weak moments. They strike when you least expect it, when you're at ease and feel you're out of danger. Marin will be charged with eliminating all of your dangerous situations. I want you to get to know him. I want you to build trust and a close relationship. I've made it clear to him what I expect. You're worried about making a misstep, I can see it in your eyes, but I assure you that for me, such an act isn't a problem if it happened. Having Granor and his ilk score a success is the problem. Their plans could have serious and perhaps deadly consequences."

"As you wish, husband..." She glanced away from Marin who stood up, but she still saw him out of the corner of her eye. He was a big, powerful and daunting man.

"Go and move your belongings in here, Marin," the prince advised. "This is your permanent new home."

"Yes, sire," he replied and left.

* * * *

Tasha left abruptly with her foul mood directed at Aron. She hadn't planned on anything further than punishing him mentally. Aron had looked at Radigan and the implication was there, again, that she was still intimately involved like an albatross hung around her neck she refused to discard. Leaving with Radigan would torment Aron, this she knew, but Aron's preoccupation with Liani had provoked Tasha. It wasn't Liani, a young friend she loved who angered her. No, Aron's undying mistrust and how easily he jumped to wrong conclusions was the problem. The rapport they'd been building always had setbacks and inevitably they were starting over, too many times. Tasha felt jealous of Liani.

"Tasha, are you vexed?" asked Radigan.

She looked at him, incredulous. He mischievously smirked back.

"Perhaps I can clarify my mood," she replied tersely. "Since you seem to have lost the capacity to reason out what is obvious, let me tell you Aron annoyed me, so I left him to stew in his silly suspicions. You're welcome to return to the camp to join him. I have no trouble walking alone."

"I have a problem with that, Tasha. Remember, Liani went alone for a walk and you can see the result. Of course I understand your mood, but I've told you I will never stop protecting you. Your safety is my goal in life."

"Your protection comes at a price, Radigan."

He laughed.

"How is this funny, sir?"

"I don't laugh for any humor of the situation. I laughed because we're irrevocably linked, Tasha. You understand me and I understand you. You're a woman who, if you so choose, no one could force to act against your will. Our times together, you can blame me as the instigator, but they wouldn't have happened without your agreement. You're trying to force something, this odd relationship you have with him. You look to change Aron, but no person can change another. He will never be me. What we have comes naturally. There's no planning our moves, practicing contrived moods or perpetrating any deceptions. Our natures are to be together and savor each other. You're strongly tempted now, Tasha. I keep telling you we're meant for each other."

She turned to him abruptly, fuming, but she didn't say anything. She couldn't really argue with what he said. He grabbed her, kissed her passionately and left her panting with desire in spite of her resistance.

"You know the truth, Tasha. It's just a matter of you admitting it to yourself. I don't pretend I'm a perfect man, but you know me completely. You know what to expect, and I can say the same about you. You're my woman. I would say my soul mate. We're both flawed people, but we can deal with it together, my darling."

She glared at him, but without any true outrage. Her anger was directed at her own turbulent feelings and the realization of the truths he spoke. This was distressing and wasn't the direction she wanted to go. Nonetheless, their path didn't go straight back to the camp and quite a while passed before they returned. Again, Tasha was in a place she tried not to be, but failed. This time, however, she looked at things differently. This intimate encounter changed her. She could no longer ignore her inner truth as Radigan so clearly demonstrated.

Aron wasn't there to see them come back from seclusion to the house, but her father was. His eyes smoldered with hatred at Radigan.

"Good evening, sir," Radigan chirped, with a bow. Tasha wouldn't look in her father's eyes. Her father took an aggressive step toward Radigan, but her mother came out of the tent at that moment.

"Hello, Radigan," she said. "Did you kids have a good walk?"

"A very good walk indeed, the best ever," he replied mirthfully. Tasha couldn't suppress a smile. She elbowed him. He simply laughed out heartily.

Her father turned away in rage and went into the tent.

She wanted to feel guilty, but each one of these stumbles seemed to bother her less and less. The time trying to mesh with Aron was looking more contrived to her. She felt badly about what her dalliance with Radigan might do to Aron's heart. He truly loved her, she had no doubts about that, but her feelings weren't the same as his. She could no longer deny it.

* * * *

Aron returned to the women and sat talking with Liani and Belisa. His distress about Tasha drained away after a time.

Enna and Biala were on night patrol and even when Wu Hang showed up to join them, Liani was remarkably ebullient, which was out of character for her and Aron noticed.

"Aron, I think my touch with the alien is somehow beneficial. I feel revived, lively, and focused more so than I think I've ever been. Do I seem different to you?" She also looked at Wu Hang.

"To me, you're ever a wonder," Wu Hang replied. "You were perfect before. If it's possible to improve on perfection, this is truly a blessing."

She gazed at him and smiled.

"Thank you, master interrogator. I didn't expect sweet words from your mouth."

"Please…Wu Hang," he replied softly. "I'd hoped you could honor my wish to put the past away. That life is over for me."

"Yes, of course, I'm sorry," she replied. "You did ask me that and it's a fair request. I'll see about doing better in the future."

Wu Hang bowed.

"Aron, did you visit with your fiancée? If so, it seems a short visit this evening. I'm pleasantly surprised you've returned to join me."

"Tasha had other plans," he replied evenly, trying not to display distress. "I did see her and we exchanged greetings."

"Greetings?" asked Belisa in puzzlement. "What does that mean, Aron?"

"If you don't wish to get into it, we understand," said Liani quickly. "We cherish what time you can spare for us."

They all turned towards another sound from Damien's equipment. Liani's eyes went glassy and she stared ahead before getting up and walking away.

"Liani, are you all right?" called Aron. Wu Hang got up and hurried after her. They followed. She led them back to Damien.

"Good, Liani, we have some matters to see about."

"Damien, why is Liani subject to your control again?"

"I'm sorry Aron. She's a necessary person to me at this moment. I'm in the middle of some difficult transitions. I'm only borrowing her, as I did before. She'll be returned to you as soon as possible. You need not fear for her. She's in no danger and there are no long term effects from her sharing."

"Sharing? Sharing what, Damien?"

"Sharing her mind, of course..."

"Damien, to my knowledge, Liani hasn't consented to do this."

"She did, but you'd have no way to know it. The computer made contact with her and the link happened afterwards."

"Computer…? I don't know that word. What does it mean?"

"I'm sorry I don't have the time right now to teach you the history of the world. If you'll excuse me..."

He turned and led Liani into his building. They tried to follow, but the invisible blocking barrier had been reactivated.

"Damien!" Aron yelled, but he was wasting his time. Damien had no interest in the peoples of the camp. Protected from Aron's force and their primitive weapons, he had a plan and was busy implementing it.

Quickly, another display in the sky of lights and sound broke out.

Agar had gone out to his balcony, high above the imperial city, for some fresh air. Night was fast approaching and Coraline came out to stand with him. He put his arm around her.

"My dear, step inside my cloak, there's a cool breeze this evening. Come and join us, Marin."

The trio gazed down at the city streets far below the ledge. Damien's light show suddenly brightened the distant sky. The prince, Coraline and Marin stared in shock and awe at the visual spectacle.

"What was that?" asked Coraline in alarm.

"I don't know," the prince replied. "It's in the direction of Aron and his people. I don't know what they've discovered. It's a daunting sight at this great distance and must be terrifying up close."

"Aron is not a cruel man, Agar. I can't imagine him planning mayhem for us or the peoples of the kingdom. I don't believe this is the work of Aron. Perhaps Galean has a hand in it. He has great knowledge and a lifetime of research. There are stories of vast power wielded in the beginning. Could this be some aspect of that?"

"It makes as much sense as anything I could think of."

He looked at Marin who shrugged. "I've not seen or heard of such, sire."

"Marin, this is a great learning moment for you. Galean was our royal scribe, yet now he's abroad and his resource to safeguard the kingdom is lost to us. I had a major role in that. It's an object lesson for both of us. I wonder whether I'll get a chance to undo the harm I've done to my father's kingdom. Having power can be a curse as much as a boon. I regret my errors and perhaps now it's too late."

Chapter Thirteen
~ The Rebirth of History ~

Aron hoped for a quick end to Damien's latest possession of Liani, but that didn't happen. The barrier remained active barring them from taking any action to free her. Wu Hang was as angry as Aron and actually tried to assault the barrier, to his detriment. At the point he tried to burst through the current, he froze mid stride suspended in the barrier and was injured. Aron and the others quickly pulled him back, but he was burned, his body smoking from the trauma and knocked unconscious. Eight powerful men got him onto a stretcher and carried him away for treatment.

Galean inspected the wounds clinically, but Aron could tell he had no idea what to do. They applied salves to the seared skin and then put him to rest.

Word spread rapidly about the predicament. Cherine arrived quickly with a troop of precision fighters at her back.

"What should we do, Aron?"

"I suspect there's nothing we can do. You saw what happened to Wu Hang when he tried to force his way through the barrier. Damien is immune to any of our weapons. His world had knowledge and power that's been lost over time. We're helpless sheep to him."

He saw the effect of his pronouncement and immediately regretted venting his worries. The troops were restless and even appeared to be frightened. Wu Hang was seen as near invincible and now was seriously injured.

Cherine looked unsure of herself.

"I'm sorry everyone. I was too quick to voice doubts. We'll find a way to overcome this obstacle. We've done it every time before," Aron added.

Cherine smiled and quickly regained her composure.

Drang-ku appeared.

"Can you go to Galean? Perhaps you can help him with knowledge of your people to aid in Wu Hang's recovery."

Drang-ku nodded and hurried off.

Radigan came to Cherine's side.

"I heard of this wrong from Damien. He's not one to be trusted. I sense he has plans which may not be favorable to us."

"He's secure in his place. We can't get to him," Aron explained.

"Did I hear he's taken Liani?"

"Yes, it's true. Her face went blank and she suddenly went to him there."

"This is dire news. Perhaps we shouldn't have our forces concentrated here where he can possibly attack us with his strange weapons and powers."

"What did you have in mind, Radigan?"

"I feel I should lead away the non combatants to a safer location."

Aron felt a twinge, but Radigan had a point. He glanced at Cherine who shrugged.

"We'll keep you informed of our progress, Aron."

He hurried away before Aron could respond.

The camp was astir and quickly many gathered their things to flee from Damien. Fear of the unknown surrounding Damien generated a great response as many wives and children tearfully parted from their husbands.

That evening, Aron walked about the now skeleton of a camp. Many soldiers had watched their families leave. Though they wanted them safe, the emotional stress of being apart left everyone on edge.

Barman stayed back with the men. Straga, however, had volunteered his forces to accompany Radigan as protectors of the civilians. Barman stood stoically with his wife as they said their goodbyes. Brock went straight to Straga.

"If you think to work your mischief while my mother is apart from my father, know that I will hunt you down and I will not be forgiving."

"You're too suspicious, Brock," Straga replied slyly. "Have I not proven I'm a changed man?"

"Not to me, Straga. You've proven nothing other than you changed your tactics to be more subtle. I'll always have my eyes on you. If you think you're the better fighter, have at it. I'll face you now or later, and you will lose your life."

Straga's eyes narrowed at the threat, but he shrugged his shoulders.

"Good fortune, Brock," he said and walked straight over to Sirina who'd watched the exchange with concern. Brock walked over to them.

"I'll be fine, son. We women will help each other. You don't need to worry."

"Mother, with the dangerous changes happening all around us, we can't afford not to worry."

Brock hugged his mother. He even hugged his younger half brothers before watching them all walk away at Straga's side. No longer merely puppets to their father, his half-brothers had developed a bond and respect with Brock.

The only women left in the camp were female fighters, like Cherine, Enna and Biala. Belisa also stayed with her corps of Arreck warriors. Tasha was gone, traveling with her family. Her goodbye with Aron had been brief and awkward. He sensed a change in her which played into his demons and felt an inevitability was unfolding he could do nothing to stop. This saddened him greatly.

Galean sent the bulk of his former staff away to safety also. A grim resolve built up amongst those who stayed back, but also a pervasive dread that doom was knocking at their door.

Damien's impervious barrier remained unchanged for a week as he pursued his secret plans. They saw one more pyrotechnic display in the sky before the barrier suddenly dissolved. Damien walked out smiling pleasantly.

"Greetings, my friends, I'm sorry to have been occupied for so long a time, but I had many duties to perform and only I to do them. Liani is a help, but she can only function on a rudimentary level for what I needed. I was fatigued, but I've recovered now."

"Where is Liani?' asked Aron coolly.

"She's resting. She too experienced strain from the work. She'll join us later."

"Are you aware your barrier injured Wu Hang?"

"I'm sorry. I assumed you all knew to stay away. When I work, the barrier activates automatically. It wasn't intended to keep you away. Let me see to his injuries."

Aron wasn't convinced he was getting the truth, but he led Damien to where Wu Hang was lying.

"Oh my," Damien exclaimed. "Your salves caused him no harm, but they did nothing for his injuries."

"We have no knowledge about such things," Galean answered, also treating Damien with suspicion.

Damien took out a device and held it over Wu Hang's injured skin. A beam of light scanned the entire surface.

"He will begin to recover quickly now. I've stimulated his healing forces of his own body. He'll be up and as good as new soon enough."

"Thank you," said Galean. "Is this thing you have something you wish share with us so we might have that healing balm for others?"

"I regret I have the only one. If there is a dire injury, simply call for me. I'll do what I can. This device has its limits. It isn't a panacea. Some injuries cannot be rectified."

"We thank you for your intercession," Galean added. "I'd like to visit with Liani when she's back up and about."

"Certainly, master scribe, you're a great comfort in her life and she cares for you greatly."

Galean got a thoughtful look as he studied Damien.

"Later, perhaps we can have a talk. I'd like to share my ideas with you all. There is much of your past you need to learn."

"As you wish, Damien..."

Damien went suddenly, without explanation, and walked swiftly out of the camp going in the direction Radigan had taken the families.

"Should we go after him, Aron" asked Brock.

"I think if he wanted to do harm, there may be little we could do to prevent him, brother."

"I will not trust him, Aron."

"None of us trust him, Brock. Don't do something foolish to provoke him. We have no defense at this point. We need to learn as much as we can and form our defenses from that new knowledge."

Brock wasn't mollified. He nodded stiffly to Aron.

Aron went down the ladder and approached the alien building just as Liani walked out. She blinked her eyes a moment before she waved to Aron.

He hurried to her.

"Liani, what happened to you? Are you harmed in some way?"

“No, Aron. I’m fine. I’m in no jeopardy from Damien. He’s a pleasure to work with. I’m fascinated with his machines and devices. He can revolutionize our world and make it a better place. He can heal in a way we cannot. You shouldn’t be so suspicious of him. He’s our friend.”

Her statement had a strange feel to it. She spoke with Liani’s voice, smiled blithely, but the real Liani was vacant, replaced by something else. Aron felt very uncomfortable about her.

“I think it will rain tonight,” she continued distractedly.

“Come with me, Liani. I’d like you to see Galean. I want to be sure you have no lingering symptoms.”

She shrugged dismissively. “As you wish, Aron...”

Again, he got the feeling she wasn’t herself. Her mannerisms, responses, and her tone were distinctly different, in an unpleasant way.

Rather than take her, Aron decided to stay back and let Galean form his own conclusions. Cherine noted his hesitation.

“This way, Liani,” she said and led her away. Liani paid no attention, and that included Aron. She would never have failed to glance at him in the past.

Brock looked at Aron.

“This just keeps getting better and better, Brock,” Aron complained.

“Maybe we should take Damien out, Aron.”

Aron chuckled. “You are consistent, brother. I always know how you think and what to expect.”

“Sometimes the simplest solution is the best one.”

“Sometimes not Brock... There’s so much we don’t know and though I agree we’re giving him a chance to gain traction, I think it’s unavoidable. It’s a risk we must take. Liani may be irreparably altered for all we know. If it can be undone, we must learn how.”

“I hope it doesn’t cost us, this waiting around for disaster to catch up to us.”

“Let’s go check on Wu Hang’s recovery.”

They walked to the hospital tent. Galean had taken Liani into another tent for his assessment. Wu Hang’s eyes were open. They walked over to where he was resting.

“You’re back with us, I see.”

“Liani just passed through. There is something wrong with her. She didn’t even glance at me. Her fear was strangely missing, but more than that, I’m now irrelevant to her. This is Damien’s work.”

"He took her into his building, Wu Hang. We were shut out so we don't know what he did to her. When she came out, she was as you see her. I hope Galean has an answer, but I doubt it."

"I will slay him," Wu Hang growled.

"You need to finish your recovery. We're trying to learn what we can about him."

"He's too dangerous to be allowed to walk freely among us, Aron."

"That's probably true, but we can do nothing at this point to prevent his intrusions."

"He is a dead man walking." The look in Wu Hang's eyes was murderous and was recovering enough to be terrifying again.

"Your skin looks much better, but you need time before you can get back on your feet. Stay here, we'll keep watching him. He's supposed to come back and have a talk with us later."

"You should trap him and slay him, Aron. He gains power by the moment. He will be beyond control soon enough, if he's not already."

"I can't disagree, Wu Hang."

"I agree with Wu Hang," Brock added.

Cherine came into the tent. "I hate to tell you this, Aron. I'm of the same opinion. Damien is going to enact some dire plan very soon. He's been making preparations since he emerged from his bastion."

Aron gazed at the three faces and had no solution, though in his heart he agreed. For him, the mitigating factor was Liani. If they could manage to kill Damien, which was no sure thing, would it sentence Liani to a life as an altered person, never able to regain normalcy.

"I'm sorry everyone. We listen to him and see what he proposes. He said he wants to educate us about our past history. I know Galean wants to hear that tale. Maybe we can pick up some useful information that will help us to create a defense."

"I don't like it, brother."

"I know you don't, Brock. I'm supposedly the leader here by everyone else's wishes, so I have to make the best decisions I can. This is what I feel is the best choice. I can't just write off Liani."

That statement sobered everyone.

"I understand," said Brock finally.

They waited for a time talking together. Wu Hang dozed off. Aron realized eventually Galean's examination of Liani would not be a short one.

"I guess we'll have to check back later to see how she is. Let's go get some food."

* * * *

Damien returned with Radigan at the meals end.

"Radigan, who's watching over the women and children...?" Cherine asked.

"Straga," he answered with a slight smile.

"They're in no danger from me," Damien piped in. "As a matter of fact, I've counseled them to return to their homes and husbands. You shouldn't live under hardship when there is no danger."

Everyone looked at him, incredulous.

"Where is Liani?" Damien asked.

As if on cue, Galean led Liani out of the tent and joined the group.

"There you are, my dear."

Liani smiled at Damien and didn't look at anyone else. Damien was smiling arrogantly; secure in the knowledge he had the upper hand. Radigan, who was watching Aron, had his own smug smile. Aron was now twice beaten, losing Tasha to Radigan and Liani to Damien.

Aron's face flushed red. Another humbling turn of events, added to his long line of setbacks. Brock tensed with anger and Aron put a hand to his arm.

"Don't," he whispered.

"Come, my friends," said Damien magnanimously. "We have much to discuss."

He walked over and put his hand to Liani's back leading her away at his side. She did not resist in any way, accepting his guidance meekly, with a slight smile on her face. Radigan walked on Damien's other side, apparently now his new ally. Damien building a following was a grim development indeed.

He was like the pied piper with a line of Aron's people trailing behind him as he walked to a small rise to have an elevated place to speak. With a confident expression, he looked at the faces staring at him for a short time to add import to the moment.. He had no fear of public speech or of swaying crowds. He looked expansively all around at the people, still holding off his speech.

An approaching sound came from behind them.

"Come forth," said Damien.

Their women and children had returned to the camp. Straga was in the lead, his face prideful and arrogant. He looked for Barmon in the crowd of men who stared back coldly.

Damien waited while families reunited. Once the general tumult died down he nodded. Straga took Sirina by the hand and pulled her forward to join him on the rise along with his sons. Radigan went into the crowd to find Tasha and led her up on the rise also. He looked triumphant and sought out Aron's face in the crowd of onlookers. Tasha saw him look and her head went down when she saw Aron, but she didn't leave Radigan's side. For all of Aron's followers, this was a display about the new order of things.

Damien put out an arm and Liani embraced him. An audible gasp erupted from the crowd at the colossal public affront to Aron who stood shaking with anger and shame. Barmon made his way to stand beside Aron and Brock who was on the verge of attack . Aron grab one of his arms and Barmon the other to keep him from reckless action.

"Greetings, my friends," said Damien releasing Liani and putting out his arms expansively. As he did so he activated equipment magnifying his voice. Behind Damien a vast screen materialized just above their heads. A scene from the ancient past displayed as if they were standing there as a part of it. On the screen, Damien was at a podium on a huge elevated stage. Arrayed around him was a throng so vast it covered the entire screen. The rabid crowd was chanting loudly and cheering in an unknown language. On the stage stood ranks of beautiful young women in white, form fitting short dresses. The dresses all had a rendering on the front of a fierce animal, in an attack position. None of Aron's people knew of that animal. All around the platform stood black clad soldiers with uniforms embossed with the same creature.

Suddenly music erupted from instruments and singers in a stirring anthem which drove the ancient crowd crazy. Damien raised fists in the air and walked along the stage inciting frenzy in the masses who answered with rabid chants and wild expressions.

Aron watched in stunned fascination. The music was on a scale never experienced; a person couldn't help but be stirred up by it. The song changed to a martial tune and the throng began to sing. Suddenly the sky was filled with a vast fleet of air vessels of various sizes. Aron couldn't believe that such things existed. When the fleet flew over the platform their engines were deafening.

The scene looked so real like they had been literally transported back in time.

Aron gazed at the flesh and blood Damien, whose eyes were aglow at the memory of his past, but also at the thought of his future.

On the screen the ancient Damien began his speech. Aron didn't need to understand the language to comprehend what he was saying. His speech incited strong responses from the crowd. With faces focused, almost insanely, their bodies swayed about accompanied with frequent chanting. Damien gestured and shouted; pointing into the crowd, he extolled them and evoked huge roars. Virtually screaming, his speech concluded with his fists pumping in the air. The crowd responded with deafening replies as the scene faded.

Damien's magic wasn't done as the music on the screen transformed into stirring song and pastoral scenes. Poignant and haunting, with the hint of something precious lost, the melody was painful in its beauty and demanding in reply. A narrator spoke, but in the old language. The scenes and the music were enough to accomplish his purpose - the ancient planet was a paradise.

The music started to crescendo as the camera view rose into space to look down on the vast blue orb of the planet. The finale of the music was an incredible series of chords that left everyone agog.

Afterwards, a huge pennant flapped on the screen and a background anthem played.

Present day Damien spoke with a greatly enhanced voice.

"You've seen the splendor that was your heritage, a gift and a boon that should have been yours, but in the past there were also small minds and jealous people, people without the capacity to comprehend the noble vision I offered to mankind. They sought their selfish own gain and had no concern about others. They were a scourge and the world is well served being rid of them. I wanted to rise up mankind to our greatest heights, but they refused my benevolence and chose instead to make war. Great power existed in those days to work ruin. Life itself could have been wiped out, but they had no pity. They cared only for destruction as they hid in their sanctuaries. That war was terrible beyond your knowing. The great cities of man, the legions of the helpless and innocent, were all consumed in the purging fires of hatred and disunity. I offered them the opportunity to be one great people.

Instead they sought to cast me down and all goodness with it. Their world would have been a nightmare of prejudice, insulation, mistrust and perpetual wars - a tragedy without precedent, which forced me to make desperate choices in the end. I cry for those who fought for me, those brave souls willing to sacrifice life itself for a higher purpose. I shed an ocean of tears over their corpses at too many funerals. I would have done anything to protect them, but our enemy was relentless, heartless and without compromise. Only one side or the other could prevail. They left us without alternatives, but to fight to the death. I will hate them for all eternity for what they did to mankind."

The background music gradually changed to a stirring refrain with a hopeful air.

"It's a miracle that I'm given a chance to rectify all of the evil that was done back then. This world can yet achieve those great goals denied to us before. What I offer you now is what I offered them, a chance to join me in crafting a new world, one where we abolish those villains who would hold us back from our rewards."

A burst of spontaneous applause swelled throughout the gathered. Not everybody responded, but a significant number did. Most of the support was centered in the former gang members, though some villagers were included. The people close to Aron stood in silence behind him. Aron was staring particularly at the women on the small rise. Tasha seemed uncomfortable. Though she allowed Radigan to hug and kiss her, she glanced at Aron's stone faced expression. Liani was dazzled and awed by the spectacle and the wonders revealed. She avidly hugged Damien who kissed her forehead and held up her hand in his.

Straga kissed Sirina romantically though she didn't cooperate. She didn't openly fight him in front of everyone, but to all was clear it wasn't her choice to be there.

"There is room for all under my banner and my protection," Damien continued. "We are all inclusive and desire to help each of you to achieve your highest abilities. There is much work to do to recover the world. I must tell you, there will be obstacles and hardships that cannot be avoided. What I promise is I'll be there to shoulder the burden as we work together to accomplish progress. I'll guide you. I'll help you recover the wonders that have been lost over the ages. I'll help you to be better than your ancestors. My help is free and my cause noble. Will you join with me? Will you pledge your utmost efforts to the cause?"

The same people roared as before, and Aron's cadre remained silent and wary.

"Do you believe in me!?"

"Yes!" came the loud reply.

Aron felt queasy along with ill feelings about the conduct of his women on the hill. He was caught in the middle of a living nightmare. What was happening couldn't be possible, yet the terrible scene unfolded before him.

He considered turning around and leaving the camp without looking back, but knew he could never escape his fate, as dim as it appeared. Damien seemed invincible, his eventual triumph guaranteed and unstoppable. Aron felt small and inadequate against such a superior opponent. Radigan and Straga standing with Damien was a logical sequence and inescapable outcome of his entire life; like he'd been fated to failure and this was the proof for all to see.

Damien triggered another display on his virtual screen, more of the stirring music and landscape scenes. This time seascapes of the great oceans displayed with powerful waves crashing against a rocky coastline; meant to dazzle the pictures hit the mark with the crowd.

"See what can be our future, my friends," Damien extolled. "This is the world as it was. I have the means to bring it back to the former splendor. It's what was meant for your lives, not this meaningless life in a wasteland. I applaud Aron who's led you to this point to free you from the royal yoke, but it's now time to turn the reins over to one more capable, one born to lead. With great humility I'll accept the mantle to guide you along the path to glory on Earth. You've had no one to show you the way. Even your names have devolved. You, the one named Abdurka, what name do you have for your people?"

Abdurka glanced at Aron before he replied.

"We're called the Amerkands."

"Your ancestors were the Americans, from a country called the United States of America. You Chenese, you're Chinese from the land of China. The Uripeans, you're Europeans from Europe. It's all been lost, but no longer. I'm here to set things right. Do you see?"

Silence... The ilk that favored Damien continued their celebratory mood and they looked at Aron's conquering forces like their loss had just been reversed.

"Who's with me?" asked Damien. The corresponding roar got louder each time he incited them. Now nearly all of the former gangs were in his camp. To Aron's surprise, the savage Brutans remained fiercely loyal. They had reformed their ranks directly behind and around Aron's Black Fist, and Cherine's masters. All of them were silent, staring at Damien.

Again, Aron saw a flash of rage cross Damien's face before his blithe smile returned. He made a point of pulling Liani close and hugging her. She smiled warmly staring in his face, like Aron no longer existed. Radigan hugged Tasha and Straga hugged Sirina. Those two women at least didn't cooperate, but endured the snub being sent to Aron.

"Do it, Aron," whispered Brock.

Aron fought the impulse, but this humiliation was too strong. He made a small signal and his entire forces, responded with a mighty martial battle shout and came to battle position. This instantly cooled the ebullience amongst Damien's new flock. Their exuberant sounds quickly died to stillness. Their glee turned to wariness.

"Thank you for your entertainment, Damien. We'll leave you now to resume our duties. As you're aware, we also have a great deal of work to do," said Aron evenly.

He made another signal and the entire command pivoted and marched quickly away. He felt endangered, like Damien would cause a lightning bolt to come from the sky and strike him down. Their families and the villagers all hurried after him. There were women amongst the gangs, widows who'd accepted new mates from those ranks. They eyed the retreating flood longingly, but their fates were now in the hands of the new order.

Aron went to the far side of the camp to consider the next step.

Galean made a bee line for Aron and the leadership group.

"This is what I suspected," he said grimly. "You saw those people of the past. They wore the symbol of the beast. I believe Damien is the person foretold in our ancient prophesies. It's him whom I believe you'll battle in the end, Aron. He's the beast."

"That doesn't seem to be much of a fight, Galean. With the powers he has available to throw against us, what could we possibly do?"

"You can't give up hope now, Aron. I admit, we're facing a far superior foe, but face him we must. There is no one else to do it. I'm convinced of that."

"Galean, we have no army. What converts we got from the wilds are halfway into his camp. It doesn't surprise me Radigan would heed his call. He's ambitious and he sees a chance to achieve new heights denied him in the service of the prince. Straga was never our friend and with him, he also sees a chance to bring us low. I'm sorry Barmon for this ill turn of events. I don't think Sirina chose him now, this was forced on her. I'll also say this to get it out in the light. Tasha seems to have made her choice. I'm assuming she's no longer my fiancée so let's leave it at that. Don't come to give me your condolences about our engagement. I lost that contest to Radigan. So be it. In truth, the struggle may have been over before it ever began. I can't really say I'm surprised. As far as Liani, I don't think she made a choice either. How he could change her into his vassal, I don't know, but we've all have seen the result. If she can still be saved, I don't know. I'll leave that to smarter people, like Galean. In the meantime, we need to swiftly take action. I think Damien will look to institute his generosity on us too, whether we want it or not. If we're meant to fall, I say we take as many of them with us as we can."

The people shouted.

"You've been faithful to me, all of you. I can't tell you how much I appreciate it. I fear you made a poor choice of who to follow. Nonetheless, we'll do whatever we can. We've got battle skills and I think we can be a dangerous foe."

Aron looked at Cherine. She took a step forward.

"We're going to quietly gather our things, eat very quickly and filter away in small groups to meet at the old Brutan camp. Once we're safely away we'll be able to craft a longer term plan. Be careful, Damien's people will be watching us. Cause no trouble and nod blithely if you're challenged about your loyalties. Those we leave behind can no longer be viewed as friends. I think there are those amongst the converts who might follow us, but we can't take any chances. If they keep to their gang loyalties, they're a danger to us. Their leaders are weak minded people who flow with the prevailing winds."

Aron went straight to his parents who were having a serious talk with Tasha's parents. Barmon and Brock were at his side. They all looked sympathetically at Barmon. He put up a hand to stop them from saying anything.

"Like Aron said, what's done is done. If there is a chance to recover my wife, I will do so, but I must focus on our survival. Aron has shown great strength, I can too. I still have my son."

"I'm sorry about our daughter, Aron," said her mother.

"You have nothing to apologize about. I need to know what you're going to do."

"I told her she can't live in our house any longer. I won't tolerate him in my presence," said her father.

"Our trouble is we just can't abandon our daughter," her mother added. "Though we won't be a party to him and his doings, we're going to remain here. If something dire occurred where Tasha needed us, we can't be away and unable to help her."

"This is a bad idea," said Aron's father.

"I agree," Aron added. "I think Damien plans on unleashing powers and forces beyond our comprehension. We all saw those scenes and the might he displayed. If he has such horrors hidden here somewhere, there is nothing we could do anyway. I don't have a plan, but I will resist as long as I still draw breath."

Aron's a sobering assessment left everyone speechless. Finally Tasha's folks shrugged.

"We'll pray for you, our dear friends. To be here was our fate. We'll have to see where it leads us."

They walked away sadly.

Cherine nodded and all of their forces dispersed quickly to fulfill their duties and make preparations for the trek.

Aron went to the hospital to talk to Wu Hang.

"I'll be up very soon," he told Aron, "but I'm like Tasha's parents. I must be here for Liani. If I can discover a means to free her, I will do so."

Aron shook his head. "I wish you were with us. I suspect we're going to have need of every fighter we can get."

"I'm always your friend and ally. I'll do what I can behind enemy lines for our cause."

"Be very careful, my friend."

"Thank you, Aron."

Chapter Fourteen

~ Repeating History ~

Aron's abrupt public departure with his supporters in the face Damien's attempt to dazzle them at his speech was a galling turn, too much for Damien to accept. He simmered as he watched the rebels march away.

This wasn't the first time in his life Damien had faced opposition, but at this point he assumed resistance was all behind him buried in the rubble of the ancient war. He realized there were still people who would still defy him and challenge his grandiose vision of a world of his own making.

"What vexes you, my lord?" asked Liani, still in his arms.

"Nothing I can't handle. Think nothing about it, my dear. We have answers for those who are unbelievers. They cannot stop us from bringing forth perfection and bliss to the world."

He looked at Radigan. Tasha was in his grasp, but she wasn't happy. Sirina wouldn't even look at Damien. She put her arms around Straga's two sons and turned her back to him.

"Come with me," said Damien. He led them off his stage into his building to a room where he pulled out dark uniforms, holdovers of the ancient war embossed with the beast, and handed them to the men. Now the army of Damien had its first two members - the first step down a path that had shattered the ancient world. For the women, he produced the same short mini-dresses with the beast logo on the chest. Liani didn't bat an eye taking the garb. Tasha hesitated briefly. Straga had to hand the dress to Sirina who took it grudgingly.

"You're the beginning," said Damien, his eyes aglow. "From this small step will blossom the transformation of the world. Mankind will finally know utopia."

Tasha eyed Damien with a concerned look. Sirina looked away. Liani beamed and hurried away to change into her new clothes.

Radigan was unusually affected by the moment and by Damien. Being an eternal cynic, the fact that Damien could interest and excite him was an accomplishment. Radigan was normally aloof, feeling superior to anyone in any situation, but Damien was operating on a vast scale of possibilities that intrigued Radigan. Adding in Damien's array of technological marvels made the potential irresistible to Radigan. With Tasha committed to him, Radigan felt emboldened to take precarious and risky steps. His horizon was suddenly brightened and his opponents lessened. Aron was finally in a seemingly no-win position. Damien had unprecedented power and the appearance of invincibility. The vision of Damien before the ancient throng in the recording still inspired Radigan.

"Go after Liani, Tasha," he whispered. "Put on this dress as a symbol of our belief in Damien's vision. I will change out of the uniform of the prince and put away for all time my link to him."

Straga pushed Sirina toward Tasha, to go with her. Reluctantly the women walked away together. They had no other choice. When they got to the room, Liani had just put on the dress. She turned to display the new look unabashedly.

"Liani, what's happened to you?" asked Tasha.

"What do you mean, Tasha? I'm unchanged in any way."

"No, Liani, you are changed. You seem a different person. What has he done to you?"

"I don't know what you mean. Our lord has shown me nothing but patience in the face of my ignorance. I'm grateful he's given us all a chance to ascend and join him at the pinnacle of human achievement. Is it not glorious to share with him in these first momentous steps on the path to greatness?"

Tasha and Sirina stared at her in disbelief. She smiled, oblivious to their worries.

"Come ladies and change quickly so we can rejoin the men. These are exciting times."

Damien's eyes glazed over when the women returned, evoking memories of his ancient predecessors. Sirina and Tasha felt shy about displaying so much leg, but Liani basked in the male attention they evoked. The old Liani would never have worn such a revealing dress.

As expected, Radigan looked dashing in his new uniform; he was a very handsome man. Straga looked much different in the uniform, like the barbarian had dissolved and a man worthy of notice had replaced him. Straga too had quickly ascribed to the new order and its potential for him.

"This is much better," said Damien. "Now you look as you should. I'm proud to have you in my company. Ladies, you look fetching. You stir the hearts of men."

"Thank you, my lord," said Liani with pride.

"Do you think we'll be like that too?" Sirina whispered to Tasha.

"I pray not, Sirina. It's a frightening prospect."

"What can we do to protect ourselves, Tasha? If I'm altered, what will become of my children, and my husband Barmon? He won't understand that I didn't choose this."

"I'm wondering about my decision too, Sirina. I did love Aron, but this thing I have with Radigan, was stubborn. I didn't want to give up what Radigan does for me. He makes me feel the way I like. I never got to such a point with Aron, but perhaps I should have taken more time and tried harder. I put the onus on Aron to outshine Radigan and merely defined myself as a fool in doing so. Aron is probably much better off with me out of his life."

"You can't possibly believe that, Tasha. Aron had so many women desiring him, but only had feelings for you."

Tears flowed in Tasha's eyes.

"I'm afraid it's too late now, Sirina."

* * * *

Aron signaled to start their trek. He arrayed the Black Fist and the masters to flank the villagers and civilians as they hurried away from Damien. The Brutans were assigned as rear guards in case Damien sent forces to attack them. Brock was in the lead riding beside Cherine. Enna and Biala had come up to ride on each side of Aron. Directly behind them was Galean and Abdurka followed by his staffers and then the civilians.

Aron rode in relative silence lost in his thoughts. Losing Tasha was a trauma he couldn't simply dismiss from his mind - a severe and ongoing emotional component which punished him painfully. Feeling rejected and inadequate was an inescapable consequent of the humiliating last few days.

"I think it will rain," said Biala.

Aron blinked, gathering his thoughts and looked up at the cloudy sky.

"You're probably right, Biala."

"Aron, we're so sorry for your pain," said Enna sympathetically.

He glanced at her. The sympathy in her eyes was meant to be comforting, and was certainly genuine, but in his current state of mind, he didn't want their pity. Pity made him feel his conclusions about his own failings were the way everyone felt about him - he was unworthy and couldn't hold his woman.

Aron couldn't manage a reply. Simply nodding at her gesture, he looked ahead again.

They traveled as rapidly as they could with such a mixture of women and their children, but it wasn't rapid. After a day of travel, they hadn't progressed anywhere near what Aron wanted. Damien was still too close for his liking. As he walked about the camp to check on them, he saw Jenn, the young widow and her little girls.

Emma ran up to him and put her arms around his leg. Winnie was sitting on her mother's lap.

"Hello, hello," said Aron gently, touching the little girl on the shoulders.

"Let go of him, Emma," said her mother. "I'm sorry Aron. My daughters like you. I hope it isn't bothersome."

"Of course not, Jenn, it's a pleasure to see you all again."

He sat down and smiled at her. Emma sat down and leaned against him. This warmed his heart and he put an arm around her little body. He kissed her on the top of her head.

"Do you fear Master Damien will strike us?" asked Jenn.

"I hope not. I think he has some ideas he wants all of us to accept. I didn't feel in a position to agree to something we don't understand. I'm afraid I allowed my concerns to make a choice for all of us."

"We were frightened by what we saw, Aron. Do you see how we followed you away without hesitation? I don't think our staying there would've led to better lives. I have a bad feeling about this man. He says noble things, but didn't seem to have the ring of truth. Does that make sense?"

"It makes perfect sense to me, Jenn. I just hope I haven't doomed us all."

"We all trust you, Aron. We're willing to trust our fates in your hands. Damien is hiding something and I think he'll work ill in the world."

"I have those same concerns, Jenn. All we can do is run away and avoid his net at this point. You say you put your trust in me, but for me it's Galean where I put my trust. Between him and Abdurka I feel we have our best hope to survive this peril."

"Galean is a great man, Aron, but you're great also. As I watch you, I sense great unrest in your soul. I think you blame yourself unfairly for things out of your control. Who could have done better than you? No one in this camp faults you for what's happened. We look instead at the weakness in those around you. They've made poor choices and will pay their prices. Don't make yourself the root of all our troubles because you're not. They're the ones who are unworthy."

Aron shrugged. Her kind words didn't alleviate his pain. Tasha was still in the arms of Radigan and vowing allegiance to Damien. She was still the love of his life, but now he wouldn't have her. There were no words that could heal that debilitating wound.

"If there is anything you need, just tell us," she added meekly.

It took a moment for him to realize what she was saying. Jenn was a young widow with children. She needed a husband to share her life, someone who as a good man who could be a good father to her daughters.

"Thank you, Jenn," he replied. "If I need something, I will let you know."

He wasn't emotionally ready to think about such things. He was too busy pining away for his lost love.

"I've got to go, Jenn. I need to talk to the staff to discuss our plans."

"Of course," she said awkwardly, like he'd rejected her. "I'm sorry we kept you."

"No Jenn," he replied tenderly. "I really do have to go. I'm going to come back when I have some time to spend with you and the girls, okay?"

She smiled timidly.

"Daddy?" asked tiny little Winny.

It brought tears to Jenn's eyes. She hugged her daughter and whispered. "No baby, Daddy is gone to heaven."

With all of the emotional wreckage Aron was dealing with, that last statement cut through it all and tugged at his heart. He felt sorrow again for the widows and for Jenn in particular. Emotions froze him in place for a time before he could manage to walk away. He felt their gaze and turned back to see three sets of eyes staring. Their struggle was brutal for so many reasons, like all of his wounds had been reopened – yet another occasion where he felt inadequate to meet their needs.

The skies opened up that night soaking the countryside. Trying to sleep in temporary tents was difficult with the strong winds whipping open the tent flaps and blowing in rain. No one was rested in the morning when they woke to gray skies and a steady drizzle.

"I wish we could sit it out here," Aron mentioned as he sat with a hot mug of coffee.

"I agree we're too close to him," Cherine replied. "It's a hardship on the children to travel in this kind of weather, but we've got no choice. In our favor, Damien doesn't have a great army at his command. That may change in the future, but for the time being I think we have the better fighting force. They outnumber us, but we know their skills. They have none anywhere near our abilities. I think Radigan can lead and Straga holds great sway amongst his ilk. Now is the time for us to put distance between us. We can begin to prepare our answer later. I think we should consider going out of the wilds. Along the frontier, the royal forces won't fight us. Actually, I suspect many would join us. That would be a good omen having our own army of trained soldiers."

"It's a nice dream, Cherine. I tend to assume the worst with what I've faced in my life. It keeps me humble and helps me be prepared for every contingency."

A rider rode up. "My lord, we've advised Trent of our approach. He said he'll be prepared for our arrival. The border area has been quiet for quite some time now."

* * * *

Agar couldn't get the strange display in the night sky out of his mind. It worried him enough he decided to go to his father.

"Be careful of Granor," said Coraline. "I know you believe he can't threaten us, but I'm a person who's very cautious. I don't want any unpleasant surprises."

"I've done many unfortunate things in my life, Coraline. My

mistakes have taught me a great deal. What Granor doesn't count on is my being anything other than the fool I was before. That strange event in the sky worries me more than Granor. I wish we had Galean here."

"We don't. He's gone. We must deal with it as best we can."

An edge to her voice surprised him. Whatever deep emotions she had, he was sensing things coming to the surface, not the least of which was "*you did this to yourself*."

"Granor's threat worries you, Coraline?"

"If it doesn't worry you, it should," she replied firmly.

The prince glanced at Marin who was always nearby. He had his usual stoic impersonal expression on his face.

"Be on your guard, Marin."

Marin nodded. The prince left the suite to head for a meeting with his father. He took his personal guards with him everywhere he went nowadays, even within the palace. Granor was in attendance with the king when Agar arrived. Granor's men were stationed at the door. They looked coolly at the prince, blocking his way into the throne room.

"Stand aside," said Agar.

"The king has ordered no one is to be admitted."

"Stand down, and stand aside," said Agar tersely. "I won't ask again."

"We have our orders, sire."

"Did those orders come from my father, or from Granor? I'll let my father tell me if I can't be admitted. If you wish to die here, we'll accommodate you."

Agar's men gave a loud martial shout and drew their weapons. Granor's men looked rattled, but held their ground.

Suddenly the door flew open.

"What is this?" shouted the king.

"Granor's men tell me you forbid me from entering, father."

"What!" the king turned angrily toward Granor who was nonplussed.

"Sire, this is just a misunderstanding. My men are jealous to safeguard you. I think they possibly overstepped their charge. It's better to be safe these days with the dangers in the kingdom. We all saw what Aron perpetrated right here in the palace."

"Your genuine concerns for my father are touching, Granor," Agar said graciously. He didn't want a fight at this point.

"Yes, thank you Granor," the king added. "Of course you're to be admitted, son. What brings you here? I see you have troops at your back. Do you wish to take the throne?"

Agar laughed heartily. "You can have the throne, father. My bringing troops have nothing to do with you or the throne."

The king looked curious. "Come in and sit with us. Would you like some wine?"

"No, thank you, father. I came about the strange array of lights in the sky the other night. I have no facts to share to explain it, but it troubles me greatly. Although it came from the area where Aron has his camp, I don't think the beam was something of his making. I've gotten disturbing stories from the frontier recently. I think there is some other peril abroad that we must consider and prepare for. Even with Galean attending Aron, what we saw is beyond the abilities of any man. Galean was a great mind, but he had no power to perform such wonders. That doesn't even include the story of an invasion from beyond the wilds. It's said that a great force of strangers, an army actually, invaded the wilds and fought a pitched battle with Aron. Aron prevailed, but at a great cost in lives and resources. As I said, I wasn't there, but this account comes supposedly from an eye witness. I believe the account to be true."

The king looked concerned.

"This is troubling news, indeed, Agar. What do you say, Granor."

"I'd heard strange stories too. I didn't put much stock in them. They had too much an air of speculation and nonsense. The borderland farmers have all sorts of superstitions and wives tales to frighten their children. What the prince says does make me believe we should reassess our thinking."

"I feel we should send new orders to the army, father. We're far to dispersed right now. We can't worry about provinces which are nuisances in flaunting us. Instead we should shift our forces so the central homeland is adequately protected and then concentrate deploying forces to ward any threat coming out of the wilds. If Aron faces another invasion and is defeated, there is no other buffer against that invading army. Preservation of the kingdom is my foremost concern."

"Good, Agar, that's exactly the conclusion you should have made. I must say the changes I see in you are remarkable. I feel much better about the future of our realm. Are you returning to the borderlands?"

"I don't see that as a wise move, or even necessary that I personally go there. Our border forces seem to have matters well in hand. We've heard no stories of clashes with Aron's rebels, and the flight of the villagers across the border has stopped. Apparently word has spread that their lives on the farms is still better than striking out into the unknown in the wilds."

He noted the surprise on Granor's face.

"Did you expect I would resume my former quest for Tasha, Granor?"

"I, eh, it was well known you hold her in high regard, sire."

"I did, and I do, but not so high as to put the realm in danger. These other developing threats require cool rational minds. The excesses of my youth can no longer rule me. Does that put your mind at ease?"

Granor made an attempt at a smile, but the gesture was forced and he was discomfited.

Agar smiled smugly and looked at his father. The king sensed a contest was in play between the two men which aroused his curiosity.

"Agar, it pleases me to hear you'll be in the palace. Would you join your parents for dinner this evening?"

"Thank you, father; that will please Coraline. As you know, she cherishes the queen and savors every moment she can share with her."

"She's a great comfort to my wife, Agar. The queen feels equally blessed to have a daughter by marriage like Coraline. I wish our daughters by birth were even a fraction of the wonderful woman as Coraline."

"Of course you should join us too, Granor," Agar added shrewdly.

"I'm honored you would think of me, my prince."

"You're a great asset to my father. How could I not be grateful to you for that?"

Granor glanced at Agar directly.

"My wife speaks so highly of you, Granor. She regrets she can find so little time to spend with you. She's pressed by a heavy schedule meeting her royal duties. Of course you understand."

Granor's eye's narrowed at the implied threat.

"Of course, sire."

"I'll be available on her behalf if you have need to correspond, or if you have some other need."

"Thank you, sire," Granor replied stiffly. He looked slightly apoplectic.

"I'm glad we're clear on that," Agar concluded frostily.

The king eyed them closely, realizing much more existed to the exchange than met the eye.

"If you're in agreement, father, I'll see to the changes I've discussed. I want to talk to the high command anyway about some other matters too."

"You have my leave, son. I'll see you at dinner tonight."

"Thank you, my king," he said with a bow. "I'll see you at dinner, Granor. Please bring a companion. Your last one was such a pleasant and a wise young lady."

"As you command, my prince, we'll be there."

Agar left the room feeling giddy, like he scored a significant triumph over Granor. He was pleased with his clever handling of a delicate matter. He'd let Granor know that his intended scandal using Coraline wasn't a piece he could bring into play and that if he tampered with Coraline, he would pay a severe price.

Agar headed for the headquarters of the army to speak with the generals.

* * * *

Damien didn't hesitate to enact his plans as quickly as possible and set about gathering every person in the surrounding area, including and especially the remaining bands which Aron hadn't managed to corral yet. He began to rapidly increase the forces loyal to him. Stupefying technical displays disarmed the weak minds from those camps. To enhance his aura and image as the world's greatest man, their enslaved women gave Damien a pool of replacements for the long lost cast of beautiful women at his back. It wasn't long before an entire cadre of women wearing the short white dresses with the beast insignia was assembled. Even though many more women were scantily clad in the revealing dresses, it didn't make Tasha any more comfortable about being forced to dress that way. Sirina hated it, but both were powerless.

Damien didn't stop with the wilds. He trained and equipped units to venture out of the wilds into the nations of the world with his message of unity and progress. Although they met with resistance and took casualties, it didn't matter to Damien. What they accomplished was spreading Damien's words and started a new flow of the curious, the weak minded, the ambitious, and those easily swayed. His location in

Aron's old camp couldn't support anywhere near the rapid incoming flood of people. This he'd anticipated and located another bunker outside of the wilds. They relocated there, though he left a significant residue of troops in case Aron tried to return.

A great deal of hardship and discord settled into the in the world - easy meat for Damien. He portrayed himself as the great hope, the alternative to everything bad in their lives, the answer and the ultimate panacea. His was a persuasive message and he was perfectly suited to deliver it to people who had no hope otherwise.

Damien continued on with more of his pyrotechnic performances. The crowds grew in size and frenzy. Word of Damien spread rapidly to both his potential converts and potential enemies, threatening people currently in power.

Tasha and Sirina worried constantly and talked quietly about what they should do.

"I can't have my sons raised in such an environment, Tasha. When they lived with Barmon, I saw how he brought out the good in them. Now they're back with Straga and all that progress is lost. I feel like we're trapped in the center of a whirlpool of disaster."

"We've got to be very careful, Sirina. You can see Liani is as bad as ever. Whatever Damien did to her may be permanent. I don't want to end up like that. We've got to bear with this until we find some safe means to escape, if there is one."

"You have Radigan as a mate. Is that any comfort?"

"My feelings for Radigan are still there, but he's so taken with the movement that's all he thinks of. He wants us to marry, but like a formality to be resolved and an achievement against Aron. I feel so badly. I lack the joy that should accompany my marriage."

"Straga wants me to pledge to him, to marry him and renounce Barmon. I don't want to, but I don't know how I can avoid it."

"Liani said Damien told her she will be his wife. She's overjoyed, but makes me sick to think of the lie it would be. The real Liani would kill herself rather than wed someone other than Aron."

Tasha paused a moment, realizing what she'd just said. Sirina looked at her sympathetically.

"I'm a fool, Sirina. Now I'm paying the price for it. What's wrong with me?"

"Nothing is wrong, Tasha. Sometimes our hearts overrule our heads.

I allowed myself to become content in my life with Straga after I was taken from Barmon. We all have our own guilt and make decisions we rue later. It doesn't matter at this point. We need to survive the here and now. That's our challenge. I hope we can find a way to help Liani, but there is some dire change in her that's beyond our understanding."

"I was angry at Aron for the attention he paid to Liani. I was jealous and I selfishly used it as an excuse to be with Radigan. Now I wish I could go back and change that day. I'd gladly see her in Aron's protective arms rather than see what's become of her with Damien. My choice of Radigan was the right one for Aron. I was never worthy of him and this stupid mistake I've made is glaring proof."

"Don't say those things, Tasha. It serves no good purpose. I know your feelings. I regret how I acted toward my true husband when we were brought back together. I was confused about my feelings, frightened about what would happen to me and my children and I wavered…a big mistake, but we can't change the past. We need to dwell on the present. We have troubles enough there."

"In a way, Sirina, this is worse than being captive in the palace. I was there totally against my will. Here, I've made a choice so I have no one but myself to blame."

The women embraced sadly.

After their move to Damien's alternative bunker, his efforts to gather his flock of followers gained momentum. In addition to curious pilgrims, Damien rapidly conscripted every male who could walk. Suddenly Radigan and Straga were generals directing large numbers of troops. Straga, instead of being a scoundrel and a mere barbarian of his former life was now a person of import. Radigan glowed with self importance and the weaker aspects of his character flourished. Straga barely contained his zeal to subjugate and intimidate.

Watching Radigan transform and evolve into a man very reminiscent of Prince Agar was a disturbing turn for Tasha. Her feelings for Radigan, which had always been one dimensional and based on certain aspects of their relationship, suddenly realized they were poor reasons for an ill conceived selection of a life partner. Sharing this new life he craved in the new world order of Damien chilled her to her core.

Damien's noble words were not reflecting in actual deeds of both himself and his camp. Contrarily, their actual deeds were bereft of any nobility at all, but rather the same seamy reality they'd left behind in the palace. Humanity was an entity for his use and nothing more.

Tasha felt trapped, but more, she felt helpless. In her mind, escaping in hopes of rejoining Aron wasn't an option, not after how she'd shamed him by publicly choosing Radigan. She couldn't even safely visit her parents. Guards had been placed on all Damien's women, who were sequestered inside the bunker, unable to leave without being taken out by Damien personally.

Liani remained oblivious to her new life. The person she'd been was gone forever. She blithely smiled and exclaimed over Damien. In those times she was alone with Tasha and Sirina, they guarded their words carefully for fear Liani would betray them. Liana was Damien's object completely now; chilling to behold and daunting to see what easily could be done to them too. Tasha's greatest fear was to lose control of her thoughts, her feelings, and her humanity, to be something less than the person she was: a pretty puppet dancing to Damien's tune. Already others of the women Damien had conscripted into his corps of background beauties were showing the same bland faces and docility as Liani. Tasha was terrified she would soon be next.

When Radigan came home to her in the evenings, she took no comfort. She was guarded with him just as much as with Liani. He totally subscribed to Damien now. She couldn't share her inner feelings for fear of the consequences. Their personal relationship was much changed, but Radigan didn't seem to notice, or to care. Damien's ways of taking ownership were manifesting in Radigan. Though he wasn't cruel to Tasha, he seemed uncaring and dismissive about her thoughts and feelings. She existed now to meet the needs of the men. Only Damien and his rise to pre-eminence in the world mattered. Whatever feelings of love he'd had, were strangely missing, replaced by this impersonal controlling aura that Tasha despised.

Sirina felt the same way. But her solace was having sons as a buffer. Their father was autocratic, and far more demanding than ever, and already he was grooming them to join Damien's army.

"Straga, your boys are too young," Sirina pleaded.

"My boys are brave," he retorted obstinately. "They will do their duty."

"Having your sons slaughtered by full grown men, how can that not strike you as idiotic?"

For some reason, her ire got through to him and he paused.

"You're right, Sirina. I momentarily lost sight of reality. The way of Damien is compelling. It's easy to be swept away."

"Not when it comes to my sons," she retorted tersely.

For a moment, the Straga who'd been her companion of the past looked back at her with sympathy and understanding, like he was awakened from a dream.

That lucid moment didn't last long, though the crisis with the boys seemed to have passed.

As time continued to pass in Damien's bunker, Sirina and Tasha felt increasing despair. Their lives were unfulfilling, unsatisfying and increasingly depressing. Meanwhile, one by one, more of their fellow female members of Damien's corps of lovelies were falling under the strange affect of Damien's machines. There were more "Liani's" and that trend was not going to stop.

One evening, Tasha decided she could wait no longer. When Radigan came home, she confronted him.

"I'm taking a risk," she started. "You have eyes. You can see what's being done to the other women. Is that how you want me, Radigan? Do you want a mindless toy? Do I deny you such that you have a need to throttle me? I don't want to live in that way. I don't want to be like Liani, lost from the world. The wonderful person she was has been lost and it's a terrible loss for humanity. Is this what you see as raising up mankind? Because Liani is no longer capable of recognizing she's being used, does that excuse it? How is this different than life under the prince? What's happened to you?"

Radigan blinked, like coming out of a coma. He paused and looked at her.

"You don't understand, Tasha."

"You don't understand, Radigan," she snapped. "You're not the one who'll be warped."

Chapter Fifteen
~ Returning Home ~

Aron stepped out of the wilds back into the borderlands region of the kingdom; a strange feeling since, in essence, he'd been driven out of his haven. His plans to build an impregnable fortress in the wilds as a bastion of safety for his people, were being abandoned out of necessity. Now he was back in open ground where the prince could take action if he so chose.

They rode to the nearest village, a place Aron had been before and talked to the local commander of the royal forces. He was surprised to see only a skeleton crew remained of the once formidable imperial army presence. A low ranking officer was left in charge. He eyed Aron's forces nervously, unsure whether to run, or run fast.

Aron brought his horse to a halt in front of the young officer and his few troops.

"What's happened here? Where is your army?"

"Most of the army has returned to the capital. It's said there's unrest all across the land. The king looks to protect the nobles. He leaves commoners on their own for protection. It doesn't surprise me."

"I see. You can stand down, soldier. We're not here to harm you. Actually we're on the run too from a new danger. I think you should join our forces for mutual defense. Alone, neither of us stands any chance against what's coming. If the rest of the borderlands deployments are like here, perhaps we can send word and gather everyone together."

"What of the prince, Aron? Yes, we all know who you are and we know the prince's grievances. Do you think he'll be tolerant of us not fulfilling his charge to bring you to justice?"

The Black Fist and the masters all laughed heartily.

“If you wish to arrest us, lieutenant, you can try,” said Trent mirthfully.

“You know what I mean,” he huffed indignantly. “The prince has a long memory for those who wrong him. You’re asking we forgo our status as loyal citizens and loyal soldiers. We’re not traitors. That’s not a small thing.”

“Calm yourself, son,” said Galean. “The world we all knew is about to end. What will come in its place, I can’t be sure. What you’re being asked is to choose between sure death sitting here like pigeons, or banding together with us for a chance at survival. We aren’t guaranteeing you’ll be safe and prosper in our ranks, but at least you’d have a fighting chance. It’s pretty clear the prince abandoned his foolish plan in coming here. You’re nothing more than a delaying force, pawns to be sacrificed until they form a defense against the enemy. Is that how you want to end your days, as meaningless fodder?”

“No, my lord,” shouted all of his men. The lieutenant shrugged in defeat.

The villagers had been standing nearby listening to the exchange. The leader stepped forward.

“All of the villages are with you, Aron. You spared us the abuse of the royal army before. After you acted, things became better very quickly. We are eternally thankful to you for that. Whatever you need, just tell us.”

Aron looked at all of the faces before him and remembered the vast throng on the screen worshipping Damien - a chilling thought. Again, people put their trust in him and Aron didn’t really want the responsibility. Damien craved the attention like Aron never would. Aron couldn’t grasp anyone would want to be where Damien was back then and where he wanted to be again.

“I don’t really have any great plans to share with you,” Aron explained honestly. “It appears we’re matched against a foe unlike any ever seen. This is your home, but I must tell you, you’re right in the path of the enemy. I say the enemy even though they haven’t yet threatened anyone. They’re design is not going to be good for people like us. Damien has his vision, but I don’t think it’s a whole lot different than the vision of the prince. I want to say you should make up your own mind about him, but I fear once you’re in his snare, there is no escape. That leaves you with making a critical decision based on my impressions. I don't like the situation, but there it is."

"What do you think we should do, Aron?"

"I haven't talked to Galean about it, but I think the entire frontier villages need to draw back and consolidate with other villages farther from the border. Unfortunately, that might start a mass relocation which reduces the ability to grow crops to feed ourselves. If Damien turns to the kingdom with the idea of invasion, the whole frontier is flatlands and poorly defensible. The retreat might end up leading us into the heart of the kingdom. Whether the prince and the royal host would treat us as friends or rebels, I can't say. All of your options are risks. Do you want to add anything, Galean?"

"I'd say you've summed it up well, Aron. This is the choice we'll offer to every village. This isn't the choice any of us would want, but circumstances dictate our moves. We're left with trying to cope."

The villagers stared glassy eyed. Finally their leader looked around.

"I think we need to move. I trust Aron's judgment about this. I don't want to stay here unprotected against whatever comes across the border."

The villagers nodded assent and immediately went to pack their things.

Aron turned to Galean. "I hope this isn't another big mistake. Maybe these people would be better off staying here. We don't know that Damien will be coming after us, and even if he did, these villagers pose no threat to him. He might just pass them by. After all, he's already got Liani, Tasha, Sirina, Radigan, Straga, and the bulk of the thugs. We're a force to be wary of, but in a real war against vast armies, we're nothing. There's nothing in our group critical to him and his purposes."

"What he fears, Aron, is our resistance. You can inspire though you don't acknowledge it. See how our passing through the realm created a groundswell of unrest against the prince and the monarchy. That is a possibility Damien has to worry about. No matter how invincible he seems with his devices, if he's isolated and alone without masses of followers, he's limited in what he can do. Granted he can cause terrible losses with his strange weapons and devises, but against all of mankind he couldn't hope to prevail. He knows this. He's busy amassing forces because he knows we won't be the only ones to fight him. All of those powerful nations Abdurka speaks of, those leaders will not simply concede their power and positions to Damien. He looks to re-fight the ancient war to have a different outcome."

"The ancient war destroyed the world," said Trent.

"His delusions don't include regrets or any sense of personal blame for what happened before. This is the true danger of Damien. He has no heart. He cares only for his selfish goals and has no conscience about who he sacrifices along the way," Galean replied soberly.

"What's our plan in the meantime, Aron?" asked Brock who'd walked over with Cherine.

"Keep moving away from him, I guess. If we can weave a network from the villagers and the remaining royal forces as we go, maybe we can provide some small defense to protect them. I'm planning on Galean discovering a means to level the fight and put us on an even footing to deter and defeat him."

Everyone chuckled, except Galean.

"Aron, don't put your faith in me because I'm just a man and eventually I'll let you down."

"I'm just a man too, Galean. You're seeing through my eyes. I keep trying to tell everybody not to put their trust in me because I don't know what to do either. I'm a glorified farmer, out of control."

It didn't take long before the villagers gathered again, ready to move.

"Aron, I'm sending messengers all along the frontier with your instructions to evacuate the border," said Cherine.

Aron nodded and signaled for the beginning of the migration.

* * * *

Prince Agar settled in to a new life at the palace. He was in the same residence, but in a radically different atmosphere. The embarrassing parade of nubile young women no longer passed through his quarters. Instead, his personal guards protecting the entrance to the suites increased in size and in belligerence. Granor's sympathizers in the palace guard could no longer even approach the princely suite. The only persons allowed to approach were single messengers, or couriers from the king himself or from the field.

Coraline was overwhelmed with Agar back in her life, and now in her face. Though she'd pined for the companionship of a spouse, the reality was now all of her private and personal time was gone. She could still spend time with the queen, but most of her other friendships were stunted, especially if those friends were male. This was a period of great change to evolve into her new roles and wasn't necessarily always movements in directions she wanted to go. Though Agar was a changed man, he was still a domineering person by nature. For his wishes to ascend and for her wishes to descend came easy. Arguing with him wasn't something she felt she could safely do.

Meanwhile Granor noted the new reality and changed his tactics accordingly. He was no fool. He abandoned his nefarious plan to ensnare Princess Coraline and use her to further his ambitions. She was too dangerous an option with the vigilant prince so close at hand. Also, Marin was not a person to trifle with.

"Coraline, have you had any further problems with Granor?" asked the prince at dinner one evening.

"No, I don't see him at all. The only time I leave our suite is to go to the queen. I'm surrounded by a full troop when I go. I'm in no danger from him, Agar."

"Good, that's one less problem to worry about. I'm still getting very disturbing reports from the borderlands. If they're true, Aron was driven out of the wilds. I would have been ecstatic to hear that last year at this time. Now I'm troubled. Whatever could defeat Aron is something of concern to all of us. The king has sent observers to assess the situation so we can properly prepare the heartland in case there is war. He gave me the choice to go or to stay. I chose to remain with you, darling."

"I'm grateful, husband." She tried to sound neutral and keep her frustration at being cooped up out of her tone. "What of the rest of the realm?"

"We pulled back the army, so those regions have nothing to complain about. They're left to their own devices at this point."

"Agar, I think that's actually a good thing and may generate good will at a time when we need their support. They won't forget all of the abuses, but with this relative freedom, it can take some of the hatred out of them."

"Perhaps, Coraline... How the world has changed. I wonder if I'd never stopped at your village I could have avoided all that's happened since then."

"A person could draw that conclusion."

"You might be Aron's wife living with him on his father's farm."

Coraline chuckled. “It would have been a much different life.”

“Would you trade for that life if you could?”

“I was always fond of Aron, but never felt I was the right woman for him. He was taken with my beauty, but we were so young then. I don’t think he ever had mature love for me. See how quickly he began to pursue Tasha.”

“Tasha,” said Agar wistfully.

“Men love her, Agar. You still do.”

“I was under her spell, but I’m finally able to look at her rationally. Coraline, I wouldn’t choose her over you.”

“I appreciate your statement, but I’m not naïve, Agar. If you could get her back, you would.”

“Perhaps not, wife... you judge me as I was. I tell you I’m changed. Someday I hope to be able to convince you of that truth.”

“I’ll be waiting for that day, Agar.”

They chuckled and embraced. To have genuine feelings and share rapport for Coraline after living a life of pretend and façade, was such a reverse in their relationship.

They heard the sound of drums in the courtyard as the troop mustered to head for the borderlands.

“Our soldiers do look good,” said Coraline as they walked out on their balcony to watch the spectacle. “I like the look of a man in uniform.” Agar stood behind her at the railing embracing her in his heavy cloak against the sharp cold gusts whipping down from the north. Her long blond hair blew across their faces. Agar kissed her neck.

Trumpets blasted and the column began to move in the direction of the main city gates. Rank after rank, the soldiers marched in perfect unison. The king and queen looked tiny standing on the steps far below acknowledging the salute of the troops. The soldiers gave a loud martial shout as they filed away. The king and queen walked back into the palace.

“Do you want to eat with them tonight, Agar?”

“It would be prudent with Granor lurking about.”

“I must tell you, Agar, I’m happy for the protection, but this life is very restricting. I only see the queen now. I did have friends you realize.”

"I hope this is only a temporary measure, my dear. As I'm able, I'll try to accompany you so you can see those friends. Will that be a problem?"

"Yes and no. If I have female friends, we won't feel free to commiserate in our conversations with you sitting right there. If I have male friends, they'll think you're jealous, and you probably would be. They'd be in fear of your wrath."

He chuckled. "I'm sure I give you plenty to commiserate about. I understand what you're saying. We'll figure out some solution, Coraline. I just don't want you in a position where Granor can make an unexpected move. With what Aron did here in the palace, I'm very wary. Trust is a rare commodity nowadays in the palace, or in the realm for that matter. Was Granor one of your male friends?"

She paused. "I didn't see him as a threat, so I guess he could have been a friend. He was usually occupied with the king, so I didn't have a great deal of contact. His proposition when we were dancing was a total surprise to me. I would never have thought that of him, and doing so in public was shocking. I didn't know how to react."

"You reacted as you should have, Coraline. You put your trust in me and now we're the better for it."

Coraline's contemplative look confused Agar. His paranoid feelings were growing with each setback. Coraline was one of the few people he felt he could trust, and yet she could have deep seated feelings and perhaps even schemes of her own. That wasn't reflected in any facts, but simply personal demons rising up to plague him.

He wavered on whether to press her for the truth. She simply got up and went to her dressing table and began to comb her beautiful long hair.

* * * *

Granor moved swiftly with his closest associates as they entered an obscure room in a little used part of the palace.

"I'm sending a fast moving squad out to the borderlands. You'll have twenty men which should be enough to deter attack from random highwaymen, but not a force large enough to evoke a response from the army troops on duty in the provinces you pass through. When you get to the border, you are to enter the wilds and seek out this enemy who has chased off Aron. I want you to make contact on my behalf to assess their intentions as well as their ability to carry out those intentions. If they are such a force as they're being portrayed, we want to be sure we're on the winning side. Do you have any questions?"

The men shook their heads.

"Move quickly and avoid drawing notice. Don't engage in fighting except to defend an attack. If you're captured by the army and questioned, I'll disavow any knowledge of you. Don't make any mistakes. Leave tonight in the dark and travel far enough to be out of the range of the city patrols. I've arranged for sympathizers to watch for you along the way. They will seek you out. Once again, be careful. We're at a vulnerable point now with the prince returned and taking up residence again. He's suspicious of everyone and that limits some of the things I planned to do. It's a setback, but we've overcome setbacks before."

The men nodded in agreement and silently left the room to return to their barracks. Granor went to his room to change clothes for his meetings with the king. Again he would take Lilith, the woman with the best mind and a sassy personality. She stood out to Granor because she could have had other options for her life, potentially better options. Yet she chose to follow Granor. Lilith was born into a family with limited means who'd managed to get her placed into service in the palace at great price hoping she could escape the poverty that was their fate.

Lilith had been a difficult servant. She questioned everything and with her sometimes sharp tongue, often suffered punishment which failed to curb her transgressions. Granor ran unto her while she was in the midst of yet another demeaning chore stemming from insolence in the face of a noble woman. She was only too eager to escape her bondage to follow Granor. The price of her commitment to him was a common one in the palace under the prince's decayed moral standard. She shrugged it off afterwards as meaningless, the price of doing business for a woman in the kingdom. Something in her dignity in spite of her circumstances caught Granor's attention and she held it from that point forward. She was one of his favorite women now and he wasn't one who put great store in any woman.

"Lilith, I'd like you to talk with Princess Coraline and the queen tonight. They'll be seated together, but I've managed that our seats will be straight across the table from them. If you can garner their favor, you can possibly work your way into Coraline's narrow circle of friends. With Agar returned, he keeps a close watch over her. I'm not sure what he's planning, but whatever it is, I need to be ready. Will you do that for me?"

"Of course, my lord..." she replied with an enigmatic smile.

"You know I'm not a lord. To tell you the truth, I wouldn't want to be a noble."

"You're a noble to me. I'm as low as you can go amongst palace denizens. What would you like me to find out from her?"

"Nothing, if you question either of them, it will put them on guard. Simply listen to what they say. You may hear some inadvertent slip of the tongue we can use to our advantage."

"Yes, master."

Granor chuckled. "Master… I think there is no man who could be your master, Lilith?"

She looked straight ahead, but the hint of a smile played on her face. She had shoulder length brown hair that women would die for, full of body and sheen, but in her life, beauty had been a curse rather than a benefit. It drew notice to her and that was usually never good in the palace. When a man looked at her, she never responded.

"I won't disappoint you, master," she added, gazing directly in his eyes.

"Wear that white dress, the one with the frills. You look angelic in that. An angel at my side is exactly what I want tonight."

* * * *

Aron's trek was slow and tedious with the large number of civilians he was accumulating along the way. Feeding so many from sparse supplies was an ongoing problem. Each village was cleaned out which sustained them in the short term, but didn't solve long term issues.

He sent Trent back as a rear guard to watch the border for any signs of pursuit from Damien's forces. He had no way to know Damien had exited the other side of the wilds to go to his new bunker.

* * * *

While Aron approached familiar grounds, Damien was dispatching probes into the adjacent nations. His converts and his army were growing incredibly fast as word of the wonders of his weapons and technology spread. His public spectacles were the routine rather than the exception. No one was allowed to approach him directly, so his aura grew about his higher state as a being of power and authority transcending that of any nation's leader. He was returned to the world to rescue it from the decay and the malaise of totalitarian dictators and autocratic rule. He was a living miracle. At least that was the story perpetuated to the masses.

What went on in private was a closely guarded secret. Many of those involved in Damien's private life were women in the same state as Liani, seemingly changed, compliant and unaware. Damien was no moral champion - no one mattered but him.

He orchestrated his sham marriage to Liani for public dissemination, but it wasn't a commitment of two people happily joined for a life journey, yet another ruse to portray him as the 'family man.' Nothing could have been farther from the truth. Liani was still held prisoner inside her mind, unable to change her state. Tasha wondered if the real Liani even knew she was now married. Damien was not a man tied to just one woman; he had a bevy of defenseless beauties caught in his artificial thrall available for his attentions. That was another way he wished to repeat history, his nefarious history.

Tasha observed it all, helpless to save Liani, or any other woman. As the number of women in Damien's cadre that still had free will and conscious awareness shrunk, Tasha's fear increased. The end of this process for her was obvious and Radigan didn't seem disposed to protect her. He was increasingly distracted about their relationship and focused on "the work." Damien's excesses escalated and became bolder since there were none who could deter him.

Tasha only had Sirina to confide in. Both were terrified and increasingly fatalistic about their future. Sirina wanted to fight for her boys to spare them service as fodder for Damien's army, but she was powerless in the face of their fate. Straga was no comfort at all. He was even worse in following Damien's way, and he too, began to emulate Damien in living life in a low way.

Both women discussed some radical alternatives, none were palatable. Among those choices were ending their lives, and the lives of Sirina's sons by suicide - a terrible dilemma with no good options.

"Aron always has found a way to save me," said Tasha sadly. "This time I'm afraid I've run out of miracles and it's due to my own mistakes. I've foolishly wounded Aron deeply so I have no right to expect any help from him. There's no one else capable of dealing with Damien."

The women stared at each other in the midst of their distress. Making a serious choice to take a life ending step was no easy decision.

With no hope and no light at the end of the tunnel, they arrived at a place of desperation.

"I'm sickened at the prospect of killing my boys," said Sirina. "I don't know if I can do it, yet for them to march off into battle as part of Damien's mob, is inconceivable. How could my life have gotten to this point? What did I do wrong to deserve it?"

"This isn't punishment for our sins, Sirina. This is just the abuse of power and nothing more. Damien isn't any nobler than the prince. There's nothing about him which I find to be higher like he wants us to think. He's a man who has control of these devices which shackle us. Without them, he wouldn't measure up to the real men, like Aron. I just can't give up hope yet. As unlikely as it would be for us to be saved, I'm sure Liani felt the same way when she was kidnapped by the Chenese. Aron found a way. As long as we're still in control of our faculties, we have hope."

"Tasha, I think that could change quickly. Damien doesn't want intelligence in his women, he wants subservience. He wants them compliant because he knows he could never win their trust and support with his character. A bevy of beautiful women standing behind him makes an impression on dull minds. That's what's important to him, the impression, the façade he perpetuates."

"As a last resort, Sirina, if our time is up and they propose to subject our minds to their machines, we should refuse them. We should demand to be put to death in lieu of their atrocities. There are plenty of other pretty faces."

"Perhaps that would shock Radigan and Straga, Tasha. I have no better idea. If we're to lose the lives we've known, I don't want to see the end for my sons if they're shipped away and sacrificed. Dying would be my choice too."

* * * *

Aron felt mixed emotions riding past his father's farm. If Coraline and Tasha had been there with him, perhaps he could have felt some joy, but there were no warm feelings for Aron at this point. Instead he felt empty and alone. His parents were riding beside him, but no one said a word, they just stared at a lifetime of memories lost. Their companion now was sadness.

Riding into their abandoned village they were amazed at how quickly the town had eroded as plants tried to reclaim the land.

"We'll camp here for the night," said Aron. Cherine nodded and called a halt to the column.

Here in Aron's old haunts, not to think of the women was impossible. Coraline the princess was not the person he'd grown up with, and Tasha, the love of his life, had forsaken him. This struck him painfully in his most vulnerable places. Even the thought of Liani, who'd been at his elbow and so important a person to him, was seemingly lost without hope of release from the strange power of Damien.

Galean, who had always been Aron's inspiration, experienced deep depression and a malaise of the soul. Liani had been a much more significant person in Galean's life than Aron had realized.

Brock made a habit of spending most of his free time with his father, Barmon, who was especially suffering from the dire turn of events. Barmon and Aron found it easy to take a fatalistic look at their futures after the humiliation in Damien's camp.

* * * *

Aron went over to sit with Brock and Barmon on this evening. They nodded acknowledgment, but no one spoke. Aron looked at Barmon as he stared away at nothing in particular. His spirit had been extracted and all that remained was a shell, one filled with rage.

Brock was angry too, but still clearly functional. Barmon had the look of someone itching for death in battle.

"Barmon, are you dealing with this?" Aron asked.

Barmon looked at him, barely able to hold back his hatred.

"Do I need to answer your question, Aron?"

"I wish there was something we could do, Barmon. I feel the same way that you do."

"Do you, Aron? You suffer, I'll grant you that, but somehow what's happened for us isn't the same. Sirina, my loving wife, was ripped away from me. When I thought I had her back in body and spirit, this outrage happened. Again I was helpless to save her. To answer your question, no I'm not handling this."

Aron paused. He wanted to give Barmon solace, but there was nothing he could say. He could find no solace for himself, much less someone else.

"I think perhaps the Black Fist should gather this evening to excise our grim feelings," said Brock.

"That's an excellent idea, brother. What do you say, Barmon?"

"It beats sitting here stewing…"

"We'll see Damien again," Aron continued. "I'll look forward to that day."

"Aye," said the other two darkly.

After the evening meal when the Black Fist gathered, it escalated as the masters quickly joined in along with Cherine, and even the villagers chose to participate. They were a people in need of catharsis and sparring vigorously was their avenue. The spirited bouts didn't solve their problems, but did ease their stress somewhat, at least for a short time.

Aron fought multiple opponents to exhaustion. Barmon was ferocious in his bouts. His fighting prowess had grown exponentially over time with expert training and steady practice. Adding in the emotions of strong hatred had made him a deadly opponent, even in practice.

Later, Aron walked into the main building where he'd been plucked by the prince and his soldiers and forced on this trying life's journey. The memory, clear as a bell, of with beautiful Coraline flirting with the prince and a sullen Tasha reacting impetuously when the others were commandeered into royal servitude, haunted him - a day Aron would gladly have excised from his life.

This version of Aron had lost his youthful optimism. Grim determination remained. He didn't feel fated to prevail in the end against Damien. All that he hoped to do was to go down in a blaze and take as many enemies with him as possible - a sad state of affairs but his reality nonetheless. He fought daily to mask pessimism from his companions. When he was looked to for inspiration and hope, he merely smiled bravely. That smile was a lie. The truth: Aron was a lot closer to Barmon's grim fatalistic state than anybody realized. They both hungered for revenge against Damien and his ilk. Nothing else in life motivated them at that point.

One exception existed for Aron, though. When he saw Jenn and her tiny daughters was virtually the only time his heart melted even slightly. She made no attempt to hide her wishes. Aron understood her very clearly, but his jumbled emotions wouldn't allow him to move on from Tasha or Liani. Jenn didn't let that deter her. She came often to dine with

Aron and the little girls would sit beside him, hug him and talk to him. This was comforting, but not enough to blot out his pain and feelings of rejection from Tasha.

Caught in a painful emotional loop, he could find no way to escape.

Cherine came over to talk to him.

"Aron, we're all very concerned for you. We understand your feelings about Tasha, but you can't allow it to define the rest of your life. She made a choice, but doesn't mean you have no choices. We're at a precarious state and need you at your best. Do you see? I don't want to seem presumptuous to force you in directions we would have you go. It stems from love and concern for you as a person. You've come to be very important in the lives of so many. Dwelling on Tasha and the past just doesn't serve a good purpose now. I'm afraid you must let it go."

"I know, Cherine. I appreciate everyone who wants to help me, but there's something I just can't put to rest. In spite of my personal woes, I can't just abandon Liani to such a fate. In her case, I don't believe she chose to follow Damien, so I can't leave her like prey caught in a spider web waiting to be devoured, I can't do it."

"What do you propose to do, Aron?"

"That's what I've been thinking about, Cherine."

Chapter Sixteen
~ Royal Maneuvers ~

The life of intrigues was not unknown in the palace and in the capital city of Nephora. Manipulations designed to gain favor, prestige, and increased power was the norm, not the aberration. The difference was the quantum shift in perceptions; for the first time, the royal class felt threatened. As impossible as it would have seemed to them not so long ago, the unexplainable events in the skies on an increasing basis hinted at momentous changes coming their way - potentially adverse changes to them and their secure positions of power.

The list of their sins was nearly endless and the thought of being subject to retribution by the aggrieved general populace was a frightening prospect. That wasn't even taking into consideration the threat of this new invasion force armed with secrets and weapons too frightening to even contemplate. Suspicions grew rapidly, as well as, alliances.

"Come, Coraline," said the queen. "I've arranged for us to take a ride out to the royal gardens to picnic and enjoy the sunshine. The tone in the palace is distressing and I think a break away from it for a day would be just the tonic we need to salve our spirits."

"Of course, your majesty," Coraline replied. "Are you including Lilith?"

"I am, unless that's a problem for you. She's a fresh face with a buoyant spirit. She brightens my day when she's around."

"I like Lilith also, my queen. I have no objection to including her. I agree she's a delight as a companion."

"I know you very well, Coraline. There is something you're not telling me. Is there something I should know about Lilith?"

"I'm sorry, my queen, I should be better at controlling my worries. It isn't Lilith I have an issue with, it's the fact she's a companion of Granor. I shouldn't say this without involving my husband first, but Agar feels Granor is working some deception and he worries the king doesn't recognize it. I don't want to wrongly accuse Granor of anything for I have no proof to present to you, but in any dealings where he's even remotely involved, I'm very wary. Lately I've picked up on some troubling implications. If Lilith is his agent, we must be careful about her. Am I making any sense to you, my queen?"

The queen frowned. "Let me tell you something, Coraline, for I trust you more than my own daughters. The king and I are not as unobservant as our son thinks. The king is constantly on his guard for schemes and ruses. It's the nature of our positions to face such things. Granor has proven himself to be very valuable and trustworthy to interests of the crown in the past. That notwithstanding, his majesty exercises caution with even his closest allies, and that includes his own children. I know you understand. Until recently, Agar had been a disappointment to us, and the possibility he might choose to accelerate his ascension to the throne was a danger we guarded against. Now we feel he's matured and evolved enough to extend him our trust. In your case, Coraline, you're a lot of the reason we feel we can trust him. You wouldn't allow him to work ill against us. That wasn't the case before you came into our lives. The king and I would trust our lives in your hands, dear, and now vicariously that includes the crown prince as a result. The king has also noted some subtle changes in Granor's behavior. He's secretly worked with Agar to screen the royal palace guards to determine how many of them might be under Granor's sway. Agar has assigned his most trusted members of his personal guards to watch the king's guards for signs of treachery. Most of the king's guards are exemplary soldiers, but the chance a few bad apples can hide among them is a possibility we won't tolerate."

"Your majesty, that makes me feel so much better to hear you say this. I've come to know you in our time together so I knew you were no fool. His majesty, the king, is another person I've come to respect. I'll be honest with you because I too trust my life in your hands. I couldn't countenance Agar's vile ways when we married, but more than that, I couldn't accept the life of the noble class in general. Their lack of regard for basic decency, their abuse of power in misusing royal assets and the populace was appalling to me. To attach myself in anyway was like tacit agreement of those ways and an impossible dilemma for me. I would never pretend I'm a perfect person as I've made grievous mistakes in my time, but I was in a position I could never accept and worried I was headed for a dark ending. I was a village girl. From my point of view, it didn't seem such a difficult task to live an upstanding and decent life, to respect others, no matter their class or station, and to try to do goodness in this world."

The queen got a sad look. "I think if women ran the world, things would be much better."

Coraline chuckled.

"I didn't mean this as a humor," said the queen, but she started to chuckle also. That led to both of the women laughing heartily about the queen's poor opinion of men running the world.

"Perhaps we should discuss this with the king to teach him the error of his ways?" asked Coraline flippantly.

They laughed again until their sides hurt.

Their door opened and Lilith walked in. She looked at them with an amused smile.

"What humor have I missed, ladies?"

"It's nothing, Lilith," the queen replied. "We were just exercising our lungs."

"As you wish, my queen," Lilith replied with a bow of her head.

"You look lovely today, Lilith," said Coraline. "You must tell me the tailor who makes your dresses. I like that design of fabric and the color choice."

"Thank you, ma'am," she answered. "She's a woman I know who lives at the edge of the city. Of course I'll introduce you if that's your wish. The other women of our party are gathered in the courtyard, my queen. We're ready to leave at your command."

"We're ready now, dear. Come along, Coraline. Today has the makings of a very pleasant day."

Marin was waiting just outside the door with a troop of Agar's guards.

"Hello, Marin," said the queen as they walked past him.

"Your majesty," he replied.

The guard's fell into step just behind the women and went down to the courtyard where the horses were tethered and ready for the ride to the royal gardens.

Coraline noticed Granor off to the side with a number of his men. Lilith never looked over in his direction.

Coraline glanced at Marin.

"We see them," he whispered. "Don't draw attention. Visit with your companions. We have your backs, ma'am."

Coraline smiled warmly. She saw him blink in reaction at her affection. It always gave her satisfaction she could so easily affect men's emotions. This had always been true in her life and even more so now that she had the added aura of fame and power.

They rode away at a steady trot. Granor dispatched his small force at a discreet distance to follow them. He watched them ride off before he turned to go into the palace for his day with the king - a frustrating prospect because now Agar attended those sessions that Granor once had to himself. His slow and patient progress making inroads into the king's confidence were threatened by Agar's keen attention to everything said and done. The king was less inclined to simply follow Granor's suggestions now, almost like Granor was thrown back to his first day of service to the king. Agar was a totally changed person. His youthful impetuousness was missing, replaced by cool calculation and savvy moves; a remarkable transformation, but for Granor a dire turn of events.

As he expected when he went into the royal throne room Agar was already there speaking with the king. They looked at Granor who smiled back placidly.

"Good morning, your majesties."

"Granor, good morning to you," the king replied. "Have you dined? There is coffee and pastries on the table. Help yourself."

"I've eaten, thank you, sire. What topic did you wish to discuss today?"

"My son feels it prudent to re-align the army. He's of the opinion that invasion is imminent from the direction of the wilds. Although we don't have enough information on our potential enemy, we've taken steps to gather that information."

Granor was surprised. "Oh, what steps, your majesty. I wasn't informed of this."

"I regret we didn't feel we had time to delay, Granor, as it was a matter of some urgency. I'm sure you understand."

"Of course, your majesty, I aim only to serve you."

The king didn't give Granor any further explanation which struck Granor as odd. Rather, the king continued to speak in low tones with his son. Agar basically ignored Granor.

Granor fidgeted while waiting to be included; another turn in events not anticipated.

When the king stood up and walked to the door with Agar, he stopped and looked back.

"Are you ill, Granor? You don't seem your normal self today."

"I'm sorry, your majesty. I wasn't sure what you desired of me. You were intent in your discussion with the crown prince."

"Well, get up. We have matters which need our attention. Come along now."

* * * *

Meanwhile, the women made the hour ride to the royal gardens. There were twenty women in the party which included the princesses, birth daughters of the queen, and various wives of nobles, confidants, and acquaintances. No men were in the group other than Marin and his guards. This was a change in routine because the queen normally included handsome young courtesans to accompany her party.

"They're nice to look at," she'd confided to Coraline to both of their amusement.

The women luxuriated in lush green surroundings spreading out blankets on the grass to sit and place picnic meals. As always, Marin stationed himself very close to Coraline. The remainder of his small force was spaced around the perimeter. Marin didn't bring a large force because a nearby army post barracks with adequate troops was available if trouble developed and the royal gardens were centered in a heavily populated area. Staging a kidnapping attempt here would be a poor choice both in terms of location and limited escape routes.

The gardens were carefully maintained and immaculately groomed. An entire host of workers were assigned to the head groundskeeper and did nothing else other than work in the gardens. Over the ages, the kings had imported rare and exotic plants from all over the kingdom. The botanical display now was colorful, the scents pleasing and the design original. The garden was one of the good things the nobility had done in the kingdom, but still self serving because the general populace wasn't allowed admittance to enjoy the splendor and the serenity of the scene.

Coraline talked and laughed with the other ladies and enjoyed the doting queen favoring her over her birth daughters. The princesses were jealous and could be petty and vindictive, but knew they were powerless to truly affect Coraline who smiled blithely and ignored their small barbs. It wasn't a situation Coraline had concocted and she felt no guilt for the dilemma of the princesses. They authored their own travails with their poor choices and character flaws.

Although she paid no attention to him outwardly, she was always aware of where Marin was. Just seeing him was reassuring and gave her a feeling of security. He was an impressive man who seemed the measure of any danger they might face. In a way he was familiar, she thought of Aron when she was near Marin. He was always stoic, seemingly unperturbed by anything, and all business. Secretly, Coraline knew he had developed feelings for her in the brief time they'd been together. On rare occasion Marin had interceded on her behalf even with the princesses. Marin wasn't royalty, but at the same time he was a man no one would trifle with. Another comfort to Coraline was that he buffered against the petty female slights of the jealous courtyard women.

On this sunny day, all seemed right with the world and hard to imagine anything other than peace and tranquility in the kingdom. That was far from the reality of the situation as the old ways were being stretched, twisted and skewed in many strange directions. Royal control over the outlying provinces had virtually been lost. Agar's ongoing realignments of the imperial army didn't offer protection for those provinces.

Granor's scouts were perched out of sight, but still nearby, monitoring the event. As usual, they saw no weaknesses in Marin's defenses.

What no one there knew was that Granor's spies weren't the only eyes on the scene. High above one of the satellites remaining from the ancient days recorded them and everything else in Nephora and sent the transmission back to Damien's new headquarters. Daily transmissions were coded and analyzed by the computers automatically and cached for later retrieval by Damien. The system assessed the data and assigned relative importance to each of the scenes - part of the battle preparation the equipment was designed for. In the case of a picnic, the system recognized there were key figures exposed and vulnerable to attack. During the war, this system could have instantly dispatched air warships, or fired from weapons batteries mounted in space on the satellite stations.

Damien hadn't yet been able to determine his available weaponry. He couldn't travel to space to inspect the stations to see what was depleted, inoperable, damaged or simply decayed over the ages. If he opted to fire on any point on the planet, he couldn't be sure if anything would happen, or if he'd blow up his own stations in the attempt. Similarly, he couldn't tell if his worldwide storage bunkers had any functional weapons remaining. The stations remained able to direct cameras at the planet so Damien could see most parts of the world. He didn't see any signs of a surviving high civilization. From what he could see on the surface, the whole world had reverted to barbarism and lost the ancient technology. He smiled at the idea he was free of viable threats at last.

Back at the palace, Agar was busily replacing Granor as his father's main counselor. He didn't look at Granor directly, but out of the corner of his eye could see the frustration Granor tried to hide. He made no accommodation to Granor, and simply dominated his father's attention and time.

It wasn't merely a blocking maneuver on his part. Agar laid out his strategy to the king about the menace in the wilds. Daily, reports came in of soldiers, villagers, and Aron's forces retreating and showing no indication they planned to make a stand.

"It would seem our friend, Aron, has opted to risk royal forgiveness rather than face this new enemy, father. It's definitely a situation we can work to our advantage any number of ways."

"I agree, Agar. This is a fortuitous turn, but I fear this strange menace. I'm told the Arreck army has redeployed. They no longer stack their defenses against us. They too feel the real danger is from the wilds. Who would have ever thought that during my reign as king the realm would experience such momentous times? I wish I could say I'm pleased about it, but if we're on the verge of a great calamity, my name will go down in infamy as the king who oversaw our ending."

"It's a grim reality, father. What do your people hear, Granor?"

"I have nothing beyond what you've been able to gather. The populace is frightened. It's a dangerous situation outside the city because now people are hoarding and fighting over food. They recognize these are not normal times and are trying to make their own attempts to survive whatever is coming. I don't think the farmers are planting crops. It's not good."

"We must maintain food supplies," the king replied thoughtfully. "We have royal reserves, but without the usual trade and the flow of foodstuffs even we could be put in jeopardy."

"I can change the orders of the royal host, father. We can send them back out to provide protection for the farms. We can't provide for the entire realm, but enough of it to keep us supplied."

"Go ahead with that idea, Agar. We'll need to keep a close watch because the situation could change rapidly. Do you have anything to add, Granor?"

"No sire. Your plans are just what I would have recommended."

"Then we're all in agreement. I have some matters to see about. I'll leave you to your work, gentlemen."

"Did you require assistance with those matters, sire?"

"No, Granor. These are minor things I can handle. You may have this day to see about your own affairs."

"Yes, sire. If you have need of me you have but to send word and I'll come immediately."

"Thank you, Granor. Son, I'll see you later for the evening meal. The queen advised me she'd be coming back in the late afternoon."

"We'll be there, father."

Granor waited a moment to see if the king would invite him also, something of an expectation until recently. Now he sensed it prudent to assume nothing.

The king went in one direction and Agar in another. Granor watched them a moment before he turned and went to his quarters. Feeling like he was followed, he glanced backward several times. He saw no one, but the feeling remained. Granor tended toward paranoia in the best of circumstances. Here where he worried his position was in danger, he was doubly cautious.

"Damn you, Agar," he muttered as he closed his door to his rooms.

* * * *

While Agar was busy with his plans, Aron slowly approached the heart of the kingdom. It was from no desire to return, but only from his concern for his followers. There was still no sign of pursuit from Damien, but that wasn't reassuring with the strange powers and devices at his disposal. Perhaps he didn't need to pursue Aron to accomplish his goals. Aron couldn't be sure.

Between retreating villagers and the massing of the remaining royal army forces, Aron's force continued to grow. By the time he left the borderland territory, the numbers were prodigious and was only because the villagers brought supplies that everybody got fed. Those supplies weren't unlimited.

"I'm surprised we haven't encountered Agar's legions yet," Galean commented after their stop for the evening. "They certainly know we're here. I wonder what it is that would occupy their attention over a chance to confront us."

"I've wondered the same thing, Galean. We're sitting ducks here."

"I'll send scouts ahead to forewarn us," said Cherine.

"Tell them not to engage. We don't want to start any fights at this point. Just come back and tell us what's ahead."

"The prince may not give us an option, Aron. He won't have forgotten his grievances against you and the rest of us. In his eyes, we're traitors and conspirators. I don't know if he realizes the threat Damien poses. The prince hasn't been known for the wisest of decisions. This time his petulance could lead to the end of us."

"I can only judge on the moves we see him making, Cherine. Because he's pulled back the army and repositioned them in a defensive array to protect the heart of the kingdom tells me he's using his head for a change. I'm not naïve to think he'll welcome us back with open arms, but I think there's a chance to work out some sort of accommodation in the meantime. When Damien comes, it will be all that any of us can cope with against his power."

"Do you have any regrets about leaving Liani behind? There is Tasha and Sirina too that are in compromised positions."

"Maybe they're better off there, Cherine. If we can't prevail, they'd be on the winning side. The people of the kingdom would suffer retribution. I didn't leave them out of spite because Tasha chose Radigan. I was only trying to save as many of the rest of us as possible."

Belisa approached flanked by Elcou and Trache and followed by the remainder of the Arreck command. "Aron, I must tell you something," she began. "I've experienced things I would never have imagined since I first met you. I learned so many lessons, not the least of which is humility. I've been brought low and I've learned to persevere and stand back up. You've been an instrument in teaching me about myself and all other peoples. You taught me courage in the face of defeat and finding a way to overcome it. You've suffered terrible emotional loss and pain I can only try to imagine when our dear Tasha went away. For that I'm truly sorry. I hope you see me as the closest of friends because you are dear to me as is no other. I love you, Aron, a human male and I truly mean it. The reason I'm here and saying these things now is I've talked with my brethren and we've come to a decision. If the future is war against Damien and his forces and terrible powers and weapons, we chose to fight with our people. I was too ashamed before to face my parents, but I'm moved by the urgency of our dire situation. Aron, I want to go home to make my stand with my people. I hope you can understand the spirit of this and not think I'm another friend casting you aside. Nothing could be farther from the truth. I'll cry at being apart from you, but it's the choice we must make while we still can."

Everybody was silent. This wasn't a turn anybody expected.

"Belisa, please don't feel I can't understand you. Your decision makes perfect sense. You should be with your people. It's been too long since you hugged your mother and father. Go with our blessing and know that I feel the same way about you. I love you too, Belisa."

Tears formed at the corner of her eyes.

"Maybe I'm just demented, but I'm not willing to concede defeat just yet. If there is a war, I can't guarantee I'll survive the first day, but what I will guarantee is I'll never give up and I'll never surrender. Tasha will be a dagger in my heart forever, but I hope the best for her. I'll never stop loving her. I hope she can find happiness in her life."

"That's a magnanimous thing to say, Aron and an example of why we all care for you so deeply. You're truly a good man."

She stepped close and they embraced. He felt his emotions welling up and hugged her tightly. She sobbed on his shoulder - a far more moving experience than he expected.

"I'm sorry, Aron," she whispered. "I was going to be strong, but I'm not. This is the hardest step I've ever had to take. I pray we will see each other again in life."

"You be very careful, darling," he replied gently. He kissed her tenderly before releasing her from his grasp. "Don't take any chances. Hurry home as fast as you can. I'll send word when I know what our situation will be concerning the prince. I would think a combined plan of defense is imperative."

"The Arreck nation stands with you, Aron," she said in a loud voice. All of the Arreck gave a martial shout. They left quickly, heading for their mountains and were gone from sight rapidly.

Aron watched them sadly and then turned to Enna and Biala.

"We're staying with you, Aron," said Enna grimly. "We miss our families too, but we made a choice to follow you to the end. If we prevail, we'll see our families again. If we're defeated, it won't matter. We'll either be dead, or slaves."

"We'll be dead," Biala added. "I won't allow them to do that to me."

Aron looked at his other friends. They were resolute, but no spark of fight lived in them. They'd all concluded a war could end only one way: badly. Trent sat silently beside Cherine; Brock was standing beside his father. Barmon's dark expression was always the same. His eyes smoldered with hatred and he clearly didn't fear death in combat. It seemed instead to be one of his goals. Aron's parents were sitting together, his father's arm around his mother. She looked on the verge of tears also. Galean had a vacant look in his eyes, like he could foresee the future and the sight of it drained away his courage. Abdurka was beside Galean lost in his thoughts, but he too looked very troubled. Drang-ku was a different person since Wu Hang had opted to stay in Damien's camp to be near to Liani. None of the Chenese felt confident any longer.

As they traveled, the accumulated royal soldiers began to look at Aron as their leader. He looked at the sea of faces staring at him which was disheartening rather than inspiring. Aron could imagine the grisly aftermath of battle with Damien's fearsome weapons and he could think of no escape from the carnage – not a feeling he could use to inspire the troops.

The members of the Black Fist and Cherine's masters were nonplussed. They drew confidence from their individual prowess and an unmatched record of successes. Aron looked at them and couldn't help but smile. They couldn't think in terms of defeat, it wasn't in their nature.

* * * *

Cherine's advance scouts weren't gone long before they returned at a gallop.

"The prince has forces moving this way. They're not arrayed in battle formations, so I don't think they're coming here to fight us. I don't think they've discovered we're here yet."

The camp went on full alert as the officers moved their troops into formation. This was open ground and no place where Aron wanted to make a stand.

"It's better if we go out to them," he said at last. "We'll take a spearhead of our elite supported by royal army troops. I hope we can avoid a fight."

Aron's troops assembled quickly. Aron rode directly beside Cherine and Barmon was riding beside Brock directly behind them. The glee Barmon's face showed for the expected fight was frightening. Aron glanced at Brock who nodded his awareness of the danger of his father going out of control.

Riding at a steady canter with no vanguard ahead of them, they traveled for only a couple of hours before seeing the flags of the royal army.

Aron made a calculated decision.

"Cherine, we're going in under a white flag."

"What?" everyone exclaimed.

"Trust me," said Aron firmly.

The two of them rode out quickly to approach the royal column. The pair and the rebel forces were spotted by the royal force. The royal commander deployed a skirmish line, but didn't attack. Aron felt vulnerable riding into the range of their archers.

When they approached the commander, Aron was shocked to see he was a man he'd met in the villages. The commander smiled wryly.

"This is a strange tactic for the rebels. Send in the leader to be exposed and vulnerable? Where did you study tactics?"

Aron chuckled. "Obviously it's an area where I need improvement. It's good to see you again."

"Cherine," said the royal commander.

She nodded.

"What can I do for you, Aron?"

"Obviously, we're not here looking for a fight. I don't know what you've heard about the wilds, but I can tell you it's much worse than you think. We face a potential enemy capable of great harm who has no conscience about striking. He has weapons from the ancient past that make him near to invulnerable."

"That is distressing news," the commander replied.

"We had no choice but to put distance between us and him. He's gathering an army and I suspect he intends to sweep over the entire world. Whether there are any capable of defeating him, I wonder. I'm sure he will come this way. I just don't know when. As impossible as it might seem, I need to strike a truce with the prince. As daunting as is the royal host, against what's coming, I fear we may all be chaff to be scattered to the winds."

"What are you doing out here, commander?" asked Cherine.

"The prince has sent the army to try to protect the farms so our food supply isn't destroyed. He hasn't made any plans against you, Aron, in a long time. I think he's finally realized his own end could be near. He's a much different man."

"Strange that it takes the threat of the end of the world for us to get sensible rule out of the monarchy," Aron muttered.

He hadn't meant it as a joke, but everyone chuckled.

"Will you allow us in your midst?" asked Cherine. "We can work together. We have considerable royal forces with us anyway."

"Who am I to stand in the way to sensible decisions," the commander replied. "For your information, Aron, no one in the army ever wanted to go on the campaign against you. We were never your enemies."

"I understand, commander. Thank you for that."

"It would be an honor to combine our camps. Cherine, I don't think you realize the legend you are in the army. My troops would cut off hands just for the chance to be near you."

"Tell them to keep their hands," she replied with a smirk. "They might need them in battle. I don't understand the attention. I'm a woman just like any other."

The men around them chuckled.

"No ma'am, you're much more than that."

She shrugged, clearly pleased.

"I'll arrange for our people to rendezvous with you. We'll have a conference to determine our next moves, commander," said Aron. "Thank you for your forbearance."

"I'll tell the cooks to prepare something special tonight." He winked at Cherine.

Aron rode back to his formation. Cherine chuckled beside him.

"What is it, Cherine?"

"Men," she replied. "Men make me chuckle. They're such louts and bone heads."

"I can't argue with that," Aron replied with a laugh.

"We're in the middle in of a campaign field and all they can think of is these silly romantic…"

"You love it, Cherine," said Aron.

"No, I don't," she huffed indignantly.

"Yes, you do," Aron replied, laughing louder.

When they rode up to the others, they looked at them curious.

"What brings this humor?" asked Brock.

"We had nothing to fear from these royal forces. All that we needed was for Cherine to make an appearance, bat her eyes and then all of those men swooned."

"Aron," she threatened. "I will take you out of that saddle and plant you into the ground."

Everyone laughed.

"We're going to have a combined camp tonight," she huffed crossly. "If any of you wish to test my patience further with this nonsense, I'm happy to stack up piles of bodies."

She looked all around at the amused faces. Wisely, none said anything.

Chapter Seventeen

~ Showdown ~

Filled with excitement, Damien walked briskly to the podium and reminisced, reliving memories about his former days of glory addressing the ancient masses. This wasn't a gathering of those former proportions, but was a start in that direction. Arrayed before him were all of the people he'd brought from Aron's camp along with the accumulated throng of converts from the surrounding nations - a sizeable gathering, already under his thrall. Crowds of the past understood the technology of the times. This assemblage was dazzled by even the merest of his technological displays. The blare from loudspeakers mystified them and amused Damien that people could be so easily swayed by explainable phenomenon, but to the crowd the exhibit was pure wizardry.

As always, his bevy of beauties marched out directly behind him and lined up across the elevated stage for maximum display to the fawning crowd. There were only three left who weren't altered by his machine other then Sirina and Tasha. Women who'd been altered stared at Damien with rapture in their eyes, like he was Adonis come down to bless them from on high. "Bless them" he did often, though they were only marginally aware of the "honor." Liani was his obedient wife now. Whatever he said became law to her. She didn't bat an eye at his outrageous behaviors, because she was incapable of normal responses and awareness. Her normal defenses were impaired.

The five remaining women who retained their faculties were living in terror of the seemingly inevitable. They made elaborate attempts to be conciliatory with the hopes of avoiding their fate. None of them had any illusions about what would happen to them eventually.

Damien looked up into the sky like he expected his air force, long destroyed and buried under the sands of time, to make a miraculous reappearance. The power of that force on this now primitive planet would have been unstoppable. In the present day sky, were only a flock of birds and a number of fluffy cumulus clouds drifting past.

Damien pushed a button which began a virtual visual display above his head accompanied by the stirring anthem of a long dead orchestra. The ancient scene panned across a vast host of singing worshippers - a very impressive display that awed the crowd, as he intended. Again the program concluded with a fly over of deafening aircraft filling the ancient skies on the screen.

His present day crowd oohed and ahhed which both amused Damien and bolstered his self confidence that at last total a victory was in his grasp.

He let the crowd cheer for a time before he put up his hand. He waited and slowly surveyed the expectant faces before speaking.

"My friends, welcome. You've made the right choice to join me here because what we will set about doing is the remaking of this world. You've seen the brutality of your governments and their indifference to you and your suffering. Not only that, you've seen their incompetence. They were never fit to rule and merely possessed the most power. Conquest of your foes doesn't mean you're the right leaders for the people. Taking advantage of the weak to perpetrate evil designs isn't the purpose of government. You aren't chattel for their amusement. You're individuals with hopes, dreams and innate nobility. We'll create true utopia. Every man, woman, and child will have dignity at last and you won't be forced to huddle in your homes frightened of abusive overlords. Each person will be free to pursue their dreams and reach their potentials. There is no limit to what we can accomplish if we but make the commitment to the cause. I offer myself humbly to you. I'm willing to pay any price to achieve our final triumph and crush the oppressors once and for all. We'll wipe away their memory and the record of their foul deeds for all time. I have knowledge and experience beyond anyone alive today. I'm uniquely qualified to be your true leader and what I offer is perfection in the world. You've seen but a small sampling of my power and my greatness. Look at these incredible women who've freely chosen to serve me with their talents, minds and loving devotion. It's beyond my belief I could be so fortunate once again in my life. Can you do less than them? Could you live with yourself if you said no where these maidens showed the courage and said yes?"

The crowd reacted to his message exactly as anticipated - like putty in his hands.

"Who has the courage to put on my uniform and go forth to face our enemies, the forces of discord and discontent?"

A great shout thundered out as many people put up their fists in acclamation.

The throng began a loud cheer and applause nodding to each other affirmatively.

Damien smiled smugly; this was too easy. The masses were sheep willing to follow him blindly.

Damien turned and nodded to Liani who was staring at him in awe. She stepped to his side as he put his arm around her. He took her hand and raised it while the crowd went wild with cheering.

Tasha was standing beside Sirina. Both looked on in horror. Tasha could only wonder what Aron would think if he saw this appalling charade. The thought pained her. Radigan was nearby totally absorbed in the spectacle and oblivious to the woman he'd chased and pursued since she'd escaped the palace from the prince. Her feelings about Radigan were transforming, but remained secondary to her fears of being altered by Damien's machine.

Tasha and Sirina smiled blithely and waved to the crowd along with the other women, pretending to be a part of Damien's aura.

Damien stepped down from the podium to greet the people in the front row. He led Liani by the hand who was dressed to dazzle and dazzle she did. The rest of the female corps followed them along the front of the crowd allowing them a glimpse of their beauty up close. A shoddy looking man reached over suddenly and touched Tasha which took everything to control herself from slugging him. Guards stepped in and pushed him back. The slow procession made their way to the end of the crowd before returning into the building away from the cacophony of the mob.

Straga walked up to them. He smiled deviously at Sirina, and even Tasha.

"You looked so beautiful I could hardly keep from rushing over to grab you in my arms, darlings."

"Thank you," Sirina replied meekly. Tasha said nothing.

"I have duties to attend to, but I'll see you and the boys tonight."

Sirina nodded.

They saw Damien coming their way and stood in silence and in trepidation.

"Greetings, my lovely flowers, you did well today. I'm pleased how you've taken to your roles in my elite corps of maidens."

"What do you want, Damien?" asked Tasha suspiciously.

"I thought to honor you by inviting you to my dinner table this evening. It's a reward for the fine job you're both doing on my behalf."

Neither woman was interested in that "honor." They'd both been "honored" before in their lives. Tasha had spent enough time in the custody of the prince to understand very well. It posed a terrible dilemma as their refusal might lead them to a trip to Damien's machine.

"Would we bring our husbands?" asked Sirina innocently. Tasha smiled at her quick thinking.

Damien scowled a moment before returning to his passive smile.

"I hadn't thought of that, but you're right. It would be appropriate to include important members of my personal staff to attend. Yes, tell them to come along also."

"We'll see you this evening, unless you have other tasks for us to handle in the meantime."

"No, you may do as you please. You served me well with the rally."

The women walked away quickly before he could change his mind.

"Very good, Sirina," Tasha whispered.

"Men are still men, Tasha. Even inflated ones like Damien can be dealt with. We still have weapons at our disposal. While we have something he wants, he makes himself vulnerable to us."

"Hopefully we can play your dangerous game and survive this nightmare."

"Tasha, we're still in grave danger. He could change us at any moment and we could live out our days like poor Liani."

"If it comes to submitting to that thing, I won't."

"Would that matter to him, Tasha? He could simply compel us. We couldn't overpower him and his troops. I don't think our husbands would side with us. They'd have us either way whether we'd lost our souls or not."

Tasha shrugged. "I thought Radigan loved me, and perhaps he does in his way, but this new lust for absolute power has taken him completely. I'm now secondary to his ambition. I honestly believe if

Damien ordered him to harm me, he would."

"I've had no illusions about Straga. Whatever small goodness I had with him is gone. This man who holds me and my boys is a stranger and a dangerous one at that. If Damien ordered him to slay me, I have no doubts he would. The boys act differently toward him too. They see the difference in him."

"There must be an answer, Sirina. I've got to believe it to maintain my resolve and my courage. Never a time in the palace did I ever feel mortally threatened like I do here. I knew I would survive there and was just a humiliating life to endure. Here, Damien is a monster."

"I agree with you, Tasha."

"Another thing I've noticed. Wu Hang stayed here because of Liani. He's plotting to do something rash. If you look in his eyes you can see desperation and that's never a good thing. As an individual man, I don't know of any who could best him, but here surrounded by Damien's growing legions, he has no chance. Even if he could spirit her away what kind of person would she be? I've seen no return of normalcy in any of the women he's afflicted."

"What do you propose? I doubt we have any way to make contact with Wu Hang. We're warded constantly by Damien's guards, not to mention the scrutiny of our husbands."

"It's a problem without a solution, Sirina."

"I'll think about it, Tasha. Perhaps an answer will come to me."

* * * *

"My prince, we received a dispatch from frontier command. Aron has met with local commanders and proposes a truce. He also hopes to meet with you personally. What answer should I take back to him?"

Agar's eyes glazed over for a number of reasons.

"Aron has come back to the kingdom?" asked Coraline curiously.

"Apparently so darling, I'm inclined to go out to meet with him."

"Is it because you want to see Tasha and Belisa again?"

Agar looked at her crossly for a moment before his expression softened.

"You worry I'll slip back into my old ways. It's a valid concern from your point of view. For me, it's a chance to prove to you I've changed. Yes, I'm curious to see them again. You'll go with me, Coraline."

"I?" she asked in surprise. "I didn't think you would allow me to travel any longer."

"I'm always vigilant about your safety, wife, but you're implying I don't trust you. I do, I trust you more so than any other person in the world. I know you want to see Aron again. I can't fault you for that."

"I'll pack my things," she said, trying to conceal her excitement at the prospect.

"This is a new reality we're facing, Coraline. We must all look at the world in a new way."

"Of course, husband, I'll be ready very soon, Agar."

An hour later, Agar left a conference with the king, and Granor.

"I'll use this opportunity to assess the state of the frontier, father. I want to hear what Aron has to say about this threat that frightens him so. It will help us with our planning."

"Good, my son. Travel with sufficient force to deter any dangers along the way. I understand you're taking our precious Princess Coraline."

"About her, I spare no expense in assuring her safety, father. She will never leave my side until she's returned safely back to the palace."

"Good, Agar. Granor, do you have anything to add?"

Granor nodded his head, trying to suppress a smug smile. Unknown to the king and the prince, Granor's messengers had returned from the wilds.

"I wish you a safe journey, my prince, to you and your lovely wife."

"I'll leave you now," said Agar.

They rode out of the main palace gates an hour later. Agar took nearly his entire elite corps. The only ones who remained behind were those he'd assigned to watch Granor and to safeguard the king and queen. The king had decided to send some of his people along too. Included in that group was an old acquaintance of Aron's, the lash master, Relak.

The prince's party traveled steadily and at a decent pace to cover ground as rapidly as possible without stressing the horses or the women. Coraline rode determinedly beside her husband. The ride was a strain for a woman who'd lived a pampered life and was a little too soft for life on the road, but Coraline was resolved to toughen up quickly. Within a week, her initial pain and saddle sores were resolved. She felt better and felt excitement for the reunion with people of her past.

"You need not pretend you're not filled with great anticipation, Coraline," said Agar as they rode along.

"I've been separated from family and friends, Agar. There's a chance I'll see my parents with Aron. Yes, it excites me."

"It isn't a problem, my darling. I hope you'll finally realize I do trust you and you can feel free to express your true feelings. I no longer have a worry if you show affection for Aron."

She looked at him skeptically. "That's an assertion I take with a grain of salt, Agar. You've never been one to show restraint when it comes to women you've claimed."

"As I said, this is a chance to prove to you I'm a much changed man."

"We'll see," she said with a chuckle. "I'm not so magnanimous about your seeing Tasha and Belisa again."

"You're jealous?" he asked, dumbfounded. "What a remarkable turn. Women jealous of me, it's a circumstance I could never have imagined with my former life."

"Words and deeds are two different things, Agar."

"This is true, darling."

They traveled for a week before nearing the large camp which held their rebel opponents.

Agar donned his dress uniform for the day they entered the camp and Coraline wore a dazzling expensive dress for the occasion.

The royal commander met them at the edge of the camp and escorted them to the center area where Coraline saw Aron standing in the midst of her village friends and relatives. Coraline cried out and jumped off her horse to race over to her mother and father. They embraced warmly and blubbered incoherencies at finally being reunited. Agar got off his horse and followed his wife.

"This is my husband, Agar, crown prince of the realm," said Coraline finally.

The prince made an elaborate bow to them.

"Greetings, prince," said Coraline's father. Her mother looked at Agar, but couldn't take her arms off her daughter. They hugged again.

Aron stood by waiting patiently. This meeting which had been fraught with uncertainty and danger was going much better than he'd anticipated.

Finally the prince, his wife, and her parents walked over to Aron.

“Sire,” said Aron with a bow. Agar smiled.

“Greetings, Aron. I’m glad to see you again, though you may not believe it. Things between us have changed a great deal.”

“You have no idea,” said Aron.

“Are you speaking about this peril in the wilds?”

“Peril is too weak a word for what we all face. Damien is a survivor from ancient times. How he’s done this, we don’t know. Galean has pondered it daily, but I’m afraid it’s beyond us. What he brings with him from those nightmare times were the seeds of destruction and annihilation. He has terrible weapons and powers at his disposal that could cause unprecedented death and destruction. What’s more fearful to me is he has no conscience, only blind ambition. Forces that fought him in the past are turned into dust. What we in the kingdom can offer as a deterrent may be a pale shade of their strength. If resolve of spirit was sufficient, perhaps we could entertain hope, but I fear what we face is slaughter against an enemy near to invincible against our primitive weapons.”

Agar’s face clouded. “I can’t judge what you’re saying because I haven’t beheld those sights, but it’s clear to me the impression it made on you. You, the Black Fist, and the masters, are our greatest fighters. If you feel you can’t prevail, it makes me believe your words about the seriousness of the imminent threat of this Damien. I accept your offer of a truce. I can also say, I’m willing to forgo those former grievances I harbored because I admit I was in the wrong about a great many things. My wife has stood by me when I was at my lowest. It’s given me the desire to be a better man for her and for the realm. I hope you can accept my apology for what I’ve done wrong in your life and in the lives of so many others. I can’t undo those past wrongs; I can only live a better life now to make amends.”

Aron was dumbfounded. This was the last possible thing he ever expected to hear from Agar.

He looked around at the equally shocked friends.

“I accept your apology, Agar. I hope you realize, we’re still patriots of the realm. We never meant to overthrow royal rule, only to protect the weak and the helpless.”

“I know that, as does my father, Aron. I hope to chart a new course of friendship and mutual respect, if you’re agreeable.”

“Certainly, Agar, we still acknowledge you as rightful heir to the throne. That isn't a problem for any of us."

"Now, I think my wife would like to greet you. I explained to her I know she has great fondness for you. There will always be a place for you in her heart."

Aron looked at Coraline. She was breathtaking, as always. She came up to Aron cautiously, but then grabbed him in a tight embrace. Aron's face flushed red and he glanced at Agar abashedly. Agar had a wry smile.

Coraline kissed him on the cheek before going back into her mother's embrace.

Agar's face had a curious expression.

"They're not here, Agar," Aron explained. "Belisa considered the probable course of events against Damien and decided to return with her warriors back to her own people to make their stand on home grounds. Tasha made a choice also. You may not know that when she lived in your suite, she had an intimate relationship with Radigan. That led to feelings for him which ultimately led to her choosing him to make her life. Radigan fell under the sway of Damien and if I understand correctly, he's now a key leader for him. I'd hoped to win her heart, but Radigan proved the better man. I could only step away and accept the inevitable. This tore out my heart, but she was convinced he was the man she wanted."

Agar was shocked. "That explains a great many things. He glanced at Coraline who was equally stunned at the news. She was not only stunned, but visibly discomfited. It wasn't difficult for Agar or Aron to realize the reason.

"I've been a fool about so many things," said Agar. "Most of my failings have been from my poor choices, but I must say, this was a surprise to me. I should've realized, but foolishly for some reason I put my trust in Radigan. Aron, I've come to know humiliation in my life. I so greatly regret the person I was and the odious things I've done. I know what I did to you and your friends are unforgiveable. Perhaps knowing that I've suffered too will give you some small solace."

"I don't rejoice in the suffering of others, Agar. At this point we can both use this as object lessons and a teaching moment. We can no longer look at things the way we want them to be, but instead we need to be able to see them for what they really are."

Agar nodded his head.

* * * *

"I don't expect you to see me as a friend, but I hope we're capable of some state of mutual respect. I have a duty to save my father's realm and to protect our subjects. Will you join us in doing that?"

"Of course, my prince, we're at your command."

They shook hands. After that, Galean made his appearance.

"Galean!" said Coraline, in joy and hugged him affectionately.

Galean turned to the prince. "Sire..."

"My father and I have yearned for your wisdom and counsel so many times, Galean. I hope you'll feel confident you're welcome back at the palace. There are no recriminations for you to worry about. As I said, I was in the wrong."

"Thank you, my prince. That's an unexpected benevolence on your part. We're grateful. As Aron said, we're still loyal citizens of the realm."

Agar turned back to Aron. "I want to say something further. The part I've played in your life shames me. I've caused you nothing but heartbreak and ruination. For that I'll be eternally sorrowful. I wish I could go back and change so many things. I grew up as an arrogant and pampered brat with no hand teaching me proper behavior. I could have all that I desired with none to stop me which led to my low ways. Again, I don't expect you to forgive me as I don't deserve forgiveness, but I wanted to make this gesture so you know how I feel now. It's too late for too many things. I pray for an opportunity in the future to do something to right this wrong."

Aron looked sad. "There are so many things all of us would change if we could. You're not alone in that, Agar."

Cherine walked up to them at that moment.

"You do seem a different person, Agar," she said boldly. "In my case, I think it will take some time for me to judge if you've truly changed. I'm sure you understand."

"Cherine, everyone knows I've wronged you grievously. I can only apologize and beg your forgiveness."

Cherine wasn't in a forgiving mood and merely shrugged.

"His majesty, my father, will be happy to see all of you," Agar added.

"You'll understand if we keep our weapons at hand," said Cherine frostily.

Agar chuckled. He reached out and took Coraline into his embrace.

"See what I've earned with my life, darling? Will I ever warrant trust again?"

"Time will show them the truth, Agar. You've convinced me. I wouldn't have thought that possible not so long ago."

"Come, my friends, let's see to getting you into camp. You've traveled far."

Aron followed the royal couple into the camp - an anticlimactic arrival after what they'd thought would happen. The new incarnation of the crown prince was a phenomenon they would all need time to digest. Abdurka was the least willing to mend fences with the prince and kept away from him as much as he could.

After an evening meal, Aron and his staff gathered to meet with Agar and the generals. A frank discussion followed as old wounds and grievances weren't so easily dismissed by the troops on either side unlike the crown prince managed.

Coraline came over with Agar and her parents to sit with Aron and his folks. Brock told the sorry tale of his mother being taken away by Straga which cast a pall over the evening instead of rejoicing at being together again. Aron felt every bit of the sting that Barmon felt as Brock told the story. He always tried not to think about Tasha, but here he couldn't help it and wondered what she was doing at the very moment with Radigan. It caused him a queasy feeling. He glanced at Barmon who had a murderous look in his eyes. Barmon looked back. With both in a dark place, they had no need of words.

"I'm still astounded to hear what Radigan has done," said Agar. "I've learned much from this painful story."

He put an arm around Coraline. She glanced at Aron who tried not to react in anyway. Sympathy was in her eyes, but was no comfort. He felt alone and the gestures of the people around him wouldn't change that.

"I think Radigan may yet be forced to stand and account for these misdeeds," Agar continued.

"He's a vassal to Damien now," said Brock. "We'll have all we can deal with just surviving, my prince. Punishing him is the least of our worries."

Agar looked directly at Aron who suddenly felt ashamed, like he'd proven a poor choice to romance any woman and here it was displayed for everyone to see. His emotions wouldn't allow him to sit idly in the company of his esteemed friends.

"I think I'll stretch my legs," he muttered. "Barmon, would you care to walk with me?"

Barmon didn't say anything. He rose up and stepped to Aron's side. They walked away, two tortured souls, toward the darkening horizon as the sun surrendered its final glimmers in a reddened sky. Large clouds approached, promising a powerful storm.

"I think we might get wet," said Aron.

"Let it come," Barmon replied. "I care not."

"I understand how you feel as I feel the same way. I wish I wasn't seen as a leader. I really have no desire to be here."

"I have no desire to be anywhere, Aron. I live to take revenge on Straga and his master, Damien, if that's possible. If not, I'm more than ready to die. Living this way is a disgrace and the sooner I can end it, the better."

"Have you given up all hope of saving them?"

Barmon's fierce scowl softened. "I was blessed to have the best wife I could hope for, even if only for a limited time. Getting her back and losing her again has gutted me. I have nothing left. There is nothing in this world for me. My hatred will destroy me, I know it, Aron. My only hope is to persevere long enough to take significant action before I go. If I lost my hatred now, I don't know what I would become. I suspect it would be nothing good."

"I'm surely an idiot, but I've got to believe we can prevail, Barmon. Through some miracle, I want to put things right. That's nothing real I can use to bring us hope, it's just my feelings. I've been through harrowing experiences and in hopeless situations before. I can only hope that yet again, some turn in the scheme of things will bring us victory in the end. I don't want to believe the world is meant to exist in the horror Damien proposes. I hope some greater power exists who watches over us all who can overcome Damien and his evil."

"For you, I hope it can happen, Aron. For me, my hope is a brave death where I take down our enemies."

"Brock is your son. Can you not think about him if he lost his father again?"

Barmon looked away. "He's a good boy grown into a good man. I'm proud of him and I'm grateful to your family for giving him a loving home and guidance. I missed his childhood, but he had a father to look up to. I can't convince you I'm on the right course because I may not be. The wound in my soul is mortal, Aron. Do you understand?"

Aron looked at him sadly. "I understand. I can't think of Tasha. I'd rather get on my horse and ride away somewhere to get lost forever. I understand when you say there's nothing in this world for you. People think I can simply pick another woman. They don't understand. I don't want another woman, but she didn't want me. How can any man cope with that? I wasn't good enough."

"War is coming, Aron. That's where I have my attention now."

"Maybe you're right, Barmon. War will certainly be consuming enough. Perhaps I can lose myself there too. Going out in a blaze is easy enough to do."

"Let's agree on it, going out in a blaze the like of which the world has never seen."

They shook hands solemnly - a death pact.

By the time they got back to their starting point, people had drifted off to their sleeping places. Aron glanced once at Coraline and the prince. Her parents were sleeping beside them. Aron placed his bedding down near his parents, but noticeably apart. Barmon slept alone too. Brock was out on guard duty.

Aron stared up at the stars. A shooting star flamed across the sky in a brilliant arc before it disappeared. Aron thought about his punishing path of his life a moment before dozing off to sleep.

Dinner with Damien was still a frightening experience for Tasha and Sirina, even with husbands at their sides. Liani was present in body, but absent in intellect. She reacted to Damien, chortling at his attempts at humor, exclaiming over his boasts and pronouncements and generally acting the banal idiot. An act as disturbing to the women as Damien's not so thinly veiled desires for them.

Radigan and Straga said nothing on their behalf, as if it was their duty to "bond" with the leader.

Finally Damien dropped the pretense.

"You should stay with me this evening. Your husbands have duties elsewhere and it would be a tragedy for you to sleep alone in your beds."

The time had come and there was no avoiding facing this dilemma.

“If we say no?” asked Tasha.

“There would be no reason to say no,” Damien replied casually.

“We’re married women,” said Sirina. “That means something to us even if it doesn’t mean anything to you.”

“Even though it wasn’t much of a ceremony, I abide by the promise I made to Radigan.”

Damien looked angry.

“We have means to relieve you of such concerns.”

Tasha felt a cold sweat and looked at a terrorized Sirina.

“Think carefully about what you say next,” said Damien.

“If you’re telling us you mean to take away our minds like you’ve done to Liani, I’ll tell you this right now, Damien. I will not end my days that way. I would rather end my life knowing who I am. If you require our obedience, that’s a terrible thing, but I’ve lived through such nightmares before in the palace. It’s you who needs to decide, Damien. We will both end our lives if you try to harm us with your machines.”

Damien looked at both of them analytically before deciding.

“I like you both. That’s why you’ve been allowed to be so close to me. I think we’ll let this matter pass for this evening. You remain who you are, but as you say, I require your obedience. I won’t allow you to question my orders ever again. If you’re called forth in the future, you’ll do so without complaint or question. You owe your highest allegiance to me. Your husband’s understand this and they agree with me. Do you agree with this? Do you accept my requirement?”

The women nodded sadly. They both looked at Liani who was oblivious to the showdown and their temporary victory.

Chapter Eighteen
~ Return to Nephora ~

Aron felt like a noose was tightening around his neck when Agar invited them to return to the palace.

"I know you have doubts, but as you've so eloquently pointed out, the old days are over for all of us. I've changed greatly to be able to look at things as they are, Aron. Now it's time for you to do the same. I've given you my pledge that you face no punishments at my hands or at my father's. Nephora is the hub of the kingdom. From there we can best react to this Damien. It's a decision only you can make for your followers, but really there is only one decision you can make."

Trent, Cherine, Abdurka, Galean, Brock, Barmon, Enna, Biala, Drang-ku and his entire staff, were all there. They looked at Aron waiting for his decision - a choice he didn't want to make. His grim memories of days in the palace were reinforced when Relak made his first appearance. To see the lash master again, only Wu Hang had seemed more intimidating.

"You may be right, Prince Agar. We probably have no other viable choice we could make. I know you'll understand when we say we'll never surrender our arms and will be vigilant at every moment."

"Of course, Aron, I wouldn't expect otherwise. You'll need that kind of vigilance against our joint enemy."

Traveling back into the city he hated was an emotional test for Aron with so many bad memories. When the palace was sighted, he couldn't help feeling queasy in his stomach. The royal army patrols saluted the prince as they rode past. Military personnel were everywhere watching every movement of everyone who passed by.

They dismounted and stood a moment staring at the doorway into the palace. Aron thought about what it took to leave that door.

"Come, Aron," said Coraline with a smile holding out her hand, like he was a frightened child. "It's all right."

Aron took a deep breath before stepping forward and Cherine fell into step beside him. The rest of Aron's staff formed up and followed behind.

They were led directly to the main council chamber where the king and the queen were waiting. They both arose. Coraline hugged the queen and introduced her parents to the royal couple.

"You should be very proud of your daughter," said the queen. "She's a remarkable young woman who's accomplished a great deal in her time here at the palace. She's overcome some daunting tests and showed courage in the face of difficult times. We're pleased to have her as a part of the royal family and my son cherishes her."

"Thank you, your majesty," said Coraline's mother. "We're just happy to be reunited with her again. Thank you for allowing us to come here in peace."

"There's been too much misunderstanding," the queen continued. "We've always wanted the best for the realm."

No one chose to contest that point, or review the actions of her son and the other nobles, but just stood mute instead.

The king looked about the rebel faces until he spotted Galean.

He smiled warmly and walked over to the scholar. "It's so good to see you again my old friend."

"I'm happy to still be among the living, your majesty," Galean replied.

"You look fit. I think your adventure has toughened you up."

"The tests of life can be a double edged sword, your majesty. I was fortunate to be surrounded by great men. Their presence lifted me up and inspired me to strive to live better."

"Well said, Galean. Can I hope to enjoy the benefit of your wise counsel again? We've missed you."

"I'll share my thoughts, but I must tell you with what we've been through, I have far less confidence in my theories. There is so much we don't know, I fear it will lead to our ends. Damien is a danger unprecedented in our lives. I don't know that my research could ever give us an answer."

"That's dire news, but it can wait for another day. We must have a banquet tonight to celebrate the return of so many brave and cherished souls to our embrace."

The king next went to Aron. "I don't know you well enough, but I hope to change that. Although you've led a rebellion against the crown, we understand your reasons. I've been told about the treachery of Radigan and how he stole away your love, Tasha. You have my sympathy. Perhaps together we can give Radigan a proper answer for his misdeeds. As far as Damien goes, I'm not willing to concede anything. If he wants war, we'll give him war."

A shout arose from the rebels and the royals both.

"I offer my services, your highness, to whatever extent I can help," Aron replied.

"Thank you, Aron. You'll be welcome to work with the general staff in defending the kingdom."

"As you command, sire..."

"Aron, I'm curious about something?" asked the queen. "You've continued to wear the uniforms of the kingdom. Why was that?"

"We never saw ourselves as traitors bent on overthrowing the government. We fought for the weak and for those who couldn't speak for themselves. Our enemies weren't people so much as the insensitive actions of people. We fought injustice."

"Honestly, we can't fault you for that, Aron. You've taken our transgressions and put them before us so they can't be ignored any longer. As my son has said, we can't undo what was wrongfully done, but we can control what we do from now on."

"If that's true, the people will gladly serve you," Aron replied. "As far as the uniforms, we had nothing else better to wear and these uniforms are very nice."

The people in the room chuckled.

"They are nice," said the queen.

The king moved on to Cherine. She had an intent steely look in her eyes.

"I want you to know that I understand your choices also, and the reasons for those choices. Although I'm heartbroken my most trusted protectors left me, I'm happy to ask you to return to my service."

Cherine stood silent for an uncomfortable moment.

"Sire, we're still loyal to the crown, but we've shared so much with Aron in his difficult journey, I can't simply cast him aside. We will serve you, but our first attention will be Aron. I hope you understand. Within the scope of our joint operations, we will look to protect you and the royal family. We won't, however, stand aside here while Aron ventures forth to face Damien. We will stand with him and our brothers in the Black Fist. I don't mean to sound resistant to your will. These are extraordinary times which call for different relationships. Do I make sense to you, your majesty?"

"You do, Cherine. I respect your judgment and your loyalty. We'll accept whatever service you're able to provide to us. Perhaps there will be a day in the future where the realm will see peace again free of the threat of Damien. Do what you must and know that we cherish the time we had with you and hope for a close relationship once again."

"You're very generous, your majesty. Thank you. We remain your loyal servants, but with a slightly different mission."

* * * *

A commotion stirred outside and everyone hurried to the windows. In the sky a bright flash of light beamed out followed by a loud boom shaking the windows and the building.

"It appears Damien sends us his greetings," said Brock.

The king looked at Galean, as if he had the answer.

"I'm sorry, your majesty. This is beyond me."

Agar walked over to his father to reassure him. Aron noticed Granor slip out of the room.

"Who is that man?" he asked Cherine softly.

"An advisor to the king... When Galean left the palace, I understand Granor stepped into the void "

"I get a bad feel about him, Cherine."

"Royal persons are not known for the best of decisions, Aron. Picking poor counselors is well within their capacities."

"I'm probably too cautious now, but I've seen too much treachery in my time. With my family here, I'm not taking any chances."

"I'll have people look into Granor and his plans. Perhaps we'll have a frank discussion with him if we find it's warranted."

"Thank you, Cherine."

Meanwhile Granor hurried to the preset meeting with his riders who recently returned from the wilds.

"What did you find?" asked Granor anxiously.

"It was unbelievable," said his lead messenger. "Had I not seen it with my own eyes, I wouldn't have believed it. The man they call the leader is Damien. He survived from the beginning times through some means we don't know of. He has powers and devices from the Great War that destroyed the world then. There is no force that could stand against such might. We spoke with his representatives and were taken before Damien. He was happy to offer us the chance to join his crusade. I looked around to see those things he wouldn't wish to reveal. He looked to dazzle us with his words, but I saw the same elements of moral decay of our own nobles. Regardless, he can't be ignored. I don't see any choice but to join his cause. To contest him is certain defeat and probable annihilation. He's gathered masses all around him from the states beyond our borders. Already he has an army large enough to face down the royal host and its growing by the day. They've fought small skirmishes against the armies of the nations, but that war has yet to start in earnest. I told him we'll pass on information about the royal army deployments and defenses. We'll organize a legion of our own which can arise behind the royal lines at critical times in the battle to disrupt and damage the cause of the king. I think it isn't necessary because they can't beat such might. Damien was very interested, and he particularly wanted information on Aron who made himself an enemy to Damien. Apparently, Damien doesn't take such things lightly."

"This is good," said Granor thoughtfully. "Aron has a gift for garnering powerful enemies. Let's go ahead with our plans to station our forces in secret places where we can illicit the maximum havoc in the kingdom at critical times. A new day is dawning and I intend to be at the forefront to claim our share of the spoils of victory. Send for Lilith and tell her to come to my quarters. I have plans for her too."

"I must tell you one other thing, Granor. To be in his presence was frightening. His secret powers are chilling enough, but I saw insanity amongst his followers given free rein. If we are choosing to ally with Damien, I wonder if he would honor any agreements he makes. He appears to have colossal contempt for everyone whether his own followers or his enemies. This is a dangerous decision you're making."

"I understand, but I suspect we have no other rational choice. As I said, I plan to be on the winning side. At this point that appears to be Damien. We'll talk again later."

* * * *

Aron nearly declined the invitation of the prince to stay in his royal suites. Cherine opted to return to the barracks with the masters. The Black Fist returned to their former barracks too. Barmon went with them and stayed with his son. Walking into the suite again was still traumatic even under different circumstances. Coraline's parents were ushered to the room where Belisa had stayed and Aron was taken to Tasha's former room. Aron's parents came with him. Aron noted Marin living in the suite and shadowing Coraline at every moment. As the warriors passed, they nodded to each other in mutual respect for their fighting prowess.

"You might as well see how the nobles live, mother," Aron said. "It's far different from our life on the farm."

"We shouldn't, son," she replied, but was obvious from her reactions she wanted to live in luxury for just this one time.

The mothers sat together to try to hide their excitement in the main sitting room. Coraline laughed at her mother's girlish enthusiasm. The queen came in to join them.

Aron knew Agar wanted to talk to him, but he pretended to be busy in conference with the two fathers.

"Son, I think the prince wishes to speak with you."

"I know, father. Although things have changed, I don't see him as a friend. I can't ignore the past. His sins are a big reason why I'm in this sorry state. I'll have to talk to him, but I'll make him wait a bit first. I know it's petty, but that's how I feel."

The father's smiled ruefully.

Aron turned his face toward the prince. He immediately walked over to them.

"Excuse me for my intrusion on your private conversation, Aron. Could I speak with you?"

Aron shrugged. The father's started to leave.

"Please stay," said Aron. It gratified Aron to see Agar wanted to speak alone, but was thwarted.

"I want to reiterate that we must reach a new level of understanding and cooperation, Aron. I do understand how difficult that is for you. Again, I don't expect forgiveness from you about the past, but at this point you must realize our private feud must be put behind us. If we can't work together, the kingdom itself could be imperiled. Although you have no regard for the nobles, they wouldn't be the only people to suffer at the hands of Damien. The common people would suffer the same fate if we're attacked. That's got to be important to you, or else I believe we have no chance."

"We may not have a chance anyway, Agar. You've only seen Damien's workings from afar. We've seen him up close. Your point about us cooperating, I've already agreed to do that. There must be something more you're looking for."

Agar seemed uncomfortable and glanced at the fathers.

"Aron, I want to ask something of you. I acknowledge I have no right to hope for your help. I'm sure there's treachery at work in the palace. I can't say for sure who's involved. I know this doesn't strike you as a surprise. There have always been intrigues against those in power. What I fear is if I'm taken out by my enemies, there is no one to protect and to look after Coraline. I don't want her to suffer and die because she is my wife. I can't be sure who I can trust. In spite of my own hand in my troubles, the problem remains. Coraline is innocent of my crimes. Will you pledge to me to give Coraline your personal protection? I have my best man, Marin, warding her, but in battle people get killed. If Marin is lost there is no one left."

"Sure," said Aron. "I would have protected her anyway, Agar. I don't know Marin, so perhaps you should introduce us. I'd hate to see him attack me out of ignorance."

"Marin knows who you are, Aron," said Agar with a chuckle. "Everyone in the realm knows you."

"I hope that's a good thing, Agar."

"From your perspective it is. From mine, not so much, but I have myself to blame. I don't know if it's too late to change. A lifetime of excessive behavior isn't washed away overnight with an apology."

"It may be a moot point, Agar, with Damien in the picture now. You mentioned the view from my perspective. I don't think you understand, I've lost so much that's irretrievable that was dear to me. I don't see anything left to be optimistic about. At this point I'm hanging on for my friends and family, not for any hope I have. You once wanted to crush my spirit into the dust. That's happened. I'm just going through the motions of living."

Agar looked genuinely remorseful.

"That's a tragedy, Aron. It may be my greatest sin, what I did to you. I wish I could go back and remove that part of my life."

"Radigan had a big hand in my downfall, Agar. He not only has my girl by her choice, he's working with Damien for domination of the world to create a society that would be a nightmare. As bad as was life under the noble's class, Damien's world would be ascension to power of the most vile in mankind. It's frightening indeed. You didn't see Liani and what he did to her. She's, well, I'm not sure what she is now. I believe she's been altered so she can't be restored. Do you understand what I'm saying?"

"I can only hear your words, Aron. Since I didn't see her, it's difficult to imagine such things. I have no trouble understanding the dire threat though. If this was done to Coraline, or my mother, I would feel helpless rage just as you do."

"We can't allow Damien to win. I understand why a great war waged against him that destroyed the world in the ancient times. Our ancestors saw the same thing we did in Damien. He's a disease that must be eradicated. I just wish we had their weapons and power."

The father's listened to the conversation intently. Their concerns were clear in the expressions on their faces. They both looked at their own wives at the prospect of Damien's depredations.

"Do you have any ideas, son?" asked Aron's father.

"I'm sorry I don't. What I've always done in the past is react to each situation. I was fortunate to have Cherine, Brock, Trent, Galean, and the others of such great skill and talents that they helped guide me into good plans. We were always facing forces with comparable weaponry though. Our strategies were based on current day tactics. Now, we have no clues to how one could defeat Damien. All we can do in the interim is to avoid battle as best we can. If some weakness reveals itself, we could try to take advantage of it. This is a poor answer to our challenge, but I have nothing else to offer you."

"I have continuous riders going to and returning from the borderlands," Agar advised. "At this point there's no sign of aggressive movements from the wilds, so for the time being it seems we have an opportunity to make preparations."

"That isn't an area I can help you with," Aron answered. "Your generals are far better equipped to build defenses and fortifications. We were never a great army as rebels. We managed to survive by avoiding confrontations against superior foes."

"Nonetheless, I'd like you and your staff to join us in our planning. Cherine, Trent, and the masters were all key members of the royal army before."

"Of course, Agar, we'll try to be helpful."

Granor watched his door open as the emissary from Damien walked in escorted by Granor's guards. He was a former resident of the wilds, a member of Straga's clan.

"Welcome," said Granor. "Is this your first time in the capital?"

"Yes, I've only crossed the border to go on raids of the villages. This was a much longer journey than I realized to come here."

"What news do you bring from Damien?"

"He's occupied presently with building his forces and dealing with skirmishes from the surrounding nations. Our forces have grown a great deal, but it takes time to train them and establish order. Damien believes he will have major engagements very soon as his enemies recognize the extreme threat to their power and they will respond forcefully. It's a move Damien's anticipated and he feels we're ready for whatever they throw at us. There will come a time to conquer this little kingdom, but he has other tasks more pressing. In the meantime, he directs you to establish and deploy a network of sympathizers to the cause so when Damien comes they'll rise up in the middle of royal defenses to cause havoc and disrupt any actions they try to take. You've made the right choice siding with Damien. There will be only one outcome to this war which is coming."

"Good," said Granor. "I gather I have authority to make plans as I see fit."

"As long as you don't alert our enemies you're free to pursue any actions on behalf of Damien."

"What did Damien say about my post-war position? Was he agreeable to giving me a status of authority and perhaps some other means of compensation?"

"Most of the things you asked for, he would allow. There are some things that he will discuss with you directly at the conclusion of hostilities."

"I look forward to that day, and to that negotiation. Do you know what he questioned?"

"I don't for certain, but I think your request to personally be allowed to execute the royal family with your own hands may not be something he favors. Though he can see them put to death, the manner of it remains in question. It would be important to achieve maximum effect from those finalizing acts. The same is true for Aron. Damien has a special interest in Aron's demise. Many of us have that same interest, we who were conquered when Aron came into the wilds and took away our former lives. Straga will be looking for Sirina's former husband, Barmon. That's a head he wants to mount outside his door on a pole."

"I see. I'm certain we can work out an agreement acceptable to both of us. Please relax and recover from your arduous trip. We'll get you back on the road as soon as you're ready."

They led the man away. The emissary gave a chilling insight into the world Damien offered. Granor's ideas were based on his personal ambitions. The gesture of personally killing the royal family had been a ploy on his part to impress Damien. Actually killing them wasn't a task he desired. Coraline was too beautiful a woman to waste in such senseless mayhem when there were so many other uses for her. Unfortunately there might be no way around it.

The door guard ushered in Lilith.

"Master," she said.

"Good evening, Lilith. I've received news from the frontier. Damien is occupied with other matters in the short term. It gives us time to consider and crystallize our plans. You've done an exceptional job with gaining the trust of the queen and Princess Coraline. I need you to get me their schedules. There will come times in the near future where we may need to be able to isolate the pair and leave them vulnerable. How is your training going with knives?"

"I've been proficient enough for quite some time to take out the women. I've improved now where I can take down guards with surprise. In a straight fight against a man, I still have a ways to go, but I'll get there. I can tell you if you gave me the order, I could arrange circumstances to allow me to bring you their pretty heads."

"Excellent, Lilith... I hope it doesn't come to beheading the royal women. What Damien wishes about them, I can't say."

"I'm ready for whatever you order."

"Stay here with me tonight, Lilith. I'm sorry I've been occupied so much recently. I'm also attentive to you, darling."

"As you wish, master..."

He smiled and she smiled back. His smile was one of seamy satisfaction while hers was contrived and intended to mislead. He wasn't a man she wanted as a consort, just merely expedient to court his affections to protect her position. She was well aware of the evolving nature of royal society and the place of a woman in the social order. She'd had plenty of practice at surviving both.

"How far ahead does the queen plan her events?"

"Recently she's done far less long term planning. She's never told us why. I get the sense she's wary, like she can sense the increase of dark plots around her. Coraline is nearly never apart from the queen, and now Agar's man, Marin, is at their backs. He is competent, and a deadly risk. He extends trust to no one. With my known ties to you, I receive special attention and vigilance. That's why I say I would need to create the right circumstances if you wish me to take some action against them. I've actually been working with my closest hand maidens in getting them the same weapons training. The queen does allow me to take up to two servants with me. With three of us, if we eliminate Marin and his guards, we could easily handle the women in the queen's party. We could leave them dead in their own blood, or I suppose it might be possible to kidnap some or all of them. I'd say killing at least some of them might be a good deterrent to resistance from the remaining women. If they know we hold their lives in our hands, I think it would be easier to control them. Do you agree?"

"You're probably right, Lilith. I must say, I'm very impressed with your grasp of such difficult matters and you're willingness to do what we must, even with the need to kill from time to time. I wouldn't have expected it from a woman."

"Thank you, master, but would you expect it from Cherine?"

"I'm happy you're on our side, Lilith. As far as Cherine, she's a rare woman. Most of us think of her as in a class of her own."

She gave him a steely, chilling and calculating look. A person in her crosshairs would be in deadly danger and he knew it. Lilith was a woman who wouldn't hesitate to kill and was confident in her abilities.

"We know Cherine and respect her greatly, master, but know that she's no longer the only woman to be wary of."

"I like that you believe in yourself, but there's a reason she's the head of the masters and universally respected. I've not seen you in action, but I caution you not to think too greatly of your prowess until you proven yourself in battle like Cherine."

Lilith got an amused smile. "I have no problem with that."

They ate dinner together. Later when they got ready to sleep, he saw how Lilith had strapped sheathes to her thighs so she had knives handy at all times. Because the blades were placed on the inner thigh there was no outward indication she was armed.

"Very clever, Lilith," he commented.

"My maidens are similarly armed. We can be a surprise in unexpected places. If opportunities present themselves, we're ready to take advantage instantly."

"This is good to know."

"We're also training with swords and other weapons. Perhaps you should come to see us."

"Perhaps I should, Lilith. You're a great asset for our cause."

"Our cause?" she muttered dismissively.

"Lilith, when it comes to Damien, we must keep up appearances. I'm not a rabid believer of his either. What I heard about his followers is contemptible. What we must acknowledge is his power. He has it and therefore becomes our focus. My desire is to carve out our niche within the world he's bringing. Just like this very moment, we will close the door for our private moments away from the façade we must wear to mollify him. Neither of us was born into prestige, riches and esteem. We must fight and scrape to earn our benefits. This was true in serving the prince and is true serving Damien. A regime change won't mean substantive differences in our personal lives. Do you see? We can still have our little pleasures, darling."

Again he was surprised by her expression. For a moment it seemed a contemptuous glance before she turned her face away. Granor wasn't sure what to make of it, or how he should respond. She was too valuable for him to lose and testing her with chastisements didn't strike him as a good approach.

"Come, my dear, enough of these worrisome thoughts. We have far more pleasant things to ponder."

She showed him no sign of genuine affection. Her reactions were mechanical, like she was doing an annoying, unavoidable household chore. He did not fail to notice. She wouldn't even look him in the eyes.

* * * *

Aron went to sleep in his bed alone, again. His parents were in the main bed in Tasha's former room while Aron slept on a small temporary bed. It had been a very long time since he'd felt anything but discouragement and despair. Optimism was a state he'd completely lost faith in. He lay staring up at the ceiling for a time before dozing off. Agar was nearby in his royal bedroom with his wife, the woman Aron had once thought was his soul mate. Occupying the same room where Tasha had been humbled and shamed was ironic, like he was supposed to simply forget and forgive. He could not.

Aron's perpetual ire simmered constantly just below the surface. All of his boyish charm and humor was long gone replaced by a grim faced man who felt hollowed out and empty. Periodically, he visited with Jenn and her little girls, but he wouldn't allow any romantic feelings to develop.

Much of his time each day was spent returning to the training pits. The masters had taken up their old roles in developing skilled fighters; though they made it clear they were followers of Aron first. The Black Fist joined the masters in their training activities with the same proviso.

Galean and his staff supplanted the temporary and inadequate replacements the king had put into the royal libraries and immediately began a new study of the ancient records from his new perspective. Liani's absence was unmistakable as she'd been a key researcher and a brilliant mind in the work. Aron went to the library frequently; to see Liani's handwriting brought back painful memories for him and for Galean. Abdurka spent his time working with Galean in research, but he also came to the pits to keep fit.

The king gave Galean full control and latitude to do whatever he felt was necessary to defend the kingdom.

In addition to the issue of coexisting with the prince, Aron was forced into another compromise: Relak sought Aron out as well as Cherine.

"I hope that our past is behind us, Aron. What you've accepted from the prince I offer also. Cherine, you continue to have my utmost respect. I did what I had to do and it was never anything personal. I was commanded by his majesty. Do you accept my offer of friendship?"

Aron eyed him grimly.

"Lash master, we all did what was required of us. Your sins are no worse than any of ours. I was a servant of his majesty too. It isn't necessary to beg any quarter from me. I have no complaint against you."

Relak looked at Aron. "You do have issue with me. I can

understand, Aron. I don't ask your forgiveness only that we move past it. Our future will require we find allies in places we never would have before. I've been told about this foreigner they called the interrogator, Wu Hang. It's said you were able to reach a point of mutual respect and cooperation. That is what I aspire to, a similar accommodation. Judge me for the man I am, not for the monster I was forced to be. If I hadn't fulfilled that role to the satisfaction of the royals, believe me they would have found another who might have been worse than I. Can you accept the hand of friendship from me, Aron?"

Aron looked at his extended hand for a moment before he shook it.

"Let's look forward to a new partnership. I marveled at the brotherhood you built so quickly with the Black Fist. I hope to achieve a similar state with you and your men. I would be proud to be included as a Black Fist."

Aron was sick at the thought, but remained neutral in his reaction and facial expression.

"I'll speak to Brock. I've passed the mantle of guiding the Black Fist to him. I'm more a figurehead now."

Chapter Nineteen

~ Savages ~

While Aron and his staff of advisors were housed in posh settings by their royal hosts, the balance of Aron's flock boarded near the palace in various inns, and homes. It wasn't a problem for many of his people, but included in his group were the Brutans; among the barbarians of the wilds, they were the most barbaric. To expect major changes in such people was expecting a great deal. Not villagers by choice, brutal ways were their culture and eventually sooner or later there would be trouble.

Initially the Brutan's were docile, but only for a limited duration. Reports of minor incidents in the immediate area began. First, small crimes and excesses occurred that individually weren't particularly worse than that of the local criminal element, but this was just the precursor in an escalation of crimes.

Aron was sparring in the pits when news came of the first serious incident. Brock and Trent were talking nearby and Cherine was conducting training not far away for a collection of recruits. Her sessions were meant for small numbers, but considerable numbers of the royal army routinely attended both to observe and participate.

The messenger, a Black Fist member, went past the royal officers in charge of the training area, past Cherine and headed straight for Aron.

"There's trouble, Aron. You need to see to this."

"What sort of trouble? Why me…?"

"An incident took place last night. We've had trouble with local residents being abused. This time the problem was much worse. An argument happened between a band of Brutans and a petty noble passing by, which became a brief brawl between them and the noble's guards. Fortunately, no serious injuries occurred because an army patrol happened past and broke up the fight before it could become deadly. That could have been the end of it, but the noble was an ass and insisted on harsh remedies. The patrol officer told him he'd need to report it to command to get an order to arrest the Brutans. The noble was intent on doing that very thing, but the Brutans weren't content to sit and wait for imprisonment. Last night, they went to the home of the noble and broke in. A fight ensued with the noble's guards trying to do their duty, but against the Brutans they had no chance. I don't know how many were killed, but it was a sizeable number. The battle put the Brutans into frenzy and they stormed the main residence, brutalizing all of the occupants. You know the kind of trophies they took to decorate their camp to frighten away enemies. There's not enough left of the noble to identify him. He's been hung out on display all over his estate along with others. We saw no women slaughtered, or children, but they weren't present anywhere. We can only assume the Brutans took them away as slaves. The royals want to attack the Brutans and wipe them out, but have no idea how difficult that would be, or how many men would be lost in the process."

"My god," said Aron, shaking his head. Cherine, Brock, and Trent had come over and heard the story.

"We must find a way to put out this fire, Aron. In reality, we need the Brutans as allies in the coming war. I worried about bringing them into civilization," said Cherine.

"Send word for Galean to meet us at the Brutan compound and then go to Agar to tell him to hold back the royal army! If the royals go in, there will be a blood bath with most of it theirs," Aron ordered.

"As you command," said the messenger as he hurried away.

Aron looked at his close friends. "It never gets easier. This dead noble may have guaranteed the defeat of the kingdom if all the allied groups fracture and devour each other. Those Brutans could do some real damage here in the middle of the capital city. This is a fight that has got to be avoided."

"The royals won't accept allowing the Brutans to avoid punishment," said Trent. "Knowing the royal class, they'll want severe punishments and probably executions."

"I know, so we need to think on our feet. That's why I wanted Galean there. Maybe he can think of a workable compromise."

"The Brutans will fight rather than relinquish their captives, Aron," Cherine added. "They don't fear fighting and dying. Slaves are a normal part of their society. If they take to the streets they'll be virtually unstoppable."

"That would seem to be an impossible dilemma," Aron replied. "I wouldn't allow them to keep slaves and when you factor in those slaves are nobility, it's a particularly delicate matter."

"Are you prepared to confront the Brutans and Agar?" asked Brock.

"Yes?" Aron replied, half heartedly.

His friends looked at each other doubtfully.

"We better hurry," said Aron finally as they jogged out of their quarters and headed for the Brutans compound. The Brutans's stronghold was close to pandemonium. Brutan fighters were formed in a solid ring around their building facing the army troops. There had already been casualties and a serious battle was about to break out.

Aron hurried to the forefront searching for the Brutan chieftain. He spotted him gesturing and shouting threats at the royal guards. Aron walked over with arms extended outward. The chieftain spotted him and turned with a snarl. A moment passed before realizing it was Aron.

The Brutan chieftain looked puzzled at Aron's bravery of facing the horde killing frenzy unarmed. The Brutan chief raised his arms and gradually the Brutans stopped snarling and went silent. All the Brutan warriors turned to look at Aron walking cautiously all the way up to the chief.

Aron stopped well within striking distance of the Brutans. The chieftain scowled.

"If you think to compel us to surrender to those royal dogs, you're mistaken, Aron."

"No," he replied evenly.

"Then why are you here?"

"I don't want to see this battle between allies. We have a terrible war ahead and can't afford to tear each other apart. We've got to find a way to live in peace in the meantime. It won't be long before Damien's forces appear on the horizon. You know this. You made a choice to follow me instead of him. Loyalty is important to the Brutans. Have you chosen to abandon me now?"

The chief pondered the dilemma Aron placed before him.

"What compromise could there be with them? That posturing buffoon of a petty noble caused all of this. He got what he deserved. The world is better without him. His woman will be much happier living as a Brutan. His children will grow to be esteemed Brutan brothers and sisters… a fulfilling and useful life instead of the arrogant decadence of their father."

"I'm not here to debate the merits of each society. You know their side will demand retribution, just as would the Brutans if this was done to you. Your people reacted too quickly and too strongly for the offense. They chose not to think with their heads and allowed themselves to be ruled by their emotions. Where is the honor in slaughtering helpless victims? They were weak, of course. No one would dispute that, but indignity is different than mortal peril. Yes, he wanted to act the fool and bring down royal wrath. Do you think I would have allowed that? Now that blood has been spilled, there's no easy solution. I can't simply say to them you can do nothing. I see the Brutans as my allies still, until you tell me otherwise. You stood with me when we were weak in front of Damien. That took real courage. What your people do with their savagery has never been what impressed me or why I wanted your loyalty. You're doggedly determined against all odds. I suspect I'll need a great deal of that with what's coming. Do you understand? Do you honestly think it's wise to hold the wife of a noble you've butchered, and his children? This isn't the wilds. You're the leader and now you must lead. Galean is on his way and you know there isn't a greater mind than his. He and I will face the prince standing at your side. We'll be looking for a suitable compromise to this sorry incident, but compromise has got to be a two way street. If you leave your people arrayed out here like this, the ones with little self control will start a fight that will lead all of us in a direction we don't want to go. You lived in the wilds according to your own rules, but you've got to move past it or there will be no more Brutans."

The chief eyed him thoughtfully. Aron could see his ire had drained.

"Let me say something else," Aron continued. "You have in your minds Brutan pride, but you've seen my life. It's been a long chain of humiliations. I've been humbled at every turn, yet you've seen fit to respect me and to pledge loyalty to me. What Brutan would endure the shame I've faced in being imprisoned wrongly, having my love choose another due to my feeble and hapless pursuit of her. Do you mean to think Brutans cannot face shame also, because what some did here was shameful? You have remedies in the tribe for the transgressions committed by your people. There must be an accounting here also. It wouldn't be because the noble didn't act foolishly, it would be because the heavy handed response of some put the entire Brutan tribe in jeopardy. A poor choice indeed and falls on you as the leader of the Brutans to see to the punishment."

The leader looked each way at the faces of his men. They didn't show hostility to Aron's words.

The arrival of the prince and his retinue rumbled in behind Aron.

"I must ask you, are the Brutans still loyal to me?" asked Aron sternly and loud enough for all to hear.

With no hesitation, they shouted a deafening martial cry and raised their weapons into the air.

"Will you walk with me, chief?"

The leader glared at Agar, but took a step to Aron's side. Aron turned and they walked slowly to the collection of leaders of the kingdom and the rebels. Aron noticed the king had come along with his son. Granor was there too, watching the proceedings calculatingly the possibilities.

Aron didn't go to the king, but approached Galean.

"Will you stand with us?"

Galean nodded and fell into step on the chief's other side as they all went to face royal authority.

Agar and his father appeared very angry.

Agar was the first to speak, but Aron held up his hand.

"Would you permit me to talk first? I want you to have all of the information you need before you say things which we cannot take back. I've asked Galean to attend because I value his thoughts at working out a solution to our joint problem. Will you have the army stand down while we discuss this problem? Brutans are quick to fight and they are deadly. If you provoke them now, it will cost a heavy price you don't fully grasp. They are fearless, feral and why they're great allies for what's coming."

Agar's eyes smoldered, thwarted in his rage, again. Recent attempts to display a new persona didn't mask the old Agar, who was still alive. His authority was being challenged and he didn't like it.

"Perhaps we could find a better place to have a conversation," said Galean amicably. "Would you allow us into your compound, chief? We'd like to verify the captives are in good health."

The chief bristled and scowled, but nodded agreement.

The party walked forward toward the compound. Aron and Galean were accompanied by Cherine, Trent, Brock, and even the Uripean women Enna and Biala. The king and prince were accompanied by several counselors, generals and also Granor.

The Brutan defense line parted wordlessly admitting the group. They went inside the building and heard a cry of anguish from the widow of the noble. Her children were huddled fearfully around her.

"Your majesty, I feared I would die here. Thank you for rescuing us."

"Be at peace, madam," the king replied. "We're here with you now."

"You weren't going to be killed," said the chief to her. She looked down at the floor in fear. "We would have cherished and nurtured you to a better life, a life with meaning and great purpose. You would have finally had a worthy husband with whom to share a good life."

"Perhaps we should attend to our meeting," said Galean carefully as they walked into another room. Enna and Biala stayed behind and sat down protectively beside the captive family.

The chief's statement surprised Aron. He'd never stopped to consider life through the eyes of barbarians - rational thoughts were unexpected and having them see any virtue in their brutal society was mindboggling.

They sat down at a great table, two sides facing each other. The king and prince weren't friendly. The Brutans were unimpressed with their dour, threatening looks.

"Would you like to make a statement, your majesty, or would you like me to speak?" asked Galean.

"Perhaps it's best if you start, Galean. If I speak now, I think it wouldn't be helpful."

"I understand your feelings, sire. We're all distressed at the outcome. I'm not here to excuse behaviors on either side. What I hope to do is establish common ground. I'm not saying there weren't transgressions which must be addressed, but there were mistakes on both sides of the dispute. Unless we can agree with this basic precept, I fear we have nowhere else to go. Are you both willing to listen and to reason this out? Your alternative is needless bloodshed of innocent people."

No one replied.

"Good," said Galean. "First I want to be sure we have the facts straight. I think each side can give their account of the events leading up to the…well, let's just say the battle. Rather than the leaders of each side speaking, I think we should hear from people who were there to give us direct accounts. I ask for no interruptions. If someone doesn't agree with the testimony, we'll talk about it at the end. None of us can say what happened because we weren't there. This can't be about royal sovereignty and attitudes. The Brutans aren't subjects of the crown. Similarly, the Brutan clans are guests in the city and must honor the code of civil conduct here. What is normal conduct in the wilds isn't true here."

Aron was surprised when Galean called in the widow who trembled terribly. Cherine stood up and steadied her.

"Everything is fine," said Cherine. "Sit down in this chair. I'll be right here with you. Tell us everything honestly about what happened to lead up to this tragedy."

The widow blinked her eyes and took a deep breath. When she started to talk she spoke softly.

"Madam, I'm sorry, but you must speak for all to hear in this room," Galean clarified.

"My family was out and about in the city as we always do… or did. We were traveling to a restaurant when we came upon a band of these men. They were blocking the road with their drunken behavior. My husband ordered them out of the way, but they turned on us in an instant. Our guards stepped forth to defend us. Before the fighting could turn deadly an army patrol came by and intervened. They ended the fight. I'm sorry to say, my husband was incensed and said some unfortunate things, derogatory things to the men. He demanded the lieutenant arrest them and haul them away to the prison. I don't know if they'd have gone away peacefully without his tirade. I was frightened, but after we left the scene, I assumed the clash was over. That night Brutans stormed our residence and overcame our guards, a terrible fight. I thought we would all be slaughtered. My husband tried to defend the family, but he was no warrior. They cut him down easily and took us, me, my family and my house staff. I haven't seen the staff to know what became of them. I heard later about the atrocities done to the dead back at the estate. They took us here and told us our old lives were over. I was terrified but I tried to be strong for my children. They were shocked by what happened and I fear they may never be the same after watching their father killed before them."

The room was deathly silent.

"Madam, I don't wish to be indelicate, but were you…touched?" asked Galean.

"Not in that way," she replied. We were roughed up a bit, but suffered no injuries."

Galean turned to the chief. "Can I ask what happened to her staff members?"

"They're unharmed also," the chief replied. "We don't abuse our captives. We absorb them into the clan. They would all have new husbands and new lives. Those husbands would protect and love them. I know our ways seem strange to you, but we had our reasons. What you see as brutality spared us untold bloodshed in fights with our neighbors in the wilds. It wasn't a place of civility. Strength was the only thing which was valued there. I think this woman spoke rightly about what happened. I have no objections to what she said."

Cherine attempted to help her to leave the room.

"May I stay your highness?" she asked. "Your deliberations are critical to my life and that of my family. I want to hear what else is presented as evidence."

"I have no objection," said the king.

"Nor I," said the clan chief.

"You must remain silent, no matter what you hear," said Galean.

"I will be silent," she replied.

They moved over to sit near the king and the prince.

"We need to speak with someone in the group involved in the fight, chief," Galean added.

The chief nodded. A Brutan left the room and came back with a warrior bearing a hostile expression and scarred from numerous fights.

"We'd like to hear your story of what happened?" asked Galean.

The warrior eyed him grimly.

"Isn't it obvious?"

"No, it's not. We weren't there."

"What did she say?"

“Speak the truth,” the chief said sharply. “She hasn’t lied to us. You better not either.”

The warrior looked like he’d been beaten with a stick.

“We were out to see this city. Perhaps we were loud, but we were causing no harm to anybody. This woman and her man came along and shamed us with insults and insolence. They looked at us like dogs to be kicked out of the way, like we have no honor. The army came along, so we ended the fight without spilling blood. This man shouted for our heads and threatened us… an intolerable affront we could not ignore. He said their army would come for us and cast us into prison for life. No Brutan would stand for that. If they want to fight, we’ll give them a fight they’ll never forget.”

“Do you know who killed the nobleman?”

“No, we all killed in the fight. Does it matter which of us? We stand together as brothers to the death. Aron knows this and it’s why we pledged to follow him. If he’s turned on us now, it will be his greatest mistake. The Brutans have long memories for crimes against us.”

Everyone looked at Aron, as if he somehow had fault here.

“I’ve turned on nobody,” Aron answered. “I’m here to listen, just like your chief. As far as I’m concerned, the Brutans are my allies and allies to the crown. Nothing has changed, but this isn’t why we’re here, is it?”

The warrior scowled, his ploy had failed. He looked at the chief.

“Is there anything else we should know?” asked Galean.

“We fought and won. We do not abide defeat.”

“If the victory was so easy, why did you defile the bodies of the slain?”

“This was our right. If they’d killed us, we would have been at their mercy. They could have dragged our dead bodies through the city streets in shame. We made a statement about Brutan might. It will deter others of these soft people from similar insults. They know now we won’t tolerate their arrogance.”

Aron glanced at the royals who seemed on the verge of attacking the warrior. The warrior glared back.

“Thank you, sir,” said Galean. “You may go.”

The warrior looked surprised and left the room, but kept his eyes on Agar the whole way out.

"Do we need to hear from others, or do you see what we have here?" asked Galean.

"I've heard enough," said the king.

"I need no further statements," said the chief.

"Would either of you like to make a statement now?"

Agar started to rise, but his father put a hand to his shoulder.

"Let me say this, my son."

The king arose slowly.

"I fear that my son and I are slaves to our emotions. We've never been forced to endure such affronts before, so I hope you will bear with me. I recognize that the chief has made an effort to be reasonable. I also acknowledge the value of the Brutan horde as allies for the war. With that being said, I look at this poor widow and I tell you, we can't accept a decision which doesn't enact appropriate punishment for what was done to her family. Your warrior has explained Brutan feelings of being dishonored. I don't dispute that. The nobles have a poor record concerning attitudes toward underlings. What we can't accept was the response. Obviously the noble didn't have forces capable of fighting the Brutans. I suspect the Brutan warriors found that out fairly quickly in the fight, but rather than use good judgment in the situation, they chose to take the lives of fathers, of soldiers who were allies, and they took his family away after killing him in front of his children! How can any group call that honorable? They were in no peril of death. You claim to live by your rules and code of honor. What do your rules say about this? What if those men took the lives of your family, chief? I'm happy to forgo any punishment of any kind as long as you can return the slain to life. Give back those grieving families their men!"

The king was shaking with rage. Agar was feral. The king then sat down.

Momentarily shaken, Galean had to compose himself again.

"What's the answer to the king's question?" asked Aron calmly. "What would Brutans face for their transgressions?"

The chief was greatly disturbed. "Our people know our rules are serious. If they transgress, they face the final outcome, they forfeit their lives."

"I'll accept that verdict to end this matter," said the king frostily. "Will this bring you closure, madam?"

The widow looked straight at the chief. “You would kill your own? I find this hard to believe.”

“The Brutan clan doesn’t shirk our responsibilities,” he replied sternly.

“Am I still subject to your custody?” she asked.

“You and all of yours will be set free, you my leave with your liege.”

The king stood up. “I will await your reply about executing your judgment. Of course we will be in attendance.”

The chief nodded darkly.

The king approached the widow, took her arm in his and led her out of the room.

“Do you want for me to stay with you?” asked Aron. “This won’t be an easy task. I’ll support you.”

“This is a Brutan matter now. It falls on me. You may leave with your friends. I’ll send word to you later.”

“I’m truly sorry, chief. I feel badly for your situation, but I feel equally bad for that poor woman. Maybe her husband was an idiot, but he didn’t deserve his fate. Now she’s a widow and her children are fatherless…a tragic circumstance...”

The chief actually looked sad.

Aron left, but he felt like he should’ve had a better alternative. Even though a better option didn’t exist didn’t change his feelings in the matter. Feeling inadequate and at fault at things happening around him, had become a part of his life. His self confidence was at a low point and wishing for an escape was an answer he could only dream about. This desperation affected him deeply and partially explained his increasing reticence and dim view of future prospects. With optimism virtually gone from his life, he sought separation as much as possible for a man in a leadership role. Increasingly he followed Barmon’s lead. Barmon spent virtually every minute of daylight in the training pits sparring against the best fighters. He fought ferociously and was a dangerous opponent even in practice. He’d reshaped himself into an elite level fighter. Fighting Cherine, the masters and the Black Fist, he finally became a regular opponent for Aron as they both tried to excise the darkness from their souls residing there like an indelible stain.

This challenge from Barmon was exactly what Aron was looking for in his goalless life.

When they were called to the final judgment of the Brutan chief, a great crowd gathered at the pits. The king and crown prince seated themselves close to react to the decision. They brought some dignitaries and family, but were attended by a large force of palace guards, Agar's personal fighters, with detachments of the royal host not far away.

The Brutans came in their entirety and were armed for battle. The situation was critically dangerous from both sides. The king brought the widow to sit to his right in the queen's place. Neither the queen nor Coraline attended.

Aron was there with the Black Fist and Cherine was at the head of the masters. Both groups chose to deploy in the arena area rather than take seats in the stands. The Brutan chief walked solemnly to the center and gazed up at the king and the widow.

"You've chosen to trust Brutan justice for your grievances. I tell you that the Brutan clan will not fail in our duty. Those of us who conducted the raid have stepped forth and acknowledged their roles for not all of them were responsible for the excesses. They all agree on who has culpability and who was at fault."

The chief nodded and a column of twenty Brutans filed into the fighting area.

"These are the men responsible and it falls on them to answer for their actions. Aron has said they would've realized quickly it wasn't a fair or honorable fight against forces far inferior to them. To continue that fight and to butcher the hapless wasn't honorable. To defile the bodies in this situation brought harm to all Brutans. It's my judgment that their lives are forfeited for risking our clan with their selfish aims. Although this man had a heavy hand in his own demise with his callous challenge to the dignity of Brutans, they responded foolishly. They agree with my pronouncement. It's not the way of the Brutans to execute our own. We allow them the right to fight to the death. It will not be a fight any of them will survive. Do you accept this as justice for your husband, madam?"

The widow nodded.

The chief turned to Aron.

"They have all requested the honor of dying in battle at your hands and at the hands of their friends in the Black Fist and from Cherine and the masters. Do you accept this sacred duty? It will be a deadly fight for we conduct battle in only one way. It will be a danger to any who join the fray. There could be casualties in your ranks. You must commit all of your forces to assure the outcome, Aron."

Aron felt trapped. This was the last thing he wanted, but there was no way out. He looked up at the gallery and saw Galean looking down sadly. He glanced at the widow who looked straight ahead and looked to be very uncomfortable with what was at hand.

Aron nodded finally.

"So be it," said the chief. "Bring forth your fury because my men will fight for their lives."

The Brutan men suddenly came over and one by one made a salute to Aron and then went down to a knee to Cherine.

"Show us no mercy," each of them said.

They went over and gathered for a moment placing their fists together before they let out the Brutan war cry and suddenly charged.

The Black Fist and the masters answered with a martial shout of their own and closed on the charging barbarians.

The battle was brutally savage. The allies found it incredibly difficult to reconcile killing men they'd fought with and trained. The fight was no easy task as the Brutans exacted numerous red ribbons on Black Fist and masters opponents alike. Some serious injuries occurred amongst allied fighters and the level of the fighting was beyond description. Carrying out the final killing blows was a painful responsibility they couldn't avoid. One by one the Brutans fell - brave in the fight to the end. In spite of the horror of their crimes, Aron felt they were a great loss for the allied cause.

When the battle was done and they were all gone the Brutans dispatched, a bloodied and bruised Aron and Cherine marched over to flank the Brutan chief. All three approached the front of the grandstand.

The chief eyed the king grimly, "our brothers have paid the price of their crimes with their lives. We've fulfilled our duties, but I tell you this. If we face any further affronts from your nobles, we'll rein down hell on you and your people the like of which you can't imagine. We're going to restrict our people to our living quarters and the fighting pits to have no contact with you and your ilk. It falls on you to restrain those appalling, arrogant and weak folk who sicken us. We've lost dearly today. It won't happen again. If you choose to exercise your own arrogance, we Brutans say come for us. We'll be waiting."

He turned abruptly and left the arena giving the king no chance to respond. Aron and Cherine marched out with him. It spoke of who they would side with if further trouble broke out.

Agar was outraged. His father put a hand on his arm.

"We must act in a different way, son. This is just one more example. We no longer have power to impose our wills. You saw that incredible fight, the best in our armies couldn't have stood up in the arena against the Brutans, the Black Fist, or the masters. We must accept what we cannot control. We must think of the needs of the kingdom."

The king looked at the widow. She had a dark expression on her face.

"Are you contented, madam? Justice has been done for your husband."

She looked at the king defiantly.

"My husband was a pompous fool. This was all needless. Am I satisfied? No, I didn't require the lives of anybody. When I was held by the Brutans, I expected to be violated, but they treated me with respect and what they said made a great deal of sense. Who knows that I might have been paired with a better man? As it is, I'm a helpless woman without a man to raise her children. What kind of life could I hope for in the kingdom?"

The king and the prince were shocked at her boldness, but knew she spoke the truth.

Chapter Twenty
~ Invictus ~

The aftermath of the 'execution battle' saw a marked increase in stress in the city and palace. The Brutan chief's threat was a serious concern. Even the prodigious numbers of the royal host weren't a safeguard against havoc the Brutans could wreak if further provoked.

City dwellers heard chilling tales about what happened at the estate of the dead noble and the grisly aftermath. Traffic in the streets noticeably decreased and some families that lived near to the Brutan compound made unplanned trips to stay with relatives out of the city.

Patrols of the royal army in the city were edgy and quick to take offense.

"Order our people to keep a low profile until this blows over," said Aron. "It would take nothing to start a serious incident and we don't need any more bloodshed."

"So far, the Brutans have kept their word. We only see them at the training pits. It's strange how they were drawn to you, Aron. We've seen another development in that they seem to have a similar respect for Relak. I think they see him as a kindred spirit, just like they did with Wu Hang. Relak has taken to the role and spends a great deal of time working with them. I think he's learned as much as he's taught. The Brutans are a unique breed, blindly loyal, and courageous to the point of disdain for danger and contempt for those not equally as brave, or committed," Trent explained. "If it weren't for their making trophies of the dead, I could respect them a great deal."

"I'd gladly ceded their loyalty to Relak and let him deal with them," Aron replied sourly.

"There is a place and purpose for everyone in the world, Aron," said

Brock.

Aron shrugged dismissively.

"My lord," said an excited messenger. "I bring word from Galean. The king has called for a meeting on an urgent matter. Galean requests that you attend with him along with the staff."

"Sure," said Aron. "Someone needs to go tell Cherine. I think everyone else is around here."

"I believe Cherine is in her quarters. On this day, she didn't arise at dawn as she always does," said Trent.

"Is she ill?"

"We don't know. We thought it best to leave her to her own schedule," Trent answered.

"I'll walk over there to check on her."

Aron walked briskly to the suite reserved for Cherine - her old quarters.

He knocked on her door.

"Cherine, it's Aron. Are you ill?"

For a moment there was no sound.

He knocked again, louder.

"Cherine, are you in there? I don't mean to disturb you, but Galean has called for us. The king has something to say."

"I'm coming, Aron, give me a moment," she said weakly.

She opened the door, looking exhausted and disheveled. Aron was at a loss for words. Cherine was always pristine and composed. He'd never seen her out of sorts like this before.

"What happened?" he asked reflexively before he could think.

"I had a difficult night," she replied. "I slept little. I'm sorry to be in this state. Give me some time to bathe and drink something."

"I'll have coffee brought and some pastries," said Aron, hanging at the door entrance.

She glanced at him. "It seems you plan to attend me here in my room, Aron. Come in. Don't just stand there letting the breeze blow in."

"I'm sorry, Cherine," he said abashedly. "I was just worried about you. I don't mean to intrude."

"Come in and close the door after you order my refreshments."

"Yes, ma'am," he replied.

Aron sat down a little later while Cherine drank strong black coffee and ate cinnamon rolls.

"I wonder what you think?" she asked staring contemplatively. "You see Cherine the consummate woman warrior, callous and calculating always, but you're seeing now another side of me. I'm still a woman and I have the feelings of a woman. I have no mate and I doubt I ever shall. My lot in life is loneliness and an empty heart."

"How can that be, Cherine? You're gorgeous, the ideal woman. Any man would give anything to have you. Because of your position, I don't believe men feel safe thinking about you in those terms. If a man were to try to woo you, they'd expect you to batter them down and maim them."

"I know that, Aron. Do you think that's how I want it? I bury my feelings, but from time to time I'm overcome with regrets. It's painful for me to watch women with their children and babies. I felt so badly for that widow who lost her husband, but at least she had a husband and she has children to comfort her in grief. My prospects are to grow old and lose my good looks alone. My best hope is to die a glorious death in battle because I have nothing else."

"That's not right, Cherine. I understand what you're saying. After I lost Tasha, I've been depressed about my future. I know how seductive it can be to lose yourself in pity and despair. If I'd known about this with you, I would have intervened before."

"What does that mean, Aron? Do you offer a few words of comfort? Does that fill my empty bed and my empty heart?"

"We've got to go now, but I want to have a long talk with you, Cherine. Will you talk with me?"

She took a long drink of coffee and looked at him.

"What do I have to lose? Whatever you want, Aron, it doesn't matter at this point."

"Go get cleaned up. I'll wait and walk with you. I'm curious what the king has to offer on this fine day."

She took some time in her bathroom. When she came out she was Cherine again in her uniform. Her stern face was back, all business and competence.

"You look good, Cherine. Are you ready to go?"

"Of course, can I ask that you keep this incident private?"

"Cherine, don't you know I'd never say anything?"

"I'm not a person to make assumptions. I speak it and then there are no questions between us."

"Cherine, you're dear to me. I thought you knew that."

She blinked her eyes.

"Be careful, Aron. I'm not fully myself. I might take your statement to draw some conclusions you don't intend."

He looked at her. "Cherine, you can draw whatever conclusions you want. I stand on my statement. You're dear to me."

He saw the hint of a smile and she looked away demurely. He'd never seen Cherine show feminine responses of any kind before.

"Aron, I have some things to say to you later, when we have your talk."

"I look forward to it."

Cherine and Aron walked to the royal throne room where guards opened the doors as they approached. The others were already gathered and Galean was speaking quietly to the king.

The crowd in the throne room all turned and looked at Aron and Cherine. Galean nodded to them as they stopped in front of the throne and bowed to the king.

"I think we're ready to begin, your majesty," said Galean.

"Thank you for coming. You'll note that I've brought the Brutan chief here to join us."

Aron looked around in surprise and saw the Brutan standing between Trent and Brock. Even Barmon had come along with his son.

"I've had to make difficult decisions and this one is most difficult. There are royal secrets, as you would suspect, but there is no greater secret than the one I'm about to share with you. I've considered the course of events and we're fast approaching a crossroads in history. The appearance of Damien has shaken us and moved me to look at all of our options. I can't say what this will mean, for in truth, I've never looked for myself. Each king of the realm going all the way back to the beginning has passed on something which perhaps has waited until now to be revealed. Even my son doesn't know about it, and he wouldn't have until the time arrived to hand him the crown. He would have been sworn to secrecy as I was, and my father and his father before."

The king went to a separate room, pulled out an ancient chest and returned to the throne room with the container. A key on a chain around his neck was used to unlock the chest. Everyone moved close as he opened the lid and retrieved a strange looking flat object. To Aron it looked like a heavy book, but it wasn't a book.

The king looked at Galean.

"I give this to you to examine. I don't know what knowledge it holds, or if there are dangers. I know of no other man better suited to discern its secrets, Galean."

Galean was instantly fascinated and put his hands on the thing.

"I don't know this material it's made of," he muttered.

He lifted the box and examined it from all sides.

"It's heavy," he added and started to fiddle with a push button on the front section. On impulse he pushed and the device suddenly opened and unfolded. A soft tone sounded before a three dimensional display appeared and projected from the thing. It looked like what they'd seen from Damien's display.

A face of a young woman appeared and she started to speak in an ancient language. They could only guess what she was saying. Her speech was brief. Next, various scenes of the ancient war displayed. The air was sucked out of the room as weapons of such power they put the survival of the world in jeopardy were demonstrated. Cities exploded and were destroyed in single blasts; soldiers were mowed down by frightening weapons. The crowd recognized forces loyal to Damien - savage in battle and exercising the same barbarism as seen in the wilds. Only they weren't marking borders to frighten away enemies, Damien's forces reveled in the slaughter; a sickening sight for all to witness.

Scene after scene displayed a wide variety of landscapes, but the battles were all the same: weapons rained down from aircraft and satellites. Land vehicles also exhibited terrifying power to slay. The terrible toll Damien exacted didn't prevent the enemy peoples from fighting united to drive him back and eventually turn the tide of the war, at great cost.

Suddenly an emblem and crest displayed on a book cover. The title at the top was *"Invictus."*

The book opened and a likeness of Damien appeared and he spoke from the book in a language unheard of. The words were unknown, but what was shown them was clear enough - a huge weapon with symbols on the tail fins and the word *"Omega."*

The "Omega" weapon dropped from a flying ship onto a great city. An image of blinding light and a rumbling sound of an explosion burst out. Just the mere echo of the fearsome event shook them to their cores. Damien chose to destroy the world rather than lose the war and surrender. The weapon wiped out civilization while Damien went into the safety of the machine which preserved him until Aron dug him out eons later. Aron felt sick at what he'd loosed upon the world.

Galean's face was ashen. "My god..."

"This is what we face?" asked the king in shock.

"His compound was found in the wilds, we stumbled onto it blindly. We didn't know what we were doing."

Cherine leaned against Aron for comfort and he put an arm around her.

"Am I the last king of the realm?" asked the king sadly.

"This is worse than I feared," Galean answered. "It isn't this terrible weaponry I'm speaking of. It's the monster who authored it. He had no conscience then and I doubt he has one now. He'll sacrifice every living being to achieve his goals. There are enough weak minds in the world to fall for his charade of a better world under his leadership. They'll flock to his call and give him an army as numerous as the stars in the sky."

"Are you saying we're doomed, Galean?" asked Agar. "Is there no hope for us?"

"I'm sorry," Galean answered. "I'm afraid this revelation has shaken me. I'm not up to brave words. I've always believed that where there is life, there also is hope. If that gives you comfort, I can't say and the best I can do right now. In my readings of our histories and prophesies, a champion defeats the beast. If we assumed Damien is the beast, my conclusion was Aron could be our savior."

Everyone in the room looked at Aron. The attention was embarrassing.

"I haven't done much of a job so far," Aron replied. "I think you need to find another person to be your savior. I'd say let Galean work with this thing. Maybe there's more we can learn that might help us."

Doubt covered all the faces in the crowd.

Galean looked at the king.

"Take it to your library, Galean. It's useless in my hands. If you can find a way for us to avoid our annihilation, let us know. Otherwise, we're fodder for the armies of Damien."

All gathered looked at the king for guidance.

"I have nothing else," he said.

Everyone filed out of the room.

"I think I'd like to have our talk, Aron," Cherine whispered. "We may have less time than I thought. I'd like to speak my piece."

Aron went with her without objection. He didn't feel like being alone at that moment.

They went back to her suite. Cherine closed and locked the door.

"I don't really want to be interrupted. I hope you don't mind."

"I'm fine with it, Cherine."

"Let me speak first, please. I may not have the courage if I let you speak first."

Aron sat down.

Cherine brought two jeweled gold chalices and poured wine for them. She took a long swig before sitting down beside him.

"I heard about you before I ever saw you, Aron. Something intrigued me about your story. You came in as a raw young peasant, bold and fearless. When I met you, I was moved by you, defiant against all odds and unwilling to bend or break under pressure. You were a natural born leader. The men came to you out of respect and it was remarkable to behold. When we first fought, you were hapless, but you improved so rapidly I was amazed. I've never seen the like before and it wasn't long before I was taxed to compete with you. Eventually you became the only man I ever feared in a fight. Radigan was nearly the best, but he wasn't your equal, Aron."

"Tasha doesn't agree with you."

"That's wrong, Aron. You use her choice to define you and it's wrong. She knew Radigan and they formed their bond without you being in the picture. I think Tasha will come to rue that decision, if she hasn't already. Regardless, I want to talk about you, not her. I realize you see her as the center of your world, but you once thought that of Coraline. My point is you can move on, Aron. There's nothing holding you back at this point other than yourself. I'm going to tell you some things I never thought I would. You see me as the warrior, but I've told you I have a heart too. You caught my attention from the start. I'm lonely, but part of the reason is my choices. I have had interest and even suitors in the past, but none were worth my notice. I've known powerful men, but that means nothing to me. You know about me and the prince and you know also about Radigan. I tell you honestly that with a choice between him and you, it is no choice. You're the winner every time. For me, being close to you was the same as for Liani. We loved you, but the situation was out of our control. Perhaps what I'm saying about my feelings strikes you as ludicrous with how you see me. That I could be a wife and bear children is my dream. Now you may speak, but I don't think I can look in your eyes for the rejection. It would be too painful."

"Cherine," he replied gently, placing his hands on her shoulders; but she continued to look away.

"I can honestly tell you I'm surprised. I didn't expect this and it isn't because I'm such a prize. I've always looked at you as out of my league. How can you not know how much you're coveted? I could tell you things men say, but…"

"What things?" she snapped brusquely.

Aron laughed. "You see why you're intimidating? My point is you're seen as a very desirable woman far and wide."

Cherine had a strange look on her face, partially of outrage, but also partly of gratification.

"Those men are louts, brainless drunks most of them. They have all the brains of a tree stump. What would you expect from them?"

Aron laughed again. "Cherine, you're asking me to take a clear look at myself. Aren't you obliged to do the same?"

She turned her face to look directly in his eyes.

"What are you saying, Aron?"

"I'm saying I'm still shocked, but I'm flattered that you would think of me in those terms. Having a wife isn't something I've thought a whole lot about lately with the direction my life was going. It isn't something I've totally dismissed. When it comes to women, I'm kind of shy. I'm too clumsy to say things right and I have a knack for making wrong impressions. I find it amazing you could see any merit in me. I'm the same clumsy farm bumpkin that you saw that first day. I've been nicked up a bit since then, but I'm no less worthy. My record speaks for itself."

Cherine smiled warmly. They stared at each other before sharing their first romantic kiss. Cherine had closed her eyes.

"That was nice, Aron," she whispered.

They kissed again and embraced. It felt good to hold a woman again.

She sat back and looked at Aron.

"If we go down this path, Aron, I want you to know that as hard as I appear on the outside and as a fighter, on the inside I still have the worries of a woman. You have the capacity to hurt me deeply because I care about you. I never allow men to get past my emotional defenses, but you did it without trying. If you…"

"Cherine, do you really think I could hurt you?"

"Never in my life have I placed my trust in a man. It frightens me, Aron. I don't like to feel vulnerable."

"You're no more vulnerable than I, Cherine. I would caution you that I've been an emotional wreck and might require some sorting out. If you can deal with that, and you can accept I'm a moron, I guess we can see about taking the next step."

"On the verge of the possible end of the world, this is not good timing, Aron."

"No argument here. I say we take it a day at a time and maybe we can both find a little happiness along the way."

"I agree."

They looked at each other again, neither of them willing to say it. Finally Cherine spoke.

"I'm not a blushing young maiden, Aron. That happened a long time ago."

He chuckled. "I guess you have the gift of reading my mind."

She shook her head and laughed.

"Men are all the same about some things."

"Is that a direction we want to go?"

She smiled.

"That's good enough for me," he said quickly.

Aron worried about leaving her suite the next morning. The fact he hadn't returned to the prince's suite and the bedroom with his parents would not go unnoticed. Additionally, the masters routinely stationed guards each night to ward Cherine. They looked at the new couple emerge together and tried to mask their surprise.

"Morning," said Aron awkwardly. They nodded in response.

"You may relay to your brothers Aron and I now have a romantic relationship. Is that clear?"

"Yes maiden," they replied.

"I don't want to hear from anybody about this. Nothing has changed for the corps. We're adults and we're allowed to have a life."

"We understand, ma'am. There will be no problems."

They walked to the royal suite to have breakfast together and were met with shocked stares and silence.

"Good morning," said Aron. "We'd like to tell you we've decided to live together. I'll be moving my things to her place. I know you all have your opinions, but it's our choice. We're both tired of being lonely."

"Son, why would you think we'd object? I've waited to have a daughter for too long for my liking. We'd be honored if Cherine becomes part of our family."

Prince Agar looked very jealous staring at Cherine. Coraline looked similarly distressed, like Aron was eternally her property.

"Did we miss breakfast?" asked Aron which broke the mood in the room and they accepted the warm expressions of congratulations from all.

"We'll have food brought in immediately," said Coraline. She hugged Aron tightly.

"I'm happy for you, Aron. It was painful to watch you suffer after Tasha. This is a good thing in your life. Cherine is unmatched in every way. You made a good choice."

Cherine became a totally different person. Letting down her guard and gruff exterior, she showed her feminine side. Aron liked what he saw. This woman at his side and her affection was intoxicating.

For the first time in a while, he felt actual pride when they went out into public and word spread. Aron endured the expected playful jests from Trent, Brock, and the other men. This was how he'd dreamed of life with Tasha.

That day, Cherine did one other shocking thing: she left her uniform in the closet and wore a stunning dress. Aron burst with excitement as she took his arm.

Their meandering path eventually led them to the library where they were greeted by Galean and Abdurka.

"Aron, I'm so happy for you," said Galean.

"Are you up to this?" asked Abdurka. "This woman is clearly beyond you."

Cherine laughed.

"Abdurka, I should have left you in that cell. I didn't learn my lesson about your nattering."

"You couldn't get along without me. I have too much knowledge and experience you need, whelp."

"I'll show you who's a whelp," Aron bellowed playfully.

"Okay, boys," said Cherine. "Galean did I hear you've made progress about the discovery?"

The smile left his face.

"I believe I have, Cherine. I was able to discover data that allowed me to do some translating. This word we saw on the cover, "*Invictus,*" comes from an ancient language called Latin. Roughly it means invincible or unconquerable. As near as I can understand, it was something from Damien, a plan he made to make them invincible. What it really meant was he wouldn't surrender. He was placed in this suspension machine that somehow preserved his life through the eons while those who survived the destruction of the weapon became our ancestors. All of those devoted followers meant nothing to him. I can only believe they employed the same control they put on Liani and the other women. It's possible people died for him who had no idea what was happening in their lives. We all derived from a common species. Apparently, the effects of that war, the weapons they used altered the survivors so we now see the wide variety of peoples. The Arreck, the Uripeans, as different as they look, they're our cousins. I suspect there are many other changed people in the world. The Chenese are another example. I don't have words for this phenomenon. I can only tell you what I suspect and what I've found. In relation to us, we must consider the type of person Damien is in our planning. He will be ruthless again because it is his nature and he'll have no concern about spending lives to beat us. He'll have no remorse for his sins. If he still has such weapons as we saw on this device, he will use them. I have no doubts about that. I'm sure none of his people understand their plight."

"Do you have any more good news, Galean?" asked Aron.

"I'm sorry, Aron. This should be a joyful time for you. These matters of Damien can wait for a day. Please come down to my office so we can open a bottle of wine I've been saving for a special occasion."

"Save it for your own good news, Galean."

"No, this is a good time. We don't have promises about our tomorrows."

They all trooped down to the lower level to his office. Galean opened the bottle and poured wine for each of them.

"This place brings back a lot of memories," Aron mused.

"Memories of Tasha?" asked Cherine.

"Tasha, Liani, Relak, and a taskmaster named Cherine."

She smiled. "I was doing my duty, Aron. You were a stranger. Believe me when I say I treated you better than most that came before the masters. You had cute eyes."

Galean and Abdurka laughed.

"Cherine, couldn't you say I was rugged or something."

"I'm sorry, Aron, it was your cute eyes."

More wine didn't dampen the laughter as Aron endured yet another round of playful verbal abuse from his friends. He didn't mind, this was so much better than grim moods.

Abdurka was particularly vocal with his taunts.

"Cherine, I think you've made a hasty decision. I'd be happy to show you an excellent option you have with a world traveler, a superb warrior and marksman, an experienced companion, and a renowned lover."

"Thank you for your kind offer, Abdurka, but I'll stick with my choice of Aron."

"You look very fetching in a dress," Abdurka added.

"Thank you."

"Galean, we'll get back to Damien later. Keep me advised. I promised to take Cherine up to the royal gardens, and then to take her rowing on the lake."

"Of course, Aron... Enjoy your time together."

"Did you want a chaperon, Cherine?" asked Abdurka. "Do you trust your virtue in Aron's hands?"

"No, thank you, Abdurka," she replied laughing. "I think you've missed the fact that I'm happily placing my virtue in his hands. This is a time in our lives to live in new ways. The same is true for me."

Abdurka smiled. "Understand when I say, we are all envious of Aron. You're a great woman and you'll be a great wife. Now with Aron as your husband, that's another matter."

"Abdurka, I am going to slug you," Aron retorted as they all laughed.

* * * *

Riding leisurely on horses, Aron and Cherine left the palace.

"The last time we rode away from the palace we were in full flight for our lives," said Aron.

"We survived, Aron. I've never regretted choosing to leave with you."

"I'm afraid life with me is going to be just what you've seen in the past, me scrambling around to put out fires and having no clue what to do next."

"Life with you is all that I want, Aron and all I ever wanted, but others were always ahead of me."

"I worry that now in a fight I'll be thinking about you, Cherine. You know how dangerous it can be to become distracted. Will that be a problem for you?"

"I can handle myself, Aron. As far as worrying about you, I always have. In every fight we've been in I've watched out for you as much as I could. You're the best fighter and would only have been a quirk if you were struck down. There is nothing any of us can do to guard against chance, stray arrows, or lucky swing of a sword."

"I guess that's true."

They rode into the serenity of the royal gardens.

"This is so beautiful and peaceful, Aron. I've always heard about the gardens, but I've never come to see them. I should have, there's a great many things in my life I should have done before now. I don't know why I waited to tell you my feelings. I guess I thought you would reject me, and then Tasha was always in the way."

"Not any more, darling."

They embraced and kissed again.

"I like kissing you," he said.

She chuckled. "I'm glad. I like kissing you also."

Suddenly a sound rumbled in the sky. Another of Damien's phenomenon boomed across the countryside with a bright flash.

"No, I haven't forgotten you, Damien," Aron muttered.

They both watched the horizon as secondary flashes and lesser booms occurred.

"I hope Galean finds some answers," said Aron. "I feel sad for the carnage Damien can rein down on us. Those pictures we saw were unbelievable."

"Yet our ancestors found a way to bring him down, Aron. Galean believes what he read in prophesies. He believes in you and so do I."

"I wish I had faith in me, Cherine."

The pleasant mood of the day had been tarnished by Damien's display; nonetheless Aron got the rowboat and took Cherine out on the water for a slow circuit along the shoreline - an ideally pleasant day. Her female mode was difficult to reconcile with the usual master fighter she displayed. Cherine was a complex person, like two separate individuals, but that wasn't a problem in Aron's mind. He still worried that a relationship with her would somehow create a vulnerability in him that would cost the allies at some point in time. Leaving her to fend in a battle seemed no longer a possibility. He could say he wouldn't be affected, but was it true? Was it true for her? Would she take action to save him that would cost her own life?

Those possibilities were just another reason for him to worry and his plate was already full.

They rowed back to the shore at dusk, which meant another hour ride back to the palace that they didn't want to do in the dark. Cherine wasn't arrayed in her uniform that held her weapons. Only Aron had weapons at hand.

"Aron, thank you for this," she said. "It's more than I could have hoped for. I love you with all my heart. I hope you can come to love me as deeply with time."

"Cherine, I do love you."

They rode into the city as light faded in the sky. The sun was resting just above the distant horizon, the end of another day for the kingdom.

Just as they saw the palace in the distance a sudden movement in an alley caught their eye. A large group of toughs threw heavy nets over them and dragged the pair out of their saddles.

Aron was surprised in the ambush before he could unsheathe any weapons to fight back. Cherine had no weapons with her.

"Cherine!" called Aron in panic. He heard her struggling. Aron got a glimpse of three women pounce and drag her off her horse unto the ground. He recognized Lilith. She clubbed Cherine unconscious with a blow to the head. She turned her face toward Aron with a smug smile.

Aron roared in rage as he was pulled down too, but the ambushers knocked him out next.

The End

Watch for the third and concluding book of the Shattered World Saga trilogy, "Savior."

About the Author

Dennis Hausker is retired from a career as a medical insurance specialist for an insurance company. Post retirement he works part time as a financial consultant and he is the finance chair person at his church. He has been married since 1968. He and his wife met at Michigan State University from which they graduated in 1969. She is a retired teacher who volunteers helping adults with learning impairments. Dennis is a veteran of the Vietnam War. He served at Long Binh as a finance clerk paying field combat units. He loves to write with his preferred genre being Epic Fantasy, although he has the goal to also write books in other genres. He is very grateful for the business partnership he has established with Melange Books in terms of their professional support services and encouraging friendly atmosphere. His hope is his stories will be captivating, unique, and compelling for the reader.

www.denniskhausker.com

Other works by the Author with Melange Books, LLC

Mortus, Book 1 of the Faenum Quest Series
The Gathering Storm, Book 2 of the Faenum Quest Series
Stirring Sagas, an author anthology
Tales of the Heart, an author anthology
Twisting Fate in R.U.S.H. anthology
Villager, Shattered World Saga, Book 1

Coming Soon!

Savior, the concluding book of the Shattered World Saga trilog

www.ingramcontent.com/pod-product-compliance
Lightning Source LLC
Chambersburg PA
CBHW031004260626
47169CB00002B/685

9781612356495